DARK
BELOVED

withdrawn
from
stock

www.penguin.co.uk

Also by Helen Falconer:

THE
CHANGELING

THE
DARK
BELOVED

HELEN FALCONER

CORGI BOOKS

CORGI BOOKS

UK | USA | Canada | Ireland | Australia
India | New Zealand | South Africa

Corgi Books is part of the Penguin Random House group of companies
whose addresses can be found at global.penguinrandomhouse.com.

www.penguin.co.uk
www.puffin.co.uk
www.ladybird.co.uk

Penguin
Random House
UK

First published 2016

001

Copyright © Helen Falconer, 2016
Cover photograph © Nargherita Introna/Archangel Images Ltd
Cover design and montage by Lisa Horton

The moral right of the author has been asserted

Typeset in 13/18 pt Adobe Caslon
Jouve (UK), Milton Keynes
Printed in Great Britain by Clays Ltd, St Ives plc

A CIP catalogue record for this book is available from the British Library

ISBN: 978-0-552-57343-6

All correspondence to:
Corgi Books
Penguin Random House Children's
80 Strand, London WC2R 0RL

MIX
Paper from
responsible sources

FSC
www.fsc.org   FSC® C018179

Penguin Random House is committed to a
sustainable future for our business, our readers
and our planet. This book is made from
Forest Stewardship Council® certified paper.

A story dedicated to Alana Quinn
9th March 2001–6th July 2005

Grá: The Irish word for love, with strong connotations of hunger and desire.

A *grá* is no ordinary, comfortable, fireside sort of a love. It is a mad love, a wild love, a hunger, a longing, a terrible insatiable desire that cannot be turned aside.

John McCarthy of Kilduff

BOOK ONE

BOOK ONE

CHAPTER ONE

Aoife couldn't sleep. Maybe because the moon was so bright.

Was Shay safely at home by now?

Was he lying awake and thinking of her at this moment, just as she was thinking of him?

She imagined the quiet farmer's son stretched out on his bed in the house out on the bog, staring out of the window at the same full moon. Kept awake by the same thoughts (he'd finally said, '*I love you, Aoife O'Connor*'). On impulse, she turned over in the bed and reached for her phone to text him, even though it was the middle of the night. But then she remembered that her phone was lost on a beach in the otherworld, and Shay Foley's phone was at the bottom of the Atlantic Ocean.

Outside the window, the moon was sinking lower and larger and more golden over the Mayo mountains, pouring into her bedroom through the bare, black branches of the ash tree. Strange – and rather sad – how the leaves were already flown. When she had left this world, it had been May: the hawthorn out, fields green and flowering. And now, after less than two days away, it was October.

No, that was wrong – it might feel to her as if she had been away for less than two days, but in this world she and Shay had been missing for five months, and everyone had thought they were dead.

And that, Aoife realized suddenly, was the real reason why she couldn't sleep – it wasn't the brightness of the sinking moon; it was because even though everything in this room belonged to her, it wasn't her bedroom any more – it was her shrine.

On the chest of drawers was an embarrassingly huge silver-framed portrait of herself – last year's school photo blown up to poster-size, smiling fakely, her long red-gold hair brushed and tied too neatly back; the collar of her polo shirt clean, white and ironed. Candles were grouped around the portrait (when she'd arrived home earlier that evening, they'd all been burning in her memory), and there was a small jade vase of autumn roses, two plaster angels, a crucifix and a *lot* of Mass cards.

It didn't stop there. Everywhere on the walls were

more photos of herself – hundreds of which she didn't even remember having been taken: childhood holidays that were only a blur in her mind. It was lovely to find her whole life had been recorded by her parents with such love, but . . .

I'm wide awake now, so I might as well do something about it.

She turned on the bedside light and got out of bed in her T-shirt. She was back from the dead, and she was here to stay, and she needed to make this room fit for a *living* teenage girl.

The first thing she did was take down the framed portrait and stick it under the bed. There was an unnerving amount of space under there – the years of clutter had been cleaned away: old sweet wrappers, dead make-up, shoes and bras too small. Next, she swept the candles and Mass cards into the top drawer of the press, where she found all her tops had been neatly folded instead of crammed in as usual. She unpinned half the photos from the wall, leaving only the ones of herself and Carla and a few other friends – the way it had used to be before.

She checked the result. It was better, but still wrong. Her books were arranged too neatly on the shelves, all the spines turned out. There were no clothes or copy books on the carpet. The badly ripped music posters had been laminated. Even her guitar had been scrubbed – *scrubbed!* – and a silver ribbon tied around its neck. The things that parents do when they think their child is dead.

She untied the ribbon, and sat down on the bed with the battered old instrument in her arms. The familiar shape and weight made her feel more like herself. She ran her fingertips gently over the strings. If it hadn't been the middle of the night, she would have struck a few chords. A lyric surfaced in her mind:

Lonely in my grave tonight,
I dream of you, I dream of flight . . .

A song for Shay, rising from her subconscious.

Outside in the night, a stick snapped and footsteps padded down the side of the house. Hastily setting aside the guitar, Aoife went to stand to one side of the window, so she could see out without being seen. A badger emerged from round the corner, plodded slowly across the garden, heaved its bulk over the wall and lumbered up the faint track that bisected the steep and stony field. Many years ago, she and Carla, in sparkly dresses with stiff wings, had pretended that very track was a fairy road. So strange how, years later, the road had turned out to be real. If she followed it now, all the way, it would take her straight across the fields as far as Lois Munnelly's bungalow – which had been built across it five years ago – then up into the mountains, across the bog, and straight to that black pool beneath the hawthorns. And then . . .

Down.

Sinking feet-first through the icy water . . .

Down.

Was the Beloved still waiting for her, under the water, his arms outstretched?

His midnight eyes.

For a long, nauseous moment she remembered how she had felt beside him at the altar, when he had pressed her fist into the empty hole behind his ribs. *No heart.*

Stop. Don't think about it.

She was safely home, and Dorocha the Beloved was far behind her – raging coldly beneath the Connacht earth. He had wanted to marry her, but Shay's love had protected her like a shield.

The badger's waddling form disappeared over the ditch at the top of the field. Fiercely shaking off the night, Aoife turned back into the room. Back into her life.

Beside the window stood her ancient PC, polished clean. She sat down on the swivel chair at the desk and touched the keyboard. It didn't respond. She sat swinging slowly from side to side, staring at the black screen. Thinking.

Her mother had strongly advised Aoife not to look at her tribute page – according to Maeve, it was 'morbid and depressing and a bit silly'. Yet now, wide awake and restless in the middle of the night, it was beyond tempting to find out what her friends had said about her when they'd thought she was dead. After all, how many teenage girls got the chance to be at their own funeral? Making up her mind, she crouched to turn the computer on under the desk, then sat back on the chair.

The ageing PC took a while to wake – its wheezing and whirring loud in the utter silence of the small stone house – but at last the screen crawled to life. She logged on to her Facebook page, and found the link – *RIP Aoife O'Connor* – which had been added to her wall five months ago, in May. There was also another link – *RIP Shay Foley*. She clicked on Shay's link first, with a sudden urge to see his face. A black-rimmed page came up, with plenty of kind and regretful messages from Gaelic football coaches and fellow players, including players from other teams:

Such great potential.
Fast, accurate, unbeatable on the ball.
His contribution will be sorely missed.

The Mayo manager had written:

A great loss. Shay Foley would surely have made the team.

In his tribute picture, he was on the GAA field, and had clearly just scored a point. The ball was sailing between the posts, and everyone else had their hands in the air. He himself was already in the act of turning away, long legs bent at the knee, one shoulder lowered – revealing the strong curve of his neck, the sloping line of his jaw. The silver earring, high in his ear. His black, cropped hair.

With a warm rush of loneliness for him in her heart, she checked her own tribute page.

Sweetest Aoife, RIP.
To our darling friend Aoife O'Connor from all your friends. We love you so much. You are in our prayers and in our hearts.

Thankfully, her tribute picture was much more flattering than the framed school photograph on the dresser – in it, she was wearing a dark turquoise dress which exactly matched her eyes, and her loose red-gold hair fell slightly curling around her pale oval face, as if she'd plaited it wet. A border of digital lilies surrounded the page, and a praying angel, wings slightly fluttering, knelt at the foot of it. Who had created this page? Carla?

She scrolled down, checking out the photos and videos.

Jessica had posted a clip that had been recorded in Jessica's bedroom a couple of years ago, of Aoife singing one of her own songs and playing her guitar. It was nice to be 'remembered' that way – but a bit of a pity the video was so old, because it meant the song was embarrassingly bad.

Jessica's best friend Aisling had put up a video of Aoife dancing like a lunatic with Carla at the last Easter disco, which was pretty hilarious.

Lois Munnelly had got in on the act, posting a photo Aoife definitely didn't remember ever being taken – of Lois, Aoife and Sinead Ferguson in blue national school uniform, with their arms around each other, acting as if they were best friends. Aoife trawled her memory. When had the three of them ever posed for a picture together? Surely they'd hated each other even way back then, when they were . . . what? Ten?

Sinead had liked and commented on the Lois picture:

Aoife, we miss you so much our darling friend, you should have confided in us, the three of us were so close, we would have helped you, I will never understand but I hope you and Shay experience true love in heaven, Your best friend, Sinead xxxxx

Ugh. Crap. This must be what her mother had been warning her about when she'd told her not to look. Obviously it hadn't taken long before Sinead had started going around claiming that Aoife and Shay had jumped off the cliff together in some kind of stupid lovers' suicide pact.

Unfortunately, it turned out that it wasn't just Sinead – underneath were about fifty similar posts, all from school friends who should have known better. Including Jessica and Aisling. Including, in fact, pretty much the whole teenage population of Kilduff:

> Rest in peace, may God heal your broken hearts, star-crossed lovers.

Ugh.

> Whatever kept you and Shay apart in life, may God fix in heaven.

Crap.

> We will never understand why you jumped, but God will understand.

Aoife scrolled on down, checking anxiously for Carla's tribute. Surely her *actual* best friend wouldn't have imagined that Aoife would be so thick as to throw herself off a cliff out of love for a boy she'd only just met. Yet however far down she scrolled – and she was scanning very fast now – she couldn't find anything from Carla, either way.

How? *Why?*

Had Carla not had one word to say about Aoife's tragic death? Posted not one picture in her memory? Surely Carla had to have said *something*. Just as Aoife was starting to feel hurt as well as confused, she thought to check her private messages on her own page.

It turned out that over the last four months, Carla had written a great deal. Hundreds of messages, in fact.

For instance, in May:

Aoife I'm not posting any stupid RIP on that stupid tribute page because I know you are alive because I know YOU ARE NOT A COMPLETE IDIOT ENOUGH TO JUMP OFF A CLIFF WITH A BOY YOU'D ONLY JUST GOT TO KNOW!! Plus obviously you would have told me if you were in love with Shay. CALL ME

In June:

A counsellor came to our school and said I was in denial and I said im not and she said you are and I said stop denying im not in denial ☺ I do know this isn't funny ☹ Aoife, if you are reading this get to a phone and CALL ME!!!!!!!!!

July:

You would have told me if you were in love with Shay, I know it

August:

Aoife if you have been kidnapped by John Joe and are reading this try to get to a phone and CALL ME!!!

September:

If you are murdered and reading this from the afterlife please give me a sign, I promise you I will avenge you

Earlier in October:

I wont be scared give me a sign

Only a few days ago, Carla had posted:

Aoife was that u moved my toothbrush to the other side of the sink??????? ☺☺☺☺ Move it again if it was you I've put it back now!!!

An hour later:

Please move it

Another hour later again:

I miss you, Aoife ☹

Aoife, smiling, with a lump in her throat, clicked her messages away. She had spoken to Carla on the phone as soon as she'd got back to the human world yesterday evening, and she couldn't wait to see her best friend in the flesh. Before leaving her own page, she altered her status, to: *I'm back, folks!!!!!* Then checked out Carla's page.

And stared.

And stared.

It was a huge shock to her, how much her best friend had changed – all the more so because it felt as if she'd last seen Carla only two days ago, rather than five months ago, in May. Back then, her best friend had been prettily plump, with soft brown hair curling to her shoulders. But in her recently updated profile picture, Carla seemed to have lost every kilo of puppy fat. She had visible cheekbones, which made her brown eyes seem huge. Her soft brown crop had grown several centimetres and had been straightened and layered, with gold and blonde highlights. Judging by another picture, where she was standing next to her mother, she had even grown a few centimetres . . .

After drinking in this transformation for a full minute, mouth open, Aoife's eyes drifted to Carla's profile details.

In a relationship with KD

16

Aoife shot upright on her chair. Surely not! Yet when she clicked 'KD', the hyperlink took her straight to Killian Doherty's profile. There was the notoriously unfaithful builder's son, as handsome as ever, with his white-blond hair and silvery grey eyes, sitting on the steps of his parents' expensive three-storey house. This was unbelievable. Never in the history of his many 'relationships' had Killian Doherty gone out with a girl for more than a week before dumping her by text. Yet Killian and Carla had got together before Aoife disappeared, and in the human world, that was . . . *Five months ago*. Unbelievable!

'*Aoife . . .*'

She glanced up from the computer: someone had just called her name – although very softly.

'*Eeee . . . fah . . .*'

She jumped up to go to her bedroom door to listen.

'*Aoife . . .*'

But it wasn't coming from her parents' bedroom across the landing, where the little girl, the real Eva O'Connor, lay asleep between them in the bed.

'*Eeee . . . fah . . .*'

17

It was coming from outside the house! With a sudden leap of her heart, Aoife ran back across the room to the window and opened it, leaning out. It was still only five in the morning, and almost moonless now, but just visible in the light from the window, grinning up at her from below, was a blonde-haired, skinny girl wearing a sheep onesie and wellington boots. If Aoife hadn't checked Facebook . . .

'*Carla! Oh my God!* Hang on a sec, I'll be right down!'

Dragging on trackies and a hoodie over her T-shirt, she jumped up onto the windowsill like a cat and, without thinking, and despite Carla's startled cry of '*Careful!*' sprang straight out of the window.

As she glided through the air, it struck her that she probably shouldn't have done this to Carla without warning. She wasn't flying, but the trajectory of her spring had taken her far out through the branches of the ash tree, and now she was passing right over Carla's astonished gaze. Pointing her feet, Aoife came down rather clumsily in the flowerbed on the near side of the garden wall, picked herself up and rushed back across the grass into her best friend's eager arms.

CHAPTER TWO

'You nearly gave me a heart attack, ya big fool!' Carla was laughing and crying at the same time, while hugging Aoife so tight she could hardly breathe. 'You could have broken your leg jumping out of the window like that!'

Aoife squeezed back just as hard, pressing her nose into the familiar fluff of Carla's threadbare sheep onesie. 'Hey, who are you calling a fool? What about you, bicycling all this way in the middle of the night when you so totally hate the dark?'

'I know it! It was beyond terrifying! I thought every sheep was a ghost and every cow was a monster, even though I don't believe in ghosts or monsters one bit! But I just kept on going!'

'And in your sheep onesie! You must be freezing!'

'I am! And I'm wrecked! And I'm starving!'

'Come in the kitchen, I'll make us hot chocolate . . .'

'Ah, chocolate, I haven't tasted chocolate in so long.'

The Facebook page had prepared Aoife to a certain extent, but it was only after she had turned on the kitchen light that she fully appreciated how much Carla had changed. It was astonishing. Even in her much-loved shabby onesie (now baggy around the middle and too short in the leg) Carla looked somehow . . . *glamorous*. Her hair was perfectly straight and silky and a gorgeous colour, like a sheaf of wheat. Her nails were shaped and painted. Even her dark eyebrows were elegantly shaped. 'Carla, you look absolutely amazing!'

With a flash of smugness, Carla checked her reflection in the window over the big stone sink. 'Thanks – it wasn't on purpose – just, my mam kept forcing things on me to cheer me up, like making me get my nails done and my hair dyed and stuff.'

'The colour really suits you!'

Another pleased glance at the window. 'And I've lost two stone.'

Aoife, in the middle of filling the kettle, turned to stare at her best friend again, in shock. 'Two stone? In such a short time? Carla, that's mad!'

Carla's head snapped back and her cheeks went pink; she opened and closed her mouth, then said in

20

a strangled voice, 'What do you mean, "in such a short time"?'

Aoife winced, knocking off the tap. 'Sorry. Totally forgot. Five months. I'm an eejit.'

'*Forgot?*' Carla's eyes, so large in her freshly thin face, glittered. 'Does it really seem like "such a short time" since you ran off on me without saying a word?'

'No . . . I mean, yes, because . . . You see . . . Oh God, this is so complicated . . .' She was desperate to tell Carla everything – but where to start? She reached up into the cupboard for a jar of drinking chocolate. 'Look, let me make this first, and then I'll explain.'

Carla said in the same tight, unhappy voice, 'Explain *what* exactly? That you were having such fabuloso fun with Shay Foley, a whole summer flew by without you noticing?'

Aoife spun round to face her, dismayed. 'No, of course not!'

But Carla's huge brown eyes were brimming with hurt and rage. 'Because it seems like a *really* long time to me.'

'Oh God, it must do, I'm so sorry . . .'

'*Sorry?*' To Aoife's horror, Carla burst into tears:

hot, desolate weeping. 'Do you know what I've been doing while you were off running around with Shay Foley in Dublin or Galway or wherever you were? I've been in absolute bits thinking you were dead! Why do you think I lost all this weight? I couldn't eat! Chocolate made me sad! The taste of it reminded me of all the picnics we'd ever had and would never have again . . .'

Aoife gave up trying to make the drinks. She went to her best friend with her arms held out – 'Oh, Carla' – but Carla shoved her away, gulping down furious tears.

'Don't you "oh, Carla" me!'

'But—'

'*Don't!* Every night I've been crying myself to sleep and then I'd dream you were alive and I'd wake up so happy and then I'd realize it was a dream and everything was horrible again!'

'I swear, I didn't realize I—'

'*You were missing for five whole months – and you didn't call me one single time to let me know you weren't dead!*'

'I'm so—'

'Don't try to hug me! I'm too mixed up in my

head and it's all your fault! I love you to bits and I'm incredibly happy you're alive, but I'm really angry with you too! How could you run away with Shay Foley *without telling me*?'

'It wasn't like that—'

'Not true!' Carla smacked her fist on the wooden counter, making a couple of dirty teaspoons jump. 'He came *back* with you! He called you from the pub last night to tell you he *loved* you! Did you think I wouldn't hear about it? This is Kilduff, for God's sake!'

Despite her grief for Carla, warmth rushed into Aoife's heart at the memory of that call, with the chink of glass and cheering in the background. *I love you, Aoife O'Connor.* (He must have finally sorted things out in his head – must have realized how crazy it was for them to be apart.) 'Look, you're right, but—'

'Do you love Shay Foley?'

Her heart grew hot. 'Yes, but—'

Carla clutched at her beautiful hair, despairing. 'Then I can't believe you didn't tell me! I've always told you how stupid crazy I was for Killian! I told you everything about everything I've ever felt about him!

Like as if you remotely care, him and me are still going out together . . .'

'I do care, and that's great! Carla, please . . .'

'. . . but even though I love him to bits, it didn't stop me caring about you the whole time, and driving him nuts being so miserable about you even though he's been really nice about it, and now it turns out you were just off somewhere being all loved up with your own boyfriend and *not thinking about me one bit*.'

'I *have* been thinking of you! I can explain!'

'*Then explain!*'

'*I will!*'

'*OK!*' After a few more wrenching sobs, Carla pulled a tissue from her onesie and blew her nose. Then rubbed the tip of her nose so hard it went bright red. Then sat down on the far side of the kitchen table and stared at Aoife with her newly enormous eyes – clearly hoping for the sort of explanation that would make things right between them. 'Well, go on then.'

Yet after all that, Aoife didn't know what to say. She was so longing to pour it out, but there seemed no believable way to tell her story. *I'm not a human like you, I'm a fairy, and I've been in the otherworld all summer.* Insane! For a desperate moment it struck her that it would be simpler to go along with the idea that she and Shay had spent the last five months living in Dublin or Galway, and just hope Carla forgave her anyway. But no. She couldn't allow Carla to think she cared so little about her, to have run off for so long without a word.

'Look, I'm going to tell you the truth, Carl, but you're going to have to make an incredibly massive effort to believe what I'm about to tell you.'

Carla looked instantly, sweetly, relieved. 'Of course I'll believe you. When did I ever not believe anything you say?'

'No, but this is genuinely unbelievable. Literally.'

Another flash of hurt. 'Just *tell* me.'

Aoife closed her eyes and opened them again. 'OK. And by the way, before I start – about Shay. I do really care about him. But I have *not* been away with him for five months. It's been, like, literally, less than two days.'

Carla stared at her. Then said: 'Less than two days.'

'Yes, I absolutely swear to the truth of that and I *promise* I couldn't get to a phone in that time, so that's why I didn't tell you about him.'

'OK. Less than two days.'

'Yes. Now, here it is. You know how I glided over your head in the garden just now?'

After a long pause Carla said, very cautiously, 'What's that got to do with anything?'

Aoife sighed. Clearly the gliding hadn't looked as impressive as it had felt. 'OK. All right. Never mind about that. Just give me a sec.' She sat down opposite Carla, and tapped her fingers thoughtfully on the wood. Then made up her mind. 'OK, how about this. Do you remember that gold locket I found in Declan Sweeney's field, with the baby picture?'

'The picture of you as a baby, you mean?'

'Yes. No. The thing is, it wasn't me.'

Carla frowned, confused. 'No, but it must have been – your name was on the locket. Eva O'Connor.'

'I'm not Eva.'

The confusion increased. 'No, but you are. Aoife is just another way of saying Eva in the west of Ireland. It's Eva on your birth cert – you showed it to me only last year, when we joined up for the handball club.'

Aoife rested her forearms on the table and leaned forward, meeting Carla's eyes – holding them, willing her to believe. 'But that wasn't my birth certificate.'

'But—'

'It was Eva's.'

'But you're—'

'Carla, please don't freak out, although I won't blame you if you do because I know this is going to sound completely insane. The real Eva O'Connor was taken by the banshee when she was four years old, and I'm the changeling – the fairy child that got left behind in her place. My parents never told the guards, because Eva was dying when the fairies took her, and they knew that for her to be safe and cured and cared for in the Land of the Young, they had to mind me and bring me up as their own.'

There was a profound, unbreathing silence in the kitchen, during which a passing shower of rain rattled the window. Carla didn't freak out, but she sat with her lips pressed together, and her dark brown eyes – so large now! – grew even larger, their anxiety morphing into pure alarm.

Aoife drew back in her chair, spreading out her hands. 'You see what I mean about being insane?'

Yet when Carla finally opened her mouth and took a breath, she said, 'I'm sorry for getting so angry with you. You should have told me sooner.'

For the second time that night, Aoife found

herself utterly taken aback by the hidden side of Carla Heffernan. First her friend had proved able for Killian – and now, able for this. 'You believe me? Carla, you're amazing!'

Carla said earnestly, 'And I want you to know it doesn't make any difference to how I feel about you – you're still the best person I know.'

'You too, Carl!' Beaming, Aoife jumped up to spoon the chocolate powder into mugs, then stood facing the table with her hand on the kettle, waiting for it to come to the boil. 'I can't tell you what a relief this is! I've so many things to tell you that I can't tell Mam or Dad because it's way too scary!'

Carla looked nervously interested. 'Really? What things?'

'Loads! I told them how the fairy world was really beautiful, but I didn't like to tell them how dangerous it was—'

'*Dangerous?*'

'Yes, seriously dangerous, like life-and-death dangerous.' A shudder ran coldly through her – Dorocha had stepped so vividly into her mind. Dark, menacing – beautiful. His midnight eyes. Her throat tight, she said, 'There was this man . . .'

'What man?'

'He was sort of in charge of the place—' She stopped, her hand to her mouth, feeling again the Beloved's eyes on her; made nauseous by that cold sensation of being dragged down into their empty darkness.

Down . . .

Down into the waste that filled his secret being.

Down . . .

Down into the emptiness behind his beauty.

No, worse: not entirely empty . . .

Carla's voice brought her back to the cheerful kitchen, with its ancient wooden dresser and uneven floor and big stone sink. 'In charge? Like a doctor, you mean?'

'God, no! Nothing like that . . .' Aoife nearly laughed – it was such an incongruous image: doctor! She made an effort to shake off the fear and smiled reassuringly at Carla, who was now looking very concerned. 'Anyway, don't worry about it, I'm safe home now. And I'd better make this hot chocolate before I tell you anything else.' The kettle boiled, and she poured the water into the cups. Outside the window, the rain had gone as quickly as it had arrived and the world was turning slightly pale: the very edges of the mountains a bluish-pink. Bringing the steaming chocolate to the table, she said, 'Just, by the way, I have absolutely sworn not to say anything to anyone about this, because Mam and Dad are worried what people will think.'

Carla nodded; she reached across and pressed Aoife's hand. 'Of course I won't tell if you don't want me too, but actually I think you're wrong to keep it a secret, because there's no need to be ashamed. If that's why you've been away, you shouldn't be afraid to tell people. I mean, it's not even that bad. It's not like believing you're the Queen of England.'

Slightly taken aback, Aoife said, 'The Queen of . . . ?'

Carla laughed a little, picking up her mug. 'I know – crazy, right? But even Auntie Ellie is fine when she remembers to take her medication.'

A wave of frustration. 'Oh, I see . . .' But then Aoife remembered how she'd thought her parents might be mad when they'd told her she was a fairy; she could hardly blame Carla for thinking she'd had some sort of nervous breakdown, like Dianne

Heffernan's fragile sister. 'Carla, I'm not like your Auntie Ellie, I promise.'

Carla said lightly, 'I know, and thank God for that – that whole English thing is very embarrassing. Irish fairies is much better.'

'I didn't mean—'

'I suppose you were found wandering around somewhere, and ended up sectioned and nobody knowing who you were? Was it Shay who rescued you?'

'Yes, but—'

Carla cried fervently, 'Oh my God, was that where he disappeared to all summer – was he searching for you? That's so romantic, he must have such a *thing* for you! Oh, I'm a fool! I can't believe I didn't think of checking the mental hospitals myself!'

Aoife protested, almost laughing, 'I've not been in mental hospital, I've been in the fairy world!'

'Don't be ashamed – lots of famous people are mentally ill . . .'

'I'm a fairy! I can prove it to you!'

'. . . and they lead really successful lives!'

Yet what exactly could she do to prove to Carla that she was a child of the Tuatha Dé Danann? She

31

wouldn't turn sixteen until next Easter, so her magic skills were only just emerging and she had very little control over them. In the otherworld, she could shoot bolts of violent power when she felt danger, when she had to protect someone – but here, safe at home in the human world, she could not feel that power in herself at all. She could open locks without keys . . . but so could ordinary thieves. If she made a deal with a human being, they were forced to keep it . . . but there was nothing obviously magical about having the gift of the gab. She had made fairy gold once . . . but like all her powers, that skill was also elusive. Although . . . Maybe if she concentrated hard enough?

Carla asked anxiously, 'What are you at?'

Aoife was digging furiously around in the pockets of her hoodie – pulling out sweet wrappers and a tissue. 'I made fairy gold before – well, fairy euros. Not that it's much good – the old stories are true: it turns to dead leaves soon as look at it. Oh, for . . . *Why does it never work when I want it to?*'

Carla sat gazing at her with tender concern – tears of pity in her eyes, as if the sight of Aoife trying to prove she was a fairy was the saddest thing she'd ever seen. 'You don't have to prove anything to me. I'm still your best friend. But, Aoife' – she glanced at the window and then at her phone – 'I'm afraid I've really got to go. Will you be all right left here by yourself or will I call your mam?'

'No, wait! Don't go! I swear I can do this!' She focused harder, squeezing her eyes tight shut, thrusting her fingers into the seams. 'I just need to concentrate harder!'

After a long silence Carla sighed and said, 'I'm so sorry, I love you loads and I understand now that you didn't mean to hurt me, but I really need to be back in bed in time for Mam to wake me up for school, or she'll take a fit and call the guards.'

'Please wait—'

'*Sweet Jesus, where did she come from?*'

Startled by Carla's cry and the crash that accompanied it, Aoife sprang to her feet with a cry of her own. But it was only Eva, clutching a filthy toy rabbit and wearing a T-shirt of Aoife's which came down to her knees. The little girl had just flung open the kitchen door, whacking it off the dresser, and now she marched to the table, scrambled up on a chair and announced in a high, clear, determined Dublin accent, 'I want Coco Pops and so does Hector!'

Aoife could have kissed the little girl's blonde curls – here was the evidence she needed, as large as life and perfectly on time. She had agreed with her parents to tell everyone that they were fostering Eva, and were in the process of adopting her. But Carla was not 'everyone'.

'OK, Carla, here's exactly what's going to prove it to you! This is the real Eva – I brought her back with me from the otherworld!'

'*What?!*'

'See, look, she's wearing that gold locket because it's hers. Tell Carla who you are, honey.'

'Hector wants Coco Pops!'

'Tell Carla who—'

'*Coco Pops!*'

'Ugh. OK, hang on.' Aoife hurried to the cupboard for the chocolate cereal that her father had been sent rushing out to buy the evening before, when Eva had refused point-blank to eat spaghetti bolognese. She grabbed a blue-striped bowl from the oak dresser, and a tin spoon from the drawer. 'Now, say your full name, honey! Tell Carla you're the human child I got swapped out for!'

'Hector wants a bowl as well!'

34

'Ah Jesus . . .'

As Aoife went back for the second bowl and spoon, Carla said softly to the little girl, 'Who are you really, baby?'

'Tell Carla, Eva!'

Eva took in Carla's sheep onesie with a disgusted expression. 'I'm not a baby, I live in Dublin. Aoife found me and brought me here on holiday. And you're a stupid sheep.'

'Aoife found . . . *What?!*' Carla's eyes fled to Aoife's, dark with horror. 'Oh my God, what did you . . . ?'

Eva was still glaring at Carla. 'I like lambs but you're a stupid sheep. I live in the house with the blue door next to the sweet shop.'

Aoife said hastily, setting both bowls on the table, 'Don't worry, she's just a bit confused. Honey, I *told* you Mam and Dad moved here ages ago.'

Eva seized the cereal packet and poured a mountain of it into her own bowl, and an equal mountain into Hector's. 'My mam in Dublin is skinny! My da has black hair! Hector wants milk!'

'Oh. My. God.' Carla looked ready to be sick. 'This is awful. Her poor parents . . .'

'Are asleep upstairs!' Aoife reassured her wildly. 'She just means they look a lot older than when she last saw them because time goes a hundred times slower in the fairy world! Honey, darling . . . *Please*. Tell Carla—'

'*Milk!*'

'Here's your milk!' Feeling slightly murderous now, Aoife slammed down the carton in front of her human counterpart. 'Tell Carla your mam and dad's real names!'

'They're called Mam and Da!'

'*Their real names!*'

Carla groaned, hands crushed to cheeks, 'Can you remember where you found her? Was it outside a school? We can sort this out. We'll explain you're mentally ill, you won't get into any trouble. I'll help you. I'll come with you, I'll stand by you—'

'*Eva? Aoife? Where have you gone?*'

'Oh, thank God, it's your mam . . .' Carla turned in huge relief to the door as Maeve's bare feet came hurrying down the stairs. 'Of course, I'm an eejit for panicking – your mam must know what's happening and she must have phoned the right people and they just haven't come yet . . .'

'Aoife? Eva?' Maeve appeared in the doorway, looking terrified, dishevelled in her old paisley dressing gown. Seeing her girls, her soft round face lit up with joy and she rushed to kiss them both. 'Oh, oh, oh, you're both still here, the two of you – it wasn't just a beautiful dream . . .'

'Mam!' The little girl stood up on her chair and threw herself into her mother's arms. 'Mam, there's a big stupid sheep in the kitchen, and it keeps on asking who I am but I won't tell it!'

Suddenly noticing Carla behind the packet of Coco Pops, Maeve looked completely panicked. 'Carla, goodness . . .'

'Where's Da? I want my da! Wake him up! I want him!'

The expression on Carla's face was wonderful to Aoife. Her best friend was staring in almost comical disbelief from her, to Maeve, to Eva, saying, 'Oh. My. *God*. This is beyond . . . When Aoife told me about Eva, I just didn't . . .'

Aoife said, grinning madly, 'Told ya!'

And Maeve, totally misunderstanding the situation, lied, 'That's right, this is our new foster daughter and we're hoping to adopt her! Isn't it funny, Carla, that she's called Eva too? It's just as well we've always called Aoife "Aoife"!'

Aoife protested in alarm, 'Mam, no, Mam, I told Carla the real truth . . .'

But already Carla was hugging Maeve, reassuring her. 'You don't need to worry – there's no need to be ashamed of Aoife being mentally ill, my Auntie Ellie is lovely! Aoife, I have to go, but your mam will take care of you now . . . Take care of her, Maeve! And congratulations on your foster daughter!' And Carla rushed out of the back door into the garden.

Aoife collapsed at the kitchen table, face in hands, hardly knowing whether to laugh or cry.

After a while Maeve sat down next to her, with Eva on her lap, and ran her fingers lovingly through Aoife's long red-gold hair. 'Oh, my love . . . So you told Carla the truth and now she thinks you had a nervous breakdown, like her mother's sister?'

Aoife groaned through her hands, 'She was just about to believe me, but then you said about Eva being fostered!'

'I'm so sorry, I thought we'd agreed to tell everyone—'

'But I had to tell *Carla*! She thought I'd been

away all summer without even letting her know where I was! Oh God . . . And now she thinks I'm completely mad.'

'Poor love. But it's probably better this way.'

Aoife straightened up, staring at her mother. 'What? Better that Carla thinks I'm *mad*?'

Maeve sighed, hugging Eva against her, her cheek pressed against the small girl's softer cheek. 'Maybe it's for the best that Carla thinks you were in hospital without anyone knowing.'

'What? *Why?*'

'Aoife, my darling . . . You have to accept, even if she believed you, no one else would.'

'I don't care about that! I want *her* to believe me!'

'But what if she did, and told someone – anyone – about you bringing a little girl home from the fairy world?'

'I swore her to secrecy!'

'But this is way too big a story for anyone to keep to themselves. And if someone in authority – like the doctor, or the guard – got to hear it, and came round to check, and they realized Eva had no birth certificate or any kind of papers . . .'

Aoife suddenly realized the danger she had placed

them in. There was a birth certificate – but it was for an Eva O'Connor born fifteen years ago. And that, as far as the world was concerned, was Aoife. 'Oh . . . Crap. Does this mean I have to let her think I'm mad?'

'I know it's horrible . . . But she'll soon see you're just your same old self, and forget about the rest.' Maeve had rearranged herself now, to have her arms safely round the two of her daughters. 'A lovely normal human girl, with a lovely new little foster sister.'

CHAPTER THREE

It wasn't as good as flying, but powering along on her old bike was definitely the next best thing. She felt light as a bird, and full of energy – on her way to meet Shay, racing up the lonely bog road, her grey hoodie and navy Canterburys thrumming in the wind as she crouched over the handlebars. A cluster of skinny sheep streamed away across the heather in bleating panic. A soft grey curtain of rain swept over the gap between the mountains, cooling her, carrying the salty smell of sea. A scrap of rainbow glittered in a patch of sky, far up and away between the rapid clouds.

(Shay had told her he would come and meet her, driving his brother's car. She'd refused to let him. 'You have to stop driving on the public roads! You're only fifteen!'

He'd said, with an odd edge to his voice, 'Not any more.'

'What?'

'I've been sixteen for a while now.'

'*What?*'

'My birthday was back in July, while we were away.' He'd sounded strangely troubled – perhaps because of how fast time had passed in the human world while they'd been gone. If they'd spent two more days in the Land of the Young, a whole year would have passed in the human world above.

When she'd got over her surprise, Aoife said: 'Makes no difference – you're still a year off legal, so I'm coming out to you anyway. Stay at the farm unless you want to walk down to the coast road to meet me.'

'Aoife, about me being sixteen—' But then he'd run out of charge.)

She herself was now fifteen and half, and her fairy strength was definitely increasing as she neared her sixteenth birthday. Even though she was now bicycling steeply uphill, she was still doing a crazy speed. Sixty kilometres an hour, seventy . . . Faster! *So good to be alive!* The road was rising to the gap between the mountains, the wind was strong in her face, the cold sweet air pouring into her lungs. The road twisted as it crested the hill . . . She didn't see the cream BMW until it was nearly upon her, when it swerved with a screech of tyres and shot off the road across a patch of grass.

'Ah, crap . . .' Fifty metres on, Aoife managed to slow enough to turn and charge back up the hill and over the top again. The driver had already backed out onto the road, and was doing a U-turn and stopping. Suddenly she recognized the car – it was the cream BMW that she'd bought with fairy gold and given to Shay's brother, John Joe. She threw down her bike and rushed to the driver's window. Her delight in seeing him made her briefly dizzy. She leaned her forehead against the vintage car; the cool of wet metal against her skin. 'I thought I'd *told* you not to come and meet me.'

Shay was winding his window down, grinning up at her. He was wearing a dark red hoodie half zipped up over a clean white T-shirt, and his black hair looked as if he'd run the clippers over it that morning. 'I'd have stayed at home all right, if I'd known some lunatic on a bike was going to try to kill me.'

She couldn't stop smiling at him like an eejit. 'How are you driving this thing anyway?'

'John Joe took the Ford because he was picking up

some tractor parts and didn't want to get this one dirty.'

'No, I mean – I thought it hadn't got an engine?'

'Oh, right . . . No, John Joe stuck one in her over the summer – found it in a breaker's yard. Here, let me out.'

She moved aside as he climbed out, then stepped back towards him. For a long moment he remained where he was, arms by his sides, looking down at her – very still and very close. His hazel eyes drifted to her mouth. She tilted her face further up to his. But then he said, in an oddly strained voice, 'Hop in the car, while I stick your bike in the back.' And turned away.

Left standing, a trickle of hurt ran through her. She felt like saying, *Hey, what's the matter with you?* but her throat felt tight and she was worried it would come out as a squeak. She turned to look at him. He was lifting her bike into the car, wrestling it to lie flat in the boot, leaning in over it. One of the pockets of his faded jeans hung loose, torn. He smiled at her again, over his shoulder. 'Go on, get in, more rain's on the way.'

She walked round the front of the car, sat in and

stared out at a grey world. OK. Grand. Even though he'd admitted to loving her, he clearly hadn't changed his mind about kissing her. *Ugh.* He was being so *stubborn* about this. Yes, his mother had been a lenanshee – a lover from the otherworld – and his besotted father had died too young: an old, old man at thirty-five. Yes, she knew Shay had inherited his mother's nature – she had seen the evidence: caterpillars in his hands became butterflies, living out their lives too fast. Yet surely it was up to *her* if she thought his love was worth the risk? Enough of this wrapping her up in cotton wool . . .

The back door of car slammed and Shay fell into the driver's seat beside her, slicking the rain from his fresh-cropped hair with both strong hands. 'So, where do you fancy going? That café on the coast road? It's a bit crap, but it's the only place round here. And you must be starving after that mad bike ride.'

She looked at him as he turned the key in the ignition – the steep, sloping line of his jaw; the slight flush on his strong cheekbones; his long black lashes; the silver earring, high in his ear. She remembered old John McCarthy, telling her in the churchyard: *A* grá *is no ordinary, comfortable, fireside sort of a love. It is a mad love, a wild love, a hunger, a longing, a terrible insatiable desire that cannot be turned aside.* If Shay still had the *grá* for her, surely he shouldn't be able to help himself, kissing her? And yet he seemed to be doing a pretty good job of self-control.

He shot her a curious glance. 'You OK? I'll pay, I've money.'

'Oh, right . . . Sorry. Sure.'

He smiled without comment, then put the car into gear and pulled off. The BMW purred smoothly over the high gap between the mountains, and the purple land and slate-grey, wind-ruffled Atlantic opened out beneath them. The road fell steeply to the sea. Changing into a lower gear, he left his hand on the stick, close to her knee. He was humming very quietly to himself – something by Christie Moore, she thought. Her eyes rested on his left wrist. Around the sun-browned skin was a paler line, where he had worn her (Eva's) golden heart locket for a while. Before giving it back to her when he'd found out what he was – a dangerous lover.

A song lyric flashed into her head, setting itself to the soft tune he was humming:

Around your wrist, a narrow line
of paler skin
because you once were mine . . .

Stop. He was hers – and she was his. The love of a lenanshee was too powerful to fade overnight. Only yesterday, measured in human time, she had stood at the altar with Dorocha the Beloved, before the whole of Tír Na nÓg. And no matter how brutally Dorocha had attempted to force on the ring, he hadn't been able to do it. She was desired by Shay. And she loved him back. Therefore no other man could steal her. That was the power of the lenanshee. This was the *grá* that had brought her safely home. If it wasn't for Shay . . . A chill ran over her skin, the hairs of her arms on end. Dorocha had said, *We are one, for all eternity.*

She shrank a little, pressing her body into the soft red leather of the seat.

Down.

Until Dorocha had taken her hand, she hadn't understood him.

Something bad, something endless . . .

She'd thought he was merely a lightweight

47

madman, come to power in a careless world. She'd imagined that after Eva was safe, she could escape him. She'd thought she was easily strong enough for Dorocha, married to him or not. But then, at the altar, when he had pushed her fist into his heart . . .

No heart.

Down.

The empty space behind his ribs. Like a dry well, into the depths of hell.

The un-empty emptiness within . . .

'Aoife? What's up?' Shay's voice, bringing her back – the interior of the car, sweet-smelling leather, polished wood. Safety. She clenched her fists to stop them trembling.

'Will he follow us, do you think?'

'Will who . . . ?' Reflexively, he glanced into the mirror at the road behind.

'Dorocha.'

Relaxing, he took the next steep downward bend. 'Are you worried about that muppet? I'd say he'd have turned up by now, if he was planning to follow us.'

'He might be waiting for something.'

He glanced at her, frowning. 'What, though? He

knows he can't have you. Even with all the druids and the dullahans and the changeling mob behind him, he couldn't control you. What chance would he have here, in this world where everyone you love will stand for you?'

She couldn't help herself. 'Including you?'

'Especially including me.'

Warmth flooded her. She said lightly, 'Good to hear it!' Although it struck her – did Shay understand what it meant to stand for her? He hadn't seen the darkness in Dorocha – only the beautiful, self-confident man who was worshipped in the Land of the Young. He hadn't heard the voice of a self-confessed murderer, only the voice of a handsome charmer who had promised Aoife's people, the Tuatha Dé Danann, to take care of the dead queen's daughter for ever – even to the point of marrying her.

Shay was saying cheerfully, 'Sure, he's a jumped-up joker with ideas above his station, and you left him standing.'

'But if—' She stopped, looking down at her hands.

Bolts of power could burst from these fingers – but not when she was near Dorocha. He drained the strength from her. The only time she had struck him was with Nuada's sword, and it was the *sword* that had flung itself at Dorocha's heart . . . *No heart*. She had escaped him at the altar because she had been able to fly – but that was only because she had made Shay kiss her; she had stolen Shay's energy, the life-force of the lenanshee . . .

She needed Shay. He was her shield. And yet . . .

It wasn't fair on him to make him feel solely responsible for her safety. If Shay Foley loved her, that was fine – more than fine. But it wasn't his *job* to love her, simply to protect her. And it would only put him in harm's way if Dorocha did come after her.

She said, 'You're right. I'm sure he's not going to follow me. And I don't care if he does. You're right. He's nothing.'

'A clown,' said Shay contemptuously.

They were at the cliffs, and he swung left along the coast road. The café he'd been talking about came into view: a lonely, shabby little building with dirty windows, caught between the vast mountainous bog and the poorly fenced cliff-top. He slowed and pulled into the empty car park just beyond – a small gravelled bite out of the orange bog – and killed the engine. Instead of getting out, he sat for a moment with his strong, square hands upon the wheel. It was as if he was planning to say something else. Something he knew she wasn't going to like.

Again, she felt that cold trickle running though her. Foreboding.

He said, still without meeting her eyes, 'Let's go get something to eat.'

Even though it was lunch time, the place was empty. The solitary woman owner was delighted to see them – dishevelled and over-excited, peppery grey hair flying out in all directions.

'Come in, sit down! What will you have? Tea? Cheese and ham toasties? The food's not fancy . . .' Her voice wavered slightly. 'I had such plans for this place, and then the recession . . . It's taking such a long time picking up . . .' She rallied. 'Tea and toasties, is it? Good choice.' She filled a huge striped teapot from the Burco boiler at the counter, brought it to their table and ran off into the back, where a wild clattering began.

Aoife waited for Shay to say what was clearly on his mind. Instead of meeting her gaze, he checked under the lid of the pot – 'Plenty of tea bags at least' – and gave the contents a long, pounding stir.

After a while she gave up waiting. 'Carla came round really early this morning. She bicycled all the way in the middle of the night, even though she's really scared of the dark.'

'Sound of her.' He replaced the lid and poured out two striped mugs of thick black liquid, pushing one towards her before heaping three spoons of sugar into his own, taking a mouthful, pulling a face, then adding another spoonful.

Aoife held her own mug in her hands for the warmth: there was nothing burning in the small iron stove and the tearoom was chilly. 'I told her the truth about where we've been.'

At last he looked up, slightly startled. 'How did that go?'

'Not great. She decided I'd been in mental hospital not knowing who I was, and it was you tracked me down and brought me home, and that's why you and me have only really been together for a couple of days.'

He laughed, shaking his head. 'Fair play to her for making sense of the unbelievable!'

'Yep.'

'Didn't you show her some of your powers?'

'Nothing worked. Anyway, Mam thinks Carla thinking I'm mad is not such a bad idea, as a cover story. She doesn't want anyone to come checking on Eva. What about your brother – what did you tell him?'

At once he dropped his eyes again, uncomfortable. 'John Joe thinks we ran off to Dublin together. I told him you're not like that, but . . . no dice. I'm really sorry about this, but you might get to hear it around the town.'

Aoife was filled with relief. Was this the thing Shay had been finding so hard to say to her? 'Don't worry about that.'

'I don't care what people say about me, but you . . .'

'Seriously, don't worry about it. I only care what Carla thinks, and I can live with her believing I'm mad. Although it is a bit annoying.' She glanced towards the kitchen – there was a faint, unfortunate smell of burning in the air, and her stomach rumbled. 'Like, she keeps texting me names of famous people who were insane. Van Gogh, Spike Milligan—'

53

'Aoife?'

'Hey, *I'm* not mad!' She looked back at him, grinning.

He said, without smiling, 'I need to tell you something.'

She felt her face fall. The trickle of anxiety running through her heart again. So this wasn't just about John Joe saying she was a slut. There was something else. 'What?'

'Aoife . . .' He reached for her hand – then flinched and pulled back before touching her.

It was exasperating. 'What? *What?* You have to stop this thing about not even touching me. You're not *that* dangerous. Didn't we—?'

'Here we are!' The woman had finally appeared with the food, and set it down with a flustered smile. Surprisingly perfect toasted cheese and ham sandwiches; piles of fresh salad, coleslaw, crisps. And a glass with a flower in it – a rosebud, still tightly furled. 'Sorry it took so long but I completely ruined the first toastie because the cat came in through the window and was after the cooked ham! The rose is by way of sorry . . . At least you're still here! I had such a big crowd last week, a minibus of ten tourists, but they all left before I could serve more than two of them.' Sighing, she scurried off.

As soon as the woman was out of earshot, Aoife finished more calmly: 'Didn't we swim together, and get buried by rocks together, and fly together? And look – not a bother on me. You've got to stop thinking I'm going to keel over if you so much as breathe on me.'

Shay gazed at her for a long moment. Then dropped his eyes and touched his finger to the rosebud, stroking it, concentrating. The rose opened, burgeoned, dropped its petals, withered on the stalk, died. Nothing left but dust in the glass. For a long moment – longer than it had taken the rose to die – Aoife sat and stared, heart pounding. Shay raised his eyes to her again – dark, haunted green.

'I was able to do it before, but never that fast. I think this is to do with turning sixteen . . . Please don't look at me like that.'

Aoife recovered herself. 'I'm not trying to look at you like anything. I don't care if you're a lenanshee. I love you. This is my decision. Here, take my hand.'

But he looked away, strong farm-boy fists clenching and unclenching on the table. 'I can't risk it. I can't—'

She cried in frustration – at him, at the situation, 'How could just holding my hand hurt me?'

'I'm not saying it would.'

'*Then do it!*'

But he said in a low, agonized voice, 'Look, it's not just about touching you.'

She was bewildered. 'I don't understand.'

Still without looking at her, his voice grew near to anger. So unlike him. 'Do you know how hard this is for me, just *being* here with you, with you looking at me like that? If I took your hand, do you know how much it would take, just to stop myself kissing you? *Do you?*'

'But—'

'*Don't look at me like that!*' He got up from his chair abruptly, slapping a ten-euro note on the table. 'Look, I'm sorry—'

'*Shay, wait!*'

As the wind chime tinkled over the door, the woman flew out of the kitchen with a massive welcoming smile – until she realized these were not new customers but her old ones leaving. Staring at the untouched food, the woman burst into tears. 'Was there something wrong? Was it what I said about the cat coming in after the ham? Oh God . . .'

Aoife was in the middle of trying not to cry herself. 'I'm sure it's lovely – I just lost my appetite.'

The woman sobbed, 'Because I took so long!'

'No, honestly, I wasn't that hungry in the first place.'

'You just can't get anyone this far back, to help. I've prayed in church!' Wiping her face on her apron, the woman began stacking their plates onto a tray. 'I've even put cakes and milk out for the fairies, in case they might take pity on me!'

'I'm really, really sorry.'

But the woman was already disappearing miserably back into the kitchen. Finally left free to step outside into the wind, Aoife stood shivering, staring in horror at the sight of her bike – no longer in the car, but leaning against the corner of the building. *Was that it then – had he gone?* No, he was still here – standing opposite the little car park on the far side of the road, looking down over the ocean. She crossed the tarmac to stand beside him. Far below their feet, the cliffs were battered by a high, grey sea.

Before she could even speak, he said rapidly, without even looking at her, 'I'm sorry I can't drive you home right now. Maybe it will get easier, but . . . This really hurts.'

'Shay, surely we can—'

'Be careful, Aoife. On the road, I mean. Don't ride too fast.'

Taken aback by the speed with which he had dismissed her, she cried, 'I won't even ask you to hold my hand again, I promise!'

'Aoife. *Please.*'

The finality in his voice was agonizing. She wanted to scream, *This hurts me too!* Instead, she ran gasping back across the road to her bike. The saddle had twisted to one side. As she was furiously adjusting it, a small white tourist bus pulled up beside her, and the door sighed back, and someone jumped down. The driver was saying, 'Toilets round the back, but I warn you, they're not very clean.'

'No, I'm going in the café.' The speaker was a girl – remarkably beautiful, in her late teens – tall and slender with long white-blonde hair. She was wearing a long white silk dress, very close-fitting.

The tour driver shook his head. 'Sorry, miss – this isn't on the schedule any more, because it can't cater for a bus-load.'

'But I'm staying here.' She had a very pretty, musical voice. 'You go on without me.'

As the bus pulled slowly away, like a curtain drawn aside, Shay was still standing at the cliff side – but this time he had his back to the sea and his eyes met Aoife's and held them. The girl in white didn't turn to go into the café but stayed where she was, staring at him, her hands lightly on her narrow hips, her silk skirt flapping around her slim bare legs. Waiting for him to notice her. Yet Shay didn't take his eyes off Aoife and, after about half a minute, the girl – with the briefest of flushed, rather resentful glances at Aoife – pushed open the door to the café and stepped into its shadowy interior, to the faint wind-brushed tinkle of the chimes.

Instantly Shay came walking across the road, his hand held out.

Aoife's heart leaped, but all he did was offer her a piece of paper, at the full stretch of his arm. 'My new number. John Joe gave me his other phone.'

She looked at it, unable to speak, gripping the cold handlebars of her bike. She wanted to ask, *What for, if you're planning never to come near me again?*

He shook the paper at her. 'In case that muppet

does come after you, Aoife. Though you don't need to be afraid of him. He can't touch you. My feelings . . . the *grá* . . . Nothing's changed . . .'

She wanted to say so much. She wanted to say, *I don't want you because you can save me from Dorocha. I want you for yourself.*

'Aoife, take it . . .'

Her voice stuck in her throat: a burning lump. She grabbed the paper, crumpling and stuffing it into the pocket of her hoodie, jumped up on the pedals and sped away into the rainy wind.

CHAPTER FOUR

Even after the long ride back to Kilduff, her eyes were still hazy with tears – and as she turned into the square, she totally upended old Mrs Munnelly, who was just stepping out off the pavement with all her shopping.

'Sorry, sorry!' Aoife screeched to a halt in a big U-turn, dropped the bike, and rushed to help Lois's grandmother to her feet. She sat the old woman on the low wall beside the shop, brushed the leaves off her tweed coat, then ran around picking up her shopping – a burst bag of potatoes, a cabbage which had rolled under a car, and finally a box of eggs, smashed. 'I'm so sorry – I've money, I'll run in and get you some more eggs.'

Mrs Munnelly said breathlessly, hand on her chest, 'It's not your fault, dear. I can't see a thing, these new bifocals, I *wish* I still had the old ones.'

Aoife felt a fuzzy dizziness for a second, perhaps from standing up too fast. The hair pricked on her arms, like someone had walked across her grave; a slight sinking feeling, like a decrease in pressure. 'I won't be a minute. I'll go and get those eggs.' She ran into the shop and down to the back. Confusingly, where the eggs had been only two days ago were boxes of plastic spiders and witch-hat fascinators. She located the eggs in the next aisle, and ran back to the till.

Two very blonde girls in green uniforms were coming away from the counter, heads down, comparing sweets. She pushed past without looking at them – then felt her arm seized. The next second, Jessica was shrieking into her face: 'It's you!'

Aoife was startled by the warmth of the greeting – and by how much the dark-haired Jessica had changed overnight. 'Oh, hi, I love your hair! I nearly didn't recognize you—'

'It's really you!' Now Jessica was clinging to her, weeping.

What was the matter with Jessica, who had last seen her only two days ago? 'Are you OK, Jess? I'm in a bit of a hurry –I just have to get these eggs—'

'But you have to stop and talk to us! You have to tell us what happened! Some people are saying you and Shay . . . But Carla says you've been ill in hospital and maybe had amnesia!'

'Aargh . . . Sorry.' She'd done it again. In the fright of knocking over Mrs Munnelly and the rush of getting the eggs, she had completely forgotten how much time had passed. Five months. Setting the eggs down on the counter, she embraced Jessica in a proper hug. 'It's so great to see you!'

'You too! I couldn't believe it when I heard you were alive! We all thought you were dead!'

'I'm so sorry . . .'

'*Sorry?*' The second girl had turned to face her now, hands on hips, stormy-faced, cat-green eyes narrow. It was Sinead, grown a lot taller and thinner, and also gone blonde – with layers – instead of the strawberry ponytail she'd had since junior infants. '*Sorry?* Do you think it's funny to go around having a tribute page up on Facebook when you're not even dead?'

Aoife smiled at Sinead brightly over Jessica's shoulder. 'Hi there – thanks for the nice comments anyway!'

'You needn't think I meant them!'

'Really, I didn't.'

Sinead spat, 'I bet half the nice stuff up there you put up yourself anyway while you were wherever you were laughing at us! And don't you go being all

63

sympathetic to her, Jess – she wasn't one small bit bothered about the rest of us when she ran off with Shay Foley, was she?'

Stepping back from Aoife's embrace, Jessica said soothingly, 'Ah now, I'm sure there's a good explanation, like Carla said . . . Aoife, did you really have a nervous breakdown?'

But Sinead wasn't about to be soothed. 'Don't fall for that one. That's just Carla trying to make out her so-called best friend didn't really dump her cold to go jaunting off with some thick one from back the bog. And us having to find stupid photos to put up on Facebook and being dragged along to endless bloody Masses to pray for her soul – some chance of saving that.'

'Ah now, Sinead . . .'

Sinead was already pulling Jessica away by the arm. 'Come *on*, we've got to get back for the last period.'

'I'm coming . . . Aoife, I'm really glad you're alive, and I hope you're feeling better! I'll talk to you later!'

Aoife cried, 'Thanks, Jess – I'll see you in school!' Then, cheerfully, with a massive wave at Sinead, 'See ya, Sinead!'

Just like the last time she was in the shop, it was John McCarthy at the till, and again, just like the last time, he looked at the coins in her hand with deep distrust, his faded eyes like pale blue marbles. He said in his quavering old man's voice, 'Fairy gold, I'm thinking?'

She smiled and paid with the couple of euros she had in her pocket. 'No – real money this time.' She had done a big shop here once before, with a hundred-euro note that had materialized in her pocket. Back then, she hadn't known that in human hands, fairy gold turned into dead leaves.

He grunted, trapping the coins beneath his palm then sweeping them into the till. 'But you're going to have to come back and pay for them eggs properly if these turn into oak leaves.'

'They won't, I promise.'

He put the box of eggs into a brown paper bag. 'I did tell them, you know.'

She held out her hand for the bag. 'Told them what?'

'That you were away with the fairies! But you were back very quick, weren't you, Miss O'Connor? You must have barely set foot in the other place.'

She stared at him, then glanced hastily around her. No one else was in the shop now, apart from a small plump man in his thirties, round-faced, balding with a bright red hair comb-over, and wearing a very old-fashioned suit. He had a trolley piled up with plastic-wrapped trays of Coca-Cola, to which he was now adding six packs of cheese and onion Taytos, and a huge tub of chocolate-chip ice cream out of the upright freezer.

She looked back at John McCarthy. 'I'm not sure what you mean.'

The old man went on as if she hadn't said anything: 'And I told everyone as how time went by a hundred times slower in the otherworld, and I said how you might forget to come home for a long, long time, but one day, maybe in fifty years' time, they'd see someone passing in the street who reminded them of you, still looking just as you looked when you were fifteen – and then, however old they'd got to be themselves, even if they were as old as I am now, they might remember old John McCarthy was after telling them you'd be back.' And finally he handed over the brown paper bag.

She seized it. 'Thanks – bye!'

'Goodbye, Aoife O'Connor. If that is your real name.'

She hurried towards the door of the shop. It was hard to tell how much the old man really knew, or whether his ramblings were more about the way he was slowly losing his mind. After all, he was convinced his nephew's wife was a lenanshee, and her love destroying his nephew. (He had accosted Aoife in the graveyard, elbows sharp in his worn black jacket: *Beware of the leannán sídhe, Aoife O'Connor. Stay away from the lover from the otherworld.*) But just because John McCarthy knew the old stories didn't mean he had any special insight into who Aoife was herself.

Behind her, as she left the shop, he was saying to the man with the comb-over: 'That better not be fairy gold, young man. I remember you from the last time, so I do.'

Mrs Munnelly was still sitting on the low stone wall where Aoife had left her, the pink back in her cheeks and now looking quite pleased with herself. 'Well, the optician woman said I'd get used to these glasses soon enough and I've never seen the world look clearer! Look at the yellow of that tree – the leaves are lovely! Oh, it's *you* . . .' And suddenly Lois's grandmother was no longer a sweet and pink old lady, but a wrinkled version of her sour grandchild, gathering her skirts as if Aoife's presence could contaminate her. 'Well, I pray you have seen the error of your ways, Aoife O'Connor, but I'm very surprised you weren't praying for your own soul at this morning's Mass. And Father Leahy so good to the two of ye, you and that boy, and holding all those special Masses for your souls over the summer, when he thought ye were both dead!'

Aoife headed grimly away, cycling with her head down. The small balding man was hurrying across the square in front of her, disappearing through the church gates, carrying his load. An odd place to be going, loaded down with crisps and ice cream – hardly the place for a picnic.

The priest himself was standing outside his house at the corner of the church lane, pointing out directions to a young woman in a small pink Fiat. As she bicycled past the car, Aoife caught sight of a fluffy white dog sitting in the back – then realized it was an outsize teddy bear, propped up in an empty child seat. The priest straightened up and stared after her, one hand raised as if wondering about calling on her to stop. But Aoife was already turning with a hiss of wet tyres on to the Clonbarra road. She didn't feel ready for Father Leahy yet. Not if he was another one who thought she and Shay had been living together all summer. And after all those Masses for the dead.

Once she was sure she was out of sight, she speeded up, past the unfinished estate, past the garage with the second-hand cars. Flying along now, left into her lane, up the long boreen. She thought suddenly – was Shay safe home? It wasn't likely he had run into a guard, but still, she should call him, to check.

No. Don't even think of calling him. You only want to hear his voice, and it's not fair on him to keep tugging at him if it hurts him so much.

Despair swept through her. It wasn't fair on her, either.

He's only trying to protect you.

Poor consolation.

He loves you.

Blinded again by tears, she powered at breakneck speed over the potholes towards home.

Her father's green Citroën wasn't here – one of the many surprising things that had happened while she was away was that James had found work as a carpenter again, making kitchens for two houses which had finally been sold on the empty estate. But her mother's Volvo was parked in the driveway and so Maeve must be back from the doctor in Clonbarra. Maeve had wanted to be certain Eva had been cured by the fairies, but she was nervous of taking her to their usual doctor in Kilduff, when she had no birth certificate or documents for her 'new' four-year-old foster daughter. So instead she'd gone further afield to a doctor who wouldn't know their family.

Aoife spun into the garden, dumped her bike, took a deep tear-filled breath through her nose, shook off her sadness and entered the kitchen through the back door.

Her mother, soft round face pale with panic, rushed to her. 'You're here! Thank God!'

Alarmed, Aoife cried, 'Mam, are you all right? Is it Eva? Was there a problem?' But the little girl was sitting at the kitchen table, eating yet more Coco Pops.

'It's not Eva, it's you! You weren't here when we got back just now! Where were you?'

'Oh, thank God . . . Then what were you so worried about? I just went out for some fresh air . . .'

Maeve gave her a look that said everything about having thought for five months that Aoife was dead.

Aoife was humbled. 'Oh. OK, sorry. Next time I'll leave a note. Eva, how was the doctor?'

Eva said loudly, through a mouthful of Coco Pops, 'He was nice and he took a picture of my insides and I'm a skeleton but Hector was invisible!'

Maeve, smiling now, dug through a shopping bag and handed Aoife a small paper bag from the Vodafone shop. 'As promised. We've put your old number on it and twenty-euro credit.'

'Oh my God! The new iPhone! But that's way, *way* expensive! You can't afford it!'

'Now your father's working, we can.'

'Oh, that's so brilliant! Thank you so much!' She was already inputting and saving Carla's number.

'I've got some of your favourite ice cream as well – chocolate chip. Do you want some now?'

'In a moment . . .' She was trying to open Facetime, but there was very little reception – only one bar coming and going. 'In a minute – save me some – I'm just going out into the front garden to get some coverage.'

When she opened the front door, a smiling young woman was standing on the doorstep, her knuckles raised to knock. She had very long, glossy blonde hair, bright red lipstick, and she was wearing a scarlet jacket and skirt with a cream blouse. For a moment Aoife couldn't work out where she'd seen her before – but then she recognized the huge white teddy bear in her arms, and the pink Fiat parked in the lane outside the gate. It was the driver who had been asking directions from the priest – clearly, still lost.

'Do you need to know the way somewhere?'

The woman said cheerfully, 'I don't think so. I think I'm already here!'

'No, I'd say you're lost. Everyone who ends up here is lost.'

'I'm looking for a Mr and Mrs O'Connor?'

'Oh! Then actually you *are* in the right place. Dad's not here, but Mam is . . .' She shouted over her shoulder, 'Mam!'

As Maeve came into the hall, the woman stepped past Aoife, still smiling, cuddling the enormous bear. 'Mrs O'Connor? I'm Deirdre Joyce. Please call me Deirdre. I'm the child welfare officer for this area, and I've come about the little girl.'

CHAPTER FIVE

Maeve remained standing with her hand against the frame of the kitchen doorway, not coming any further, saying in a horrified voice, 'Child welfare?'

'There's no need for any alarm!' The woman in the scarlet suit shifted the huge teddy bear to her left arm, and pulled out a laminated ID card which was on a chain around her neck – holding it up rather like a priest brandishing a crucifix against a vampire. 'My only concern is the safety of the child. Where is the little girl in question?'

'Why? Why do you want to see my daughter?'

Deirdre Joyce sighed and pursed her bright red lips, and even rolled her eyes slightly – as if having to explain herself was a terrible bore. 'This morning, Mrs O'Connor, you brought a little girl to a medical clinic in Clonbarra . . .'

'I brought my *daughter* to the doctor – my foster daughter – for a confidential visit!'

'There is no "confidential" if a crime is suspected.'

'*Crime?*'

'Everything is inter-connected now, Mrs O'Connor – computer systems, patients' records. How do you think we keep track of you all? When the receptionist entered your four-year-old "foster daughter's" details into their system, the computer returned hospital files on a fifteen-year-old Eva Sarah O'Connor, who also has parents called Maeve and James O'Connor, and who also lives in Kilduff! I assume this is the young lady in question, who was brought into casualty to be checked for concussion ten years ago?' And the welfare officer cocked her head enquiringly towards Aoife, who suddenly remembered that trip to the hospital – she had hurled herself headfirst out of the ash tree in a wild attempt to 'fly'. (She'd only been in the human world for a year, and must have still known, deep down, who she really was . . .)

Seeing what was coming, Maeve was saying despairingly, 'That's right, that's our oldest daughter, Aoife. It's such a coincidence the girls have the same name!'

'Exactly what the receptionist thought! And she thought it was even more of a coincidence that they have the same health insurance number! Which is why she contacted my department! I am here to examine the young child's birth certificate and foster papers.'

Maeve's eyes met Aoife's, dazed with horror – this was exactly what she had feared: that someone in authority would come round to check and find her two daughters had only one birth certificate between them. 'Birth certificate . . . Foster papers . . . I'm not sure where I've put them – they could be anywhere. My husband isn't home now . . . he might know where they are. Can you come back later, after we've had a chance to look?'

The welfare officer smiled at Maeve in the exact same way Aoife had smiled at Sinead Ferguson in the shop – cheerful, bright, and not even pretending to be genuine. 'My sole concern is for the child in question. If you cannot produce valid papers then I must interview her to ascertain her identity. If the child corroborates your story, you will have twenty-four hours to provide the correct documentation. Now – may I speak with the child in private?'

Aoife had a sudden very bad feeling about this. 'Mam, I don't think—'

Her mother was saying nervously, moving back against the kitchen door, 'Eva's got a *very* vivid imagination.'

From inside the kitchen, Eva shouted, 'Milk!'

'Ah, *there* she is.' Deirdre Joyce shoved straight past Maeve, pushing the door closed behind her. Her voice came through the wood: 'Hello, little girl! Would you like to play with this beautiful teddy bear?'

'Wait, stop!' But as Aoife went to rush after the woman into the kitchen, Maeve held her back.

'There's no point interfering,' she whispered frantically. 'It will only look even more suspicious.'

Aoife whispered back, equally frantic, 'But I really don't think you should allow her to ask Eva any questions. You don't know what she's going to say . . .'

'It's fine. She's four. If she talks about the fairy world, it will just sound like a little girl making up wild stories. At least she'll say I'm her mother, and then we'll have a day to figure out what to do.' Maeve clutched her cheeks in desperation. 'Oh God, what *are* we going to do?'

The warped wooden door had not quite closed, and Aoife peered nervously through the crack.

Deirdre Joyce had settled into a seat beside Eva; she was holding up a mobile phone and taking a picture. 'So you're the lovely, clever little girl I've been hearing all about? Look at the camera, pet! And you're having Coco Pops *and* chocolate-chip ice cream for your dinner – what a healthy combination, what a lucky girl you are, being so well looked after.' She sat the huge teddy bear on the polished oak table. 'Isn't Mr White a beautiful teddy? He's come all the way from Clonbarra, especially to see you.'

Eva, busy feeding Coco Pops and ice cream to her filthy toy rabbit, glared in disgust at the enormous bear. 'Mr White?'

'That's right!'

'What a silly name.'

'It's because he's so clean! Isn't he lovely? What is your rabbit called? He looks like he could do with a wash.'

'Hector. And Hector doesn't like white. He likes grey.'

'Ha-ha-ha!'

'That's a silly laugh. Are you a banshee? I don't want to be stolen by the fairies again.'

The welfare officer's smile grew wider and slightly

predatory, showing small white teeth. 'I can assure you, little girl, I am not a banshee – I'm absolutely real.'

Eva looked dubious. 'The banshee was real.'

'I'm not a banshee, little girl.'

'I think you're a banshee.'

'What's your name, little girl?'

'You're a banshee.'

'*I'm not a banshee!*' Deirdre Joyce paused, and took a deep calming breath, still determinedly smiling. 'How do you like your new mummy and daddy?'

Surprised, Eva said, 'They're not my new mummy and daddy! Mam and Da live in Dublin in the house with the blue door and my dad has black hair and I'm only here on holiday because Aoife found me and said I had to come with her!'

Maeve, unable to stay listening to this any longer, threw open the kitchen door, crying, 'I can explain! She doesn't understand!'

Eva cried gleefully, 'In Dublin, Mam was skinny!'

'*I can explain . . .*'

But Deirdre Joyce was already on her feet, whipping out her mobile, triumphantly punching buttons. 'There'll be plenty of time to explain, Mrs O'Connor.

If at all possible, I will arrange an emergency hearing for early next week.'

'*What?*'

The woman said into the phone, 'Put me through to the Gardaí station in Clonbarra . . .'

'No, don't – this isn't what it looks like!'

Deirdre Joyce turned her back, one hand covering her other ear. 'Mrs O'Connor, let me make this call in peace.'

Maeve seized her arm. 'She's my daughter! I mean, my foster daughter! You're making a terrible mistake!'

'Let go of me, Mrs O'Connor. Clonbarra station? I need to arrange safe transport for a child.'

'*No! Don't take her away again! I can explain!*'

Eva, realizing that something had gone very wrong, started to cry, and Maeve swept her weeping daughter up into her arms ('Everything will be fine, sweetie!'), clinging desperately to the child as if she thought it was the last time she might ever hold her. 'Please, Deirdre, listen to me!'

Standing trembling in the kitchen doorway, Aoife could feel herself going cold inside; her vision darkening. Something was happening to her . . . Her fairy power . . . Ice pouring into her veins . . . Hands hurting fiercely . . .

The woman in the scarlet suit was saying loudly: 'Clonbarra station? Deirdre Joyce, child welfare officer. Put me through to Chief Inspector Delaney, please. Yes, I'll hold.'

And now Eva was reaching out her arms to Aoife, over her mother's shoulder, her little face twisted with panic. *'Don't let that lady take me!'* (The coal-eyed banshee in her blood-red cloak, demanding that Aoife hand over the human child. *Come with me, sheóg . . .*)

'Ah, Chief Inspec—'

'You can't take her!' Aoife's power burst out of her in a violent uncontrolled shock-wave, hurling the woman screaming headfirst into the ceiling, whirling around in spread-eagled circles, shrieking dementedly like someone on a roller coaster, while Maeve, also screaming, backed up against the dresser with Eva clutched against her, staring up in terror at the demonic vision.

'Banshee!' howled Eva, pointing.

With one more convulsive twist, Deirdre Joyce crashed onto the table on her back, sending the milk jug and Coco Pops flying, and lay there silent, eyes closed, the back of her glossy perm resting in Eva's bowl of ice cream. The big white teddy toppled to the floor.

Eva instantly stopped crying and shouted indignantly, 'Mam! She's lying on Hector! Make her get off!'

'Oh my God . . . Oh my God . . .' Maeve was breathless and panting and terrified. 'Oh my God, is she . . . ?'

But already Deirdre Joyce was sitting up, tenderly holding the back of her head. Her nose was scratched red by the broken light bulb; all the buttons had come off her jacket and her phone was in pieces across the floor. 'What happened?' She took her hand from her head and looked in astonishment at her palm, now sticky with ice cream. 'Why am I here?'

Maeve, still flattened against the dresser, found her voice and gasped hopefully, 'I don't know why you're here! You just came in and took a bit of a fit! Can't you remember anything?'

'A fit? But . . .' Deirdre Joyce was looking around now, and finding herself among broken crockery covered in Coco Pops and ice cream. A moment later, her face cleared and eyes bulged, and she jabbed her forefinger at Maeve. '*You know well who I am and you attacked me!*' Leaping off the table, she rushed for the door, shrieking at Aoife, 'Let me out! I am the child welfare officer for this region! My office knows where I am!' She tried to push past, but Aoife, still shaky from the violent discharge of her fairy power, gripped the doorframe and stood firm. The ice was seeping into her blood again . . . *No, don't use it. You could have killed her. You're not in the otherworld now. Different rules.*

'Let me out!' Deirdre Joyce was shrieking in her face. 'That child is not safe with that woman! I have to call the guards!'

Aoife said, through gritted teeth, 'I can't let you do that . . .' Yet how could she stop this woman, in a world where people like Deirdre Joyce held all the real power? And then it came to her, with sweet relief. 'Unless you *promise* me not to call the guards.'

Deirdre Joyce blinked and jerked back her head, looking utterly amazed at Aoife foolishness. 'Yes, fine, I promise!' she cried untruthfully. 'I won't tell anyone! I wasn't going to anyway!'

Aoife said hastily, 'No, I mean, say "It's a deal."'

(Dave Ferguson had said *It's a deal* and then he'd had to sell Aoife the cream vintage BMW – for fairy gold.)

Deirdre Joyce nodded so hard, drops of ice cream flew from her blonde bob. 'It's a deal! Now let me out!'

'No, wait, let me think . . .'

The woman looked terrified again. 'You said you'd let me out!'

'I will, it's a deal, but . . .' While she was about it, she might as well sort out the whole thing in one go. 'And promise me you'll write in your report that Eva Sarah O'Connor is my parents' fully and completely adopted daughter and everything is in order.'

'Yes! Yes!' The welfare officer beamed with relief. 'Just as soon as I get back to the office! The quicker you let me out the quicker I can write my report!'

'Then say "It's a deal"!'

The woman squealed: *'It's a deal!'*

'Thank you.' Aoife stood back and she raced hysterically down the hall and out across the garden, where the rain was now bucketing down, to the little pink Fiat at the gate, jumped in, did a screeching three-point turn and roared away, bouncing furiously over the potholes.

When the noise of the engine had been swallowed to nothing by the hiss of the downpour, Aoife closed the front door and went smiling back into the kitchen. Maeve was standing in exactly the same place, against the dresser, her face sheet-white, Eva still clutched in her arms. 'Mam, it's all right now, she's gone.'

Maeve didn't move – rather, she flinched further back. She said in a trembling tone, 'Oh God, what are we going to tell the guards, oh God, this is a nightmare . . .'

Aoife, who had been about to hug her mother with relief, stopped where she was. 'Oh, I see – no, it's grand. She made a deal not to tell them.'

'Of *course* she did – that's the only way she thought she could get out of the house alive!'

Aoife said patiently, 'I *know* that, but she can't go back on it, trust me. If a human makes a deal with a fairy, they can't change their mind. And she's also going to write in her report that Eva is adopted, so you can totally relax now! Seriously, Mam, trust me on this. I swear to you. It's OK.'

Maeve stared at Aoife for a long, long moment, her arms still tight around her human daughter. Then her shoulders relaxed very slightly, as if maybe she was able to believe what her fairy daughter was saying to her. But tightened again as she burst out: 'But that woman. What happened to her? She flew right up in the air! And then . . .' She stared wildly up at the shattered light fitting dangling from the plaster. '*She actually broke the bulb!*'

'I know – I'm sorry, I didn't mean to do it – it just burst out of me when I thought she was going to do something to hurt Eva . . .'

(Eva squeaked, 'Put me down! I want Hector!')

Maeve hugged the wriggling child fiercely to her chest, caressing her soft blonde curls. 'But you could have killed her. When she fell on the table, I really thought she was dead . . .'

'She was grand! And everything's fine! Mam?' She needed Maeve to stop staring at her in that way. 'Mam?' She also needed her mother to stop holding Eva so tightly, and cringing against the dresser as if . . .

As if it wasn't only the welfare officer that was the threat. As if the human child needed protecting from the fairy child. The *alien* child.

Aoife's heart twisted.

'Aoife! Where are you going?'

'Out.'

'No! Come back!'

She leaned over the handlebars of the bike, flying along under the falling leaves. She wanted Shay. She had to talk to Shay. Only he would understand what it was like, not to truly belong in this world – not to be human. She had his phone number! Letting the bike drift into the side of the boreen, into a gateway, she pulled her new iPhone out of her hoodie, and took out the crumpled paper with his number.

But then, before uncrumpling it, stopped. He had said so painfully, *This really hurts.* Sounding almost angry with her, as if she didn't – *couldn't* – possibly understand . . . Eyes blurry, she shoved his number back in her pocket again. If this situation was hurting him anywhere near as much as it was hurting her, she should let him go . . . Oh God. She needed to talk to someone who loved her in a simple, uncomplicated way . . .

Carla.

Carla should be back from school by now.

Aoife didn't have to scroll for the number – it was the only one stored so far. Carla picked up on the second ring. 'Hi, Carl!'

'Jessica, hi! You've got a new phone!'

'It's Aoife, ya fool.'

'How are you feeling, Jessica? Any better?'

'It's *Aoife*. Are you in?'

'Hang on . . .' Carla's voice faded into the background, then came back. 'Sorry, Jessica, we're just about to eat so you can't come round.'

'*Carla, it's Aoife.*'

Another pause, longer this time. At the other end of the phone, the sound of movement, a door closing. Aoife, her phone to her ear, got off her bike and leaned it against the five-barred gate.

When Carla spoke again, it was very quietly. 'Are you still there?'

'Yes. This is Aoife, by the way.'

'I know that.'

'Well, that's a relief. So, what's going on?'

Another pause, and more movement. A tap running. Clearly Carla was in the toilet, and running water to cover her voice. She came back on the phone. 'To be honest, my mam's a bit angry with you. I've tried telling her you were in a mental hospital and Shay only found you two days ago, but she still thinks you and him probably spent the whole five months together because of how you left at the same time and came back at the same time, and so now she thinks you're still lying to me and that's made her even angrier and now she says I can't see you at all. Sorry.'

A feeling of resigned sadness swept over Aoife. Since junior infants, Carla's house had been Aoife's 'other home'. Almost every other day she had eaten or even slept there. Dianne Heffernan even liked to joke that she was Aoife's 'other mammy'. But now Dianne, as well as Maeve, felt the need to protect her human daughter from this strange, unknown girl who was Aoife.

'Oh, I see.'

Carla said, 'Obviously, I *will* see you . . .'

'Well, obviously.'

'But just not here. Are you well enough to leave your house?'

'Carla, I'm not really that ill . . .'

'Of course you're not – not any more, just so long as you take your medication! Have you taken it today?'

Aoife sighed. Maeve thought this was a good thing. 'Yes.'

'Perfect! Then you'll be grand. I'm going to

Killian's in an hour – why don't you meet me there, if your mam thinks you're OK to be out by yourself? I've explained it all to him as well, and I've told him you're not *scarily* mad, and you're getting over it anyway, and he's really sympathetic. So we don't have to talk about it at all – we can just hang out and chat about normal stuff.'

'Oh, Carla . . .' She did so want to see her, but the thought of meeting Killian made her cringe. Whether the builder's son believed Carla or Dianne, either way he was bound to find the whole Aoife thing pretty damn hilarious – however 'sympathetic' he was pretending to be for Carla's sake. 'I'd love to hang out, but not tonight.'

Carla sighed. 'OK, I guess it is a bit too soon for you to be out and about in the normal worl— Ha ha, in Kilduff, I mean.'

'Sure.'

'No, wait, don't go yet – listen. *Listen.*'

'I'm still here.'

'About Mam. She loves you. She's just – hurt, you know? And trying to protect me even though she's completely wrong.'

'I know.'

'Aoife . . . ?'

'Yes?'

'She'll come round when she realizes you really, *really* believe you're a fairy. And she won't mind that – it's not like she's not used to it with Auntie Ellie. And even if everyone else thinks you ran off with Shay, they'll get over it. As soon as you're feeling completely better, you and me, Killian and Shay – we'll all go out together. As a foursome. People will get used to it. They get used to anything in Kilduff, and they're only delighted to have life made interesting for them. What do you think?'

Aoife's heart swelled with sorrow. She opened her mouth to say, *Me and Shay, we're not seeing each other any more. Because it really hurts.*

'Aoife?'

'It's OK. I'll call you later. Bye . . .'

Carla cried anxiously, 'Hey, wait!'

'What?'

'I love you!'

'Love you too, Carl.'

'Take care of yourself. Don't forget to take your medication. And if your mam says it's OK for you to be out, I'll be at Killian's . . .'

As soon as Aoife got off the phone, she saw she'd received several texts from Maeve. Instead of reading them, she leaned her folded arms on the top bar of the gate, staring across the field. The rain had stopped for a while, and all was glimmering. There were sheep: peaceful humps of doing nothing. A strip of brighter grass ran across the far side of the field, from ditch to distant gate. The fairy road, cutting its way from her parents' house across the land towards the distant mountains and the hawthorn pool. Blocked only by Lois Munnelly's new-built bungalow, on the far side of the Clonbarra road. If she wanted to follow the fairy road all the way . . .

She supposed she would have to knock on Lois's front door and ask permission to walk through the house.

But that would be too weird. And she didn't want to go back.

She didn't want to go home either, not right now. She got on her bike, and travelled on.

She didn't take the fairy road, but somehow she found herself back at the hawthorn circle, anyway – heading left for Clonbarra then cutting right up the ancient bog road; dumping her bike on the verge; following the stony track across the bog; climbing the sheep-trodden pathways of the hill. The circle of tightly woven thorns was even more bare of leaves than when she and Shay had come home this way yesterday. The red berries had shrivelled in the cutting October wind. The thorns didn't want to let her through, but she put up her hood, and pushed and struggled her way in – tearing strips out of her hoodie and trackie bottoms.

Inside, the black pool lay flat, surrounded by the blossoms of last summer. Sprinkled with the tiny brown boats of curling leaves. She lay flat on her stomach, on the rotting blossoms – the stench was rich and sickly – and, after a moment's hesitation, dipped in her hand. And arm. Up to the elbow, before she could feel the soft mud.

Then sat up, wiping the mud off her hand onto the dead leaves.

Down.

But the pool was closed to her, as it had been before – back in May – when she'd seen the lost child out on the bog and chased after her into the hawthorn circle. Eva had been gone by the time she reached the pool, and by then the water had been shallow . . .

And that, she realized suddenly, was strange.

Caitlin and Ultan had been drawn back to the otherworld by their sheógs – the human children for whom they'd been exchanged. Ultan had 'drowned' in a bog pool and Caitlin in a well, before waking up again in the Land of the Young. Yet when she herself had followed Eva, her own sheóg, the pool had stayed closed to her. Why? Was it because Shay had already been in love with her – his desire protecting her from Dorocha?

He says he loves but cannot stay . . .

Oh, it was cruel.

Down.

She pulled off her trainers and trackie bottoms and slipped her feet into the pool. And stood up. It came to her knees. Her toes curled in the soft mud. She walked from one side to the other. It was a little deeper in the middle – halfway up her thighs. She dug around with her foot. Somewhere here was a gateway to the Land of the Young, that paradise buried beneath the wilds of Connacht. The world to which she belonged. The world where her fairy mother would not have shrunk from her, as Maeve had done, as if Aoife's power was a dark and frightening thing . . .

If she could only remember her fairy mother, just a little.

Down.

But when she tried, here and now, standing at the gate between the worlds, only terrible memories and thoughts arose. The queen's silver blood, spangled across the black sheets of her bed in the crystal minaret. Stabbed by the Beloved, in his jealous rage.

Down.

The red blood of the priest, her mother's lover, running for ever down the city walls. Murdered by the Beloved, and blamed for her mother's death.

Down.

(Dorocha the Beloved. His midnight eyes.)

Shivering, she climbed out of the pool, dried her legs on her trackies and pulled them damply on again.

On the way back along the Clonbarra road towards Kilduff, speeding through the deepening dusk, she passed yet another large outcrop of hawthorn – she hadn't noticed it earlier, but now there was a tractor parked in the road beside it and there were two farmers – one of whom she didn't recognize, but the other was Declan Sweeney – regarding the large tree in the beam of the tractor's headlights. As she neared them – slowing down to look normal – Declan was saying: 'But it must have been here before. And you can't chop it down even if it is after being in the way of the gate – it's pure bad luck.'

'Well, maybe it isn't hawthorn.'

'It is, Eoghan.'

'Then how is there mistletoe with him? I've never seen a mistletoe wrap himself around a hawthorn tree.'

Aoife slowed down even further. Something flickered in her mind from yesterday: throwing aside the crown of hawthorn and mistletoe as she and Shay walked down this road. But it had been such a little, little thing . . .

Declan Sweeney suddenly noticed her watching and smiled shyly. 'Welcome home, Aoife. Still love the lambs?'

Declan Sweeney always said the same thing to her, *Still love the lambs?* He'd brought a lamb to the

95

house once, for her mother to show her – a long time ago, when she was very sick. Although of course, she knew now that child hadn't been her. That had been the real Eva. The human child.

She bicycled on, through the purple dusk.

Halfway down the boreen, headlights suddenly threw Aoife's shadow in front of her, and a horn beeped. She looked over her shoulder, then coasted into a gateway to allow her father's Citroën to pass. He pulled up beside her, and stuck his head out of the window. 'Thank the Lord – I've been all over Mayo and I thought I was going to have to go home to your mother without having found you. She's been really, really worried about you.' By the shake in his voice, it was quite clear that he'd been really, really worried himself.

'It's only about six.'

'And dark. You've no lights on your bike – it's not safe, my love.'

'It wasn't so dark when I left the house.'

'Because you've been gone for hours. Aoife, we love you so much. *Please* don't do this to us, running off without telling us where you're going.'

'I'm back now, aren't I?'

'You are, and don't ever be afraid to come home.

If the guards come, we'll think of something to tell them, we'll sort it out—'

A flash of frustration. 'That wasn't why I went out! There's nothing to sort! I've sorted it already! The guards *won't* come, because I did a deal with that woman and she has to stick to it! I told Mam that and she must have told you. Why won't you both believe me?' She was tempted to jerk the bike round and go powering off again.

As if he'd guessed her thoughts, he scrambled out of the small green car – with difficulty, as always, because he was far too big for it. 'Stop, stop! Of course we believe you . . .'

She shrugged off his clumsy attempt at an embrace. 'No you don't! Maybe I should go back to the fairy world, where people understand magic . . .'

This time he refused to let her push him away, hugging her so tight she was squashed out of enough breath for speaking, and for a long while not saying anything himself. Until, in a voice thick with tears: 'What do you mean, where you belong? This is where you belong! Oh, darling child. Come home to us. Come home.'

*

Maeve also held her for a long, long time on her return.

But still, there was tension in the house. Her father constantly going to the door to look out. Her mother flinching at every gust of wind in the trees. Nervously expecting the guards to arrive.

Later, in her room, Aoife pulled out her phone to read through her mother's texts from earlier. All of them saying how much Maeve loved her.

There was also one from Carla, received only minutes before, which somehow she hadn't noticed – this phone had a different and softer alert noise than her old one: she would have to turn it up.

at Killians, he says if you're allowed, come round ☺☺☺

Killian was obviously keen to have a laugh at her expense. Another text popped in before she could think of a diplomatic reply:

he says he'll keep quiet and go in another room and wont get in the way of us talking ☺☺☺

To her surprise, Aoife found herself beginning to think she had underestimated the builder's son. After all, here he was with Carla, still going out with her after five months – nearly five months longer than he'd been in any previous relationship. And he was saying he'd keep out of her and Aoife's way, just to please Carla. Well, good for him. But still, he was Killian . . . She texted:

no, you're grand. ☺☺☺

And Carla replied:

ok if you not feeling the best ☹ love ya! ☺☺☺
stay safe I'll see you tomorrow xxxxxxxxxxxx

While Aoife had the phone in her hand, she decided to input the number Shay had given her. Just in case. She dug out the piece of paper, then noticed there was something on the other side and unfolded it. It opened into an A4 painting of a girl with red-gold hair.

Her heart grew hot. The last time she'd seen this

picture, Shay had seized the artist's sketchpad from her and tossed it into the back seat of the old red Ford, saying: *You don't want to be looking at my old rubbish.*

Why had he given her this? Had he wanted to show Aoife how much he cared about her? Or was he just getting rid of everything that could remind him of her?

Well, she was keeping this – it was beautiful.

In her still ridiculously tidy desk drawer was a roll of sticky tape. She stuck the picture to a clean patch of wall below her windowsill, picked up her guitar and sat facing it. The girl in the picture had her back to the artist, but she was unavoidably Aoife – and running up the hill towards the hawthorn circle, exactly the place where she'd just been.

She ran her fingers over the strings of her guitar, thinking of the lyric that had come to her earlier:

Around your wrist, a narrow line
of paler skin
because you once were mine . . .

And then added:

The windswept cliffs, the cool grey sea,
It hurts me when he looks at me

The words kept rising into her mind, like grey gulls over the edge of a cliff:

Looks at me and looks away
Saying he loves
but cannot stay

But finally, gazing at the picture right before her instead of at the picture in her head, she returned to the first lyric she had ever written about him:

I dream of this:
Under the hawthorns he raises me with a kiss . . .

The first lyric, and the truest.

CHAPTER SIX

'How about some Weetabix and a banana? It's so much healthier for you. You can't live on sugar.'

'*Hector wants . . .*'

Aoife rolled her eyes, and reached down the Coco Pops. She took the Weetabix packet for herself and threw five into the bowl – she was always starving these days – and chopped in three bananas. 'Come on, Eva – look at me, I'm eating loads of the healthy stuff for *my* breakfast.'

'Don't care!'

'Don't you want to grow up into a big strong girl like me?'

'No! I want to stay the way I am for ever!'

Aoife paused, in the act of slopping milk into her bowl. 'Really? Just four years old for ever?'

'Yes!'

'You don't want to grow up?'

'No, I'm a good girl, and Morfesa said I could stay the way I am for ever if came to his party . . .' Eva hesitated, and looked confused, casting a glance around the kitchen as if expecting the old druid from the Land of the Young to suddenly appear in his white robes.

'What party, honey?' It was the first time the little girl had even spoken of the fairy world since coming home.

'Nothing! I want cartoons!' Eva shoved her bowl aside, scrambled down to the floor and disappeared into the hall, Hector tucked under her arm.

Aoife found her in the back room, furiously attempting to turn the television on by pressing a non-existent button – the way she must have learned to turn it on eleven years ago. 'Here.' Aoife found the remote, and got up a cartoon on Netflix. Eva scrambled into the deep wing-back armchair by the bookcase, and sat with her legs stretched out, heels just over the edge of the cushion.

Leaning on the back of the chair, Aoife looked down at the little girl's blonde curls and wondered what Morfesa had said to Eva. Clearly, something about never growing up – but what was special about that, in the Land of the Young? Everyone there stayed the age they were, unless they were sent to the human world. She herself would still be only four years old if she'd remained at her fairy mother's side. And with that thought came another memory of the queen – not a real memory, but one given her by Dorocha.

So many fairy mothers neglect their children. But your mother brought you everywhere with her, even when she went to walk in the surface world to wash her hair in the soft water of the bog pools – and there you would age a day every time. In the end she stopped bringing you to the surface. She was right. She was immortal. Why would paradise need a second queen? It would only make trouble.

If Dorocha was telling the truth, the queen had never intended Aoife to grow up – nor to find her powers. Strange thought. Her fairy mother, although fond of her, had wanted her to stay a powerless child for ever. She reached down to brush Eva's short curls back from her forehead. 'Wouldn't you like to be old enough to go to school, with all the other little girls? My friend Carla has a sister your age and I'm sure she'd love to meet you.'

Tilting back her head, Eva looked up Aoife with pale, ice-blue eyes. 'What's her name?'

'Zoe.'

'Is she going to grow up?'

'She is.'

'Will she be a doctor?'

Aoife said, surprised, 'Maybe. Why a doctor?'

'Doctors are nice.' And Eva went back to watching cartoons, Hector tucked comfortably under her chin.

Back up in her bedroom, Aoife opened the drawers of the press until she found the clothes she was looking for – neatly folded away in drawer of their own, along with her school books.

'You're in your school uniform!' Maeve was in the hallway as Aoife came down the stairs, on her way to the back room with a cup of tea in hand. She stared up at Aoife in open surprise – she herself was still in her blue paisley dressing gown, hair an unbrushed mess. 'I didn't think you'd want—'

'Why not?' Aoife hopped down the last two steps, school bag in hand. 'I've got to go back to school sometime. No point sitting around and doing nothing all day while everyone else gets on with their lives. If I'm going to act normal, the sooner I start, the better.'

Her mother winced guiltily. 'Oh, Aoife . . . Just let me get dressed and wake your dad to mind Eva, and I'll drive you and we'll talk. And you need a packed lunch—'

'Already done. Mam, don't fuss, I'll take the bike.' She went to the coat hooks, where her school coat had clearly hung all summer – another little shrine to her memory, when her parents had thought she was dead. She pulled on the washed-and-pressed jacket and shouldered the bag of books.

'Aoife . . .' Maeve was between her and the door.

'Mam, I really need to get going.'

With a sudden pounce, and a rather wild look in her blue eyes, Maeve seized both of Aoife's hands. 'Look, I'm *sorry* how I kept on acting like the guards were going to come.'

Aoife stood looking down at her mother's hands, so tightly intertwined with hers – Maeve's plump and pink; her own slender and pale. 'It's fine.'

'Darling, look at me.'

She did. Her mother's eyes were so like Eva's, and were now filled with tears.

'Darling, I'm so grateful to you for saving Eva from that woman and I'm so sorry I didn't believe you about the deal.'

Smiling now, Aoife managed to extricate one of

her hands so she could unlatch the door. 'Really, don't worry about it.'

Still keeping a tight grip on the other hand, Maeve said, 'And I'm *so* glad I have a fairy for a daughter, and I'm so sorry I didn't trust you and got stupid and frightened. I'll learn. You'll have to show me everything you can do.'

There was a warm, pleasant feeling in Aoife's heart. 'Mam, everything's fine – don't worry about it.'

Maeve squeezed Aoife's hand very tight before finally releasing her to the day. 'I love you, my fairy daughter. I really do.'

The autumn morning had barely yet broken when she left the house – the sky still a sickly yellow-grey, and the fields dully glimmering with last night's rain. The fairy road was a silvery strip of dew, running up Declan Sweeney's steep and stony field.

Fetching the bike out of the shed, she checked the tyres. They were bald already, after only a day's use – she had to stop riding so fast: they'd burst on her soon like the last pair. But once outside in the lane, she threw her leg over the saddle, and despite her best intentions sprinted wildly all the way to the

Clonbarra road, flying over the potholes. Then slowed to a less entertaining, human pace, through Kilduff, left at the shop and up the hill to school.

She heard Lois before she saw her, the girl's voice high and trembling with excitement:

'You don't understand, I just *knew* – it was like we had an instant connection – oh my God, he was *pure gorgeous.*'

Aoife stopped dead where she was, her school bag half off her shoulder. Where Lois was, so would be Sinead. Aoife looked carefully round the corner. By the grey metal lockers, a group of girls were clustered around Lois Munnelly – they were out of her line of sight, but she could see them reflected like ghosts in the steamed-up windows, beyond which the increasingly heavy rain poured into the school courtyard.

Jessica was saying anxiously, 'I still don't think you should have let him into your house, not if you didn't know him.'

'But it was like I knew him.' Lois's voice was dreamy and soft. 'Even though we'd never met before.'

Sinead said, 'Well, what was he doing in your garden?'

'He'd been walking the fields between our house and the mountains checking on all the old stone things on the way because he was a . . . Oh God, what did he say he was? Something with a really long name.'

'Psychopathic lunatic.'

'No! Beginning with "A".'

'Axe-murderer.'

'*Stop.*'

Jessica said helpfully, 'Archaeologist?'

Lois's reflection nodded vigorously, tight black curls bobbing. 'Something like that.'

'How old was he?'

'Twenty? Not even. *Anyway*, it started raining, and he asked to come in, and I made him a cup of tea while it stopped, and he wanted to know all about me, and who did I like at school, and what I do with my friends, and I told him about the boring old Halloween disco—'

Sinead's voice protested in alarm – or mock alarm, 'God's sake, Lois, what are you at? It's like one of those teenage snuff movies – he's going to come in a mask and hunt us down and kill us all one by one.'

'*Stop!* And then, when the rain eased up, he said

he had to go on, he had a meeting in Kilduff, and we had a laugh about it being bad luck to leave by a different door than he came in by, but he went out of the front door anyway and went off down the road towards Kilduff, and he was looking back at me all the time and waving . . .'

Jessica and Jessica's best friend Aisling sighed at the same time: '*Aaaah!*'

'I *know*, it was *so romantic*.'

Sinead said, 'Well, if you run off with some weird guy, at least send us a postcard to let us know you're still alive.'

'Excuse me! I'm not some careless slut like Aoife O'Connor, thank you very much . . .'

Aoife found her own arm suddenly and forcefully linked. She was being dragged away down the corridor by Carla, who was hissing at her, 'What are you doing here? You need to be at home resting.'

'You did say *see you tomorrow* . . .'

'I meant *after* school! You're not well enough for this! Surely to God your parents would let you stay off until after the Halloween break?'

'But that's ages away.'

'What are you on about? It's next week!'

'Oh . . .' Of course it was – this was October, and that explained the plastic spiders in the shop, and the witch-hat fascinators. If she'd stopped another day in the otherworld, she'd have missed Christmas. (Terrifying to think: if she'd been gone a few months, she'd have missed her whole life here.)

Carla said, 'I really don't think this is a good idea, but if your parents are cool with it – look, just stick tight by me and don't mind anyone or get stressed out. I've told everyone it was just a nervous breakdown, but you might hear a bit of—'

'Really, it's OK. I don't care what people like Sinead are saying.'

'If she gives you a hard time, I'm going to punch her out.'

'Do not! I can fight my own battles.'

As she continued to hurry Aoife along the corridor, Carla said kindly, 'No you can't – you're in a highly fragile state and I'm going to look after you. Come on, maths is first lesson.'

'Hang on, I need to go back and put my books in my locker.'

'You don't have a locker any more.'

'What? *Why?*'

'Because you were dead, that's why! Dead people don't get lockers! You'll have to drag your bag around with you until they sort one out. Anyway, your books will be the wrong ones now – we're not doing junior cert any more.'

'Aren't we? Oh, of course—'

'Aoife! Hey, Aoife!'

The shout came from a group of little kids Aoife didn't recognize. She craned to look back at them, puzzled. 'Who are that lot?'

'Nobody. First years.'

'Oh, sweet, they're so small!'

'Yay, small like head lice.'

'Aoife and Shay, sitting in a tree, kay eye ess ess eye en gee!'

'See what I mean? They're so much cheekier now than we were back then. Where is Shay, by the way? Is he coming in today as well?'

'I think so.'

Carla slowed her pace and looked at her searchingly. 'You don't know? He wouldn't leave you to do this on your own. You surely told him you were coming in?'

'No . . .' She had *thought* about texting him to say

she'd be there – because where could be the harm in seeing each other across a crowded classroom? But she had stopped herself in time. *It's not fair to keep on tugging at him.*

Carla was looking at her even more closely, with deep concern. 'Is everything OK between you? You haven't split up already? I thought you were mad in love with each other . . .'

Aoife said, blinking back tears, 'We are . . .'

A deep voice cried, 'Well, look who's back!'

'Pay no attention.' Carla picked up the pace again, hustling Aoife past a group of tall, lanky boys who were swivelling their heads to stare at her. She didn't recognize them any more than she had recognized the first years. The boy who had shouted out was six foot tall and heavily spotted, with greasy brown hair, and she'd never seen him before in her life . . .

Although a moment later, she realized that in fact she'd known him for ever: he was the butcher's son, Lorcan McNally. It was just that the last time she'd seen him, he had been extremely short and extremely fat. And now she realized she knew all the other lads as well – they were all from her year – but it was really confusing because they had grown so tall and skinny, seemingly overnight. That was what happened when you went away for a couple of days in the teenage growth-spurt years and came back to find five months had passed.

And there was Shay! So tall, with cropped black hair. Turning now to see what the others were looking at . . . She realized suddenly how much she'd prayed he would be here . . .

It wasn't him. It was Killian's cousin Darragh Clarke, standing a good fifteen centimetres taller than when she had seen him last. He peeled away from the group of gaping, grinning boys and came towards her, inserting himself in her and Carla's way. 'So, what's the story?' Not only had he grown, his voice had dropped an octave since she'd last heard him speak.

Carla tried to drag Aoife past him. 'I've told you, and she doesn't want to talk to you!'

He blocked their path, resting his hand against the wall. 'Easy, tiger, I'm not going to steal your cub. So, Miss O'Connor, what happened?'

'She's in a fragile state and she doesn't want to talk about it!'

Darragh leaned in closer. 'I hear Shay Foley is

taking your break-up so bad, he's dropped out of school so he never has to see a certain gorgeous girl again.'

'They haven't broken' – Carla's eyes slid sideways to Aoife and her sentence faded to a question – 'up?'

Aoife was unable to speak – she felt breathless and sick, like she'd taken a punch to the gut. *He was so desperate not to see her, he'd dropped out of school?*

Darragh was laughing. 'Oh dear, didn't Aoife tell you? Quite a habit with her, isn't it, keeping secrets from her best friend? Well, in the interests of openness and transparency, let me help: John Joe brought Lorcan's dad a trailer-load of lambs for slaughter this morning and told him Shay's jacked in lessons to work on the farm.'

Carla's expression hardened. She said grimly to Aoife, 'Toilets.'

'Good stuff.' Darragh nodded cheerfully. 'Get the full story out of her, and then I'll get the full story out of Killian after he gets it out of you.'

'Look, I know you're not well and you're not totally responsible for everything you do, but are you

115

determined to make me look like a complete idiot? Why didn't you tell me you'd finished with him?'

Aoife leaned against the bathroom wall with her hands over her face, trying not to cry. 'I didn't finish with him. I love him.'

'Then why is he so miserable he doesn't even want to see you?'

'It's complicated . . .'

'Oh God . . .' The anger melted out of Carla's voice. 'Don't cry. Did he dump you? The bastard! I'm sorry. Here . . .'

'He's not a bastard, he's just trying to do the right thing.' Aoife mopped her eyes with the length of toilet roll Carla had pressed into her hands, and blew her nose. 'Crap, I can't believe he's dropped out of school.'

Carla gave her another length of the roll. 'What do you mean *do the right thing*? What's happened between you? *Tell me.*'

'I can't – you'll just think I'm being mad again.'

'Tell me!'

Aoife cried despairingly, 'OK, it's because his mother was a lenanshee, and so is he. If a lenanshee falls in love with you, and you with them, they can destroy you entirely, you end up living out your dreams really fast and then—'

Carla interrupted, with a catch in her voice, 'Yes, I know what a lenanshee is.'

It was Aoife's turn to be taken aback. 'You do?'

Carla leaned against the basin, arms folded, eyes lowered to her shoes. She said quietly, 'Old John McCarthy is always going on about his nephew's wife being a lenanshee. He said it's her fault his nephew is wasting away doing nothing but writing poetry, because she's a lover from the otherworld, and once the lenanshee has a *grá* for you, you're doomed to do great things then go to an early grave.'

Aoife agreed eagerly, 'Yes, he told me that too – I didn't believe it until . . .'

Carla raised her eyes to her, damp with sympathy. 'But Doctor Burke says Andrew McCarthy has multiple sclerosis.'

'Oh.' Aoife's heart sank again.

'Seriously, Aoife, you can't do this to Shay Foley. You can't be after breaking up with him . . .'

'*I didn't!*'

'. . . just because you've got it in your head he's a

lenanshee. Try to remember the fairy thing is all in your—' The school bell blared out from speakers set high in the wall. Carla sighed and picked her books up off the basin. 'Come on, we'll talk about this later. Miss O'Shea is a luna— Sorry, I mean, she gets very cross if anyone's late.'

But instead of following, Aoife turned to the mirror over the sink, sadly pushing back her tear-sticky hair. 'You go on. I want to wash my face, I'm a mess.'

Carla hesitated behind her – clearly reluctant to leave a mentally unbalanced Aoife unattended; clearly worried about being late for maths. 'Be quick, I'll wait.'

'No, go.'

'I don't want to leave you—'

'Go on, I'll be grand.'

Carla sighed, giving in. 'OK, OK, just don't go wandering off anywhere. I'll save you a seat. Be quick.' The door swung shut.

Aoife splashed her blotched face with cold water and fixed her long red-gold ponytail. No point walking around looking like a mess, however she felt inside. Although hopefully by now everyone would be in class, and she could slip out of school without being seen.

The clouds had burst as she hurried across the teachers' car park to the bike shed. Now a solid grey downpour was rattling the corrugated-tin roof. Sitting beside the bike rack on an upturned blue plastic milk crate, waiting for the weather to pass over, she got out her phone and texted Carla:

sorry had to go home, I call you after school

Then sat staring at the screen for a while – but of course, Carla's phone would be turned off in class. She texted Shay. She didn't want to tug at him. But she couldn't leave things the way they were.

don't drop out. I wont come near u. i wont even look at u.

Again, she sat staring at the screen. Again, nothing.

Outside, the downpour was getting heavier, thundering on the corrugated tin, dripping in long silver streams through holes in the rust. The school building was almost invisible through the curtain of water pouring from the sky. Aoife turned up her school coat collar against the cold; she rested her elbows on her knees; she tried not to listen for the beep of an incoming message from the phone in her pocket. If Shay was out on the bog, he might be out of range. Or maybe he was sitting on the tractor, thinking about her text, deciding whether or not to answer . . . A cold drip fell on her neck, bringing her back to where she was – a leaking bike shed in the school grounds. Shivering, she moved the crate into a drier corner at the far end of the bike rack, then zipped open her school bag to dig out her packed lunch. However bad she was feeling, the amount of calories she needed to consume these days was absurd – her metabolism must be racing since her powers had started to develop.

She was halfway through her second ham sandwich when Killian hurtled into the bike shed on his blue racing bike – no longer bright brand new, like the last time she'd seen it, but battered, muddy and scratched. He swung in a wide skittering circle, jumped off, tossed his bike into the rack beside Aoife's, scowled out at the rain – his school coat was soaked – and finally noticed Aoife sitting in the corner, trying but failing to be invisible (clearly, not a power of hers). He caught his breath loudly, silver-grey eyes widening with surprise.

For a few seconds Aoife could only stare silently back at him, halted in mid-bite of her sandwich.

Even though she'd seen his updated image on his Facebook page, it was still shocking how much Killian had grown since she'd seen him last – almost as much as his cousin Darragh. And he looked older in other ways as well: less boy band, more male model. His trademark floppy hair had been cropped short, and his face was thinner; his cheekbones now high and sharp; cheeks slightly hollow. Something about him touched her heart like a freezing hand . . .

Down.

Something about . . .

Down.

His face . . .

Stop that. Killian's hair wasn't the blackened red of dying coals, but white-blond: the colour of Mayo sand. The eyes of the Beloved were the inky blue of midnight, flecked through with tiny golden stars. Killian's eyes were silvery grey, like a cold low-lying mist on a winter's day.

And yet . . .

'This is a surprise. What are you doing here?' Killian pulled off his wet coat and gave it a strong shake, before hanging it on the handlebars of his bike.

'Eating,' said Aoife, continuing to do so.

'Then don't let me interrupt you.' He threw his leg over the crossbar of his blue racer and sat balanced astride the saddle, toes on the ground, arms folded.

She frowned at him. 'Aren't you going into class? The bell went ages ago.'

'Right back at you.'

She took out a third sandwich. She had packed a big lunch. 'I prefer it out here.'

'Hanging out in the bike shed, eating like a pig? Is this a symptom of your unstable mental condition?'

She looked at him.

He smiled back at her in a surprisingly friendly fashion, running one hand through his wet fair hair, spiking it up. 'Don't get me wrong, I don't really think you're mad. I'm just interested. Tell me about where you went this summer.'

She stuffed down the last piece of crust. 'I don't want to talk about it.'

He nodded, still very friendly. 'I can understand that. That was a pretty unbelievable story you were telling Carla— It's all right, don't worry!' He raised his hand as Aoife looked up sharply. 'Everyone else, she's just saying it was a nervous breakdown. It's only me she was telling about your fairy delusion, and she's sworn me to secrecy – and don't get thick with her about it, she had to tell someone or she'd have had a breakdown herself. She's had a rough summer.'

Again, she felt she might have got Killian wrong. She'd never liked him – especially since he'd lied to Carla about Aoife fancying him last May. But here he was, being genuinely concerned for Carla. And not even being that mean about the 'fairy delusion'. 'I'm not cross with her for telling you and I know she's been miserable, thinking I was dead. I feel crap about that. I just didn't have a way to contact her.'

'No mobile phone network?'

'No . . .'

'The fairy world must be very old tech. But couldn't you have just used magic?'

Annoyed at herself for letting her guard down, Aoife started packing her lunchbox back into her bag.

Killian watched her, swinging his foot, brushing

the sole of his trainer against the ground, to and fro. He said, 'Satisfy my curiosity. What was this fairy world like? Is it better than this world?'

She stood up, shouldering the bag. He also slipped off his bike and stood up. 'Wait, don't run off on me. I like the fairy thing. I was googling it last night. Is there really a whole different world under the surface of Connacht?'

'I have to go now.'

'No, wait, I'm not ripping the piss, I think it's interesting. Can you really make fairy gold? I'd like to do that. Sometimes I almost feel like I could . . . I have some skills myself – I always know who's texting me even before I look, I don't know how . . .'

She made to move past him, to get her own bike, but he put his hand on her arm. His touch made the hairs on the back of her arm stand up, right through her jacket, and she shook him off sharply, with a shudder of revulsion.

He looked surprisingly hurt. 'Hey – do you hate me that much?'

'Sorry . . .' She had to stop thinking how the builder's son reminded her of Dorocha. It was ridiculous. 'Of course I don't hate you.'

'But you don't like me?'

'Of course I like you – you're . . .' His hand was on her arm again, and she pressed her lips together, steeling herself not to react.

He was smiling into her face. 'Good, because I like you too, fairy girl.' And his perfect mouth came close to hers.

She jumped back in absolute horror. 'What are you doing? Get off me! I don't mean that way! I like you because you're Carla's boyfriend!'

'Fine, grand.' But he was still smiling at her, unbothered, elbows akimbo. 'I get it – Carla's your best friend, and you girls stick together. But you know, down the road—'

'Don't you dare dump her!'

He laughed, holding up his hands, palms out. 'Aoife, come on. I'm not even sixteen yet. I'm hardly going to be going out with some girl I met in school for the rest of my life.'

'She really cares about you!'

'And I care about her, and I don't want to hurt her – she's sweet. She's maybe the sweetest girl I've ever been out with. But one day I'm going to *have* to hurt her—'

The dark power burst out of her.

Killian screamed long and loud, slapping his hand to his chest then crashing sideways, striking his head off the sharp metal corner of the bike rack – which was when the scream cut off abruptly, like a door slammed shut on a raucous party.

Aoife couldn't physically move. Her vision was spotted black. She was going to be sick. She'd had no idea what she'd been just about to do . . . It was only when he said, *I'm going to have to hurt her* . . . Killian lay on the damp floor unmoving, a little streak of blood running out from under his hair. *She'd killed Killian Doherty* . . .

He rolled over onto his face, groaning.

'Oh, thank—!' Dizzy with relief, Aoife rushed over to him.

'What happened to me?' He was struggling into a sitting position, feeling the back of his head. 'I feel really weird.'

Aoife crouched in front of him, holding up three fingers. Her hand was trembling, weak from the discharge of power. 'How many?'

He glanced dismissively. 'Three. Last thing I remember . . .' He frowned and took his hand from the back of his head, then looked startled at the dab of blood on his fingertips. 'I'm bleeding!' His eyes focused on her, shocked. 'Jesus, Aoife! What did you push me for?'

'I'm sorry, I didn't mean to—'

'*Jesus, Aoife* . . .' He was on his feet, now – spitting fury. 'I can't believe I was trying to be nice to you! I can't believe Carla said you're not dangerous! Jesus Christ, you're *insane* . . .' And he raced away across the courtyard, splashing blindly through the rain.

CHAPTER SEVEN

Crouched over the handlebars, she hurtled across the flooded yard, out of the school gates and down the hill towards Kilduff.

First the welfare officer, then Killian. He was right – she was literally insane. She couldn't protect people by going around acting like a lunatic! Flinging Deirdre Joyce to the ceiling! Her mother was right – she could have killed the woman! And it was beyond crazy to attack Killian, just because – *one day I'm going to have to hurt her* – he'd been talking about splitting up with Carla. Killian wasn't some evil demon – *something about his face* – he was an annoying, selfish teenage boy who might one day break her best friend's heart . . . until Carla realized what a jerk he was and found someone new.

There was no heroism in battering mere humans with fairy power.

If she couldn't control herself, she needed some sort of help.

Maybe she should take pills, like Carla's Auntie Ellie?

Hot and sweating, despite the rain, she turned her focus to slowing down before she reached Kilduff, so as not to knock anyone over this time round. She was still going about thirty kilometres an hour as she swept past the shop and across the square, heading out down the Clonbarra road. Yet by the time she passed the empty estate, she found herself slowing further . . .

Stopping. U-turn. Riding back.

When she reached the church, the porch door was ajar. Perhaps she had noticed subconsciously that the church was open, and that's what had prompted her to turn round. She left her bike, leaning it against one of the fancier tombs – one with a door and a railing around it. It was the Doherty resting place. Killian's grandparents, Joseph and Betsy, lay there. What would they have thought if they had known how close their handsome grandson had been to joining them, at Aoife's hands?

Entering the porch, she dipped her fingers in the small font of holy water and crossed herself. The glass doors to the interior were locked, but she touched her finger to the brass keyhole and the mechanism clicked open. (She felt momentarily smug – now, that was the sort of magic power that made life easier.) Stepping into the aisle, she crossed herself again, and dipped her knee to the altar. Then sat down in the nearest pew. Then knelt on the embroidered prayer cushion, with her hands resting on the back of the pew in front. Then restlessly took off her school coat, which was still dripping. Then, still unable to settle, checked her phone. Still nothing from either Carla or Shay.

Through the stained-glass windows on either side of the church, and the rose window high above the altar, struck coloured bars of light. Under the rose hung a wooden Christ, much larger than life, arms spread upon the cross, head drooping under His heavy crown of thorns. Gazing at Him, Aoife folded her hands again, and tried to imitate His stillness. The Catholic church was a part of her family life, the same as nearly every family in Kilduff. She had never thought about whether she believed in God – she had just always assumed she did. She had been baptized; she had made her Holy Communion, and her

Confirmation. Her mother had brought her to church every Sunday since she was a child. She had accepted without question that Jesus Christ was her saviour.

And now she needed Him to save her.

She said, in her mind, to the man on the cross: *Father, I know not what I do. Save me from myself. Whoever I am.*

In the still, cold silence of the church, the wooden man gazed down.

I don't want to kill anyone. Save me. Take away from me this dark, unholy power.

The man's eyes were weary. Was He even listening?

Lowering her gaze, she recited the first part of the rosary, under her breath: 'I believe in the Holy Spirit, the Holy Catholic Church . . .' In the stony cold, her breath came out in smoky wisps, condensing on the air. 'I believe in the communion of Saints, the forgiveness of sins, the resurrection of the body and life everlasting. Amen.'

As she finished, a jaunty tune sprang into her head – for a moment she wondered who it was by, before she realized it was one of her own. It was the song that had formed itself in her head the last time she was in this church. And now the lyrics were coming back to her as well:

Your God says he's the holy one,
But you know he's not the only one . . .

She couldn't block out the annoying tune, because it was coming from inside her head, and she couldn't pray until it stopped. She rested her forehead on the polished rail of the pew in front of her, waiting for it to end.

I think he's just the lonely one,
Maybe he's the phoney one . . .

At last it died away, and her head went quiet. Her eyes still closed, she said loudly: 'Glory be to the Father, and to the Son, and to the Holy Spirit. As it was in the beginning, is now, and ever shall be, world without end. Amen.'

A hand touched her arm, and she shook it off with a startled yelp, then saw who it belonged to and sprang to her feet. 'Sorry, Father, I didn't see it was you.'

'And I'm sorry if I disturbed you, Aoife. Please sit down again.' The priest lowered himself into the pew in front of her, settling himself sideways, his long thin legs stretched out, feet resting in the aisle. Under the hem of his black robes he was wearing surprisingly expensive-looking trainers. He raised his eyes to hers – dark and small in his clean-shaven face. He didn't smile, but then, he had always been a cold, dry man. 'Welcome to the House of God, Aoife.' His voice, like hers, came out in small white puffs, like a man smoking outside a pub. 'And may I ask, how did you get in?'

'The door was left open – I thought it was OK to come in, I'm going now. I'm sorry for disturbing you – it's just, the door was left open and it was raining out.'

He remained sitting. 'The door is always open to those who seek God's help.'

'I know, but—'

'Sit down, Aoife.'

She sat. She had been raised to show respect to the priest. Besides, she knew how good Father Leahy had been when she was 'dead' – visiting her parents almost every week, saying Mass for the peaceful repose of her and Shay Foley's souls – assuring everyone that the angels had brought the star-crossed lovers straight to the feet of God.

When she had settled herself, he said, 'Good. Now – tell me why you are here.'

'No reason, Father.' She knew it sounded ignorant, but it was God she had come to ask for help. Not this dry, cold priest, who would think she was mad if she told him one word of the truth.

The priest continued to study her, unsmiling. 'But you came in here to pray?'

'Yes, but—'

'Tell me why.'

Her heart sank and she squirmed slightly in her seat. She should have understood. Father Leahy was clearly wanting to hear all about her five months away with Shay Foley. He wouldn't have been impressed by Carla's 'nervous breakdown' story, even if he had heard it. He must want her to explain how she could do something so sinful – run off with a boy, and her not even sixteen, and never make contact with her parents to say where she'd gone. He must be expecting her to make a very long, very interesting, confession.

The priest was still gazing at her with his small dark eyes. Disapproving. Cold. Fascinated.

She was mortified to feel herself blushing. 'I know it looks bad, Father, but it didn't happen the way you think.'

He raised thin eyebrows. 'And what exactly do I think?'

'I . . .' Her voice faded; she looked down into her lap. This was awful, knowing what was in his old-fashioned head and having no way of disproving it. 'I can't talk about this.'

'You mean, you can't tell me the truth.'

She didn't answer.

He put his white hand on the polished rail of the pew between them. 'But what if I already know the truth?'

Her cheeks grew hot. 'You don't, Father, because it's definitely not what you think.'

'Mm.' As if to buy himself time to consider what he was going to say next, the priest rummaged for something in his robe, took out a handkerchief – a cotton one – and blew his nose. He said eventually, 'It might surprise you to hear this, but I know all about you.'

'Really, Father, you don't.'

He folded the handkerchief carefully back into his pocket. 'I do, Aoife. In fact, I've known for years.'

'No, seriously, you— *What?*' She stared at the priest blankly, completely thrown off track.

His eyes moved across her face, studying it like a strange, unfamiliar object. 'That's right, Aoife. Years and years. Yet I hid the truth – even from myself.'

The rhythm of Aoife's heart quickened slightly. She sat up straight, saying nothing, only listening.

The priest smiled dryly, dipping his head – acknowledging that he had won her full attention. 'Yesterday, a welfare officer asked me for directions to your house. Do you remember? You were cycling by at the time, and I signalled for you to stop.'

'Sorry, Father.' A knee-jerk reaction, while she desperately tried to work out what was going on.

He waved her fake apology away. 'I wanted to introduce you to the woman in the car. She was asking about Maeve and James O'Connor's four-year-old daughter, Eva. And I wanted to prove to her that you weren't four but fifteen.'

'That's right, I . . .'

The priest held up his soft white hand. 'Less than

an hour later, I met the same woman again – this time in the garage, where we were both buying petrol. I asked if she'd found the child she was looking for. She showed me a picture she had taken on her phone, of the child in question sitting at your kitchen table. "The child is adopted and everything is in order," she said. "The child is adopted and everything is in order." She didn't seem able to say anything else. She paid for her petrol and drove away.'

Aoife kept her expression deliberately blank. Inside, she was dancing. She'd been right: the welfare officer couldn't break the deal. Eva was officially safe. She said boldly, 'The fact is, Father – my parents have adopted a little girl. They didn't like to say anything until the whole thing was finalized, but now that everything is in order, I think it's OK to tell everyone.'

The priest again went through the elaborate process of retrieving his handkerchief and blowing his nose. Then he said, 'When James O'Connor was in his twenties, he moved to Dublin.'

Once more, Aoife was thrown by his reply. It seemed to have no bearing on what they'd just been talking about. 'I know, Father.'

'Later, James's parents moved to Australia to be with his sister, their daughter. For years the O'Connor family home stood empty.'

'I know, Father.'

'Then one day James and his Dublin wife came home with their own daughter, Eva. She was very sick. No one was allowed in to see her, because of the risk of infection. But everyone believed the O'Connors had brought the little girl home to die.'

'I know they did, Father. But then I got better.' Why was Father Leahy telling her this old story about her own childhood? As far as he and Kilduff was concerned, the dying child had been her. No one in the town had seen the original Eva – that was why it had been so easy for her parents to pass the fairy child off as the human child.

The priest said coolly, 'There was only one man that your parents dared to let into the house, because they believed the power of God was stronger than the risk of infection. I prayed with them at her bed-side for over an hour. I will never forget that little face – such a beautiful child, with short blonde hair and ice-blue eyes.'

Aoife gazed at him steadily, the small hairs on the back of her neck rising.

'Months later, Maeve O'Connor brought Eva to Mass. Not only was the little girl so full of life and health she couldn't sit still, but she had bright red hair instead of blonde.'

'Young children change—'

He raised his hand to silence her. 'I know. And the child had been sick. And I'd only seen her the once. That's what I told myself. Until yesterday, when that woman showed me the picture she'd taken on her phone. And there was the face I had never forgotten. Those eyes – unforgettable. As pale as ice. Eva O'Connor – still only four years old.'

Aoife stared at him, her heart beating very fast, a bird in a cage.

He smiled at her briefly. 'I may be a priest, Aoife, but I am a Mayo man. I know what happened eleven years ago. I know you are the changeling child.'

After the shock, Aoife experienced a deep hot feeling of relief. At last, here was someone other than her parents who knew who she was. Someone she could talk to in confidence – because a priest couldn't break the secrets of the confessional. Someone who could absolve her of past sins. Who could help her with the darkness.

In the cold, stone silence of the church, the wooden man gazed down with His weary eyes. Was this how He had answered her prayer? Father Leahy was saying nothing, his own head tilted to one side in much the same way as the carved Jesus – waiting for her to speak.

She blurted out: 'I don't want to hurt anyone, Father, but I have this power, and it bursts out of me if I sense danger, if I feel the need to protect someone. I haven't done anything too terrible yet, but I'm scared I might. It's like having something inside me that doesn't know how to behave—'

He interrupted, 'Like an animal.'

She stopped. Then said, uncomfortably, 'Yes.'

'I'm not surprised by what you're telling me.'

'You're not?' This wasn't quite the help she'd been looking for. And he had spoken so coldly. 'What do you mean?'

He said, 'You are a fairy, Aoife. You are from a pagan race. You have not received God's grace. You are not a Christian.'

140

The feeling of relief drained away as fast as it had come. Something she had never understood before clicked into place. The hostility with which Father Leahy had watched her down the years. His hesitation over giving her the communion wafer. His narrow, suspicious gaze – the same one that rested on her now. *You are not a Christian.* She said, deeply offended, 'I am a Christian, I'm a Catholic. I did my Holy Communion.'

'You were not baptized.'

'Yes, I was— Oh.' It was true, the real Eva's baptismal certificate wasn't hers, any more than Eva's birth certificate was hers. It had happened before the banshee came.

Father Leahy's dark, cold eyes rested on Aoife's face. 'If you wish me to help you, Aoife, and cast out this dark magic from your soul, you will have to believe in the one true God.'

In her head, the inner tune piped up again: *Your God says he's the holy one, but you know he's not the only one . . .* She said loudly, to drown it out, 'Of course I believe in Him!'

Father Leahy bowed his head. 'Then the next step is baptism, to purify your soul.'

141

'Purify . . . ?' The tune in her head redoubled in volume, singing crossly: *Maybe he's the phoney one!!*

The priest said thoughtfully, more to himself than to her, 'With His help, I am certain I can make room in your heart for His glory. Didn't Saint Patrick meet with the fairies and preach to them?' He stood up, holding out his hand to usher her with him. 'Come. Let us try what we can do to ensure you a place in heaven.'

For a moment she was so angry at the implication that she was beyond God's grace (how different was the priest behaving from Sinead?) that she nearly refused him and walked out. But at the same time she had come in here to beg God for help – and this seemed to be what was on offer, in answer to her prayer. She got to her feet, and followed him.

The priest left her standing by the font, while he went to fetch the baptismal service. As soon as he'd disappeared into the vestry, she lifted the wooden lid to peep inside – the stone bowl was full of dimpled water. White mist rose from it, in the cold air. Would Father Leahy pour it over her head, like he did with the babies? The little ones always screamed their heads off. She dipped in a finger. Not too bad.

Quite warm, actually, considering how cold the church was. Did the water get heated somehow, for christenings? It wasn't a question she'd ever asked herself. Maybe in the vestry, Father Leahy had flicked on some switch. A few bubbles were rising to the surface, like an electric kettle only just starting to heat up. Hearing a noise from the vestry, she hastily resettled the lid and sat in the nearest pew.

After her baptism, would she be a changed person? She felt a stab of fright – maybe her powers would disappear. (But wasn't that what she wanted? *Evil witch*, Killian had called her.)

Before she could think it through further, Father Leahy reappeared with a small leather book open in his hand. He lifted the lid off the font, beckoning Aoife to his side. She found herself walking towards him very slowly. Then she decided it was ridiculous to be afraid of a little water. Baptism was symbolic – a way of admitting her into the Catholic religion, so the priest could then advise her with a clear conscience.

The wooden man gazed down.

Father Leahy placed his hand on the back of her neck, saying rapidly in the flat, nasal monotone of his sermons: 'Almighty and ever-living God, you sent your only Son into the world to cast out the spirit of evil. We pray for this child: set her free from original sin and send your Holy Spirit to dwell within her. We ask this through Christ our Lord.'

Giving no warning, he pushed Aoife's head towards the water. Without really meaning to, she pushed back against him. There were more bubbles rising now – bigger ones, and it was confusing. And the steam felt very warm on her face. The priest's grip tightened further. His fingers were like pincers. 'I baptize you in the name of the Father and of the Son and of the Holy Ghost . . .'

Again, he thrust Aoife's head down towards the water. Under her horrified eyes, the font was now bubbling furiously. She struggled, fought, cried out. Father Leahy pushed harder, a steely powerful hold on her neck, shouting: 'Bless this water in which she will be baptized! We ask this through Christ our Lord!'

'No! Stop! No!' The steam was scalding her – she was going to be scarred for life . . .

'Our Father in heaven, bless this child and rescue her from sin! I baptize you in the name of the Father and of the Son and of the Holy—'

Exerting all her changeling strength, Aoife flung the priest from her just before he plunged her face into the boiling water. He crashed through the air, landing sprawled on the carpeted altar steps, crying out in shock and terror.

Horrified, Aoife rushed to help him up. 'Father, I'm so sorry, are you all right? Let me help you up—'

But when she tried to get hold of him, he shrank away from her, crying, 'Don't touch me!'

'I didn't mean to hurt you, Father. It was only because something went wrong with the water . . .'

His eyes darted past her, then enlarged in utter horror. '*God have mercy on our souls!*' The font was bubbling over, pouring boiling water across the floor, steaming in huge white clouds that filled the church. The priest shuffled frantically on his backside towards the altar, casting his eyes up to the giant wooden man. 'Save me! Save your servant, O Lord! *Our Father! Blessed Virgin! Cast out the power of Satan, the spirit of evil!*'

'Father . . .'

Fumbling for the crucifix around his neck, he brandished it frantically at Aoife, the thin chain straining tightly around his neck. 'Deliver us from the kingdom of darkness!'

'Father, it's only me, Aoife . . .'

Panting, he huddled against the altar. 'Get away from me, demon, in the name of God!'

'Father!'

'Get out of my church! Get out!'

CHAPTER EIGHT

Standing the back room of her parents' house, Aoife tore book after book from the shelves, flipping through, finding nothing useful, discarding them in despair on the floor. All these faded paperbacks and ripped hardbacks, hundreds and hundreds of them acquired by her father from car boot sales and house clearances and the back rooms of junk shops. Stacked in every corner of the room, piled under the television, on the windowsill, on top of the cabinet with the glass doors (which itself was crammed with more books, instead of china ornaments) . . .

All these years, James O'Connor had been trying to find out to what manner of place the fairies had taken his human daughter.

Now Aoife O'Connor, his fairy daughter, was trying to find out what manner of creature she was.

Surely I'm not some Godless monster . . .

But a terrible memory came back to her – of Caitlin, the big ugly changeling girl, saying of the priest in Ballinadreen: *And the stupid man got out his cross like we were in the Dracula film and started praying over me, so I pointed at him to see what would happen and he went up in flames.*

If fire had been Aoife's power, instead of brute knock-out force, would Killian have gone up in flames like Caitlin's priest?

The bookshelf was getting empty now, and she turned to another one beside the fireplace. Country stories, ancient history, mixed up together, crammed upside down and sideways into the shelves. *Folklore and Fable* looked promising . . . But it was just about leprechauns in stupid hats. *Ugh.*

The next torn paperback was the *Lebor Gabála Érenn*. It fell open at a page with the corner turned down, revealing the passage her father had read to her last May, about the arrival of the Tuatha Dé Danann in Ireland, thousands of years ago:

They landed with horror, with lofty deed,
in their cloud of mighty combat of spectres,
upon a mountain of Conmaicne of Connacht . . .

Without ships, a ruthless course
the truth was not known beneath the sky of stars,
whether they were of heaven or of earth.

Aoife thought grimly: *Or of hell.*

Every reference she had already found claimed that the Tuatha Dé Danann had spent only a few years in Connacht before disappearing down through the stone circles and hawthorn circles into the other-world. The *under*world. Why had they chosen to live beneath the earth, with the dark creatures?

Down.

Were they of the dark themselves, and not the light? Were they of life – or of death?

An ancient maroon hardback was jammed side-ways between the top shelf and the low ceiling. *A Most Comprehensive Catalogue of Ye Irish Fairies.* The pages stiff and wrinkled, half of them stuck together. Hundreds of colour plates of peculiar creatures . . . Including a coloured illustration of a small, wizened being covered in coarse orange hair.

GROGOCH: Half human, half fairy. Hermit by habit. A venomous spite of priests.

Aoife paused over the volume, peeling apart more pages, intrigued, flipping back towards the beginning. She'd seen one of these creatures in the underworld, in the zoo outside the pyramid city of Falias. Maybe this account was more accurate than the rest?

CU-SIDHE, OR 'COOSHEE': Fairy dog, many times the size of a human-world dog. Dark green in colour, with bone-white eyes and yellow teeth.

There was no picture with this piece of text – some of the plates were loose, and maybe this one had fallen out. But she had no problem picturing the giant dog in her mind. She had rescued Eva from a pack of them, and then tamed them. She hoped the zookeeper was looking after the ones who had survived their subsequent battle with the dullahans.

POOKA: Takes on the shape of the victim's loved one, to lure them close enough to swallow the head.

Here the illustration was still glued in – a huge, hulking figure, covered in thick black fur, with grotesquely twisted horns and clawed hands. Red eyes burned on either side of its gaping snout; it had no tongue but its mouth was crammed top and bottom as far back as its throat with row after row of thin triangular teeth, like a hideous cheese grater. She'd seen one of these monsters too – at a distance, luckily: it had been eating the enormous cat that had killed poor Donal.

DULLAHAN: Decapitated, the dullahan carries his head for a lantern, and if he calls on a mortal by name, the mortal must follow to his death.

In the black-and-white illustration, a hooded figure held up a rotting head, tongue lolling and maggots falling from its eyes. She had come far too close to these terrifying creatures – Dorocha's coachman was one of them. And she'd heard a horde of them call Shay Foley's name, at Dorocha's bidding – when the Beloved had been unable to force his ring onto her finger.

(But she had kissed Shay, and he had kissed her back, and they had flown to safety. *Shay*— Stop. Try not to think about him – too painful.)

Swiping the back of her wrist across her eyes, she

turned more pages. And her heart, already aching at the thought of Shay, grew tight with fear. A beautiful young man with hair the blackened red of dying coals and starry ink-blue eyes was smiling up at her . . . Her eyes fled to the text.

FEAR DOROCHA: Servant to the Queen of Rebirth, who captured the Dark Man in the wilderness and made him her Beloved. At her request, he fetches down mortal men to the underworld for her amusement.

Here the entry ended, but Aoife knew the rest of the story, of which this writer was clearly ignorant. Dorocha had murdered the queen when she refused to marry him – as he had threatened to murder Aoife, if she didn't . . .

Merge with him.

From the page, his eyes gazed up at her.

His midnight eyes . . .

She threw the book to the floor, overwhelmed and panicky – heart beating too fast – trapped, like a bird flown by accident into a room and unable to find a window.

All children need to grow up, even the daughters of queens. So I brought you to the surface myself, after your mother's death.

It was true: he had carried her to this house, himself, in his black coach, along the fairy road . . .

It had been a rainy day in spring . . .

And the banshee had brought her into this very room – she remembered it now – only there were far fewer books and the couch was by the window, and a little girl her own age was lying on it, fast asleep. The banshee had cut Aoife's tender palm with a knife; and she had cut the human child's little hand as well, and merged their red and silver blood . . . But still the human child did not wake up. And then the banshee had left, carrying the other little girl. And the woman asleep in the chair had woken up suddenly, and when she saw Aoife, she'd started screaming – and a man came in crying 'Where is she?' And Aoife, the changeling child, was desperate to get out, glass and china breaking, trying to fly out of the window, but the shutters were closed and the latch was made of iron, and she had no power over it . . . *She had to get out, she didn't belong here, these people were strangers, she wanted her fairy mother, she wanted her mother, but her mother was . . .*

Gone. Dead. Murdered.

Silver blood staining the black sheets of her bed.

And her fairy mother had not gone to heaven, no one had even talked about heaven, and nor had she been buried because she could not be reborn, because she had been murdered with an iron knife. Instead, her people had carried her away. The ships, with their gold and emerald sails, disappearing into the mist . . . Distant voices raised in weeping. They had taken her mother, wrapped in green silk, to the islands, where she would lie for ever on a great flat rock. Washed clean at high tide by the cold grey sea. But never changing. For ever dead. *She would never see her fairy mother again.*

'Aoife?'

With a wild cry, she dropped her armful of books.

Her father was standing in the doorway, staring in bewilderment at the mess – hundreds of books lying everywhere on the threadbare carpet; face down, crumpled, torn. He cried, 'What is it? What's happened?'

'Nothing! Nothing!' She tried to get herself back under control. 'I was just looking for something. I'm sorry, I'll pick these up right now.'

Behind him in the hall, there was a bustle of Maeve and Eva, and bags of shopping disappearing into the kitchen. He came into the room, closing the door behind him. 'Aoife, what's the matter?'

She was on her knees on the floor, picking up all the useless information – traveller's tales from a world where none of these writers had travelled. 'Nothing.'

'Come here to me . . .' He pulled her to her feet and insisted on embracing her, awkwardly like in the lane, holding her too tight against him so that her nose was pressed into his big shoulder. Now he was working, he smelled again of wood-dust, as he always used to before the recession. 'Tell me what's happened, my love.'

She gave up trying to get away, and sobbed into his shirt, 'I need to know who I am!'

'Ssh, ssh. You're my daughter, that's who you are.'

'I'm evil—'

'That's rubbish!'

'I can't control my power. I could have killed that woman who came for Eva.'

'Sure, I would have killed her myself if I was there—'

'No, you *wouldn't*! I'm talking *literally*. And it's

getting worse – I burst out at Killian Doherty because he talked about hurting Carla, even though he didn't mean anything more than splitting up with her—'

'Killian Doherty?' Her father's shoulders tensed anxiously beneath his shirt.

'He got a cut on the back of his head and he thinks I'm an evil witch.'

The shoulders relaxed. 'As long as you haven't spoiled his lovely looks.'

'Dad, this isn't funny. I threw Father Leahy across the church.'

'*You threw Father Leahy . . . ?*' This time he stopped embracing her – he pulled back and held her with one hand on each of her shoulders, face drawn tight with shock.

Aoife hated the scared expression in his eyes. 'He's OK, he's not hurt – but he knew I was a changeling!'

'*What?*'

'Because you let him in to see Eva when she was dying, and he always suspected she wasn't me, and now he *knows* because the welfare officer told him you have a four-year-old adopted child and showed him Eva's picture on her phone!'

'Oh my God.' For a moment he was breathless with shock . . . but then recovered. 'He can't do anything about it – no one would believe him in a month of Sundays. Darling child, *why* did you throw him across the church?'

'Because he tried to baptize me and the water started boiling!'

'*What?*'

'And I had to stop him, and now he thinks I'm a creature of Satan and he told me never to come into the church again!'

Staring at her, James O'Connor repeated, 'The water did *what?*'

Despairing, she tore herself away and threw herself into the old wing-backed armchair by the fireplace; the one her father always sat in when he was reading his way through these countless useless books. Huddled sideways, head on her knees, she sobbed, 'I'm a monster!'

'Oh, Aoife, my love, my love.' He crouched heavily on the hearthrug right in front of her. 'Of course you're not a monster.'

'I am!'

'Aoife, you're my lovely daughter.'

'I'm so afraid of killing someone!'

He shook his head emphatically. 'You won't do that.'

'But how do you *know*?'

'Because I know *you*.'

'Father Leahy think I'm evil!'

'Father Leahy is a superstitious man who thinks good and evil is down to which God you worship.'

'*What?*' She looked up at him – tear-stained; shocked. 'But you and Mam are Catholics?'

As he knelt before her, his brown eyes were on a level with hers. He said earnestly: 'We are, of course – but how different is the Catholic religion from the old religions? Aren't so many of our churches built on the same stone raths where people worshipped the ancient gods? The Tuatha Dé Danann believed in Danu, the goddess of rebirth. Life dies, goes into the ground, and is reborn. I've thought about this so much since the banshee took Eva, trying to figure out where and why she'd gone . . . Think about it, Aoife! The body of Christ becomes bread and wine. How is that not a religion of rebirth? It's

Halloween next week. The church call it Allhallows Eve – the evening before the Day of the Saints. But in ancient times it was called Samhain, the Festival of the Dead – a celebration of the end of the harvest and the beginning of winter. The season when the fabric between this world and the otherworld is at its thinnest: the green shoots above and the roots beneath—'

She interrupted in a panic, 'But which of those worlds do I belong to? Who *am* I?'

He put his hand on her arm, stroking it. 'My love, you're *Aoife*, the same as you've always been. It's not whether you're fairy or human – it's who you are inside, who you are in your heart. It's everyone you love, and everyone who loves you – these are the things that make you who you are.'

Carla finally answered her, clearly having just turned on her phone after school.

No worries, Killian said he saw you in the bike shed so I knew you gone home. How are you feeling??? ☺☺☺

Smiley faces. Had Killian said nothing? Aoife, lying on her bed propped up on one elbow, texted:

so how is Killian? OK?

did you hear?

Hear what?

banged his head coming off his bike ☹ but he OK! ☺☺

Aoife stared at the screen for a moment. OK. Killian must have thought better of mentioning what had happened in the bike shed – perhaps he was worried that if he told on Aoife, then she would tell on him for trying to shift her. That was good – he was clearly afraid of losing Carla. She texted:

poor old Killian ☹

no, worries, he's grand. and he just did you a big favour . . .

?????

u want to come round tomorrow? ☺☺☺☺☺ ☺
☺☺☺

Again, Aoife stared at her phone in utter surprise.
Then tapped:

what about your mam?
Killian was just here and told mam that I'm right
and he talked to you about the fairies and you are
totally mad! ☺☺☺

Aoife, feeling rather ambiguous about this, texted
back:

Excellent ☺

BTW SORRY I TOLD KILLIAN ABOUT THE
FAIRY THING but he has not told anyone else
except you (but you already kno) and mam who I
already told because I had to explain to her but I
swear NOBODY ELSE!!! ☺??

Aoife paused before texting back:

☺!!

☺☺☺!!!!! and Aoife please text Shay and tell him you know he's not a bad fairy because he isn't I KNOW U THINK THIS BUT I SWEAR ON MY LIFE AS YOUR BEST FRIEND ITS NOT TRUE and when you are better you will regret it if you don't listen to me, I love you and I am telling you this FOR YOUR OWN GOOD

Aoife paused for longer this time, before replying:

I love you too

This was followed by silence. It was probably dinner time in Carla's house, when her mother forcibly removed all mobiles. Even her husband's, when he was home from England where he worked as an engineer.

Aoife was just finishing her own dinner, sitting at the kitchen table with her parents and Eva, when the iPhone finally beeped again. She glanced at the screen casually, then – heart missing a beat – jumped up and ran out of the kitchen. She had to be by herself when she opened this.

Shay had texted:

> sorry was out on the bog just saw yr text don't worry about school

Standing in the hall, she typed back quickly:

> no please dont drop out, I won't come near you

There was a long pause – so long, she wondered if he was out of range again. And hoped he was, rather than ignoring her. (Maeve called from the kitchen, 'Are you all right?') But eventually:

> Aoife im grand

Immediately, despite her own vow not to tug at him, she texted back:

> please please this is crazy, surely we can still see each other, just in class? we don't even need to

talk. I know this is hard but I think it is more hard not seeing you, don't you feel the same way? please don't do this

She waited a long time, in the shadowy hall. But no answer.

Later, she was watching television with Eva – or rather, Eva was sitting on her lap watching cartoons on Netflix, and Aoife was just staring into nothing – when the phone finally beeped again. She shifted Eva onto her left knee to dig it out of her pocket.

It was Carla.

Love you too! did you text Shay yet? ☺

Aoife considered her reply. The truth would have to do.

I did. He not got back.

He will ☺ crap reception on bog

he wont but it's fine

No no no no no he will you are most gorgeous girl in Kilduff! ☺☺

ha ha no you definitely the most gorgeous!!! ☺☺☺

Ha ha, you seriously are mad! Bring Eva tomorrow, Zoe can't wait ☺☺

Yay! Will do, I promise her ride on bike ☺☺☺

And at least that was something – she was welcome in her 'other home' again.

Aoife was up in her room with the light off and nearly asleep, before Shay finally replied. She grabbed her phone from the floor beside the bed. His text said:

night night, Aoife

Like a ghostly hand touching her hair. *Goodnight. I can't help thinking of you. Goodbye. Goodnight.*

CHAPTER NINE

Eva was sitting on the carpeted steps of the Heffer-nans' split-level living room, having an earnest conversation with Zoe about Halloween costumes. Zoe had produced a battered pair of fairy wings – the ones Carla used to wear as a little girl – and a witch's hat.

Eva flatly rejected the whole idea. 'Fairies don't have wings.'

Zoe – at four, the cut of Carla at that age: soft brown hair, brown eyes and a cute, chubby little face under the pointed hat – looked at Eva in astonishment. 'Yes they do, they do have wings.'

'They don't.'

'*They do.*'

'Nope. Aoife's a fairy and she doesn't have wings.'

Aoife was sitting with her arms around her knees on the long blue leather sofa beside the patio doors, eating her way through a plate of Oreos and Kimberleys. She glanced at Carla to see if she was listening – but Carla, stretched out beside her, seemed to be happily absorbed in Snapchat, firing out a series of pictures of herself stuffing three Oreos into her mouth at once.

Zoe spotted Eva's obvious mistake and pounced, triumphant. 'Aoife isn't a fairy, she's from Kilduff!'

With a quick check at Aoife, Eva countered, 'No, she *is* a fairy because she threw the banshee up in the air.'

At this, Carla also shot Aoife a look from under her eyelashes and, just as quickly, looked away again – clearly not wanting to embarrass her by openly noticing how Eva was mimicking her delusions.

Zoe said firmly, 'No she didn't.'

Eva stood her ground. 'Yes she did.'

'No she didn't. What's a banshee?'

'A woman in red who cries in the night and steals little girls like you right out of their bedrooms.'

Caught off guard by this unexpected attack, Zoe raised her voice in trembling protest. 'There's no such thing!'

Eva, watching closely for Zoe's reaction, pressed home her advantage: 'Yes there is, and if you're a very good little girl, she brings you to a great big party where stinky old men dressed all in white—'

'*Carla, Eva's being mean to me!*'

Aoife said hastily, 'Eva, don't be mean to Zoe.'

Carla set aside her phone with a sigh. 'No she isn't, Zoe, and she's new here and you have to be nice to her. Have a— Jesus, Aoife!' The plate was empty: while listening to Eva – and wondering what was real, and what fantasy – Aoife had absently eaten everything.

'*Aoife's eaten all the biscuits!*' Now the little girls were hopping up and down in front of the sofa, united in outrage. '*Aoife's eaten all the Oreos!*'

Aoife protested, half laughing – but slightly mortified: 'Not just me – Carla too!'

'I had, like, *three*!' Carla was completely taken aback. 'And you've eaten all four Kit-Kats as well! And the Mars bar! God almighty, what are you – a gang of teenage boys? I'll go and see if there's anything left in the cupboard . . .'

'*Aoife's a greedy pig!*'

'Eva, quit it, I'm not a pig, I'm your big sister – you have to stick up for me.'

'*My big sister's a big greedy pig!*'

'Mine too,' said Zoe consolingly, happy to smooth over their recent differences.

Carla, returning with ginger biscuits and a packet of Penguins, shook the whole lot out onto the empty plate and gave it to the two little girls. 'Take this, and keep it well away from Aoife.'

'*She's a big greedy pig!*'

'Oh, go sit in the corner, you brats.' Carla plonked herself down on the sofa again, adding to Aoife: 'They're right, though. Jesus, I'd love to be able to eat anything I want and stay as thin as you.'

Aoife examined her best friend, smiling – she found it hard to get used to how like a model Carla looked, with her beautifully groomed hair and expensive make-up. And so slender. 'What are you on about? There's not a pick on you these days.'

'There is, actually.' Carla plumped up a cushion and settled herself sideways for a chat. 'I've put on half a kilo since you came back.'

'That's nothing!'

'Nothing if it stopped there, but it won't, and it's your fault for not being dead after all.'

'I'm really sorry about that.'

Carla pulled a face. 'I suppose I forgive you. And

at least I know Killian loved me before I lost all the weight, so hopefully he won't mind me getting fat again.'

'Stop that! You were never fat!'

'And talking about love – Shay?'

And just like that, the lightness went out of Aoife; all the fun switched off.

Moments later, Carla was saying anxiously: 'Aoife . . . ?'

Aoife leaned back her head against the firm leather of the couch. (*Night night?* What had he been trying to say? *I'm thinking of you?* Or: *Please leave me alone?*) 'Really, it's OK, I'll be all right in a minute.'

'If you'd just get over this . . . *thing* . . . about him.'

'Do you mind if we don't talk about it?'

'But we have to – it's not fair on him.'

Aoife let her head fall to one side, meeting Carla's deep brown gaze.

Carla sighed, and rested her elbow on the back of the sofa, and her cheek on her folded fist. 'OK, fine. Let's say you don't get any better. Let's say you're always going to think you're a fairy. Let's say nothing's going to change your mind.'

'Sorry.'

'It's OK.' Over Carla's shoulder, through the patio doors, a warm rush of sunshine came over the lilac mountains; a river of gold from a lowering sun. The back of Carla's house faced west, in the direction of the sea. Somewhere up there, the cliffs; a lonely farm . . .

Carla was saying in a practical voice, 'If that's what we're stuck with, we'll just have to work around it.'

Aoife brought her eyes back to Carla's face. 'Work around . . . ?'

'Your belief system. Well, more like work *with* it. So you're thinking that Shay Foley's mother was some sort of a fairy?'

Aoife sat up. 'A lenanshee.' She knew Carla was only humouring her, but it still felt important to get it right.

Carla nodded. 'A lenanshee. Sorry, I knew that. OK, grand. And this lenanshee's love was so powerful it destroyed Shay's dad . . . Hang on, is that why we're saying Shay's mother killed herself, God rest her soul?'

In for a penny . . . 'Moira Foley didn't kill herself. When she jumped off the cliff, she went back to the underworld. That's a log of wood buried in her grave in Kilduff. It's an old fairy trick.'

Carla stared at her, then lowered her head, poking her finger through a hole in the seam of her trackies, making it larger. Then recovered, and looked up again with a sweet smile. 'OK. But what I was going to say was – Shay's dad was human, wasn't he? So maybe so is Shay.'

'No, Shay is a lenanshee. There was a' – *devil* – 'man who tried to marry me, but he couldn't because Shay loved me, and if a lenanshee has a *grá* for you, no one can take you away.' *And she had made Shay kiss her, and they had flown . . . So high, so far, from one world to the next . . .*

Carla was nodding earnestly. 'OK, so we're agreed he's a lenanshee. OK. What sort of a fairy are you? Good, I assume?'

'I'm a child of the Tuatha Dé Danann, the people of Danu.'

'Oh, I've heard of them! No wait . . . It's the name of a pub in Clonbarra. Anyway, the Tuatha Dé Danann . . . Are they powerful?'

'I think so. They're gone to the Blessed Isles now. It's only us changelings left behind in the otherworld – the children of the people of Danu.' It actually was a relief to talk about it, despite knowing that Carla thought she was making it all up. She had avoided telling Maeve and James about her fairy parents – it would feel unkind, as if she was judging the O'Connors for being too ordinary. 'My fairy mother was the queen of the people of Danu.'

Carla's eyes widened a fraction. 'Really? You're a fairy princess?'

'A queen. My mother was murdered, and I've been crowned.'

Carla looked even better pleased. 'Excellent. So you're a fairy queen. That's perfect. So, here's what you have to do: you have to tell yourself that lenanshee power can't affect you. I mean, in your belief system you've got to be pretty amazingly powerful. And in your world, Shay might be a lenanshee, but he has to be half ordinary human, because of his dad. You think a half ordinary human, half lenanshee could mess with a full-on fairy queen? I don't think so.'

For a long, long moment Aoife looked at Carla with much the same astonishment as Zoe had looked at Eva when Eva had announced that fairies didn't have wings. Paradigm shift.

Then she said, 'Carla, you truly are amazing. Look after Eva for me.'

Faster, faster, out across the empty bog. Up over the gap between the high shoulders of the mountains, the rusty heather glowing pink in the blaze of the declining sun. A wilder, different sort of happiness was filling her than when she'd last made this bicycle ride. Then, she had been sure of him. Now, she had to argue with him. But it was OK. Everything would be OK.

Because Carla was right and Shay was wrong – the lenanshee boy couldn't harm her.

Her fairy mother had been queen of the Tuatha Dé Danann. She was powerful already, even *before* she'd turned sixteen. The one time she had kissed Shay properly, she had become filled with his energy and had flown, up into the shining sky. She had been that caterpillar-turned-butterfly. That girl-turned-bird. And she hadn't died. She didn't *need* protecting from Shay's love. She must have been mad – *genuinely* mad – to let him imagine that he could burn her up! Why had she allowed him to turn away from her – when it was so crazily painful to them both?

She should have just kissed him, the way she'd made him kiss her before, in the temple when they'd had to escape her wedding to Dorocha. Ah, that sense of flight . . . Exploding up the walls of the pyramid city, into the glorious blue-gold sky above . . . Brushing shoulders with eagles . . .

Earthbound, she headed at a ridiculously happy speed downhill, towards the distant sea. The sun was getting lower, long streaks of gold and crimson in the sky. How wonderful it would be to fly into a sunset. She and Shay could do it, together. They could do *anything* together . . .

He and his brother must be back from the bog by now, and John Joe would have headed out to the pub, leaving Shay by himself on the small, remote farm. She could tap on the window. She pictured him sitting at the kitchen table – and then looking up and seeing her looking in. She would know, from the way his face changed, what was in his heart. He would be so glad to see her . . . And then, when she explained—

'Crap!' She had reached the edge of the land already – and she was travelling far too fast. She swung dangerously left onto the coast road, leaning almost horizontally. The tyres, already worn paper-thin over the last few days, exploded into shreds, and with a terrible screeching of metal, the bike lost its grip on the tarmac and skidded sideways towards the edge of the cliff, where the low metal barrier had rusted and broken away. 'Crap! *Crap!*' She threw herself recklessly to the ground, sliding with the bike across the gravel, still in the same direction . . .

She closed her eyes, bracing herself for the feeling of the ground disappearing from beneath her.

She slowed. Stopped.

Still sweating, she opened her eyes. She was so close to the edge that by simply lifting her head she could see down to the waves crashing against the base of the cliff, foaming pink in the sunset light, a hundred metres below. She might have managed to glide down on the wind, but at the bottom she would have been broken against the rocks by the massive waves.

Moments later, the rush of adrenalin subsided, and pain flooded her body. Gasping, she sat up to check her injuries. The sleeve had been nearly ripped off her hoodie and her right shoulder was an agonizing mess of torn flesh and silvery blood. Black spots drifted in across her vision; she turned her eyes away, feeling slightly sick.

The bike itself lay in the middle of the narrow road, snapped spokes sticking out at every angle. After the black spots had disappeared, she got shakily to her feet and limped over to pick it up. She could have wept, looking at it. She'd had it since her eleventh birthday. Now its wheels were buckled, handlebars twisted. She wouldn't even be able to push it home. She dragged it to the bog side of the road and laid it in the ditch – tenderly, as if burying a childhood pet.

She would have to walk the rest of the way to Shay's. Although she couldn't see him, not looking like this: bloodied and in bits. Maybe she could wash herself down in a stream. Or maybe she could use the ladies' in the grubby, deserted little café where she had met him two days ago. She could see the building in the distance.

Halfway to the café, her left hip began to feel like it was on fire. She pulled out the elastic waistband of her trackies and peered at the damage. It was horribly grazed, the top layer of skin gone. Suddenly she felt so dizzy she had to sit down on a stone by the side of the road, and put her head between her knees, to breathe. Her phone buzzed while she was slumped there; without lifting her head, she slid it out of her pocket (relieved to see that the screen hadn't been cracked in the accident). Carla had messaged:

> good for you but you crazy biking it! where are you now? text him to meet you!

Aoife texted back:

> thank you so much for everything!

> TEXT HIM TO MEET YOU!!

> OK OK ☺

And although she'd only been trying to mollify Carla, texting Shay didn't seem so bad an idea. She tapped out: *I've had an accident please can I have a lift* . . . Then erased the text – she didn't want him panicking and speeding like a lunatic on the public road. *My bike is fecked, I need a lift* . . . That was more like it.

> Hi sorry to bother but I need help. I'm down near

the café on the coast road and my tyre is punc-
tured and I need a lift

However much he thought it would hurt him to
be near her and not touch her, he'd hardly refuse to
help. And then, once he was there, she could con-
vince him . . . This time she wouldn't be taking *No*
for an answer.

She sat staring at the screen, smiling. Waiting.

No reply.

He couldn't be ignoring a cry for help. He must
be out of range. She slipped the phone back into her
pocket and got to her feet and walked on up the coast
road in the direction of the farm.

A thin, misty rain was falling, wetting her hair
and clothes, slowly cleaning away the silvery blood
from her exposed shoulder, but leaving the ripped
flesh still studded with crumbs of dirt and gravel.
She would be passing the café shortly – she might as
well get cleaned up anyway. The toilets were round
the back and she could get to them without going
through the front and scaring that poor lonely woman
with the state of her.

Although, as she neared the small one-storey

building, she found herself wondering if she had come to the right place. The front of the shop was gleaming. Not only had its dirty windows been washed, but the peeling yellow window frames, door and fascia board had been re-painted a charming pastel blue. Hanging baskets of Michaelmas daisies dangled, swinging in the chill sea breeze. A new blackboard outside the door announced: RITA'S CAFÉ! LOBSTER SOUP! FRESH CRAB SALAD! HOME-MADE BREAD AND CAKES! REAL LEMONADE! Amazingly, there was a tour bus with a foreign registration drawn up in the little car park.

Aoife was so absorbed in the change, she forgot about going round the back to the yard and instead walked straight into the café. The inside had been cleaned and painted as well, and there were oil cloths and little vases of fresh flowers on all the tables. Instead of burned toast, the air was filled with gentle cooking smells and the scent of turf from the small iron stove. And crowding every table were tourists – one of whom, a woman with a grey bun, glanced towards the door with a smile . . . then let out a thin scream. The next moment thirty pairs of eyes were staring at Aoife in horror. And an instant after that, a beautiful waitress with a long white-blonde pony-tail and shining eyes came bustling across the café and hurried Aoife gently but firmly between the tables towards the back door, away from the startled customers.

'You poor thing, what happened to you? Did something attack you? I didn't think there were monsters out on the bog!'

'No – what? Oh, you're joking . . . It's grand – I'm sorry I freaked everyone out, I just fell off my bike.'

'Is there someone you'd like me to call to take you away?'

'No, really, I'm grand! If I could just get cleaned up in the bathroom.'

'Of course you can, before you go again.' She hurried Aoife across the rain-swept yard to the toilets. 'There's plenty of towels in there, use as many as you like. I'll just run and let everyone know you're not dying yet . . .' And the waitress was gone again.

Aoife was left standing alone in a sparkling white space. The toilets were as scrubbed and clean as the rest of the place, with a pile of white towels sitting on a small blue cupboard and a soap dispenser by the sink. She ran the water, and it was hot. She washed the dirt from her face, combed her fingers through her matted hair, then soaped a clean towel and dabbed cautiously at her shoulder, easing the tiny pebbles out of the damaged flesh. Then washed her hip.

'Rita, she's the owner, she sent you a cup of tea with sugar in it – great for the shock, says she!' The girl was back already, not just with a big mug of tea but with a plate of chocolate biscuits, which she balanced on the edge of the sink. 'How are you feeling now?'

'Grand, thanks a million. Oh, it's *you*!' Now Aoife had a chance to look at the girl properly, she recognized her – it was the girl who had jumped off the bus just as she and Shay were leaving the café before. Beautiful – mesmerizingly beautiful. Hair like fresh cream and eyes the silver grey of sunlit rain. 'Are you working here now?'

'I am! And you are . . . ?'

'Aoife.'

'Aoife!' The girl seemed oddly amused by this. 'How strange, I had it in my head you were called something different altogether.'

'You must be mixing me up with someone else. Although I did see you before.'

'When you were younger?'

'No, just the day before yesterday, when I was coming out of this café and you got off the bus.' Aoife was astonished all over again. 'I can't believe that was only two days ago! The place looks so different now!'

The girl beamed. 'It's nice, isn't it? It was hard work, but I'm super-efficient, and I had a lot of help from my friends.'

'It's extraordinary!'

'Thank you! Rita says I'm a gift from heaven! She said she'd been praying to the universe for help, and suddenly there I was, like magic!' The girl was smiling at Aoife as she chatted on – even her voice was beautiful: soft and sweet and winning. 'You're right, by the way – I did see you when I got off the bus! But I wasn't able to pay you much attention, because I was so distracted by that boy! I've never seen one so handsome in all my years. Such strong cheekbones, and such black, black hair, and his eyes so green and somehow golden-brown at the same time, and he has such a very, very kissable mouth— Oh!' The girl clapped her hand to her own mouth as if mortified, although she was still smiling widely behind her fingers. 'I'm such a fool, I shouldn't have said anything! You're not in love with him, are you?'

'You're grand . . .' The happiness bubbled up in Aoife's heart as she took a sip of the tea. *That gorgeous boy* – how true! She was tempted to confide: *I do love him, and he loves me.* Instead she grinned back at the waitress. 'I'm just on my way to see him now, actually, though he doesn't know I'm coming.'

'Oh, poor you.' The girl put her head on one side, so that her blonde ponytail fell over her shoulder, and clicked her tongue sympathetically. 'I thought you were over him, but I suppose that's not very likely.'

Aoife put down the tea. 'You thought . . . What?' A cool chill fluttered through her; the happiness bubbles subsiding.

'Oops!' The waitress caught the precariously balanced mug before it tipped sideways into the sink, then turned her attention back to Aoife, saying cheerfully, 'I mean, I don't blame you for chasing – he is amazingly gorgeous! And such a nice name . . . *Shay Foley.*' She breathed it out like music. 'And he has such a lovely way of speaking too – so soft, like rain on heather—'

'You've been talking to him?'

'Of course! You rushed off and left him standing there like a fool, so I brought him in for a piece of cake to cheer him up, but actually he didn't need cheering up – though he ate the cake all right! No, he said it was all for the best, and he was ready to move on.'

She was going blind . . . She gripped the edge of the sink, leaning heavily on it. A sheet of painful black sliding down like a guillotine over her vision . . .

The waitress's lovely voice was babbling on in her ears: 'Anyway, we got talking about life and ourselves, and we agreed that we're definitely kindred spirits. Isn't it so handy – he only lives back the road from here? We're meeting up again tomorrow . . .' In the distance, beyond the yard, the café chimes tinkled. 'Yikes, better go! Are you going to be all right? Hello? Are you all right?'

With great difficulty, Aoife opened her eyes. The electric light appeared utterly blinding. Her eyes hurt. *Everything hurt.*

The waitress had moved away and was standing in the doorway, holding Aoife's un-drunk tea and uneaten chocolate biscuits. 'Are you feeling better now?'

Aoife cleared her throat and answered hoarsely, 'Yes.'

'You still look very pale. Are you sure you don't want me to call someone to bring you home?'

'No. I'll be grand.'

'Are you sure? Oh, that bell!' And the mesmerizing girl was gone, sprinting across the yard towards the back door of the café.

Aoife remained where she was, holding onto the sink, staring at her white face in the mirror, waiting for the tears to come. But the tears stayed lodged painfully in her lungs, like stones; like gravel in the flesh. *I'm so sad, I can't even cry . . . I have to go home . . .* But the thought of walking back alone through the dark, through the cold wind and lonely rain . . .

She had been so happy on the way here. But now . . .

She needed help. She needed comfort. She needed . . .

She took out her phone, and called Maeve. 'Mam? I've had a bit of an accident and I've written off my bike . . .'

'Oh my God, darling, where are you?'

When her mother's Volvo screeched up twenty minutes later, Aoife was sitting by the side of the road in the rain with her broken bike in the ditch beside her.

Maeve leaped out of the car and rushed to help. 'Oh, darling! Oh, your poor bike . . . Don't worry, we can buy you another one. Ah, darling, don't cry, don't cry . . . I know you really loved that old thing, but it's had a good innings. I've brought you a change of clothes, you can take off your wet ones in the car. Oh, your poor arm! Oh, your hip!'

In the car, Eva was snoring in a new child's seat in the back, her mouth slackly open and her nose turned up.

Maeve settled Aoife into the front, patting at her wounds with antiseptic wipes, helping her on with dry trackies and socks, wrapping a big fluffy blanket around the rest of her, unscrewing a Thermos of hot homemade soup. Kissing her cheek.

Mother's love.

In the early evening, while Aoife was sitting in bed with a pile of pillows behind her and drinking yet more of Maeve's chicken soup, her phone pinged. She reached for it painfully – then forgot her pain.

Shay had texted:

Are you hurt?

But before she could work out how to answer, he texted again:

Heard you had a tip on the bike!

And all the joy went out of her. He must have been with that girl again, or at least talking to her on the phone. And the waitress had told him about the accident, and now he knew Aoife had been on her way to see him, and he must know she knew about the girl, and yet no explanation, no excuses, nothing but this: **Are you hurt?**

Of course she was hurt. She texted back:

No, not hurt.

A long pause.

Night night, Aoife.

CHAPTER TEN

Carla said, 'But you must go, you can't just *languish*. You *have* to go – it will cheer you up. Ah, come *on*, who else am I going to get ready with?'

Aoife was lying flat on her back on her bed – still aching: skin, bones and heart. 'Why don't you get ready with Jessica and Aisling?'

'Because they're each other's best friends and you're mine! Listen to me – Shay Foley's not going to be there. Discos aren't his thing, you know how quiet he is. And dancing will cheer you up, I swear. There'll be other boys—'

'I don't want other boys.'

'Sure you do. And don't bother about Sinead going around calling you a slut – nobody cares.'

'Nor do I. It's not that . . . Look, please don't make me.'

Carla must have heard her despair, because she abandoned the pep talk and said much more gently, 'OK, I know I sound like I don't understand, but seriously, I don't believe this thing about Shay taking off after some other girl.'

Aoife breathed in through her nose. It was an effort to speak normally, because of the unshed tears still embedded in her lungs. On an outward breath she said, 'If you saw how beautiful she was, you'd believe it.'

'Bullshit. *You're* the most beautiful girl I've ever seen – counting films.'

Aoife closed her eyes. 'Trust me, this girl gives a whole different meaning to the word "beautiful".'

Carla's voice went up a key – something between sympathy and renewed frustration. 'Look, try to remember I *can't* trust your world view at the moment, and nor should you. We have to trust mine instead. So listen: this isn't Shay Foley's style. No offence to Killian – I love him to bits – but I'm certain that Shay is a zillion times as loyal. If he did get talking to some other girl, he was probably just being polite and she was just being all pathetically excited because he wasn't as awful to her as most teenage boys usually are.'

For a moment part of her believed – or maybe just *wanted* to believe – what Carla was telling her. Could the Shay she knew – so courageously loyal to her in the otherworld – fall for another girl, and over night?

It seemed impossible. Yet nor was he the quiet, reserved famer's boy that Carla assumed him to be – he was a lenanshee, driven by deeper and more dangerous desires than any human lad. Maybe he couldn't live without love. Maybe in order to protect Aoife, he had to give his heart to someone else. And that girl was so beautiful, and so sure of him—

'Aoife! Hello? Disco!'

Aoife reached for another excuse. 'I fell off my bike, I'm in bits.'

Carla lost patience and played her trump card. 'Aoife, don't be a buzz-kill. I missed every single disco last summer because of you – even the one Killian insisted on going to, and in the end he went by himself and I was terrified he'd shift Sinead. So you *owe* me enough to stagger along to this one. Even if you've broken both legs.'

'Aaargh . . . Sorry about the summer. Grand, I'll come.'

Carla said cheerfully, 'Good! I'll come to yours after school tomorrow to get ready. Can your parents drop us in and can I stay over? Mam's going to Nan's with Zoe and she won't be back until tomorrow, and Dad's off in England again working, the poor man.

What will we go as? Aisling's lost her head and is going full-on as a Frankenstein nurse, the mad fool. Jessica's dressing up as a witch – she has this tiny little witch's-hat fascinator she got in McCarthy's shop, quite sweet. I'm thinking black cat. What about you?'

Aoife changed her phone to her other hand because her grazed right shoulder was aching so badly, just from the act of holding it. She tried not to sound too pathetic. 'Not sure. I hadn't got anything in mind.'

'I'll bring over the usual stuff.'

Carla arrived in the middle of Saturday afternoon with a huge black plastic sack of clothes slung over her shoulder. She stared around Aoife's bedroom in shock. It was the first time she'd been in it since before Aoife had disappeared. 'Your room's so neat – what happened to it?'

'Mam tidied it. Does it still look neat to you? I've been trying to get it back to normal.'

'No, don't, leave it as it is, it looks great. Such a lot of floor space. I must tidy my own room – it makes it so much easier to walk around.' As she finished speaking, Carla upended the sack all over the carpet – short black dresses, high heels, tights, cracked Halloween masks, huge mouse ears, a pair of smaller cat's ears, a squashed witch's hat, a nurse's outfit and a black-and-white cow suit complete with pink rubber udders. She pulled out Aoife's make-up drawer and tipped its contents out onto the desk, sticking the keyboard up out of the way on top of the computer. 'Any purple lipstick? What do you think of the cat idea? Too yesterday? Are witches boring or sexy? What do you think of the mouse ears? Let's have some music.'

'Not One Direction.'

'Don't panic, I'm so over that. Have you any Flat Out?'

'Who?'

'*What?*' Carla was clearly as shocked as she was gratified by being more in the musical know than Aoife. 'I can't believe you haven't heard of Flat Out! They're HUGE in Mayo. Here, I have them on my phone.' Carla swept her fingers over the screen, found what she was looking for, propped the phone against the computer, turned up the volume and shouted over the music enthusiastically at Aoife: 'God, this is so great, you and me just being back to normal again!'

Aoife said, with an equal rush of enthusiasm, 'Isn't it!' Because it was great, it was *lovely*, to have this moment – a step back into her safe human childhood, when she knew she was loved by everyone she loved.

'So – you want to go as a cat? I have these two little black dresses, and some cool heels. Actually, there's only one set of cat ears, but I can be the mouse.'

'I can be the mouse, I don't mind.'

'Sure? We can swap them about. I don't suppose anyone will be able to tell the difference anyway.' Carla's tone changed, this time to one of horror: 'Aargh, that's . . . You poor thing! You didn't tell me you'd hurt yourself *that* badly!'

Aoife was pulling her T-shirt off over her head – carefully, so as not to scrape off any fresh scabs. 'It is a bit gross, isn't it? Look at my hip—'

'Put it away! Jesus! How fast were you going, ya fool? Have you been to the doctor?'

'What could he do? I cleaned it, and then Mam cleaned it – it's grand, healing up fine.'

Carla studied Aoife's grazes doubtfully. 'OK. But it makes it tricky with the dress – it has straps. You really need to cover up, it's not a good look. Have you a black cardigan?'

'I might have, but since Mam tidied everything I've no idea where anything is.'

Carla stuck in her head in the wardrobe – 'She did a really good job, didn't she? I might tidy mine' – and rifled through the hangers and the hanging shelves. Then cried out, 'Oh. *My. GOD.*'

Aoife, who had been flicking through Carla's playlist for any other new bands she might have missed, looked up in surprise.

'Oh. My. God.' Carla, turning to face her, was shaking the creases out of a very beautiful dress. The hem had been dipped in dark blue dye, and from this embroidered rays of gold shot up to the paler rose-pink of the shoulders: the sun rising from the sea. 'Aoife, this is *gorgeous.* Where did you even get this? What's it doing just stuffed in a bag like old rubbish?'

It had been the plainest, least bridal-like gown that she could find in her fairy mother's chambers, when Dorocha insisted she dress herself for their wedding. He had wanted her to show herself off as a joyful, willing bride. He had been quietly angry at the plainness of her choice. (But back in Mayo, Shay had smiled at her in the pouring rain, his hazel eyes flicking over her, head to toe. He'd said: *I like that dress on you, even if you do look like a drowned rat.*)

Aoife grabbed the dress from Carla and thrust it

back into the wardrobe, stuffing it behind the hanging shelves. 'Don't mind that, I don't like it – it was only there till I could get rid of it properly.'

'*Seriously?* But it's . . .' Carla caught the look on Aoife's face and coolly switched subject without missing a beat. 'Lois is going around all miserable because her archaeologist never got back in touch, but Sinead is still convinced he'll come to the ball and axe-murder the lot of us. And talking of Sinead, she's doing a line with Darragh – did you know?'

'Again? Poor old Darragh, what an eejit.'

'I know it.' Carla began pulling out the drawers of the press. 'It's, like, the fifth time she's snapped her fingers for him only a short time after dumping him. I don't know why he goes running back every time. You're right, he is a complete eejit. Oh, look – a black cardigan, all neatly folded! In the *cardigan* drawer, no less!'

In Kilduff parish hall, Freddie Mercury screeched from ancient speakers, just as he had the year before and the year before that. Four little vampires were already flinging themselves around, waist-deep in dry ice. Ultra-violet strobe lights whirled in semi-darkness. On stage, the metalwork teacher from the school was bent over the decks, with a knife buried in his head. Fourth-year zombies cruised the walls, but there seemed to be a shortage of girls their age. A table was set up along the back wall with the usual fare – sandwiches, soft drinks, bars and biscuits.

To the right of the table, the missing fifteen- and sixteen-year-old girls were gathered in a tight group, their backs to the room. Nearly all of them in short black dresses and very high heels.

A handsome cloaked and booted warlock was heading towards Aoife and Carla; he shouted over the crackling music, 'I thought you weren't coming!' and flung his arms enthusiastically around Carla, who laughed, clearly delighted by Killian's over-the-top behaviour. 'Course I was coming – why wouldn't I come? You're looking great!'

'Come and dance!' He was completely and deliberately blanking Aoife – no doubt thinking of it as punishment for what had happened in the bike shed.

Carla, too busy fixing one of her shoes to notice, straightened up and teetered happily off with him. 'OK, but don't rush me, these heels are really high!'

A firm hand gripped Aoife's arm and spun her round. It was one of the zombies, wearing a hideous rubber mask. Tall with cropped black hair. He bent to murmur in her ear, lifting the mask from his mouth: 'See, like you, I'm back from the dead . . .'

It was Darragh.

Aoife's heart was beating too fast. The same as in school, she had mistaken Killian's cousin for Shay – his height, his black cropped hair. She plastered on a smile. 'Hi!'

He grinned, and pulled the mask back down, saying in a more muffled voice, 'Hi yourself. Rocking the witch look.'

'What do you mean? I'm a cat!' Carla had kindly insisted that Aoife have first turn with the cat's ears.

'Of course you are! Better again. Would you like to dance as well? Or may I escort you to the bar for a drink? There's a splendid array to choose from – Coke, orange, lemon. And if you care to follow me into a dark corner, I'll whip out the hip flask that I have concealed in my pocket.'

'Mm . . . I don't think so.'

He grinned at her, taking the mask off altogether and leaving it to hang on the elastic round his neck, running his hand across his dark hair. 'Really, it's just a hip flask.'

She laughed, despite herself. 'But I thought you were here with Sinead . . .'

He shrugged, a wry smile. 'You did? Me too.'

'Couldn't she come?'

'No, she's here all right.' He nodded towards the jostling crowd of girls near the table. 'Just not with me.'

'Oh, you mean she's hanging with Lois. I thought you meant she'd abandoned you for another—'

'Look again.'

And now that Aoife looked, she realized there was a boy in the mix – tall and black-haired like Darragh, his back to the wall and almost hidden from view by the crowd of the high-heeled girls pressed around him. Sinead was busy fighting her way into the scrum, wearing a shorter black dress than anyone else. Lois was right behind her.

Darragh said, 'There she goes, after fresh blood. Amazing to think that only yesterday she told me if she was still single by the time she was thirty, then she'd marry me. I was so happy – it was like we were the new Carla and Killian . . . What *is* going on with my cousin, by the way? He's acting very monogamous tonight. Did you threaten to cut off his boy-bits if he didn't behave himself with Carla? Is that one of the tricks they teach you in prison?'

Still staring at the group of girls, she said vaguely, 'Prison?'

'Surely that's where you've been all summer?'

'Oh . . . Yes.' Slowly it was becoming obvious – how had she not realized it already; known it in her blood, from the moment she set foot in this place? That dark head visible among the cat's ears and witch-hat fascinators. It was Shay. He was here after all, at the centre of a laughing, flirting throng . . .

Darragh said irritably, 'Feck's sake, Aoife, I'm talking to you.'

She shivered, and pulled her eyes away. 'What?'

He seemed genuinely annoyed. 'Stop staring at Shay Foley.'

'Oh . . .' Helplessly, her eyes were drawn back to the scrum by the wall. It was impossible to see the girl he was actually with . . . Was this what the waitress had meant when she said she was meeting him tomorrow? No white-blonde head in sight . . .

Darragh said, 'I don't know what aftershave he has on, but I'm definitely asking for it for Christmas. *Aoife!*'

She blinked, looked back at Darragh, forcing a smile. 'Sorry. What did you say?'

'That's better. Remember your pride. Don't be like me with Sinead, breaking up and getting back together until I can't remember if it's off or on. Running back to her every time she clicks her fingers and everyone calling me a total eejit – yes they do, don't lie to me, you've probably said it yourself. Now, how about that drink?'

Aoife made a huge effort to pull herself together. 'OK. Why not?'

As they walked across the dance floor, through the dry ice and whirling vampires, Darragh slipped his arm round her back. She nearly pulled away – then didn't. Darragh was right – she needed to show some pride, whatever the truth. They passed Killian – leaping up and down, flapping his arms, teeth and eyes shining a peculiar white in the ultra-violet strobes. Carla grinned and rolled her eyes very slightly at them – then noted that Darragh had his arm round Aoife and nodded her approval. Darragh tightened his grip, pulling Aoife against him. When she looked up at him, he raised his dark eyebrows. 'You're limping, madam. Heels too tight?'

'No, I fell off my bike a couple of days ago and my hip is sore. Mind my shoulder, actually.'

He changed the position of his grip. 'Cats really shouldn't ride bikes.'

'I guess not.'

They were getting closer to the table of food and drink. She couldn't look at Shay. She *wouldn't* look at Shay.

She did look at him.

He had made a minimal nod to Halloween by dressing all in black: a close-fitting black shirt, black jeans. The beautiful girl from the café wasn't anywhere to be seen – only Aisling and Lois Munnelly, pressed up against him on either side, both chatting away eagerly. Instead of the ubiquitous short black dress Aisling was wearing a blood-stained nurse's outfit and had a rubber scar on her cheek. As Aoife watched, Sinead fought her way to the front of the throng of girls and got right in Shay's face, gazing up at him, laughing gaily with one hand on his arm. Lois glared at Sinead.

Look away.

Darragh met her eyes with a slight shake of his head. 'Coke?'

'Club Orange.'

'Here you go.' He released her shoulders to pour the drink, and handed her the plastic cup.

She took it – 'Thanks' – and limped away towards the edge of the dance floor. Killian was still bopping wildly around Carla. Darragh followed and positioned himself beside her.

'Want to join those two?'

'Not right now.'

'I promise I don't dance like a demented Labrador. Unlike my cousin I'm actually quite cool.'

'I'm sure you are.' She smiled up at him. The summer had given something more to Darragh than centimetres – he was definitely more civilized than he used to be.

He smiled back at her. 'So – try me for size?'

She hesitated.

Behind her, a low voice said, 'Aoife?'

For a moment she didn't move; she was still looking at Darragh, although not really seeing him any more – just vaguely conscious of him rolling his eyes and saying, 'Oh, for feck's . . .'

She turned round.

He was standing a little back from her, his hands

203

in his pockets. His eyes glittered green then black in the sweeping strobes. He said, 'Are you all right?'

Behind her, Darragh snapped, 'Of *course* she's all right – now go away and stop annoying us.'

Shay's gaze flicked to him very briefly, then settled again on Aoife enquiringly, one eyebrow raised slightly higher than the other. 'I saw you limping. Are you all right?'

She said firmly, to keep the shake out of her voice, 'I'm grand. Why wouldn't I be all right? Are you all right?'

'See? She's grand. Now back off.'

Shay took a step towards her, ignoring Darragh utterly this time. 'I was in Rita's café with John Joe for our tea last night and the waitress said you'd come in to get cleaned up after falling off your bike. But she made it sound like nothing. She didn't tell me you'd been hurt.'

She stared at him, searching his face for the truth – a lightness flowing into her heart, lifting it. Was Carla right, as always? Had the girl been just 'pathetically excited' by having a teenage boy talk to her politely?

(Darragh said, 'Aoife?' And then: 'Fine then.

I'll just be standing quietly over there when you need me.')

Shay still didn't take his green eyes off her face. 'Where does it hurt? Tell me.'

She realized she was holding her breath, and let it out on a sigh. 'My hip. And my shoulder.'

'This one?' He slipped his strong square hand under her cardigan, cupping his palm over on her right shoulder.

At the unexpectedness of his touching her skin – something he had never done before, not so deliberately, just to touch – she trembled, and warmth came flooding through her. His palm felt hot to her – a stinging, startling heat. 'Oh . . .'

His gaze grew concerned. 'That hurts?'

She lied, 'No, it's grand.'

'Good.' Still holding her eyes with his, he slowly placed his other hand on her hip. The same heat, searing right through the black dress. She stood firm, lips pressed together, eyes wide. He said, 'Listen to me. I shouldn't have come tonight. I just thought . . . I don't know . . . that Carla would drag you here and I'd miss seeing you. And I thought, it would be grand – I wouldn't have to come near you at all.

There'll be a big crowd, and I'd just see you – you know – across a crowded room . . .' He laughed, not very happily. 'But look at me. I can't do this.'

(Oh, the heat . . .) She said, 'You're wrong.'

'I'm not. I only meant to look at you across a room, and I had to come and talk to you. I only meant to touch you for a moment, and I can't take my hands off you . . .'

'You don't have to. There's no need for you to worry about hurting me. You're a lenanshee, but I'm the queen of the Tuatha Dé Danann. I'm not even sixteen yet, and I'm already more powerful than any other changeling. You can't hurt me, even if you wanted to.'

His dark green eyes on hers. The golden depths of them, lighting up. 'It's true . . . You were crowned . . . Does it make a difference? I don't know . . .'

'I know it. *I know it.*'

'Do you? Is it true?' His curved mouth, hesitating over hers. His strong hands pressing on her shoulder, and her hip. Her skin scorching, enough to bring tears to her eyes . . .

'It's true!' Yet her voice came out as a gasp of

pain – she couldn't help herself, her flesh was on fire . . .

And he flinched back, releasing her. 'I'm hurting you!'

She gasped, 'You weren't . . .' She was shaking, heart pounding.

'Why didn't you *say*?' His eyes had gone dark again. He shoved his fists into his pockets. 'I'm sorry. I should have known. I'm going now—'

'*Don't leave me!*'

'Aoife, I'm going. I have to go.' And he *was* going. He was walking away. The gaggle of girls by the wall were grinning and beckoning to him – Lois, Sinead, Aisling . . . She wanted to run after him, grab him, make him see. Kiss him, despite himself . . .

Everyone watching. Pride.

Darragh was standing by the food and drinks table, eating a sandwich; he gave her a slight wave as she fled past him towards the ladies'.

CHAPTER ELEVEN

A group of second years were hogging the mirrors above the row of sinks, gossiping and fixing their make-up. She slipped into the cubicle nearest the door; closed and locked it. The pain was fading . . . She pulled aside the cardigan and the strap of the black dress to look. And cried out in wonder, under her breath.

Laid across her shoulder, across the wound, was a clear, strong handprint. No scars remained; only the scarlet outline of his hand. Trembling, she placed her own hand over the mark of his, spreading out her fingers in the exact same way, but was not able to cover it completely. The intense heat of his energy radiated from her skin, heating her palm. It gave her a dizzy rush, a feeling of lightness . . .

She lifted the black dress to check her hip – the grazes were gone from there too. Only the mark of a broad, square palm, fingers spread out.

He had healed her.

She tugged down her skirt, closed the lid of the toilet seat and sat on it, staring at the back of the door.

He hadn't damaged her. He had *healed* her.

The chattering second years had finished beautifying themselves. Loud music blasted in as they left the bathroom, then cut off as they let the door slam shut.

Aoife got to her feet. She had to go to him, to tell him.

Before she could open the cubicle door, the outer door of the bathroom opened again. Two pairs of feet crossed the floor, followed by the noise of a tap being turned on, and the gasping sound of someone splashing their face with cold water.

Over the noise of the tap Jessica's voice was asking, 'Are you all right?'

The sound of paper towels being ripped from the holder. Aisling's voice answered, slightly muffled: 'Ugh. I feel so ugly. Did you see how beautiful she looked? No wonder Shay didn't have eyes for anyone else. I hate this stupid outfit!'

'It's original!'

'If only I was gorgeous like *her*.'

'Ah now, Aisling, you are!'

'Good joke. I mean, it was like she put a spell on him. He just kept staring and staring at her . . . Why can't I do that to a boy?'

Hidden in the cubicle, Aoife couldn't help smiling – her heart, a small balloon of pleasure coming untied.

A blast of Britney as the door opened and slammed again. Sinead called cheerfully, 'Oh my God, did you see what Aisling was wearing? Oh, hi, um . . .'

Jessica said, 'Aisling worked really hard on her outfit she didn't just throw on a black dress and a fascinator same as the rest of us.'

Without even pausing, Sinead said, 'Aren't you great, Aisling, and your costume is fabulous. I can't believe Shay didn't fall for you instead of going off with that absolute whore in her fancy white silk dress.'

Another brief blast of music, and now Lois's voice was squealing, 'Shay's slow-dancing with her now and everyone's watching them like they're that one from Dirty Dancing!'

'Who is she, anyway? Did you find out?' Sinead asked.

Lois said, 'Apparently she's that new waitress

from that café up near the Glen. I guess that's how he knew her – he lives only up the road.'

Inside the cubicle, Aoife had to stop herself crying out with the agony. Her heart was made of glass, cracks shivering across it; she put her hand to her chest, as if that way she could protect it from falling to pieces.

Jessica was saying, 'He's just gone so impossibly gorgeous since he turned sixteen.'

'And he knows it,' Sinead said. 'I blame that Aoife O'Connor. No doubt she was telling him how fabulous he was all summer. Slut.'

'Ah, now!'

'She *is* a slut and you know it. Did you not see her going after Darragh Clarke?'

'He seemed to be going after *her*—'

'Bullshit. He's a boy – he hasn't got a mind of his own, he goes where he's led. But I'm not letting her get her hooks into him – she'll only give him a big head. There's nothing worse than a boy who knows he's devastatingly good-looking.'

Sinking back down onto the toilet seat, Aoife sat with her head in her hands, tears sliding down under her fingers and winding their way around her wrists.

Another blast of music – Britney had been replaced by the Red Hot Chili Peppers. Lorcan's voice called, 'Lois, there's this guy out front says you hired him to give everyone trips around the square in a Halloween coach?'

A moment of astonishment in the bathroom, before Lois said, 'Bullshit, and this is the ladies' – go away and shut the door.'

The music continued in the background: the door was being held open. 'He definitely says you hired him as entertainment for the disco. He must be a friend of Paddy Duffy the undertaker, because he has that horse-drawn carriage Paddy uses for the traveller funerals, and he has it all dickied up for Halloween with skulls and stuff.'

'Nothing to do with me.' Lois was clearly mystified.

'Sure, whatever. I'm only here because he said someone should go and fetch you out to him, because you might like a free spin before he got going with everyone else, but if you're not interested—'

'No, wait! What does he look like?'

'Tall, very dark red hair?'

Lois screamed: '*Oh my God!! Tell him I'll be right out!!*'

'Grand, so . . .' The music cut off.

In the bathroom, Lois was still screaming, '*Oh my God, he came! I can't believe he came!* Quick, give me make-up . . .'

Sinead was saying urgently, 'Who came? Who is it?'

'The guy who came to my back door! He's really interested in me! Oh God, he's so beautiful . . .'

'The *axe-murderer*?'

'Ha, ha, *in your face*, Sinead Ferguson. Lend me your foundation.'

Sinead snapped, 'No, it'd be a waste.'

'*Give it to me!*'

'What's the point? You're only going to be chopped up into little pieces and stuffed in a bin bag.'

'*GIVE IT TO ME!* And that mascara, which is actually mine.'

Sinead said bad-temperedly, 'Fine, take it, but I'm telling you the next person doing your foundation will be Paddy Duffy himself.'

Lois chanted, 'You're *so* jealous! So, *so* jealous!'

'Lois, he's turned up to see you *in a funeral carriage*. Could he make his intentions any clearer?'

'Don't be ridiculous! You heard Lorcan – it's a bit of craic for Halloween. I was telling your man how boring the disco was. It's so nice of him to say this was my idea! Come on, girls, let's go! This'll be fun . . .'

With much chattering and laughing, the bathroom emptied.

Just before the door closed, Aoife heard Sinead saying: 'Make sure to keep your phone on so we can track your body by the GPS.'

And Lois gloating: 'Oh, you're so, *so* jealous!'

Silence.

Aoife took her head from her hands; stood up; let herself out of the cubicle. For a while she stood staring into the mirrors above the sinks. Her mascara was streaked across her cheeks by tears – she pulled off a paper towel, wetted it and scrubbed away the black marks. Her shoulder was visible in the mirror – the mark of his hand. She hesitated, then touched it again; it was still very warm.

He had healed her body. His parting gift.

She jerked her cardigan back into position. Pride.

The hall was shaking, the music turned up full, but there were only two people dancing – very slowly, circling the centre of the floor. Shay had his arms around the girl from the café. She had on the white silk dress which she'd been wearing when she got down off the bus; her feet were bare. She was leaning against him, her forehead resting on his shoulder. His eyes were also closed; his curved mouth pressed to the girl's pale white-blonde hair. Her dress clung and swung around her slender figure – she shone like a ghost in the ultra-violet strobe, a flickering white against his black. The perfect match in every way.

Don't cry, Aoife. Pride. *Pride.*

Blinking back tears, she took out her phone and texted Carla, who she couldn't see anywhere:

got to go sorry c u tmw

Out on the floor, the girl took Shay's dark head between her hands and tilted it down towards her. His eyes were still closed. He kissed her, very softly and purposefully, on the lips. No resistance at all. Wasn't he afraid of destroying her with his love? Clearly, his desire for her outweighed all caution. The girl smiled and drew her fingers down the strong curve of his neck. He groaned softly, as if her light touch had inflicted pain.

Aoife fled.

The steps were thronged by excited party-goers. Below in the lane sat Paddy Duffy's large black coach. On the box sat a man wearing a hooded cloak, holding a white whip. Between his feet a Halloween pumpkin glowed, and other smaller pumpkins dangled from hooks at each end of the box. The sides of the carriage were decorated with skulls sporting grey tufts of hair. Paddy's two huge strong carthorses – usually unflappable – were shifting restlessly between the shafts; black ears fearfully flattened, nostrils scarlet.

Aoife kept to one side, hand shielding her face, hiding tears. The crowd grew thicker, the nearer she got to the bottom of the steps – everyone, including Carla and Killian in his vampire outfit, was queuing. Lois was fighting her way to the front. 'Let me through! He's *my* friend!'

A man wearing an undertaker's top hat pulled right down over his face was leaning out of the coach door, yelling in the style of a fairground hustler: 'Roll up! Roll up! Rides for all! Rides to the underworld! Get your one-way tickets here!'

From the middle of the crowd Killian yelled out, 'How much for two tickets?'

The hustler shouted back, 'Two for the price of one, because I feel like I know you from somewhere, young man!' Then dropped his voice a little, and said chirpily, 'Well, good evening, Father . . .'

Father Leahy – presumably come down from the priest's house to check on all the excitement at the parish hall – was standing at the door of the coach, saying loudly in his dull, nasal, sermonizing voice, 'Young man, you're on church property. I trust you have insurance for this?'

'All signed and sealed, Father! And I'm expecting no complaints from the church.'

'Your coachman knows how to handle the horses?'

'He was born to it, Father! Do you want first ride? Ah, now, don't go!'

The priest had turned away, a cold smile on his face. Aoife – now at the foot of the steps – shrank against the corner as he passed her, climbing the steps towards the hall. He didn't glance in her direction, but he drew his robes close around him as if suddenly detecting an evil presence. She jumped down the last step and hurried away, up the ill-lit lane towards the square.

'Hey, you there in the cat's ears!'

She couldn't be the only one wearing cat's ears.

'*Hey, Aoife O'Connor! Come for a spin, why don't ya!*'

This time she froze by the graveyard wall, hairs pricking on the back of her neck.

'Aoife! *Ee . . . fah!*'

Now the voice had turned softer, smoother . . . Captivating . . .

Sick to her stomach with dread, slowly, she turned.

Leaning in the open doorway of the coach, looking straight at her, the top hat now tilted far back on his head . . .

Aoife's knees gave way, and she grabbed the stones of the wall beside her to keep herself on her feet, forcing herself to stay standing until the first icy shock-wave of fear had passed through her. Her body paralysed. Her mind swimming in terrified circles . . .

Dorocha was beaming. 'Come hither, young lady, for the trip of a lifetime!'

Move, Aoife, move, run . . .

What to do, where to go? Stay strong. *Focus.* Once before, she had escaped him . . . Yet that was when Shay had his desire for her, protecting her with the *grá*, his lenánshee love. Shay Foley was lost to her now – dancing in the parish hall, oblivious, his curved mouth buried in another girl's hair.

He had abandoned her.

'Hey, hey!' Lois had finally made it the front of the queue. 'You said I could have first ride! You promised!' She tried to clamber up the steps of the coach in her high heels, slipping and sliding, holding out her hand for Dorocha to help her up.

'Ah, Lois! Faithful servant! The first to welcome me down the fairy road and open her doors for me so kindly! Do you want a one-way ticket to the Festival of the Dead?'

'Yes, yes, I do!'

'Then come with me and off we go!'

To groans of impatience from those who had been waiting longer, he reached for Lois's hand and pulled the eager girl up the steps and into the interior. 'Drive on, coachman! We're off to the Festival of the Dead!' On the box, the dullahan driver – his orange rotting head between his feet – cracked his white whip. The horses whinnied nervously and tossed their big heads. The grey skulls knocked like knuckles against the woodwork and, with much creaking of brass and leather, the coach rolled slowly forwards – Dorocha leaning at an angle out of the door, gripping the frame with one hand and the brim of his undertaker's hat with the other. As the horses picked up speed towards where Aoife stood frozen, he flourished the hat, crying gleefully, 'And now, my queen!'

Instantly unfreezing, Aoife kicked off her high heels, sprinted down by the graveyard wall and round the corner, across the empty square. She strained for speed, but by the time she'd reached the far corner, the coach had burst from the entrance to lane. Round the pub, up towards the bog, cold rough gravel under her bare feet – had she lost them? – but the rattle of wheels and the drumming of hooves were coming fast behind; horses gasping with the strain, finding it hard going up the hill . . .

If she could reach the bog before she was caught,

if she could cut across the soft heather where the heavy wheels would sink and horses founder . . .

Closer came the horses.

She mustn't let him catch her, mustn't let him put his hands upon her . . .

She could hear his voice now, howling over the thunder of wheels: 'Aoibheal!' The name her fairy mother had given her. The mother Dorocha had murdered. 'Aoibheal, come here to me!'

And Lois's voice ringing out as well, high-pitched: 'Who are you calling? Who's out there?'

'*Aoibheal!*'

But the cries and the rumble of the wheels were falling behind. The slope was too steep for two horses dragging the big heavy undertaker's coach behind them. *I'm out-pacing him* . . . Twenty metres ahead was one last solitary house – its outside lights whitening the night – and beyond that the darkness of the bog. She was pulling ahead . . . *Nearly there.*

Behind, the door of the coach crashed open, and booted feet landed on the road, then came racing after her at terrible speed. Faster, so much faster than the horses. *Faster than her.* She made a furious, terrified effort to redouble her speed . . .

Run, Aoife, run.

Hands of steel grabbed her shoulders, and his fingers were sinking into her flesh.

She was struggling, kicking, falling.

Down.

The strength being sucked out of her. He was drinking her in through his hands . . .

Down.

. . . as if his fingers were straws, and she a long, cool drink of blood.

CHAPTER TWELVE

Dorocha said, very slowly and seriously, 'Look . . . at . . . me.'

Aoife kept her eyes crushed shut. *Don't look at him.* That moment on the altar, when he had thrust her fist into the hole where his heart should have been . . . *No heart.* She was going to fall into that bottomless pit . . . *Eternity.* Don't look into his eyes . . . *Down.*

This was no handsome, charming man. He was a black hole, full of the ghosts of long-dead stars. *Un-empty emptiness . . .*

She was being pulled towards him. She was growing weaker. Weaker. Don't look into his eyes . . . I'm . . . *Don't fall.*

'Look at me, Aoibheal.'

Shay, help me. I think he is the devil . . . .

But Shay was dancing, and she was on her own. Darkness began to come and go, flashes of consciousness passing across her mind like strobe lights in a disco . . .

The girl in white . . .

He was dancing . . .

How was it possible that Shay had abandoned her?

'Look at me, Aoibheal.'

Eternity in his arms . . .

'For the third time. Look at me, Aoibheal.'

Helplessly, she did.

Grinning, he winked at her. Then let go of her shoulders and did a full twirl, arms above his head. 'So, what do you think of my Halloween outfit?' The outside lights of the last house on the road poured a faint skim of brightness over him. He was still wearing the linen shirt stained with his own blood, and his long black coat and soft red boots. But he had amused himself by adding other mocking details: Paddy Duffy's undertaker's hat, which now had real spiders poised around the brim; a necklace of human teeth; a blank human eye, fastened to his lapel with a long silver pin. (Oh God . . . The horror . . . Whose corpse was lying desecrated in Paddy Duffy's funeral home?) Aoife backed up against the stone wall of the field behind, the brambles sticking into her legs and arms. She clenched her fists, desperate to feel a rush of power – as when the welfare officer had come for Eva, or Killian had threatened Carla.

Nothing.

'Come, my queen.' His tone was hushed; a mockery of an undertaker's voice. He leaned forward to slide his arm round her back. With the other hand he removed her cat's ears and tossed them into the field behind, saying, 'Not very regal! We will find you a tiara of sapphires instead, my queen.'

She tried to say, *I don't want your jewels*. But what little strength she had left, his touch was draining from her. Feeling her slump against him, he laughed and gathered her into his arms like an armful of grass, then half supported, half lifted her into the coach.

Lois was sitting bolt upright in the corner, looking furious. 'Where did she come from? What are you bringing her on the ride for? I thought this trip was just for you and me!'

Dorocha said with exaggerated patience, 'But Lois, this is Aoibheal.'

'No it's not, she's *Aoife*! And you won't like her, she's a slut, always after other people's boyfriends . . .'

He laid Aoife gently down on the other seat, then leaned out to close the door. 'Lois, I can assure you – whether I get to like her or not – this is Aoibheal. She may have been going incognito among you, but she is the queen of the underworld.'

'Oh . . . What?' Lois was confused but hopeful. 'You mean . . . Is this a Halloween game, like Dungeons and Dragons?'

'That's right.' Settling himself next to her, Dorocha gazed fondly into Lois's round, anxious face; he touched her under her chin, very lightly, with the tip of his long forefinger. 'It's all one big game, my lovely Lois.'

Lois flushed with pleasure; she said weakly, 'But why does it have to be her who plays the part of Aoibheal? Why can't I be your queen?'

Dorocha withdrew his finger and leaned out of the window, crying, 'Coachman! Drive on!' The whip cracked, the horses jerked forwards, and the coach rumbled into the driveway of the last house, drove in a circle around the lawn (living room curtains being furiously jerked aside), then out of the gate again, back towards Kilduff. After which Dorocha brought his attention back to Lois – who was staring open-mouthed out of the window, clearly shaken at the way the coachman had just driven right over someone else's carefully mown grass. 'Lois, I adore you . . .'

Immediately she turned to him, all smiles – the churned-up lawn forgotten. 'Do you?'

'But everyone has to do what they do best. And what you can do best for me is to be my gift to the druids, who have asked me to bring them a teenage human girl as a sacrifice—'

She emitted a shrill, startled giggle. Then said uncertainly, 'What?'

'Let me explain again. I am on a mission from the druids to bring back a teenage human girl for their festival.' Again Dorocha touched the girl's soft chin, tickling her very lightly under it. 'My sweet one, say you'll be my gift to them!'

Her doubts softened by his endearment, Lois simpered, 'Sweet one? Oh, you're such a messer . . .'

'Sweet and tasty! Yum-yum! Ah, she's smiling! Come on, say you will!'

'Oh, *you* . . . OK, whatever!' relented Lois, laughing. 'I'll be your human sacrifice!'

Lying on the hard wooden bench, watching

Dorocha make Lois his adoring pawn, Aoife focused on breathing slow and deep. She had to make a move soon. She had to get stronger. She had to persuade Lois out of the coach. She struggled; managed to half sit up. 'Lois, you need to get out. Now.' Her voice was slurred – soft and croaky.

Lois stopped giggling with Dorocha and bristled at Aoife, black curls bouncing. 'What? No! And quit talking like a zombie on Xanax – you don't sound scary, you just sound stupid, you can't act.'

Dorocha winked at Aoife. 'You see? Lois doesn't want to get out. She wants to feel the cold stone knife pushing slowly, slowly, through her skin, the fat, the flesh, the ribs, tickling the skin of her heart just before the druid . . .'

Lois said, giggling again, 'I know it's Halloween, but . . .'

'. . . plunges in the knife!'

Lois squealed with infatuated pleasure, 'Eeugh, gross!'

The coach had re-entered the square and was nearing the church again. A handful of cars were crossing their path – parents arriving to collect the disco-goers, forcing the horses to slow to walking speed. A knot of older teenagers were gathered at the top of the parish lane, watching for the return of the coach, their shadows thrown long and black by the solitary streetlight on the corner. Carla was waiting, with Killian's arm around her. Sinead was there, looking at Killian, and Darragh as well, a cigarette glowing between his lips, patiently being ignored by Sinead.

Dorocha pressed his face to the window, gazing with sudden interest. 'Lois, who is that remarkable-looking boy with the very pale hair? He does remind me of someone . . .'

'Killian Doherty? He's an awful tart, and his girlfriend is a penance. Can we go round again before you give them their go?'

He drew back from the window, smiling at her fondly. 'Of course we can. Together, you and I, we can go round and round.'

'Really?' Lois glowed, enchanted. 'Thank you so much . . . Can we drop Aoife – I mean, Aoibheal – off first?'

A stir rippled through the group of teenagers as it became clear that the coach was not going to stop on the corner, or follow the cars down the lane to the hall. Lois's phone rang; without taking her eyes from Dorocha, she put it to her ear and rolled her eyes. 'Sinead, stop bothering me, we're having great craic. No, he's lovely. Stop trying to spoil things for me. No, I'm not going to get out – we're going around again—'

Aoife said, louder than before, 'Lois, Sinead's right, get out now.'

'Bye, Sinead – and *in your face*!' Clicking off the phone, Lois turned on Aoife crossly. 'No, *you* get out! Go on, go chase after Darragh or Killian, or whoever you're hot for tonight— Hey, where are we going?'

They had passed the entrance to the lane, but instead of going around the square, the coach had carried straight on down the Clonbarra road and was now picking up speed – the horses trotting past the empty estate, cantering as they reached the garage . . . Galloping now, the wheels spurting gravel and squelching in mud . . .

Lois was beaming, bouncing up and down, hanging onto the edge of the wooden seat. 'Oh, oh, the road's so bumpy! How far are we going?'

'As far as your house, my dear.' Dorocha had his arm hooked over the back of the seat behind her; his dark blue eyes, resting on the human girl, were narrow with amusement.

She was thrilled. 'Really? Are you going to come in?'

'I am indeed.'

'Yay! I'll text Mam to tell her she doesn't have to fetch me — she'll be delighted.' Her thumbs tap-tapped away happily at her phone as she bounced. 'I can't wait to see Mam and Dad's face when they see us roll up in this! Let's drop Aoife first, she's on the way. Here's her turning— Oh!' The coach had swept past the lane to Aoife's house. 'You passed it! Can he turn round? Seriously, Mam won't want me bringing her home with me; my nan thinks she's an awful heathen . . . OK, fine, but we'll have to leave her in the coach while we have our tea.'

The cold glass of the window trembled against Aoife's cheek, vibrating with the speed of their going. In the small stone house at the bottom of the lane, James and Maeve O'Connor would be waiting for her to text them to pick her up from the disco. If she could just somehow open the door, jump out . . . But she couldn't leave Lois, she had to help Lois. Lois thought Dorocha was joking, but the druids did sacrifice teenage girls; the changeling girl Caitlin had been afraid of them for that very reason . . .

God, help me help Lois.

But God had turned His back on her. The water had boiled in the font.

Shay, help me . . .

How could Shay Foley have abandoned her? It didn't make any sense . . . Dancing with that girl. That girl. She slipped her fingers under her cardigan, slid them over her shoulder, where he had touched her to heal her. Still hot, even now. She angled her hand to cover the print of his. The heat of him rising from her skin. The touch of his touch, seeping into her.

'Oh, hi, Mam, did you get my message? You're going to get a real surprise! Not far away . . .' Lois rang off, then said nervously, checking out of the window at the black hedges flashing by, 'We're nearly there – aren't we going a bit fast?'

'Are we, my lovely Lois?'

She giggled wildly. 'Oh!'

The warmth of Shay leaking up into her hand, wrist, trickling into her blood, crawling into her heart . . . The last of his *grá* for her.

'That's mine up ahead – tell your driver to slow down, we're going to miss it, we're going to— *Oh!*'

At the last moment the coach swung violently to the right, whip cracking and horses screaming, wheels half off the ground, and went thundering up a neat gravelled driveway straight towards the Munnellys' small modern bungalow.

'*The horses are bolting! We're going to crash into my house!*'

'I thought you didn't want to miss it,' said Dorocha cheerfully. 'And who in their right mind builds their house on a fairy road?'

'*We're going to crash!!*'

A sensor light flared, illuminating the porch. For one moment it did seem they were going to smash straight between the plastic columns into the front door, but at the last instant the galloping horses took a sharp left across the lawn, sending a small fountain and a hundred plaster gnomes flying. In the living room, turning from the television, startled faces . . .

Lois howled in horror, '*The lawn!*'

Dorocha shouted out of the window, up to the coachman, 'Get off the lawn!'

The coach took a sharp right, straight through the closed French windows of the conservatory . . .

'Not the house!'

. . . in a massive shower of glass and plastic, turning over a potted palm tree, the television, the drinks cabinet . . .

'No! The sun room!'

. . . the wheels of the coach mired in cane furniture, horses screaming, struggling to get through. In the archway that led to the living room, Jane and Peter Munnelly standing clutching their heads and howling in distress . . . Lois's grandmother, her pink face distorted with horror in the background . . .

Still holding her shoulder, Aoife made a weak effort to stand up. Now was her chance to get out, and take Lois with her.

'Let me past!' Lois shoved Aoife aside, reaching for the coach door, crying over her shoulder to Dorocha: *'Come on, quick – let's go!'*

But before Lois could turn the handle, the wheels came free and the coach shot through the back wall of the conservatory, across a rockery and then – the horses sweating, dragging and shrieking under the persistent whip, bloody spittle flying from their mouths – squeezed between the tightly planted border of conifers, over a low stone wall and line of barbed wire, into a field of sheep that scattered, onwards up the steep moonlit hill towards the mountains . . .

Lois sank to the floor, arms over her head, wailing, *'We're all going to die!'*

Dorocha pulled her up onto the seat beside him. 'Calm down, my sacrificial lamb. You're safe with me.'

She clung to him. *'Save me!'*

'Ssh, shh, of course I'll save you.'

'Don't let me die!'

He roared with laughter. 'Now why would I let you die, my lovely Lois? Not yet, anyway.'

Drawing on the last remnants of Shay's energy, Aoife made one more desperate effort. 'Lois, you have to get out!' Staggering upright, she dragged the human girl from her seat and pushed her against the door, throwing it open. 'Jump!'

'What are you doing?' howled Lois, clinging to the door frame as the field went flying past beneath the wheels.

Aoife shoved her as hard as she could. 'Get out!'

'Stop pushing me! You're crazy!'

Dorocha was amused. 'Aoibheal, really, don't be so cruel to the girl. How many times does she have to tell you, she doesn't want to get out? Lois, my love, come here to me . . .'

'She's trying to kill me! Stop her!' But Lois's fingers were slipping, and with one more fierce shove, Aoife hurled her out of the coach, then flung herself out as well, crashing on top of the screaming girl, grabbing her and rolling over and over with her down the hard stony hill, arms wrapped around Lois's head, taking the battering of the rocks on her own arms. The coach thundered on up the hill, door slamming to and fro. The headless coachman – hood fallen from his shoulders – was standing up on the box, hauling on the reins, trying to turn them back. But Paddy's screaming, bolting carthorses snapped the reins in their terror and – their heads now unrestrained by the coachman's inhuman strength – went pounding on up the steep slope towards the moonlit sky, dragging the coach by its shafts behind them, disappearing with it over a ragged hedge of brambles into the next field.

As the thunder of the wheels grew fainter and fainter, Aoife rose to her knees. Lois remained flat on her back – eyes closed, face white as milk in the moonlight.

'Lois?'

'Aaargh . . .'

'Oh, thank God. Are you all right?' She slipped one hand under Lois's shoulders, thinking of trying to move her out of the bed of thistles in which the girl was lying.

Lois shuddered and flinched. 'Don't touch me. My arm . . . My leg . . .'

Aoife moved her hands away hastily. 'Are they broken?'

'Please don't kill me . . .'

'No one's trying to kill you – he's gone, you're safe now.' Far below at the foot of the hill, outside lights were springing on at the back of the bungalow; she could hear thin distant cries. 'Have you your phone? Let me ring your parents, tell them where you are – they'll call an ambulance. Is it in your pocket?'

'*Don't touch me!*' With surprising energy, Lois rolled sideways across the thistles, scrambling to her feet, kicking off her one remaining high heel. 'You're a psycho!'

'OK, good, I'm glad you're OK, but call them anyway—'

'You were determined to get rid of me, weren't you? You're not just a slut, you're an evil vicious whore!'

Aoife cried in astonishment, 'Lois, I was trying to save you!'

Staring up the hill to where the coach had disappeared, Lois wailed miserably, 'And now he's gone without me!'

'Are you mad? You could have been killed!'

'Yes, by *you*! Don't try to follow me!' And Lois went scampering away – '*Mam! Dad! Help! Ow!*' – barefoot over the thistles and stones, down the long dark field towards the lights.

Left alone on the hill, Aoife collapsed on the grass, exhausted, her forehead resting on her knees. Behind, over the mountains, the moon was riding high – every rock and clump of thistles throwing its hard inky shadow over the grey grass. Lois's dark little shape zigzagged at surprising speed down the hill until she reached the conifers and scrambled over the fence into her garden, into the embrace of the electric lights and her parents running frantically to meet her.

In the pocket of Aoife's cardigan, her mobile beeped. She pulled it out – the screen was shattered, but thankfully it was still working. The text was from Maeve:

Ready to be picked up yet?

She texted back:

Not yet. Having great craic.

Then, with a sigh, sank her head into her arms. A shower of hair fell around her shoulders, coming loose from its tie – glinting dark silver in the moonlight, instead of red-gold. A cool wind blew over her back, making her shiver in her thin cardigan. She raised her head, pulled the short dress down over her knees. Time to go home. Maybe slip back to the parish hall so Maeve could pick her up from there? A long shadow lay on the ground beside her. She looked at it for a while, then, with the faintest of hopes, pressed her hand to her shoulder. But the skin was cold now. The last of Shay's warmth was gone. She was on her own. As calmly as possible, she got to her feet and turned round.

He was standing just above her on the moonlit hill, on a small tussock of earth and grass, his arms folded. As soon as she had turned to face him, he winked and took a step towards her.

Don't let him touch you. She took a hasty stride back, nearly falling.

'Oops, mind yourself!' He was laughing, raising his hands, palm out. 'Relax, my queen. I'm not going to come near you! I've only come to talk.'

She could run, but she knew now that he was so much faster . . . She stood with her fists clenching by her sides. *Show no fear.* He didn't know about Shay and the girl in white. As far as Dorocha was concerned, Shay's *grá* was still her shield: the Beloved could not force her to marry him. 'Talk about what?'

He sat down on the tussock, perched with arms around his knees, his dark coat spread out about him. The moonlight brightened his pale skin, deepening the inky blue of his eyes to black, whitening his copper lashes, casting shadows beneath his high cheekbones. His hat was on his lap, the spiders balanced precariously around the rim. 'About you, for one thing. I'm curious about you, Aoibheal. You just

240

risked life and limb to save a stupid human girl who had nothing good to say about you.'

'I could hardly let you hand her to the druids as a sacrifice!' Even though she suspected him of being . . .

Empty . . .

. . . she was shaken by this glimpse into his nothingness – the fact that he couldn't even understand why she would want to save silly, foolish Lois Munnelly. It was unnerving, the ignorance that underpinned his evil.

Dorocha was shaking his head. 'But she was human! Aoibheal, you have to grow up – you need to break your ties with this world.'

She said angrily, 'It was you who sent me here when I was four!'

He tutted, flicking at a spider that had crawled off onto his knee, herding it with cupped hand back onto his hat. 'I should have chosen your parents more carefully – I didn't realize you were going to be so badly brought up.'

'They're *good* parents!'

'Exactly. Anyway, enough of your personal failings. What I'm *really* here to talk about is your lenanshee boy. How did you like Shay Foley's sweet lover, Aoibheal? His hungry, heart-sucking demon? She always steals the most beautiful boy from the dance – and so I sent her here, to Kilduff, because who could be more beautiful than a lenanshee boy of sixteen? She is so happy with my gift to her, and he is deep in love . . .'

The blow to Aoife's heart was so great, she staggered; the field seemed to shift beneath her feet. She should have known . . . Why hadn't she listened to Carla? Carla had said, *This isn't Shay Foley's style.* How could Carla have been so wise, and she so blind? Shay would never have left her for another girl. She should have known something must be wrong. Instead, she had abandoned him . . . She cried hoarsely: 'Where has she taken him?'

Dorocha shrugged, spreading out his hands. 'Too late now, I'm afraid. My pretty demon will never let him go, and his heart is hers for ever. It's a shame, Aoibheal. I *was* going to bring you with me to Falias. I thought you might like to join the party.'

She seized at this strange, amazing straw. If she could get to Shay, she could simply kiss him, and they could fly to freedom. 'I would, I'll come with you to Falias – it's such a beautiful city!'

But he pulled a long face at her, his lower lip thrust out. 'Mm, no, sorry, changed my mind.'

'No! *Why?*'

He was shaking his head. 'Blame that Lois. Or rather, blame yourself. Look at all the fuss you made to save that stupid girl, when I had specially promised the druids a teenage girl for their festival – and now Morfesa will get in one of his foul moods and mutter on about every time he ever did my bidding against his better judgement, and how I always try to force the hand of fate. All this mindless rushing to rescue people, Aoife – it makes such a mess of things.'

'I won't try anything!'

'Very amusing. No, I've decided to lock the fairy road against you until my sweet demon has finally tired of him, and drained his heart and crushed the dried husk of it into a thousand pieces. Literally. Now, now, Aoibheal . . .' He raised his hands sharply. 'Don't even think of attacking me – you know I'll break you like a twig.'

She pulled back. *Stay calm.* Nails sunk into her palms. *Be in control.* She said slowly, measuring her words, 'How could I rescue him, even if I wanted to?

You said yourself, it's too late. He loves her now, and he won't want to come away with me – and if she breaks his heart, it's none of my business. Maybe I'd like to watch.'

He looked highly amused. 'Vengeful, Aoibheal? Hell has no fury like a woman scorned?'

'Exactly.'

He seemed to reconsider. 'I approve this spite. Maybe if you ask me nicely.'

'Please bring me.'

'Oh, I misspoke – I meant to say "beg", not "ask".'

'Please, please bring me!'

'On your knees, Aoibheal . . . Ah, good girl, that's right.'

'Please!'

'Please, my Lord.'

'Please, my Lord.'

He laughed. 'No.'

And he was gone.

CHAPTER THIRTEEN

She ran headlong down the hill across the thistles and the rocks, running as the crow flies, over the hedges and ditches, nearly crippling herself on an unexpected barbed-wire fence, splashing through wet mud in her bare feet, ripping herself on brambles.

Dorocha had locked her out. One hope remained – maybe the dance in this world had not ended. If the music was still playing on, if Shay and his demon lover were still in each other's arms, and she could warn him . . . (And if he wouldn't listen? She would *make* him listen.)

A last ditch and she had reached the road. As she sprinted at changeling speed towards Kilduff, a Gardaí car rushed past her in the other direction, siren blazing, and turned into the Munnellys' driveway. She fled on, past her own boreen, past the garage, past the empty estate. No cars passing, or parked ahead of her in the square. No distant sound of music . . .

Yet the lane to the parish hall was not deserted.

On the corner, under the streetlight, a solitary girl in a black dress stood shivering, swaying on her high heels and holding a second pair dangling in one hand. *'You're safe!'* Carla rushed to her, clinging to her, the high heels in her hand hitting Aoife on the back. 'Oh, thank God! Thank God!'

Aoife gasped, 'Is everyone gone? Is Shay gone?'

'A Gardaí car went by and everyone heard there'd been a crash outside Lois Munnelly's and I was so scared you'd been hurt.' She pulled back hastily, digging into her bag for her ringing phone.

'Carla, is everyone gone?'

'The last ones just left, and Father Leahy's gone home so I guess it's all locked up. *Damn*, I left my coat in the hall! At least I've got your shoes. Wait!' Gripping Aoife's wrist with one hand and holding the phone to her ear with the other, Carla said with impressive calm, 'Hi, Mam. Yes, just on my way back to Aoife's now . . . Give my love to Nan! See you and Zoe tomorrow.'

Aoife's phone was ringing in her cardigan pocket. Maeve. She rejected the call, then texted quickly:

I'm ok

'Carla, I have to go to the hall.'

Carla wouldn't let go of her wrist. 'I told you, it's all locked up, everyone's gone.'

'But did you see Shay leave? Have you been standing here the whole time? Did he pass you?'

'No, but even if he's still— *Come back!*'

He had to be there, he *had* to be.

Chasing after her, Carla cried, 'Aoife, I've something to tell you. That girl from the café—'

'That's why I have to find him!'

'No, no! If it's true, you can't go running around after him, it's crazy, you'll only make yourself twice as miserable! Oh, for— *Wait for me!*'

At the top of the steps, the small postern door of the parish hall swung open under her hand – not because of her magic, but because it was already unlocked. *Someone was still here.* But she paused, her foot on the threshold, heart thumping, summoning her strength, fighting the urge to go rushing in headlong, not knowing what manner of demon this was – or if it might use Shay as a human shield.

Go carefully, quietly.

Carla came panting up behind her. 'Oh, they forgot to lock it – at least now I can get my coat.'

'Ssh.' Aoife held her back, one hand on her arm. The double doors into the hall ahead of them were moving very slightly, as if creaking in a breeze.

'Really, I don't think anyone's here. Father Leahy just forgot to lock up, that's all – there's no lights on.'

'Ssh! Please. Stay here and keep quiet. Shay's in terrible danger from that girl.'

'You mean, from that *waitress*?'

'She's a demon – she's going to destroy him.'

Carla squeaked, '*What?*' And then, remembering immediately that her best friend was delusional, added sympathetically, 'Oh, Aoife . . .'

'Stay here.' Aoife stepped softly into the lobby. The small glass panels set in the hall doors glimmered then darkened, glimmered and darkened – catching the moonlight that flowed through the open door behind her.

Carla persisted in following, although she had lowered her voice to a whisper. 'Really, there's no one here. *Oh!*'

Inside the hall, the lights had sprung on – although not the very bright overheads suspended from the high ceiling, but the low-level emergency ones set around the walls. 'Stay back and don't move.' Aoife hurried softly to the doors and peered in through one of the glass panels.

The dimly lit hall was empty.

A split second later, the person who had turned on the lights passed across her field of vision, heading away from the switches by the door down to the back of the hall. It was a small, plump, balding man with a bright red comb-over, wearing a very old-fashioned suit – the same man whom she had last seen carrying a huge amount of ice cream, Cokes and crisps out of the shop, across the square into the churchyard. Reaching the food and drinks table, he shook out a large black plastic sack and began scooping into it the leftovers from the party.

A strange, distant bell rang in Aoife's mind. (Old John McCarthy in the shop: *That better not be fairy gold, young man. I remember you from the last time, so I do.* And Ultan in the otherworld, telling her: *Some of the older changelings like to get their hands on human food . . . Everyone knows one or two of them are sneaking it in from above.*)

Getting her breath back, Carla whispered, 'It's

only one of the parents come back in to clean up. I guess they couldn't find the main light switch. I'm going in to get my coat.'

Aoife stopped her from pushing open the door. 'Wait. I want to see—'

'He's cleaning up!'

The man wasn't cleaning up. He was leaving the dried-up sandwiches and crumbled half-eaten buns on the table, and helping himself to the untouched food and drink – cans first, then crisps and chocolate. As Aoife watched – and as Carla made impatient noises at her side – he folded the tin-foil platter around the untouched layer of the green Halloween cake and placed it in his sack with care; then stashed away a tray of egg mayonnaise sandwiches still sealed in cling-film, then a similar tray of ham sandwiches. Reaching a packet of Kimberleys, he appeared to hesitate, then ripped it open and stuffed several into his mouth, as if starving. Then stood there, chewing his way through them, his head on one side as if contemplating life.

Carla lost patience and shoved at the door. 'Come on, I need my coat . . .'

The man spun round to face them.

Aoife seized Carla and hustled her back into a

corner of the lobby, between a set of lockers and a mop bucket, hissing, 'Don't let him see us!'

'What are you doing? He's just a—'

Aoife slammed her hand over Carla's mouth. *'Keep quiet and stay completely still!'*

Moments later, the man came barging out through the swing doors, his black plastic rubbish sack slung over his shoulder. His round, pink face was made rounder by having cheeks full of biscuits. He passed close by them in the dark lobby, thrust his munching head out into the night to check the coast was clear, then left. The sack was so full, he had difficulty getting it out through the narrow postern doorway – for a moment it caught behind him on the frame.

Carla was already pushing Aoife off her. 'You luna— See, nothing to worry about! Just wait here a sec and I'll be back . . .' and she ran into the hall for her coat.

Aoife fled the other way, out into the lane. The little man *had* to be one of those older changelings from the otherworld. And if he was smuggling human goods, then he had to know a secret way down to the Land of the Young; a road unknown even to Dorocha – and therefore, still unlocked.

The changeling was gone from view already . . .
But the small side-gate to the graveyard was swinging.
Aoife darted across the lane and through the gate,
and paused, listening for the sound of hurrying
feet. Nothing but the rustle of the wind in the yew
trees, and the squeak of rust as the lychgate closed
again behind her. The streetlight on the corner over
the wall suddenly went out, dying in a few seconds to
a dull red. But then the moon swung from behind the
clouds, lighting the grey, leaning stones.

Avoiding the crunching gravel of the path, Aoife
hurried on her bare feet up the grassy slope. Here
were the traveller tombs. Angels stood guard with
widespread wings; groups of pale children were clustered around their feet – cherubim, holding stone
books engraved with the names of the dead. And
there was the man, a long way off, dodging along
between the graves, his black sack over his shoulder.
She ducked behind an angel. *Don't let him see you.*
There were rumours in the otherworld – these smugglers kept their ways secret by cutting the throat of
anyone, changeling or human, who dared to follow
them. A swooping darkness passed over, like the
shadow of a vast black bird – the moon disappearing

behind the clouds. She left the safety of the angel and ran as quietly as she could after the man. It was hard not to fall, dodging in and out between the grave surrounds. Presently, she *did* fall – her foot going down a hole. Wincing, she remained very still on her hands and knees, listening intently.

Then the moon burst out again and she found herself staring at Shay's parents' grave:

HERE LIES MOIRA FOLEY,

BELOVED WIFE OF EAMONN FOLEY,

BELOVED MOTHER OF JOHN JOE AND SEAMUS FOLEY.

Though it wasn't Shay's mother – it was a log of wood, a fairy trick. Shay's lenanshee mother was in the fairy world.

HERE LIES EAMONN FOLEY,

BELOVED FATHER OF JOHN JOE AND SEAMUS FOLEY.

Eamonn Foley was buried here, for sure. His life drained from him by his lenanshee wife. Dying an old, old man at the age of thirty-five.

Aoife cocked her head, alerted. Behind her, in the

direction of the church, a slow, steady creaking, as of a door opening. She leaped to her feet, racing towards the porch. It was open, but once more the inner door was locked. She placed her hand on the lock, expecting it to click like the last time – but it resisted her, her energy sparking painfully back at her, hurting her all the way up to her elbow like an electric shock. *Iron.* Father Leahy must have changed the lock from brass to iron, knowing it would keep un-Christian creatures out . . .

But that was good. It showed the changeling man could not have passed this way.

She ran back out of the porch and stood listening again . . .

Again, a door creaking.

Hard by the church porch stood the Doherty tomb, where Killian's paternal grandparents lay at rest. She ran round to the front. The wooden door of the sepulchre was closing . . . She darted forward, leaping over the railing to grasp the edge of the door. It fought against her, crushing her fingers against the frame. She exerted all her changeling strength, set-ting her power against the magic spell. Gradually the door yielded to her – and finally surrendered and became an ordinary lump of wood on hinges. She wrenched it open. Blackness. She dug out her phone. The battery was dying, and the torch scattered only the faintest of beams, barely penetrating the empty room. She stepped in, casting the fading torchlight around her.

Instead of a stone sarcophagus, a set of steps disappeared from the centre of the floor, down into darkness.

Icy air rushed up towards her from the depths.

Down.

The hairs on her neck rising, she stood staring into the depths. The faint beam of her phone illuminated the first ten stone steps. After that the descent was shrouded in impenetrable black. Behind her, the door swung creakily closed.

Down.

Below, was the changeling man lying in wait – to cut her throat?

Down.

Below, in the bowels of the earth, was the demon girl who had taken Shay.

Down.

The light trembled in her hand, fading, fading . . . Only five steps visible now. The otherworld under

Connacht was a wide country. These steps would probably not even lead to Falias – the tunnel through the sea-cave had brought her to a completely different city. How long would it take her to find her way across the wilderness to the city of Falias, without a map, unaided? Days? Weeks? And then, even if it was possible, how long would it take her to find Shay, and rescue him, and bring him home? A month? Longer?

A mere six months was fifty years in the human world. A lifetime. Carla would be seventy-four. She would never see her parents again – only return to find their graves.

She brought her dying phone close to her face, and with grieving fingers texted Maeve:

got to go, don't worry xxx BRB

She hit send.
Down.

END OF BOOK ONE

BOOK TWO

BOOK TWO

CHAPTER ONE

Down, down . . .

The steps quickly became very steep, with a long drop from one to the next, so narrow that there was barely room to set her heel, let alone her whole foot. Worse, they were getting dangerously slippery – covered in a slimy coating of thick moss.

Aoife negotiated them very slowly, pressing her hands hard against the earthen walls to stop herself falling. The light from her phone was still just working, showing her the way. Beetles and woodlice pattered, dislodged by her fingers.

Down.

Fingers stroked her arm. A shrivelled arm, thin and black in the moonlight.

'No! Get away!' Almost weeping with terror, she beat the hand back; it snapped and fell. Not an arm – a tree root.

Shuddering, heart pounding, sweat prickling, she stood still clinging to the earthen wall, steadying herself. Willing her heart to calm. If she was afraid of roots, how was she going to save Shay from an actual demon? She had to leave fear behind her, in the human world. Beneath her feet, the steps continued on down, each now no more than five centimetres deep. If she kept trying to descend on foot, she would fall. Very carefully, she sat down. Then, using her hands, lowered herself cautiously from step to step like a toddler negotiating a flight of stairs.

Down.

Each step seemed to tilt forwards slightly, and they were still covered with the wet slippery moss that made it impossible to get a proper grip. The light from her phone faded; then, finally, it was gone. With no light at all, even her sharp fairy night vision could not help her. She lowered herself blindly from step to step, feeling her way, her hands and feet slipping and sliding dangerously on the moss, her short black dress rucking up around her hips.

Down, down.

How far, how deep? This was going on for ever.

She had to go faster . . . Shay needed her . . .

Maybe she should just throw herself down. No,

that was stupid – if she broke her leg, she would lie here in this dark for ever . . .

She started counting the steps to keep her frantic mind occupied.

Fifty . . . sixty . . .

One hundred.

One hundred and ten . . .

Shay, I'm coming!

Please God, if you love me, keep Shay safe until I can rescue him. Merciful God, protect him. Our Father who art in heaven . . .

But the priest had locked the church against her with an iron key.

(*Maybe he's the phoney one . . .*)

Please God, even if you don't love me, keep Shay safe. Keep *everyone* I love safe. Let my parents understand that I had to go, and I will try my best to get home before they grow old . . . Let Eva be safe. Let Carla not be too unhappy . . .

She was suddenly overwhelmed by guilt – Carla would be so terrified, left alone in the middle of the night, not knowing where Aoife had gone. The street-light was off, and Carla was so scared of the dark, and she would have to make her own way home across the empty square and up the hill, past whispering hedges and heavily breathing cows. Oh, Carla . . . Forgive me . . . Just remember I'm mad, I know not what I do . . .

And she must be mad. And she didn't know what she was doing. To find Shay, she must go to Dorocha . . . Dorocha, who longed to crush Aoife into his emptiness – thrusting her fist into the hole behind his ribs; dragging her . . .

Down.

She had to save Shay.

Down.

Far below, a movement in the darkness. A scraping and a pattering. She paused, leaning forward to listen, gripping the edge of the step. How far ahead of her was the changeling man? Would he really cut her throat if he caught her following him? Too dreadful to die for some stupid reason in some black hole, so far from doing what she had come to do . . .

Nothing below her but silence. She got ready to move on.

But then, the same sounds – nearer now – a loud scuffling, and getting louder. Coming up towards her very fast. She held her breath, hairs standing up on the back of her neck. Nearer, nearer . . . Tiny scratchy claws rushed up her right leg, a sleek furry body pushed past under her arm, whipping her with its tail. Throwing herself to one side, Aoife lost her grip and slid bumpily down the steps, crying out, her dress rucking higher up under her armpits, her naked backbone scraping agonizingly over the sharp stone of the nearly vertical staircase, sliding faster and faster . . .

Finally she managed to roll over onto her stomach and, digging her fingers into the carpet of wet moss, slowed her momentum bit by bit, until at last she stopped sliding and lay face down on the stairs – dizzy with the pain and shock. Gradually her panting eased and all was silence again. Silence and darkness. It took a moment to orientate herself – in the utter blackness, it was hard for her mind to tell which way was up. Then she got to her knees, wriggled the dress down over her hips, and got back into a sitting position. She prodded around with her feet, feeling for the invisible, slippery steps. Then prepared herself to carry on.

Onwards and downwards.

No, stop again . . .

Far below, more scuffling in the dark. She braced herself for another rat to come racing past her. But this time the creature was moving much more slowly – padding slowly and softly up the stairs towards her. Heavy – more like the badger that had crossed her garden on her first night home.

Aoife got to her feet, very slowly, flattening herself sideways against the earthen wall, making herself as small as possible.

Below, in the dark, all movement ceased.

She waited, breathing as quietly as she could.

A few seconds later, the padding began again. Closer, nearly upon her. She held her breath. The creature was passing her now, rubbing against her in the narrow space. She could feel its rough bulk pressing against her knees and thighs.

A man's voice muttered softly, somewhere near her waist, 'Knife . . .'

Not a creature – a man. *The man.*

Skin crawling, Aoife pressed her back even harder to the wall. The body leaning against her knees tensed, as if it had sensed her slight movement; shifted position, the pressure on her thighs increasing. A hand passed across her dress, paused, fingering it . . .

The light of a match flared briefly, blinding her before it went out; the man's voice was shouting, '*I know you, you dirty devil!*' and the next moment her head was dragged sideways by the hair and coldness streaked across under her chin. With a horrified cry, Aoife smashed her elbow at where she hoped the man's face would be in the dark, then tried to leap over him, risking a headlong fall down the steps. A hand seized her leg, jerking her foot out from under her, twisting her in mid-air. Falling onto her back, she kicked out fiercely with her right foot, connecting with something hard. With a deep howl, his body crashed on top of her, crushing her under his bulk; a knee in her stomach, a calloused hand thrusting her chin back, the cold sharp blade across her throat again, pressing, pressing. She grabbed for the knife, forcing it away, the razor-sharp edge slicing across her thumb—

Light burst across the darkness.

Her fairy blood was pouring from her hand, and by its silver glow (so bright, now that she was in the otherworld again) the changeling man's face sprang into view, his small eyes blazing with fear – and then relief. 'A fellow changeling, by Danu – you've silver blood!' He lowered the knife and climbed off her, adjusting his red comb-over back over his bald spot and saying chattily, 'Sorry about that, but I knew your face from McCarthy's shop and I couldn't take a chance on your not being a pooka, this place being infested with them . . .'

Aoife was also filled with relief – at least he hadn't been trying to kill her just for following him. The rumours of smuggler savagery must be untrue. She got back into a sitting position. 'Is this the way to Falias? I have to get there fast.'

He seemed anxious to explain himself. 'Wait till I tell you! Them pookas are awful tricky buggers. They come on you in the shape of someone you know from the human world, and then, if you don't cut their throat straight away before they change – *bam!* Your head is in its stomach.'

The blood was still leaking from Aoife's thumb – she bit the edges of the wound to stem the flow. 'Is this the way to Falias? I can't wait around.'

'I cut my own grandmother's throat once. Snap decision. Her or me.'

Briefly shocked out of her single-minded focus on getting to Dorocha, Aoife said, '*What?*'

'Got your attention now, have I?' Delighted, the man settled his plump backside on the step above. 'Like I said, it was a snap decision. You can never be *sure* it's a pooka and not the real person – and the old dear sounded absolutely terrified when I went at her with the knife. "No, Mícheál, no, it's Nana, don't hurt me!" But I asked myself, what would the old lady be doing down here in the otherworld? And as soon as I had her throat cut ear to ear, the pooka turned back into her natural form. I was sweating with relief, so I was! Big as a bull, horns and all – black blood spurting everywhere. I stank of it for a week. So make sure to remember – if you see someone you love from the human world wandering around down here, definitely kill them. Anyone you know but don't love, probably kill them anyway – the pooka might just have it wrong about how much you care. Strangers are OK.'

Trying to be polite, Aoife said, 'I'll remember. Is this the way to Falias?'

With a sigh, the man said, 'Has anyone ever told you that you have a one-track mind? Yes, this is the way to Falias.'

'Thank you.' She set off down the steps. The flow

of blood from her hand was lessening now – still dripping silver drops that glimmered like fallen sequins, but shedding very little light. She should get as far as she could while she could still see.

The man shouted anxiously after her, 'Stop! Wait!'

She called back in exasperation, 'I can't – I have to save a boy I know! He's been stolen by a demon girl!'

'You'll never find him if you go on alone!'

She slowed, looking over her shoulder. The man was pulling a small copper lamp from his pocket; he struck a match neatly off the wall, replacing the gathering black with a flickering orange. 'I don't know a thing about demon girls, but I do know all about pookas, and you're fair set to get eaten by one if you go on alone. I know every inch of this road myself, so usually I save the candle. But for you, I'll make an exception.'

'Thank you.' She started to descend again.

'Hold your horses!' He bounced down towards her on his plump bottom. 'Let me go first – the road divides a lot, and if you go the wrong way, you'll end up in a pooka's nest, being reborn as a pooka baby.

'Tis a fate worse than death.' As she moved aside to let him squeeze past her, he paused, awkwardly leaning on one elbow, holding out his hand. 'Name's Mícheál Costello. I'm sorry to hear about your boy . . . It's hard to break your human ties, isn't it, even though we're not supposed to sneak back home?'

'Aoife O'Connor.' She was beginning to like this little man, despite his frustrating, time-wasting chattiness. She held out her left hand; the one not still dripping little splashes of silver blood. 'And I don't break my ties to anyone – human or fairy.'

He grinned and nodded. 'Fair play to you, girleen. And I'm Mícheál Costello, and I won't be betraying you to anyone either, for using the secret ways.' He took her hand and shook it. His palm was calloused with hard work; perhaps in his previous life he had been a farmer. Then he turned over onto his stomach, and – lantern raised in his left hand – began half scrambling, half sliding backwards down the steps, remarkably fast for a small, fat man, changeling or not. He called up to her, 'It's not an easy road, this one. Stick close to me and watch where I put my feet!'

Aoife also turned on her front and followed in the

same way. It was far easier with the lamp below her, its light glancing off the walls. Also, by mimicking his movements, she could find the least slippery places for her feet.

I'm coming, Shay!

But then they were stopping again – the sack of party food had been left lying against the wall, and Mícheál had paused to sling it over his shoulder, grunting at the weight, gripping it in the same hand as the lantern to leave his other hand free. Before continuing, he looked back up at her, small bright eyes blinking.

'Just to let you know, I wouldn't have left your body lying cold on the stairs for any passing pooka to eat. If I'd killed you and you'd turned out to be yourself, not a pooka, I would have taken you out into the forest and buried you deep enough for nothing nasty to dig you up, and you'd have been reborn as yourself some day, after being a butterfly or a bird.'

'Thank you, I appreciate it. Can we—?'

'I know it might seem mad to you, big men needing their little treats so much they're prepared to be killed by a pooka getting them and maybe risk killing their own grandmother . . .'

Was he ever, ever going to stop talking? 'I don't think it's mad. Can we go now, please?'

He shook his head, grimacing. 'You do think it's mad. And so do I. But we can't help still loving our Kimberleys and our Taytos, and our Barry's Tea. I suppose it's the taste of childhood, somehow. The things our human mothers gave us.' And shouldering his black plastic sack of childhood memories, Mícheál Costello carried on sliding down into the dark.

CHAPTER TWO

Aoife was glad she'd waited for him. The staircase divided at least fifty times, but each time – left or right – Mícheál Costello seemed confident about which way to go. And mercifully, he didn't stop to talk again, seemingly saving his breath for the long descent – although nimble enough, the little man was already panting heavily. Despite the increased speed, it still felt like they'd been sliding for hours before he gasped up to her, 'Nearly there!'

'Oh, thank God.'

A green glittering mist was rolling up to meet them and the steps had got wider and less steep. Mícheál Costello rolled over into a sitting position, reorganized his sack and lamp, and carried on down on foot, saying breathlessly over his shoulder, 'And all without meeting a pooka, thanks be to Danu.'

Aoife hurried eagerly after him. 'Falias?'

'Ah no, we've a small bit to go yet, before the city.'

'How far?'

'A week's walk, if you want to go it alone.'

'A *week*?' Tears of horror rushed into Aoife eyes. Even if she found Shay in Falias, two years would have already passed in the surface world . . .

'But stay with me, and I'll get you there in a day.'

'A day . . . Oh God . . .' Better, but the disappointment was still crushing.

The little man glanced back at her in exasperation. 'Be grateful, girleen. It's the best offer you're going to get – they don't do trains in the Land of the Young.' And he would say no more.

After another turn, the staircase became a short, sandy passageway; the green vapour was pouring in through a low arched opening just ahead of them. The man dropped to his hands and knees, disappearing into the mist. 'Mind your head!' Hunkering down, Aoife crept after him, and when she stood up again on the far side of the arch, his plump little figure was wading away through the mist, which was only knee-deep. They were in an underground cavern now, down the centre of which ran the source of the sparkling green haze – a river of phosphorescence, which poured out from under a high protrusion of rock some distance off, ran the entire length of the cavern and flowed out again under another, similar, shelf. Lying low in the river, barely visible in the thick vapour rolling off the water, was a long green-painted boat, its prow carved in the likeness of a cooshee's head.

Aoife felt light with relief as she ran to admire the neat fifteen-footer. 'A boat – and it's beautiful!' It was – there were green silk cushions on all its seats and two sets of long, strong mahogany oars.

The small man beamed at her proudly, patting the cooshee figurehead's snarling snout as if it were a real fairy dog rather than a wooden carving with white alabaster stones for eyes and gold-painted teeth. 'Like her? I bought her off a man in Falias for six packets of Kimberleys, ten boxes of Barry's and a six-pack of cheese and onion Taytos. She's magic as well as beautiful. She knows her own way home to Falias, and she fixes herself if she gets a leak.'

'And I have a special power that will help us get there much sooner than a day! I can make boats, cars – anything – go really fast!'

He nodded brightly. 'Grand stuff, girleen. Speed is a handy power to be having.' But instead of step-ping aboard, he leaned in over the side of the boat

274

and lifted out a bundle of sticks, quickly arranging them into a small pyramid on the bank.

Aoife, already preparing to untie the rope by which the stern was tightly tethered to a thin stalagmite, stared in shock. 'Hey, what are you doing?'

'Don't worry, we can jump in and cast off if a pooka appears. They hate the water, it burns them up – just like this!' He tilted the candle of his lamp to kindle the sticks, and the little pile crackled up in flames.

'No, but . . . Why are you lighting a fire?'

He reached into the boat again, and took out a small copper pan, which he dipped into the river. 'Tea-break. I've been promising myself a nice cup of Barry's and a couple of biscuits all the way down from the surface.'

'What . . . No . . . *What?* I'm in a hurry!'

'So you keep telling me, girleen.' Mícheál set the pan of green, glittering water on the fire. 'But there'll be no hurrying on my account until after I've had me tea, so if you want to go by boat rather than walk for a week, I suggest you stop complaining and join me.'

'Oh God . . .'

'Don't let the colour of the water put you off – she

makes a lovely brew. Reminds me of the tea we used to make out of the black bog water when we were above in the Glen, cutting the turf.'

She seized on this fact of geography to stir his compassion. 'The boy I'm looking for is from near the Glen!'

At last the little man looked up from poking the fire. His small bright eyes were round with surprise. 'Well, I'll be . . . What's the name?'

'He's a Foley!'

The man's interest faded slightly. 'That's not near the Glen – the Foleys are from the next valley. Anyways, it makes no difference – if you're going demon-hunting, you'll manage a whole lot better with a nice cup of Barry's and a few biscuits inside you.' And he pulled out of his sack in quick succession: a clay mug, a box of tea bags, milk, sugar and the already open packet of Kimberleys, which he held out to Aoife. 'Come on, cheer yourself up.'

Aoife surrendered; she moved closer to the fire, taking the packet of biscuits from him, saying miserably, 'Thank you.' It was obvious that whatever she tried, they were going nowhere until Mícheál Costello's tea break was over – yet sticking with him was clearly her best, and maybe only, option. Also, there was no avoiding the fact that she was very, very hungry. *Starving.* Maybe he was right – she'd run better on a little basic fuel.

While he was blowing on the fire to get the water boiling, Aoife rapidly ate her way through the soft marshmallow biscuits – crouching by the boat, looking around the cavern. Up-lit by the peculiar light of the glittering mist, stalactites dripped from the roof, meeting stalagmites to form giant wasp-waisted columns. The cavern walls were lined with shadowy archways of various heights; within were ghostly glimpses of other stairways, some leading up and others down.

'Danu's sake!' On a high note of alarm, Mícheál grabbed the Kimberleys off her, and handed her a packet of Rich Tea instead. 'Have these if you're *that* hungry! Them Kimberleys are a big favourite and the brothers won't be thanking me if I arrive back with none left.'

'Sorry.' Unable to stop eating now she'd started, Aoife stuffed three of plainer biscuits into her mouth one after the other, and then another three.

Mícheál huffed and puffed, tucking the packet of

Kimberleys away into the sack. 'Umph. You're grand, but you can thank Danu it was me you ran into and not some other smuggler – there's many who would have lost their temper entirely over a Kimberley. Lucky for you, I'm a reasonable chap. *Too* reasonable, to be honest – I know the other lads call me soft behind my back. They'd not be overly pleased with me for not killing you in the first place. No one's supposed to know about the secret ways but us smugglers.'

'Really?' So the rumours were true – she might indeed have died in that black hole, so far from saving Shay. 'Then thanks for not trying to kill me. At least, after you realized I wasn't a pooka.'

'No problem. Just don't touch the ice cream. Wee Peter's very, very fond of his ice cream. Lovely, lovely man – but not if you mess with his ice cream.'

She crammed in another biscuit. 'You smuggle ice cream?'

'I do.' He sounded smug.

She couldn't help but be interested. 'Doesn't it melt?'

'Nope. Keeping things cold is my special power.' He ripped the cellophane off a box of Barry's Tea, threw six bags into the boiling pan, added milk and sugar, poured out a cup and passed it to Aoife, saying, 'There now, take that and I'll drink from the pan . . . *Mary, Mother of God, a pooka!*'

From somewhere deep within the walls of the chapel had risen a wild, ghostly wail. The little man shot upright, staring around fiercely with his small eyes. Aoife did the same, hairs prickling up her arms. The wail died away. The pale green mist flowed up and down the many staircases, faintly visible through the shadowy archways. The two of them remained on their feet – tense, listening. But apart from the soft whispering of the water, all was now silence.

Mícheál Costello relaxed. 'Don't worry, I'd say we're grand – I'd say it's gone another— *Mother of God!*'

Again, the wordless, heart-wrenching cry – much closer now, high and trembling, shrieking out from within the cavern's walls.

With an irritated sigh, Mícheál threw aside the dregs of his tea, and began packing up the tea things into his sack. 'Grand, you've got your wish, girleen – we're moving on. Get in and I'll untie us.' He kicked the glowing embers of the fire into the river, where they fizzed and sank, and stashed away the plastic sack in a small hold in the stern of the boat. Relieved, Aoife climbed in and sat on one of the centre seats, looking towards the dark exits in the walls as she waited for Mícheál to cast off. There was no repeated wail. The mist ebbed in and out of the archways like a sparkling green tide flowing into many caves. Crouching by the stalagmite, Mícheál was muttering to himself, 'Come on, come on . . .' He wasn't having an easy time with the knot – it had been drawn tight as the boat strained to go with the current. He fumbled impatiently at it, with square, calloused fingers. 'Mary and Joseph . . .'

Was that a slight movement?

She whispered, 'Mícheál.'

The small man looked up sharply. 'What?'

'Over there . . .'

'Where?'

'*There.*' It was only a shadow in the lurid low-lying mist, but she was sure some creature was crawling on its belly, out from under the arch from which they themselves had emerged a short while ago. With a gasp, Mícheál Costello saw it too – he jumped into the boat and dragged Aoife down beside him. Then raised his head a few centimetres to peer over the side with his round, bright eyes.

'Hmm. Small. Either a baby pooka, or it's in human form already. Damn that knot – we could have been gone by now.'

The creature was getting slowly to its feet out of the low-lying mist. Aoife caught her breath. 'Oh God . . .'

The little man stiffened, whipping out his long knife. 'Who is it? That boy you're chasing after?'

'No . . .'

He whistled quietly. 'Ah, I see her now! A girl – and a pretty one.'

'But it's impossible . . . It can't be . . .'

'Your sister?'

'My best friend – but don't do anything yet, supposing she really—'

He shook his head with grim satisfaction. 'Nope, the more you love 'em, the more certain it's a pooka. Right, this is what we're going to do: we're going to work as a team. Pretend you're glad to see her and call her over, then I'll leap up and cut her throat.' He winked encouragement, testing the blade of his knife with his thumb. 'Come on, don't look so worried – it's not your friend. How could anyone have found their way down all those twists and turns without a guide? Call her!'

Heart pounding, Aoife steeled herself to lure Carla to her doom. Mícheál was right – and it wasn't just the impossibility of Carla negotiating all those dividing stairways on her own. Carla was terrified of the dark. How could she have summoned up the courage to follow Aoife in the first place? Through a graveyard, into an open tomb . . . No. There could be only one explanation. Behind that dear, familiar face were the sharp, hideous horns, the twisted claws, the hideous tooth-crammed mouth of a pooka.

Cautiously Aoife took another peek over the side.

The pooka that was Carla looked muddy, dishevelled and very scared. She was still wearing her mouse ears, and also the Superdry jacket which the real Carla had gone to find in the parish hall. Her expensive make-up was in ruins. Peering through the mist in the direction of the boat, clearly attracted by the movement of Aoife's head, she began crying out in a wavering voice, 'Aoife? Is that you?'

The little man hissed urgently in Aoife's ear,

'Go on! Speak to her! Call her over, and then I'll have her.'

'Aoife? If that's you in the boat, please don't hide from me – it's not funny. I've come such a long way to find you, and I thought there were ghosts and my phone broke and I've been so scared in the dark . . .' The voice that sounded so much like Carla's was cracking with fear; she was drawing nearer to the river.

Bristling with excitement, Mícheál whispered, 'Here she comes now! As soon as she's in slashing distance—'

'But supposing she really is—'

'Do it! Then I'll slice her throat from ear to ear!'

Aoife's mental image of the pooka was instantly swept aside by the even more hideous mental image of Carla lying dead with her throat cut, and she made her own snap decision. Rising to her knees, she screamed, 'If you're really Carla, go back the way you came! You're in terrible danger!'

Carla's scared face transformed with joy – she rushed towards the boat with her arms held out. 'There you are, thank God! Why did you run off on me? I've been so afraid!'

'No! Listen to me! Don't come any further!'

'Come closer, my dear!' Mícheál Costello shot to his feet, a ghastly parody of a welcoming smile on his plump face, his knife held behind his back. 'Do come and join us! I've heard so much about you from your lovely best friend here!'

The small man succeeded spectacularly where Aoife had failed – Carla stopped dead where she was, looking in horror from one to the other of them. 'Aoife, what are you doing here with that lunatic?'

'Carla, I'm *begging* you! If you really are you, go home! *Now.*'

But the pooka – or Carla – took another step forwards, her face setting into an expression of terrified determination. 'Has this man kidnapped you?'

Mícheál Costello had his foot on the rim of the boat now, grinning and beckoning with his free hand in a way that could only be described as creepy. 'Come closer to us, Aoife's best friend. Closer, closer.'

Aoife gripped him by the back of his jacket. 'No, wait – I don't think—'

'*Closer, little friend!*'

Carla pulled out her phone (which looked extremely broken), took yet another step towards them and announced in a high, strained voice: 'You let my best friend out of that boat – the guards are on their way and I'm calling them again right now!'

Suddenly shedding his jacket, Mícheál Costello sprang from the boat and raced towards the girl with his knife raised above his head, howling, 'Die! Die, ya filthy rotten—!'

Cowering, Carla screamed, '*Oh my God!*'

'*NO!*' Leaping from the boat, Aoife threw herself upon the little man, bringing him crashing to the floor.

'*I don't want to die!*' shrieked Carla.

'That's what my grandmother said!' roared Mícheál Costello, still wriggling forwards on his elbows, desperately reaching for his knife as it skittered away from him into the mist. 'Before she tried to bite my head off!'

'Stop! Stop!' Aoife clung fiercely to his plump legs. 'She's not your grandmother! Look at her! She hasn't changed!'

'*I'm not your grandmother!*' wept Carla, who by now was obviously – surely, even to the most paranoid of pooka hunters – just a teenage girl in paroxysms of real terror. '*Please don't kill me! Please, please, please, please, please . . .*'

'SHE'S NOT A POOKA!'

'Oh, for . . .' But the little man had stopped struggling. He said irritably, 'Danu's sake, I guess you're right. If this one was going to bite my head off, she'd have done it by now.'

Aoife still clung on. 'You promise not to do anything? You really mean it – I'm right?'

'Yes, yes, you're right. Now let go of my legs – this is extremely embarrassing.'

She released him with great caution, but all he did was sit up, adjusting his comb-over and saying grumpily, 'And by the way, when I say you were right, even a stopped clock is right twice a day, and I hope you know that was a completely unjustifiable risk to take on the battlefield, and if we're going to keep journeying together, then next time you have to let me do what I have to do, or our partnership is over and you can walk the rest of the way.'

Aoife was already kneeling at Carla's side, hugging her distraught friend. 'Darling, you can relax now – everything's fine, you're safe. Mícheál's very sorry—'

'*He tried to kill me!*'

'Ssh, ssh, everything's fine – he thought you were a shape-shifter just pretending to be you—'

'*He's a delusional psycho!*'

'He's not – relax, please. Here, give me a hug, you poor thing . . .'

Slowly, while Aoife held her tight (and Mícheál Costello sat with his back to them in the boat, trying not to look guilty, and stuffing his face with biscuits), Carla's shrieks ebbed to moans, although mainly because her voice was simply giving up.

But then a different voice chimed in. 'Carlie? Can I have a hug too?'

At the sound of that high, sweet voice, Carla broke away from Aoife's embrace and twisted round to stare behind her, choking out in disbelief: '*Zoe?*'

The little girl was leaning in one of the many archways along the walls – although not the one which led to the surface. She was wearing a fluffy white baby-lamb onesie – a miniature of the one beloved by her big sister – and she was smiling and sucking her thumb.

('Zoe?' said Aoife, stunned.)

'Zoe?' Carla rose to her knees. 'Oh my God, what are you doing here? You're supposed to be with Mam at Nan's house—'

Aoife snapped out of her stupor. '*Don't touch her! Mícheál, cast off!*'

'Hug me, Carlie!' The little girl had left the shelter of the archway and was trotting trustfully towards her big sister, offering up her arms for an embrace. 'Give me a hug!'

Mícheál was wrestling wildly with the knot as Aoife dragged a freshly screaming Carla backwards into the boat. He howled, 'I can't undo it! I've lost my knife! Ah, sweet Danu . . .'

Carla fought furiously to get out of the boat. 'Let me out – you're crazy – what are you doing, it's Zoe!'

'Stay down!' Holding the human girl back with one hand, Aoife leaned at full stretch towards the rope. If her power could work on locks . . . The loop at the far end of the rope unravelled and the boat swung violently out into the centre of the current.

'Thank Danu!' panted Mícheál Costello, seizing a pair of oars and starting to row vigorously, sending the boat shooting down the centre of the current.

The little girl in her baby-lamb onesie was racing along the bank beside them, smiling and waving. 'Carlie, don't you love me? Give me a hug!'

Carla made a frantic effort to throw herself over the side into the river. 'Stop the boat! Aoife, I'm begging you – it's Zoe, we can't leave her, she'll never find her way home, you've known her since she was a little baby, she loves you . . .'

Aoife threw her arms around Carla's waist, hauling her back. 'It's not Zoe, it can't possibly be her – she's at your nan's house, ages away from Kilduff!'

'It's Zoe!'

'It's a shape-shifter!'

'Aoife, this shape-shifting thing is a delusion! You and that lunatic are both mentally ill! Let me go! Zoe!'

Between the current and Mícheál Costello's furious rowing, the boat was rapidly gathering pace. The little girl was having to run faster now – very, very fast for a four-year-old. 'Carlie? Don't you love me? Give me a hug!'

'I'm not going anywhere without you!' Carla hung desperately out over the side of the boat, reaching out. 'Get to that rock up ahead as fast as you can! Climb! You can jump into the boat!'

The little girl glanced where Carla was pointing – and her brown eyes widened with sudden understanding. Despite the shortness of her plump legs, she put on an astonishing burst of speed, racing ahead of the boat towards the rocky shelf under which the fast-flowing river left the cavern. Seeing what was happening, Mícheál Costello tried desperately to row faster, to beat the child to the exit. He roared at Aoife, 'Get the other oars!'

Aoife scrambled for them, but it was too late – the little girl had already gained the rocky overhang, and was leaping and scrambling up it like a mountain goat.

'Danu help us, Danu help us!' Now Mícheál was trying to turn the boat and, with Aoife's inexpert help, he actually succeeded – but it made no difference: the current was stronger than their combined efforts, and swept them on, stern first, towards the overhang where the child stood poised, thumb in her mouth again, looking anxiously at the fast-flowing river beneath her feet. With a war-like cry, Mícheál rushed past Aoife and fell to his knees in the stern, clutching one of the oars like a weapon under his arm, resting the shaft of it on the back of the boat like a knight in a tournament going in to joust, his comb-over blowing behind him like a bright flag of war. In his panic, he was now praying to another God, more familiar from his human days: *'Our Father who art in Heaven . . . Deliver us from evil . . .'*

Aoife, on her feet, raised her hands above her head, willing a bolt of power to blast from her fingers, to knock the tiny child from her high perch. Snap decision. Come on . . . She could feel the power growing in her hands and arms, bubbling, ready to burst out . . . And yet . . . And yet . . . *This is Zoe . . . I've known her since she was a little baby . . . I can't kill Zoe . . .*

The child wept shrilly, 'Carlie! I'm scared of the water! Where are you going? Don't leave me!'

Carla pushed past Aoife, screaming: 'Zoe, jump as we pass under! I'll catch you!'

'I can't! I might fall in!'

'You can swim, you know you can, I taught you myself! Jump!'

'I can't!' But with a terrified cry, Zoe jumped.

The transformation happened in mid-air. The lamb onesie ripped apart, and from its scattering fragments burst a monstrous creature with curved horns and massive claws, thickly covered in black fur; deep scarlet eyes burned on either side of its blunt snout; its gaping mouth appeared to have no tongue but instead was crammed top and bottom, as far back as its throat, with row upon row of thin, triangular teeth like a monstrous cheese-grater . . . It came crashing down on the boat, then screamed with rage as it put its clawed foot straight through the side into the water. The boat lurched. Carla rolled howling under a seat. Mícheál Costello was on his feet, swinging the oar like a hurley stick. The pooka knocked it aside, then grabbed him by the front of his shirt with one clawed hand, opening its vast jaw wide, cramming the little man's head into its maw, the red threads of his comb-over catching in its serrated rows of teeth.

Aoife's power burst out of her, slamming the pooka full in its chest. With a roar, it threw the man to the floor and sprang over his body towards her. She hit it with a second, lesser, bolt of power, then – as the beast staggered – snatched up her own oar and ran forwards, thrusting it against the mighty chest. Off-balance, the pooka crashed backwards into the river, sending up a fountain of green spray – and there it rolled, screaming in agony, thrashing, buckled arms and legs pounding the water. It was as if it had fallen in a bath of acid. Its thick black hair was peeling off in handfuls, clumps of it swirling away on the surface of the water. The boat slid on, turning in the current. The pooka, howling in agony, grabbed for the cooshee figurehead on the prow, but Aoife pivoted on one foot and slashed down with the blade of the oar, slicing off three massive claws, black blood spurting. Yowling, the monster grabbed for the side of the boat with its other clawed hand, trying to haul itself aboard. But Carla was beside Aoife now, on her feet, wielding an oar of her own – together, they battered at the monster's ghastly face from which the rest of the hair was sliding away, leaving only black, bubbling, melting flesh behind. The current swung the boat right round. The dying pooka grabbed for the rope trailing from the stern, missed, and disappeared face down in the water with a despairing cry.

And Aoife pulled Carla to the floor just in time to avoid being slammed clean out of the craft as it rushed under the overhanging rock into darkness.

CHAPTER THREE

For the next few seconds Aoife just lay holding Carla against her, huddled under the prow. The shaking girl clung to her in stricken, panting silence as the boat rushed smoothly on, carried by the fast-flowing current. The tunnel they were passing through was very narrow; the walls flashed by centimetres from the gunwales, and the roof hung so low above them that Aoife could have touched it by reaching up a hand. The phosphorescence glittered off the wet curved rock, enclosing them in a cylinder of flickering green.

Slowly Aoife's heart and mind steadied.

At least they were on the move again. And in the right direction – Mícheál had said the boat knew its own way to Falias. She could hear the little man behind her, muttering quietly to himself in the stern. She should go back and make sure he was not too badly injured. After that, when she'd recovered her strength from the encounter with the monster, she would concentrate on making the boat go faster – driving it on with the power of her mind.

Shay, I'm coming to find you.

Although . . .

A desperate, frustrating realization. She couldn't bring Carla with her on such a dangerous journey. Before she went any further, she had to get her best friend home – right now. It was a miracle the human girl hadn't been killed already.

She closed her eyes and spoke to him in her head. *Forgive me, Shay, but I can't keep Carla from her family for months on end, maybe for ever, and I can't have her risk her life for you. I'll be as quick as I can, I swear.*

And then, still with her eyes closed, she focused on her power to control the speed of any vehicle. Could she put the boat in reverse? She thought strongly: *Go back.* In response, the boat merely rushed on a little faster. Perhaps it needed room to turn – how much further would they have to go for that? She needed to check with Mícheál.

Carla wailed suddenly against her neck, '*Oh my God, what just happened and where is this place? What happened to Zoe?*'

Aoife hugged her tighter, smoothing the glossy

hair. 'Ssh. That wasn't Zoe. That was a shape-shifting monster that looked like Zoe. The real Zoe's with your mam at your nan's house.'

'I can't believe it, it's impossible, you went down through a grave . . .'

'I'll explain everything, I promise. Look, will you be OK by yourself just for a moment?'

'No, I won't! Where are you going?'

'Just to see how Mícheál is and if he knows how soon we can turn the boat round.'

'But he's a lunatic!'

'Don't worry, I swear he's not dangerous.'

'He tried to kill me!'

'I told you – only because he thought you were a shape-shifting monster – it's an easy mistake to make down here. Look, I promise I'll be right back.'

'No, no, don't go, don't leave me . . . Oh God, be careful!'

Aoife turned over onto her front and crawled towards the stern, sliding snake-like over the seats – not daring to raise her head more than a few centimetres for fear of the low stone roof, which was rushing past dangerously fast just above them. To her right there was a leaking hole in the side of the boat where the pooka had put its foot through the boards – it was smaller than before, slowly fixing itself as Mícheál had told her it would. On the far side of the third seat, the little man was lying very still on his side in a pool of green water. He had gone silent now. His shirt had been ripped nearly off his back.

For a moment Aoife's vision blurred with grief. But surely Mícheál could not be dead? The other smugglers might call him 'soft' behind his back, but he was definitely one of the toughest people she'd ever met . . .

Yet as she wriggled in beside him, Aoife's hopes faded. Not just Mícheál's shirt but his flesh had been shredded by the claws of the pooka. The green puddle in which he was lying was swirling with silver spirals – his fairy blood, pouring out of deep holes sunk between his ribs. A lot of blood. Too much blood. With sinking heart, she eased off her cardigan to make a pillow for his head, raising it out of the puddle. He was so badly injured, it seemed better to leave him where he was, rather than put him through the agony of being dragged over the seats to the drier end of the boat. The man opened his eyes and smiled weakly at her; he made an effort to button up his torn shirt, but before he could manage it, his hand slid back limply to his side. Aoife did up the shirt for him, using the few remaining buttons – covering the worst of his wounds. As she was doing so, she said brightly, 'We'll soon get you to dry land. And then we can sort you out.'

He made another effort to fix his shirt for himself; his hand came upon hers as she was doing up the last of the buttons. He took hold of her thumb; he whispered, 'Bury me deep.'

A lump came into Aoife's throat. She said cheerfully, 'Nobody's burying anybody. You're going to be just fine.'

Mícheál slid his hand fully over hers. 'Darling Maud—'

'It's Aoife.'

As soon as the words were out of her mouth, she regretted saying them, for a look of such disappointment crossed his face. He peered at her, slightly lifting his head – then let it fall back and closed his eyes, saying weakly, 'Stupid. Stupid. My darling is in heaven.' But he kept hold of Aoife's hand.

She returned the pressure of his fingers. 'I'm

sorry. Your wife must have died so young.' On impulse, she leaned forward and kissed his forehead very lightly, brushing it with her lips.

A shiver went through him. 'Young?' He frowned. But then smiled, as if a pleasant thought had come to mind. 'Yes, she did. She *did* die young, in a way.' His voice grew suddenly stronger, as if her kiss had breathed life into him – even though she was not who he wanted her to be. He said, 'I didn't mean to leave my wife, you see. I followed a sheóg and fell into a bog hole and thought I was drowned, and then I was here. And I was lost and afraid, and so lonely for my wife. Then I heard a rumour of the secret road, but it was months before I discovered the lads who used it, and months again before they trusted me with their secret, and that was only because of promising to bring Wee Peter back ice cream. Did you know time goes a hundred times faster in the human world?'

'I do know it.'

'Never forget it – never stay here too long. By the time I got home, over seventy years had passed and my wife was an old, old woman of ninety-six.'

Aoife said again, feeling the terrible inadequacy of her words, 'I'm so sorry.'

Mícheál shook his head slightly, as if her sympathy wasn't needed. 'I went out to our farm and I climbed in through the window and sat on her bed. And when she woke up, she thought she was young again, because I was still young myself, and we talked as if we were still in the good old days.' He smiled again. 'We talked about how many children we wanted to have – six! – and what would be their names. And then I held her, and she died very happy, she died very young. She's that way in heaven now, please God.'

Aoife repeated hopefully, 'Please God.'

The smile faded and he looked troubled. 'I'm glad I saw her that day, because I know I'll never see her again.'

'You will one day in heaven, please God.' She couldn't seem to come up with anything better than the platitudes everyone used at funerals. Yet even these very ordinary words of comfort seemed to unsettle the dying man. He tightened his grasp on her hand, and beads of sweat sprang through his skin and ran down his face.

'No,' he said loudly. '*Reborn*. I will only be *reborn*.' Then his voice failed, and he muttered something else which she couldn't catch. She bent low, holding back her long red hair with her free hand, bringing her ear close to his mouth.

'Say again?'

Mícheál took a deep, gravelly breath, making a painful attempt to fill his lungs. Aoife could hear the air hissing out of them, not through his mouth but bubbling out through the holes in his ribs. He said with great difficulty, 'Bury me deep.'

'Oh, Mícheál, don't say that . . .'

'*Deep*, where the pooka can't get to me.'

'Mícheál . . .'

'I don't want to be reborn as a pooka. I want worms, and then plants, and then birds. Bury me deep. *Promise me.*'

She groaned, 'I promise.'

'Thank you.' He loosened his grip, his hand sliding from hers. Shivering, she dipped a corner of her black dress into the pool of water around him and used it to wipe the hot sweat from his forehead. He smiled at her touch, closing his eyes.

'You said you were coming straight back!' Carla appeared, still trembling with fear, at Aoife's shoulder; her eyes fell on the man lying in the water and she groaned with fresh horror: 'Oh my God . . . Is he . . . ?'

Without opening his eyes, he murmured, 'Maud? Is that you?'

'Who's Mau—?'

Aoife grabbed Carla by the wrist, putting her finger to her lips.

Carla, with a startled glance, fell silent.

In her silence, Mícheál Costello was smiling again. 'Maud? Is that really you? Maud?' He opened his eyes once more, squinting and shielding them with his hand as if the weak light had become suddenly, dazzlingly, bright. 'Maud! Oh, this light, this light . . .' It wasn't obvious if he was looking at Carla or somewhere slightly beyond her, into the shadows. He cried, raising himself on one elbow, *'Maud! Oh, this light!'*

And seconds later the light did indeed become dazzling, to them all – the boat had swept out of the pallid shadows of the tunnel into hot, brilliant sunshine, and the river turned pure sapphire under an azure sky.

And Carla said, faintly, staring around, 'Oh. My. God. This *cannot* be real. Oh. Oh. This is absolutely . . . This *cannot* be real.'

*

302

Seconds later, the boat began sinking. The hole in its side was still too large to cope with a sudden influx of new water pouring into the river, coming from a waterfall that was crashing down the cliffs behind them.

Grabbing the oars, Aoife steered into the reedy shallows then jumped out and – with Carla's help – dragged the water-logged craft up onto a grassy bank, over which blossoming fruit trees spread their branches. In the bottom of his much-loved boat lay Mícheál Costello, his face sun-dappled by the light shadows of the flowering canopy swaying over him. He was smiling as if he was very happy. The boat continued to heal itself, the broken boards gently slipping back into place and knitting together like bone.

After gazing for a long traumatized moment at both the smiling dead man and the mysteriously self-healing boat, Carla went to throw herself down under the nearest tree, lying flat on her back on the grass, staring up through the branches at the azure sky. A few seconds later, she pulled off her mouse ears and unzipped her Superdry coat.

Aoife stood anxiously over her. 'Are you feeling

OK? I hate to say this, but we don't have time for a rest.'

Carla said in a tight, trembling voice: 'Please, just let me try to recover here for one minute. I can't get my head around anything, and if I even think about it, my head's going to explode.'

Aoife dropped guiltily to her knees beside her. 'Oh God, I'm so sorry about all this. I can't believe you followed me . . .'

Carla laughed rather wildly, still without opening her eyes. The next moment she sat up and grabbed Aoife by her cardigan and wailed into her face, '*You went down into a grave! In the middle of the night! On Halloween!*'

'I'm so sorry – it's just I had to get here really fast . . .'

'*And I slipped down a hole and fell about a million miles, and when I stopped falling, all I could see were these shiny dots in the dark, and all I could do was keep crawling after them . . .*'

So that's how Carla had picked her pathway down the constantly dividing staircase – by following the trail of Aoife's silver blood. If Mícheál Costello hadn't slashed his knife across Aoife's thumb, the human girl would have ended up in a pooka's nest. Shaken by the horror of what could have happened, Aoife rocked Carla in her arms. 'Hush, hush. You're here now – you're safe now and I'm going to have you home in no time.'

'*And then that little lunatic tried to cut my throat. And then I had to kill a terrible monster!*'

'Carla, you're the bravest, most fantastic friend anyone could ever have, and I swear to you, I'm going to make this up to you. Are you ready to move yet? I'm going to get home immediately.'

'No, don't make me go anywhere yet – my legs are jelly and if I move an inch, I'm going to be sick. *Please.*' And Carla threw herself back on the soft grass again, laying the back of her hand across her eyes.

There seemed no point in trying to move her. Aoife sat down on the soft green grass beside her. 'I suppose we have to wait while the boat fixes itself, anyway.'

Carla said, with a slight whimper, 'Exactly. Just while the boat is magically fixing itself.'

Waiting for Carla to recover, Aoife leaned against the slender trunk of the tree behind. Under her bare feet and legs and palms, the grass felt cool and soothing. Above, through the blossoms, arched a cloudless azure sky, criss-crossed with rainbows. Everywhere, the flowering fruit trees swayed, slender and supple and loud with birds. Behind, a limestone cliff sloped upwards to the sky, covered in vines from which, at every shake of the breeze, blue butterflies rose in clouds. It wasn't a cliff, of course – it was a ruined city, higher even than Falias or Gorias, and carved out of limestone rather than rose quartz. The river bubbled brightly out of the small green archway through which they'd come, the water turning from emerald to sapphire as it flowed into the sunshine. There, the stream merged with a waterfall that plunged in a long streak of rainbow spray down the face of the abandoned city, and then flowed away between banks of tall bulrushes towards a distant shining glimpse of lake.

A deep sense of belonging flooded Aoife's heart. Despite its many horrors, this was her world. The sun was hot upon her head. Everywhere the scent of flowers infused the air. Her eyes drooped . . .

He was dancing . . . He was dancing . . . his lips buried in her white-blonde hair . . .

The flood of sheer grief shook her physically

awake. What was she doing, drowsing here in the sun, while Shay was in danger? 'Carla, we have to go – now!'

'Aoife, please, I'm still trying to get my head around all this—'

'Carla, *NOW*.'

The boat had just finished fixing itself. Crouching, Aoife ran her hands quickly across the hull; she couldn't even feel the join. Inside, even the green silk cushions were neatly arranged. Amazing magic. All she had to do now was get Carla safely back through the tunnel, and then she could head for Falias.

But first there was the matter of the dead man, still stretched out in the bottom of the boat.

Carla had joined her, staring again at Mícheál Costello – her make-up was ruined and she kept on hiccoughing, but she seemed to be gradually calming down. A moment later, her tendency to common sense even managed to reassert itself. 'OK – is there somewhere to bring him, like a funeral home?'

Bury me deep, where the pooka can't get to me.

'No, Carla, there's no funeral homes – this is the fairy world.'

'Oh, OK.'

'OK . . . ?' Carla's sudden acceptance of the truth was oddly disconcerting.

Carla said, with another hiccough, 'Once you eliminate the impossible, whatever remains, no matter how improbable, must be the truth.'

'*What?*'

'Sherlock Holmes. And I'm sorry for not believing you before, but, you know, improbable is a bit of an understatement. So, what are we going to do with him?'

'I promised to bury him. Oh God . . .' A wave of panic swept through Aoife. She hadn't thought her promise through. If she had to dig a whole adult grave single-handed, and deep enough to keep away the pookas, it would take her all day . . .

Carla was taken aback. 'Bury him – here? *Now?*'

'It's what fairies do for each other, so they can be transformed and then reborn . . .'

'Oh Jesus . . . OK. Right. We're in the fairy world. Sorry. Still adjusting to the new reality.'

'And you have to help me bury him, Carl – I can't do it all by myself.' Two of the oars were still unbroken from fighting the pooka – she grabbed one of them and ran with it to the nearest level piece of ground. Lifting the oar over her head, she drove the sharp blade down into the earth. It sank in a couple of centimetres.

Carla was looking horrified. 'But we can't just bury him here without letting anyone know!'

'His wife is dead and he has no children! No one else will mind!' This time, by forcing the oar in at an angle, Aoife managed to lever out a good slice of dark earth. She wrenched the oar out of the soil and rammed it in again. The blade snapped. 'Crap! This is going to take for ever! Please help me, and then I promise you I'll get you home!' She rushed back to the boat for the last oar.

When she returned, Carla was standing over the miserably small dent in the earth, with her arms folded. 'But we don't even have a coffin.'

'We don't want him in a coffin – he's better off like this! He'll come up quicker then, as flowers and then bees, and then he'll be a bird and . . .' She rammed the oar into the earth. The blade also snapped. '*Oh my God, what am I going to do!*'

Carla said unhelpfully, 'Do you remember the hamster's funeral when the cat brought him back into the kitchen while we were still having the tea and sandwiches?'

Aoife groaned and fell to her knees, digging frantically with her hands, trying to lever out the tough tree root which had snapped the last of the oars. 'I do, and that's exactly why you have to help me. I promised Mícheál I'd bury him really deep so no pooka will ever eat him . . . Help me – you have to help me!'

'*Then stop digging now!*'

Startled, Aoife looked up.

Carla unfolded her arms and pointed down the river. 'There's a lake just there ahead. If we really have to do this, how about we take the poor man out in the boat and find a deep spot and give him a burial "at sea"?'

Aoife stared at her. 'But to be reborn he has to be transformed through living things . . .'

Carla looked slightly smug. 'I'm not pretending to be an expert on this, and I know I've only just got here – but fish and water lilies and swans are living things, aren't they? And the pooka definitely won't get at him if he's at the bottom of a lake. I mean, look what happened to that monster when it fell in the water. Filthy beast – we gave its face a good washing, didn't we?'

In the centre of the lake, they crossed Mícheál Costello's stiffening hands on his chest, and fitted a bulrush cross between his calloused fingers. Then fixed his bright red comb-over to lie flat across his scalp.

Kneeling over him, Carla intoned, 'Hail Mary, full of grace, Our Lord is with thee, blessed art thou among women, and blessed is the fruit of thy womb, Jesus. Come on, Aoife, ten Hail Marys. Hail Mary, full of grace . . .'

In every direction, leafy green oak forests stretched to the horizon; in the distance beyond, white gleaming mountains rose. Directly above, an eagle circled, sailing very high – a golden winged dot.

Aoife joined in the prayer: 'Our Lord is with thee . . .'

After they had completed ten Hail Marys, they lifted Mícheál Costello's short plump body between them, and lowered him carefully over the side of the boat. Alarmingly, he floated for a while beside them, his shirt and trouser legs swollen with air. Swans gathered around them in a circle, dipping their heads, paddling with quiet feet in the sapphire water. Mayflies drifted, and a silver salmon jumped and fell back again, causing a loud splash which rocked the body slightly.

Carla said one more Hail Mary, persuasively.

As she finished, Mícheál Costello tilted sideways, rolled and sank.

The water was so clear that by leaning over the side of the boat they could watch him gliding down through the water in his white shirt and old-fashioned black trousers. His arms were out sideways now, wafting up and down gently like he was flying. An arrow-shaped swarm of silvery fish followed him at a respectful distance. When he was nearly at the bottom of the lake, one arm dropped and he rolled again, coming gracefully in to land on his back, where he rested spread-eagled on the stones, gazing blindly up towards the light.

Carla whispered once more, 'Hail Mary, full of grace, Our Lord is with thee . . .'

The fish drew cautiously closer, circling him, a glittering aura.

CHAPTER FOUR

It was simple. She could do this. First she had to turn the boat, drive it against the current through the long tunnel, then bring Carla up the staircase to the surface world, carefully noting every twist and turn. The way would be open for them – she had broken the magic that had held the tomb door closed.

And then . . . back down . . .

The whole journey might take three, four hours . . .

I'm so sorry, Shay. As soon as I've sent Carla safely home, I'm coming to save you. I swear. Somehow, somehow, I'm going to save you, Shay . . .

Carla, sitting on the seat just behind her, asked anxiously, 'What are you doing now?'

'Ssh, let me concentrate.' Aoife was crouching in the prow of the boat, one hand on the carved neck of the cooshee figurehead, the fingertips of the other hand pressed to her forehead. 'I'm turning the boat round to take you home. It's one of my powers.'

'*You have powers?* Oh, sorry . . .' Carla's voice dropped from astonished squeak to humble apology. 'Of course you do. You told me. Sorry. Still adjusting.'

Yet when Aoife looked up, the boat was travelling in the same direction as before, at the same steady pace, towards the far end of the lake where oak forests ran down to the glittering water. 'Hey!' She slapped the side of the boat, hard. 'Turn round!' The craft quivered as if annoyed, and simply sped up, leaving a deeper v-shaped wake behind them. Aoife slapped it again, much harder. '*Turn round!* Ah, that's better . . .' The boat was finally paying attention, swinging in a wide, leisurely arc, sending a criss-cross of bright ripples across the shining water. But before completing the circle it stopped turning, and headed straight for the forested bank. '*Whoa – wait, stop!*'

Ignoring her, the cooshee craft plunged on between the trees – down a hidden dimpled waterway, where gold-green branches arched across the water. The speed of their going pushed their wake up over the weedy rocks, wetting the tangled roots of trees. In impotent fury, Aoife beat on the back of the cooshee's carved, curved neck. '*Stop! Stop!*' The cooshee thrust its head forward very slightly, elongating its neck, as the deep oak forests rushed past on either side, taking them further and further away from the limestone city.

With a groan, Aoife leaned her forehead against the figurehead, and closed her eyes.

OK.

OK.

So the boat was not under her control. But at least it was heading for Falias. In that case she would have to get Carla home from there, through the queen's pool, under the hawthorns that crowned her mother's tower. Where Dorocha walked the crystal balconies, gazing out over golden days and velvet nights . . . *Waiting for his sweet demon to be done, and Shay's heart to be broken beyond salvation . . .*

But she had the upper hand. She was here without Dorocha's knowledge. She had the advantage of surprise. She was going to save Shay. And she was going to get Carla home. She could do this . . . *She could.* (But oh, the stupid, cruel mistakes she had already made. Abandoning Shay, when she should have known he would never leave her unless a spell had been cast on him. Breaking the magic charm on the tomb door, and never imagining her best friend would have the courage to open it and follow her down.)

'Aoife?' Carla was beginning to sound scared again. 'Did your powers not work?'

Aoife groaned, and pressed her cheek to the cooshee's neck, trying to take comfort from the painted fur, as if it were one of her living dogs – the ones she'd had to leave in the zoo after they had followed her to Falias. 'I'm so sorry. I guess my powers aren't as strong as I thought they were.'

'Oh God . . . Then where are we going – do you know?'

'Mícheál told me the boat knows its own way back to the only proper city here, so I guess that's where it's going. I promise I'll get you home from there instead.' Although how was she going to get Carla to the queen's pool while Dorocha was in her mother's chambers? *Every road I need to take lies through him. He threatens everything I love. My powers aren't as strong as I thought they were.* A deep sob was forming in her chest; she swallowed furiously, and choked out, 'I'm so sorry this is taking so long.'

Carla said in a quavering voice, 'It's OK – we've

got a bit of time before Mam hits the panic button – she's at Nan's overnight and tomorrow is Sunday and she'll think I'm still with you . . . Which I am, of course. And Dad's working in England for the whole week. What time is it anyway?' She checked her mobile, pulling it out of her jacket, which was bundled on the seat beside her. 'Oh, I broke my phone when I fell. You?'

'Out of charge. Carla, about the time . . .'

Catching Aoife's anxious tone, the girl looked up sharply – her brown eyes widened and she hit her palm off her forehead. 'Crap. Don't say it. I know what you're going to say because of course you've already told me, I just didn't listen. Time goes ten times faster in the human world than down here . . . *Crap*.' Automatically, Carla checked her broken phone again, then shoved it back into her jacket in disgust. 'How long have we been gone, do you think? Five hours? Aargh, that's . . .' Tears rushed into her eyes. 'Oh, poor Mam – two days, she'll be in bits . . .'

'A hundred times – I'm so sorry.'

'What?'

'One hour is a hundred hours.'

For a long, long moment Carla stared at her – brain busy calculating, in rising horror. Finally she blurted: 'Fifty days? That's . . . *Nearly Christmas already!* Oh dear God, poor Mam, poor Dad, poor Zoe . . .' The sobs came pouring out.

Aoife cried, heart breaking for her, 'Look, I texted my mam that I was going again, so I'm sure she'll guess you've followed me and she'll let Dianne know where you are!'

'Aoife, this is my *mam* you're talking about! Do you seriously think she's going to believe in some absolute, crazy, lunatic— *Oh God, Killian!*' Her sobs redoubled. 'He'll think I'm dead! That green-eyed bitch will be round there every day comforting him!'

Aoife protested, 'He won't go off with Sinead – he loves you, he told me you were the sweetest girl he'd ever been out with.'

'So what? He always knows when Sinead's just about to text him! He must have a special alert assigned to her, though he *swears* he doesn't – he just laughs and says it's magic!' And Carla buried her head in her arms, and wept for a good long while, until finally she shuddered out a sigh and raised her head, saying grimly, 'Oh well. Maybe Mam *will* believe your mam, in a sort of a way – at least, just enough not to totally kill herself with despair. And me and Killian weren't ever going to last anyway.'

Aoife said instantly, 'You were . . . I mean, you will.'

Carla gave her a weak smile. 'No we weren't, and we won't. Here . . .' And she pulled Aoife onto the seat beside her. 'I'm being a selfish pig weeping about Killian, when you and Shay have just split up. Though I still can't believe he would go off with that—' She stopped. Breathed deeply in. 'OK. Right. That's something else I didn't listen to, isn't it?'

Aoife had her face buried in her hands, elbows on knees, fingertips pressed to her eyelids, crushing back the tears. She sobbed: 'You said it yourself – he wasn't like that. I should have listened to you. I'm a fool, and now he's been taken by a demon, and he thinks he's in love with her, and she's going to break his heart in some terrible real way, and I don't know what I can do to stop her, or if anything can stop her – I don't know, I don't know anything, I don't know how to save him . . .'

I'm not as strong as I thought I was. Even this boat defeats me.

The overspill of tears pooled in her palms, ran

down the inside of her wrists. 'I don't know if I can save him, Carla. The truth is, I don't think I can. He might not even let me rescue him if he thinks he's in love with her . . . But I'm going to try so hard to get you home, Carla, I swear I am!'

After a while Aoife felt Carla's arm slip around her.

The boat fled on at a furious pace between the high banks. Great shafts of sunlight broke between the oak trees, setting golden gates across their path. The two girls in short black dresses sat leaning against each other – Aoife with her head now on Carla's shoulder – as the cooshee boat broke through gate after intangible gate. There seemed no end to this endless shining road – just the high earthy banks and the overhanging trees.

In the end Carla said very lightly, giving Aoife's shoulders a little squeeze, 'If we were back in Kilduff now, this is the point where I'd suggest we eat ten dozen chocolate bars and a tub of ice cream. I don't suppose we'll be passing a shop any time soon?'

Aoife sighed. 'No, but . . .'

Kneeling on a bed of green cushions in the stern, Carla rummaged through Mícheál Costello's black bin bag of food, then – with a grunt of satisfaction – ripped open a six-pack of Dairy Milk. 'How come your man brought all this with him – is there no food here?'

Aoife sat on the seat facing her, chin on hands. 'There's plenty, but there's a group of older changelings who like to smuggle sweets down from the human world. They've never lost their taste for factory flavourings.'

'Good for them. Here . . .' Carla tossed her a chocolate bar.

'I don't feel like . . .' But of course, she did: as soon as it was in her hand, she was starving as always.

'Coke? Club lemon?'

'Coke.'

'There you are. Full fat, plenty of caffeine, none of that zero crap.' Carla passed her the can. 'Get that into you –everything will seem a lot more do-able once you've got your blood sugar up.'

Aoife cracked open the can – surprisingly cold, as if fresh from the fridge – drained it, and ate the chocolate bar in two bites. Probably not the complete solution to defeating demons, but Carla was right – she did feel better for it. Although still starving.

Carla was nodding encouragingly. 'Good woman. How about a sandwich? You probably could do with some protein as well.' She had pulled two tin-foil trays out of the sack, and set about tearing off the clingfilm. 'Ham or egg mayo? Have one of each.'

'OK.' Aoife began to eat her way steadily through both trays of sandwiches, which Carla had rested on the seat beside her.

'Oh, lookie here – Oreo biscuits! Take a few of these.'

'Thanks.' It was bizarre. Here she was, in the middle of the most terrifying time of her life, having an ordinary picnic on a river with her best friend – just as if they were little girls again, when they used to paddle a cheap rubber dinghy up and down the shallow stream behind Carla's house while stuffing their faces with picnic food identical to this.

Carla was peeping under the lid of the huge plastic tub of ice cream. 'Chocolate chip. We'd better eat it quick, it's beginning to melt. I'm amazed it even lasted this long, if your man brought it all the way from Kilduff. Ah, a packet of plastic spoons! Here . . .'

Aoife prodded the surprisingly firm contents of the container with one of the spoons. 'Keeping things cold was Mícheál's special power. I guess the power stops working now he's . . . being transformed.'

'Maybe being a fish for a while will suit him, then. They're cold-blooded, aren't they? How does that rebirth thing work, by the way?'

Aoife paused with her first spoonful of ice cream halfway to her mouth. 'I'm not quite sure, to be honest. All I've been told is, fairies don't die. They get transformed. I haven't actually seen it happen, but I saw something really amazing when . . .'

'When what?'

Aoife cleared her throat, blinking back the sudden onrush of grief that had stopped her speaking. She left the plastic spoon stuck upright in the ice cream. 'When me and Shay came here before . . .'

Shay, I'm coming and I will do the best I can to save you . . .

Carla shovelled ice cream into herself very rapidly. 'I really do want to know, but not if you can't bear to talk about it.'

'No. It's OK.' It was good to remember. And not just because it gave her the chance to talk about Shay, in better times. By the time Donal died, he had been gone so long from the human world – it felt important to speak his name aloud. 'This dear little boy helped us when we first got here. His name was Donal, and he was adorable and he saved our lives – twice, actually. First by finding us buried under rocks. And then with this juice he made out of hawthorn berries – very, very strong. Don't ever touch it, by the way, unless you're ninety-nine per cent dead and need it to come round. But then something terrible happened. This enormous cat attacked him . . .'

Carla, who had been listening with great interest, nearly choked on the ice cream. 'What attacked *who*?'

'A cat attacked Donal, and killed him, right in front of us—'

'*There are lions?*' Carla threw a terrified glance into the deep woods rushing by.

'This wasn't a lion, it was a cat-sidhe – a fairy cat – a white domestic cat, just very, very big.'

'Big enough to kill a *child*?'

'About two metres long.'

'Oh good God. Poor kid.'

'I know, it was beyond awful. And I didn't understand my powers at all then – I didn't even know I had half of them – and I couldn't do anything. But there was this one good thing. Shay kissed Donal as he was dying, and after we buried him, his grave transformed so fast, it was beautiful – flowers and apple trees grew overnight, and the apples were so incredibly sweet, and bees and birds flocked to them.'

Carla was slightly unconvinced. 'That's good.'

'Really, it *was* good. I think the idea is, you get absorbed into other living creatures and then get reborn as one of their babies, and so on until you come back as whatever you started out as. If Shay hadn't been a lenanshee, Donal's transformation would be taking a lot longer.' With a catch in her throat, she added, 'Ah, that little boy was sweet. You'd have loved him if you'd met him. I hope he comes back as himself soon.'

For a while Carla gazed thoughtfully at her knees, clearly considering the science of rebirth – then abruptly lay back on the pile of green silk cushions, hitching up her short black skirt to expose her now very slim legs all the way to the top of her thighs. 'This weather is fabulous. Come on, stretch out your legs like me. We'll both be gorgeous by the time we get home – the only ones in Mayo with a genuine tan instead of the dodgy streaky stuff.'

When Aoife didn't answer, Carla turned her head to meet her eyes. 'I haven't lost it and I'm not being incredibly brave, or blasé, or callous. I'm still petrified and I absolutely realize that this is a dangerous place, and I know you must be in bits about Shay. But we've been awake for a long time, and it can't just be me that's exhausted. It's good we've got some food inside us. Now we need some sleep. Whatever comes next, we'll be the better for it.'

'Carla, you're amazing—'

'I'm not, I'm just boringly sensible. Now come and lie down.'

Obediently Aoife went to settle beside Carla on the cushions – although sitting stiffly upright, with her arms around her knees. She couldn't imagine how she could ever sleep again.

After a while, still wakeful herself, Carla murmured: 'Robin.' The small bird was perched at the far end of the boat, on the long nose of the cooshee figurehead. 'Oh, that's sweet . . .' The red-breasted bird had fluttered the length of the boat and was now pecking sandwich crumbs around Aoife's bare feet. Occasionally it stopped to fix tiny bright green eyes on Aoife, its head on one side.

On impulse, Aoife held out her hand, forefinger extended. The robin hopped up onto her knuckle, scratchy little claws digging in.

Carla smiled, rising on her elbow. 'Is that him, do you think?'

'Him?'

'Donal. That little boy. Didn't you say birds were eating the apples?'

'Oh . . . That's a lovely thought. I wish it was possible to know.' She moved her finger to bring the robin closer. It put its head on one side, and stared at her closely. Its eyes were brilliant green, as Donal's had been before death (no, transformation) closed them. 'Donal?'

But with a feathered shrug, the robin hopped back down among the crumbs, and continued pecking busily around her toes.

Carla had flopped onto her back again, face uptilted to the sun, eyes closed, the soft green shadows of the oak trees rushing over her bare skin. A kingfisher flashed over – a blink of electric blue – and the sun came and went in sweeps of heat.

With a sigh, Aoife lay down beside her friend. Maybe it was better to get some rest before Falias.

When they got there, she would figure out what to do, and how to persuade Shay to leave a girl so beautiful, he would surely refuse . . .

Taking Aoife's hand and lacing their fingers together, Carla said sleepily, 'Don't worry. We'll save Shay, the two of us. Didn't we already kill a pooka? You and me?'

All at once Aoife was amazed by the memory. 'That's so true! You smacked it across its head with the oar! You actually got in the last blow!'

Carla smirked with pride. 'I did.' Then shuddered, eyes squeezed shut. 'Ugh, it was so disgusting when all its black fur started peeling off . . . I can't imagine any demon comes worse than that. Look out, you bad things! Here we come!'

'Oh, Carla . . .' Warm tears rose into Aoife's eyes. There was something so natural and comforting about her best friend being here in this world with her, promising to help her like the two of them had been helping each other ever since they were little girls. Since they'd paddled up and down the stream behind Carla's house. Or, in Declan Sweeney's field, wandered up the fairy road holding hands, playing a game that they never realized would turn real. 'It's all right – I'm going to have to fight my own battles from now on. But thank you so much . . .'

There was no answer.

Aoife tilted her head back further on the cushions, gazing up. The canopy of leaves rushed overhead, sunlight pouring through in through every gap, blinding her in golden bursts. The air was pleasantly hot even in the passing shade, a soft breeze flowing over her face and bare legs and arms.

No sound but the swishing of the water around the boat, and the ceaseless singing of the birds, and Carla's soft regular breathing.

Aoife closed her eyes.

CHAPTER FIVE

When she woke, it was night. Through the black net of trees, the sky was ink; a fat moon sailed in and out of view, shedding buttery light.

She sat up slowly, coming to herself.

The boat was still moving rapidly through thick forest. The river rushed on between the banks; the trees crowded densely to the edge, a deep blue-black. Over the surface of the water flickered sharp-edged shadows – bats. Curled up on the cushions beside Aoife, Carla was snoring softly, her hair spread out over the cushions; her Superdry jacket was pulled up over her shoulders.

Where were they now? There was no way of telling. The only sound was the hiss of the boat cutting through the water, and the squeaking of the bats. The tip of a branch brushed against Aoife's bare arm, scratching her. And suddenly she was alert, sniffing deeply at the warm night air. Instead of the leafy sweetness of the oak woods, an acrid scent of resin stung her nostrils. She reached out her hand, and when the next branch touched her fingers, she pulled off a few leaves. Not leaves – needles. Not oak trees, but conifers. She rubbed the greenery between her fingertips and inhaled its scent. Poisonous.

Yew trees.

Falias was surrounded by yew trees . . . Ahead, the waterway widened. A tingle of anticipation ran across her skin.

If this was the same yew forest she had travelled through before, any moment now she would see the glow of the mighty pyramid city, carved from a single crystal of rose quartz, every bronze door and golden window gleaming like a jewel. Brilliant as a bonfire in the velvet night.

The boat swept out from under the yews into a wide, dark, empty plain, where the butter-moon had just sunk behind distant cliffs, leaving only a lick of cream, rapidly fading. The river circled to the left, bubbling up around smooth boulders. Despairing, Aoife leaned her forehead on her knees. She had been so sure . . . Without raising her head, she turned her face to the right, staring out over Carla's sleeping body into the night.

High in the air, a pale blue circle flickered, hovering above the valley like the spaceship in an old movie. Above the circle floated a thin finger of silver, pointing directly up at the black velvet sky, sequinned with stars. Aoife lifted her head, staring. Below the circle of blue, a pyramid of darkness . . . The river turned to the right and poured like molten grey metal under the stars across the flat dark plain, towards the circle and its faint blue light. Towards the mighty city of Falias, all its fires extinguished in the night, dark and cold and camouflaged against the ring of marble cliffs behind.

Minutes later, Carla stirred beside her and sat up, hair sticking to her face, rubbing her cheeks, yawning till her jaw cracked. 'I can't believe we slept until it got dark.'

'It's OK, we're nearly there – look, there it is – Falias!'

'Where?' Carla peered blindly into the darkness.

'There – two, three kilometres?'

'Can't see a thing.'

Aoife had forgotten: changeling eyes were much sharper than human eyes, especially in the dark. But back in the direction from which they had come, the cliffs were faintly rimmed in darkest turquoise. 'You'll see it soon – I think it's nearly dawn.'

'*Dawn?*' Shocked, Carla again automatically reached for her phone, then remembered it was broken. And then, yet again bursting into tears, remembered why it would have been no good to her anyway. 'We've been gone for nearly a day! One day is a hundred days! November, December, January...' She grabbed her jacket and pressed it over her face, muffling her hysterical sobs.

Aoife groaned, 'I'm so, so sorry...'

'Poor Mam, poor Dad, I can't bear to think what they're going through... And Killian's sure to be with Sinead by now...' Carla wept for a bit longer and then, with her face still buried in the material, breathed a long, deep, shuddering sigh. 'Oh well. As Mam says, no point worrying about things we can't do anything about.' Then she sobbed again – a helpless, painful sound, as if something that should have stayed stuck together had torn apart in her chest. 'Oh, Mam. Poor Mam. I just hope she's taking that advice for herself.' And then wiped her face in a final fashion and said sadly, 'Only, she never does.'

Over the yew-topped cliffs, a first flush of pink

was leaking up behind the turquoise – the rim of new dawn, softening the edges of the world. The boat rushed on across the plain, drawing ever closer to Falias. The topmost layers of the city were slowly warming with the dim early light.

Carla, now able to see the outline ahead of them, murmured sadly but with increasing interest, 'That's Falias? It's so beautiful!'

There was as yet no sign of city life. Only, very far above, the bluebell lamps of lenanshee quarters, shining out softly and coldly over the valley. Aoife stared up at the pale azure light. Shay's mother lived there – perhaps she would help her? Yet she had once told Shay to stay away from Aoife. And the lenan-shees were themselves dark creatures, with dangerous passions. Beautiful, but more of the darkness than the light.

Above the layer of azure was a layer of darkness – the stables where the dullahan coachman kept Dorocha's real coach and horses. And further above rose her own mother's crystal minaret, crowned with hawthorn, poised at the summit of the rose-quartz city, catching the very first glint of the new day – a solitary spark, like the match Mícheál Costello had struck from the wall. With sudden foreboding, Aoife crouched lower in the boat. Perhaps Dorocha was there even now, standing on the same balcony where she'd come upon him once before, at dawn.

(She'd asked him then: *Have you been here all night?*

And he had smiled at her, and said: *I never sleep.* His beautiful eyes on her, rich with stars like the midnight sky.)

Could he see her now, in this little boat, a dark speck running across the plain towards the city? The bottom of the valley was still sunk in night. But Dorocha had said to Caitlin, the ugly changeling girl: *I can see better and further in the dark than I can in daylight, and I can see better in daylight than any other being.*

Above the hawthorn summit, against the paling sky, a mighty bird circled – but not a golden eagle; this bird was bigger than an eagle, and its wings as black as the fading night. Far off across the purple-shadowed plain, a high coarse howling and screaming rose.

Carla flinched: 'Jesus!'

Clustered almost a kilometre away was a

ramshackle collection of huge wooden cages, char-coal-coloured scrapheaps in the early dawn. Relieved, Aoife said, 'Oh, it's OK, that's the zoo – all the beasts are safely locked up.'

'Are you sure?'

'Pretty sure . . .' Although the cages *were* flimsy. Over the other howls, she could hear the cooshees barking and – even at this distance – the thud and creak of the demon dogs throwing themselves against the bars. She felt a deep rush of gladness to know that her dogs were still alive – her violent, loyal dogs, with their dark green fur and bone-white eyes and yellow teeth. She hadn't liked leaving the seven cooshees with the zookeeper – she hadn't been sure she could trust Seán Burke to feed them or tend their wounds after the battle they had fought with the dullahans. Now yet more animal voices were joining in the howling – screams and roars and grunts. She thought with some satisfaction: *Seán Burke must be finding it hard to sleep.* But then she realized she didn't want the zookeeper awake and on the prowl, and again crouched low in the boat, this time pulling Carla down beside her. 'Keep out of sight for a bit – there's someone whose attention I don't want to attract.'

'Who?'

'A spy for Dorocha. Nasty little old man.'

'And who's Dorocha?'

Aoife shivered. It was strange: she had told Carla so much, and yet nothing about Dorocha . . . And she still didn't want to talk about him. 'He's a man I met here. Sort of in charge of this place. I think he knows where the demon has taken Shay. If he finds out I'm on my way, he might warn her.'

Unexpectedly, the boat looped away to the left, leaving the main river for a narrow tributary that snaked through massive fields of barley, silvery pink in the mixture of starlight and early dawn. Here, the slender green-painted craft rode low between steep banks, and the cooshee's head seemed to dip, snout skimming the dark water. Above their heads, the barley stalks stood high, a silhouette of spears, blocking the view from both the zoo and the city. When Falias finally became visible again, they were directly beneath the shadow of its walls, out of sight of the tower. The boat swung smoothly into the moat that ringed the city's foot; they were still shielded from the zoo by the high outer bank.

Aoife began looking out for a place to stop and tie

up – steps, or maybe a water gate. Just ahead of them, a cluster of blossoming hawthorn trees overhung the river, branches trailing in the water, the roots breaching the walls, cracking the quartz like an eggshell, forming a small beach out of crumbled crystal. Aoife mentally willed the boat to stop at the little landing place, but it continued to ignore her and swept wilfully on, rounding the next corner. From here, far off she could see lights burning – a row of orange paper lanterns strung across the width of the river. The boat, which had been moving steadily down the centre of the current, slowed and pulled in tight to the wall, where the shadows were impenetrable. 'Oh, come *on*.' Aoife slapped the stern of the boat in her frustration.

The boat shuddered and crept forwards, under the dark walls; it was moving at less than walking pace now – a mere crawl – inching along. Drops of water showered on their heads from above; the quartz city was carved with vines and flowers and figures, and whispering rivulets spilled down from the cupped hands of one gargoyle to another – endlessly pouring from the hawthorn pool at the summit of the city. In daylight, the rivulets would shine crimson – the water was stained with the blood of her mother's lover, murdered on the pretext of having killed the queen, and hurled by Dorocha down the city walls.

A small indignant flurry erupted in the dark bottom of the boat, and the robin hopped up onto Aoife's knee, shaking droplets of the falling water from its feathers. Carla whispered: 'He came all this way with us! I bet it *is* that that little boy. He definitely seems to know you.' The robin studied the human girl, head on one side, then fluttered up onto the figurehead, where it perched between the cooshee's ears, shoulders hunched, gazing ahead like a tiny lookout.

As they drew nearer to the orange lights, it became apparent that the paper lanterns weren't suspended on a string but were placed along the parapet of a stone bridge – the entrance to the city. More light was beginning to leak into the valley now, as somewhere on the far side of the cliffs the sun broke free of a concealed horizon. There was a bad smell in the air, as of rotting meat, and Carla wrinkled her nose and gagged. 'What is that *stink*?'

Only metres ahead, a set of steps led up the walls

onto the bridge, and Aoife was already beginning to hope that the postern door in the bronze city gates would have been left unguarded, when the boat stopped altogether, pulling in behind a sloping block of rose quartz that jutted out at an angle into the water. The nose of the figurehead stuck out a few centimetres past the buttress – but remained concealed in the darkness, helped by another hawthorn tree that had taken root in the fractured crystal, forming a natural screen.

As soon as it was clear that they were going no further, Aoife said, 'Right – wait here. I'll swim to the bridge and check the coast is clear.'

But before she could swing her leg over the side, Carla grabbed her wrist, whispering, 'No, wait. Maybe the boat's hiding on purpose, like when it took that roundabout route through the barley fields.'

'You think it did that because it was deliberately hiding?'

'You said it was magic – it must know what it's doing . . .'

And as soon as Carla had said it, it *was* obvious. She'd been about to make another really stupid

340

mistake. 'Oh, you're right. It must be part of its magic, to avoid getting caught.'

Carla said lightly, 'I'm *always* right, if you haven't already noticed.'

'I have noticed. Stay here, I'll try and see what the boat is hiding from.' Aoife crawled cautiously up to the prow and knelt behind the cooshee's arched neck, peering through the thorny blossoming branches. In the early light, a small figure was hobbling down the road that led from the zoo. The hairs on the back of her neck pricked. Judging by the stick and the limp, it was the zookeeper – although both his head and body seemed an odd shape.

Behind her, Carla whispered, 'See anything?'

'Dorocha's spy. Stay out of sight.'

Seán Burke was drawing close to the far end of the bridge, where the orange glow of the lanterns made him visible. He looked busy, as if on his way to do something important, and he was misshapen because he was swamped inside a huge, roughly made black fur coat and wearing a peaked fur hat far too big for his head – it had a long pointed brim with a bone-white button stitched to either side of it. The coat had yellowy bone toggles, like a duffel coat, and the hat had a stiff fringe of thin yellow tassels.

Not tassels.

Teeth.

Not toggles.

Claws.

Not black fur, but inky green.

Something flipped over inside Aoife's stomach; she was flooded with a nauseous surge of rage. She started to stand up. Carla dragged her back down. 'What are you *doing*? I thought you wanted to stay out of his sight!'

Aoife hissed through clenched teeth: 'I'm going to kill that evil bollox, right now. He's murdered one of my cooshees. He's wearing its skin for a coat and its head for a hat. My poor brave dogs—'

'*Stay down, he'll see us!*'

Seán Burke had reached the bridge, but now he paused, peering over the parapet across the dark water. The button eyes, glazed orange by the lantern-light, also gazed blindly in the boat's direction from each side of the cooshee head that he was wearing for a hat. Ice thickened in Aoife's veins. Her power was flooding her . . . With one quick blast . . .

Yet Carla was right. Attacking the zookeeper would just give them away. And Seán Burke was hardly a worthy foe – just an evil, feeble, hobbling old man. She dug her fingernails painfully into her palms, holding back the icy rush.

The old man stopped looking and went hobbling on over the bridge, only his head and shoulders visible above the parapet, the tap of his stick ringing out loud and hollow. Every time he passed a glowing paper lantern he would pause and, with a quick furtive glance towards the city gates, raise his stick to shoulder height as if he longed to knock the thing into the river, but dare not. The seventh time he acted out this little pantomime, he flinched and stopped mid-swing, hastily lowering his stick. A tall hooded figure was moving smoothly towards him from the direction of the gates – so tall it was visible from the waist up. The little zookeeper ducked his head obsequiously. 'Good morning, my lord.' His thin voice quavered through the purple air.

The figure pushed back its hood – around the headless stump of its neck revolved a cloud of darkness: flies. The dullahan picked up the lantern that the zookeeper had been threatening to knock into the river and, cupping it in black-gloved hands, turned it to gaze up-river – bringing rotting eyes and a maggoty mouth into view. Instantly Aoife understood the smell of death that tainted the air – the glowing paper lanterns were a row of dullahan heads, left out on the parapet to guard the city, watching the road across the plain.

Behind Aoife, Carla gave a little moan.

Aoife glanced round, finger to lips – her friend had gone deathly white, biting her lips to stifle her terror; eyes huge with fear at the sight of the headless monster holding its head in their direction.

The old man was shrilling, "'Tis grand to see so many of ye on guard, my Lord! No calling the queen by name, mind, if she does turn up. If anyone's with her, by all means call them – but not the queen. The Beloved wants her alive, for his own purposes, whatever they might be these days – which is none of my business! I have a special cage set aside in case she does appear. We'll tie her hand and foot and keep her bedded in straw with a grogoch to watch over her, and keep her as hungry as her dogs until the Beloved returns from whatever dark secret place he's retired to while Morfesa gets over his rage. Ah, but when the Beloved returns it will be a mighty celebration, and we'll all wear cooshee fur and drink and dance.'

Aoife clenched her hands tighter, listening intently. So Dorocha was gone from Falias – and even the zookeeper did not know where.

The dullahan carefully replaced its stinking head on the stone parapet, then stretched out its right arm to the side, hand forming a black-gloved fist. Seán Burke flinched away as a leathery black creature swooped down the city walls, the speed of its descent disturbing the flies that clustered around the dullahan's neck, sending them briefly buzzing in all directions; it settled itself on the outstretched forearm, gripping it with bony feet and hands. It was a hideous creature, not a bird but a crouching old man with a few greasy strings of hair dangling from its scalp – an emaciated version of the zookeeper himself. Its horny mouth was slightly beaked, and as well as wizened arms it had leathery wings, which it flattened like a cloak around its shrivelled body. Perched on the dullahan's arm, it turned its bald head from side to side, showing twisted, pointed teeth, before fixing its hooded eyes on the buttress behind which the boat had concealed itself.

The robin, which had hopped up into the hawthorn tree, crouched low in the bush, pressing its breast to the thorns.

The zookeeper recovered his equilibrium and began edging carefully round the hideous apparition and its master. 'Good birdeen! Are you watching out as well? Nothing like the eyes and ears of the sluagh! I'll be leaving ye then, to take a turn of the city streets. You'll wait here till nightfall, my Lord? After that, I might bring the cat-sidhes down. Ah, Jaysus!' The creature had swung its beak to snap at him, before rotating its head back again to gaze intently up-river. 'Nice chatting to ye – great craic.' And Seán Burke was gone, the tap of his stick fading away into silence.

On the bridge, the dullahan remained stationary against the emerging dawn, its hood pushed back and the flies gradually settling back into their usual pattern, circling the raw stump of its neck. The creature the zookeeper had referred to as 'the sluagh' stepped from the dullahan's arm onto the parapet, where it stood shuffling from one clawed foot to the other.

The boat remained very still. The robin crouched. No sound but the drip, drip, drip of the tainted water down the walls and the click of the leathery creature's claws on the stone parapet. Aoife's mind spun, turning over ways of escape. It was a serious setback that Dorocha was away – she was sure that wherever Dorocha was, there the demon and Shay would be – but at least it meant that this was the perfect time to take Carla to the queen's tower. Perhaps if they slipped into the moat and swam under water . . . If it was only her, she would risk it, but Carla was human and slower – and if the dullahan spotted her, it might call her name, and then Carla would die. Maybe she could launch a surprise attack on the two creatures guarding the bridge. But it might not be just the pair of them on guard. The other dullahans were unlikely to have strayed far from their own heads.

Beneath her knees, the boat trembled, and edged forward a little. With a jolt of panic, she gripped both sides, shouting at it angrily in her mind, *Hold still!* Up on the bridge, the bird-like creature's head snapped round, staring straight at their hiding place. The robin in the hawthorn bush crouched lower. The boat paused . . . then edged out another centimetre. Behind her, Carla nervously sucked in her breath. Aoife screamed again silently: *Hold still! Hold still!* On the bridge, the creature lifted its wings away from its sides; the beaked head thrust forwards; it rose slightly on its clawed toes.

The robin broke cover, streaming in a bolt of red and brown towards the far bank. Instantly the sluagh lost interest in the emerging cooshee head and sprang after the tiny bird with an ear-piercing howl of greed. At the same moment the craft darted from its hiding place and headed straight for the bridge, shooting between the thick supporting columns and out again on the other side, racing down the centre of the water, the cooshee's head straining forwards.

Clinging to the cooshee's neck, Aoife looked back in terror to see if they were being followed. Carla was hunched down between the seats, moaning with fear. The robin was still flying, a tiny fluttering thing against the pale dawn sky; just above it, the sluagh was turning in a slow black-winged spiral, closing steadily on the small struggling dot. Then, just before the inevitable kill, a second predator came swooping down from the lavender sky – faster than the sluagh and every bit as deadly to its prey: a golden eagle, brilliant as metal in the first rays of dawn.

The sluagh, realizing it was about to be robbed of its victim, folded back its wings and dropped. Too late – the eagle shot past and, with a fierce cry of triumph, seized the robin in its claw and was gone, back up into the sunlit heavens with its kill.

Carla sobbed, and Aoife's throat tightened with sorrow.

The bridge was getting smaller in the distance. The dullahan was slowly turning in their direction. The sluagh had started after the eagle, but that mighty predator was now a distant streak of gold, and the hideous winged creature suddenly spotted the fleeing boat below, and with thumping strokes of its wings began descending, clawed hands and feet outstretched.

Carla shrieked in despair, arms over her head.

The boat sped on round the corner of the pyramid, and they were out of sight – but not for long. The slow whump of leathery wings was growing steadily louder; the creature's shadow stretched from round the corner, a long black finger on the crimson water. Aoife raised her hands, feeling the icy power rush into them . . .

The boat turned sharp left, heading at full speed

for the city walls and, as Carla screamed again . . .
rushed straight on. What had seemed like a solid
wall had been a pink and white curtain of real
flowers, perfectly camouflaged against the rose-
quartz carvings. Now they were travelling at great
speed down a narrow canal between high walls; seconds later, the faint dawn light was left behind and
they continued racing forwards in absolute darkness,
then took another abrupt left. There followed a long
series of sickening corners, before the craft stopped
so suddenly that Aoife would have been hurled headfirst into the water had she not had her arms wrapped
around the cooshee's neck.

Still clinging to the prow, she gasped over her
shoulder into the impenetrable dark, 'Carla? Are you
all right?'

After a few alarming seconds of silence Carla
finally replied, her voice hoarse and trembling with
fear: 'Aoife, what *was* that thing?'

'I don't know. I've never seen one before. Are you
all right?'

'I think so . . . Did we get away before it saw us?'

'We're safe here for the minute, probably.' Aoife
peered intently around into the black, waiting for her

changeling eyes to pick up any drop of light. The darkness remained absolute in most directions. But slowly she began to make out fine lines of glimmer, several metres above her head – pale and ghostly scratches on the surface of the dark.

Carla was whispering, 'Where are we? I can't see a thing . . .'

'Wait a moment.' The surroundings were increasingly taking shape. There was a narrow wharf, from which stone steps led up into a darkness fractured by the four lines of light, two vertical, two horizontal. 'There's a door at the top of some steps.'

'How can you see that?'

'Fairy vision.' A metal ring was set into the mossy stone. She reached out her arm and gripped it, pulling the craft in alongside the steps, then forwards along the wall. When the stern was in line with the ring, she tied the rope to it.

Carla's voice came again, nervously, 'What are you doing now?'

'Tying us up. Wait here – I'm just going to check the lie of the land.'

'Oh God . . . Don't leave me.'

'I won't. I'll be back in two seconds.' Aoife stepped

out onto the narrow wharf – slippery with algae under her bare feet – and made her way very softly up the steps. At the top, she put one eye to the thread of light, but all she could see was the light itself. She pushed against the door; it moved, the hair-line fracture widening to a centimetre.

She was looking into a large shadowy cellar, roughly carved out of the same solid crystal as the whole city and lit by a single guttering candle set at the far end of a long counter, which was also made of crystal. At the far end of the cellar, a street door was bolted and barred several times across. A man in a dirty white linen apron, which was nearly pulled up to his armpits, and sporting a bushy beard the colour of marmalade, was sweeping the white stone floor with a besom, stirring up a great cloud of sand and dust. He was nearer seven foot tall than six – and with shoulders a good metre wide.

Aoife drew the door softly closed, and descended the steps again.

In the dark, Carla sounded scared. 'Is that still you?'

'It is.'

'I can't see a thing. What's happening?'

To get closer to her, Aoife sat for a moment on the

edge of the wharf, her feet in the warm water. 'The boat brought us where Mícheál would have gone if he hadn't died . . . I mean, if he wasn't being transformed. It's the smugglers' bar, where they sell the human food. There's only one man in there right now, but he's a big one and I don't know what he's going to make of us walking in by his back door and asking to go out the front.'

'Well, we can't just sit here in the dark for the rest of our lives. And we have to tell *someone* the poor man is dead, God rest his soul, and where he's buried. And give them the rest of his stuff.'

Aoife stirred her feet slowly in the water, thinking about what Mícheál Costello had told her. He was sure the other smugglers called him 'soft' behind his back. In the darkness, his voice seemed to whisper in her ear: *They'd not be overly pleased with me for not killing you in the first place. No one's supposed to know about the secret ways but us smugglers.*

But here they were with no way back, and she needed to get Carla to the tower before Dorocha returned. 'OK, you're right, maybe that's the best thing. I'll go in and tell the man in there what happened, and hand the bag over. You wait here in the boat.'

Carla said with heavy sarcasm, 'Ha ha. *Not*.'

Aoife was thrown. 'What? No, I'm serious. I don't know how he's going to react, and I'm not putting you in danger. If there's a problem, I can deal with it, and then I'll come back and get you.'

'No, Aoife. There is absolutely *no way* I'm going to sit out here in the pitch black not knowing what's happening to you in there. What if you don't come back? What then? Do I look after myself? How much chance do I have of surviving in this world without you? I'd be like that robin, eaten alive.'

A brief silence fell between them.

Carla, clearly – like Aoife – thinking of the robin, murmured quietly, 'Oh, the poor little thing. Do you think . . . ?'

'I don't know. I don't know.' Aoife was picturing in her mind's eye that struggling dot against the sky – and she felt an overwhelming wave of grief for its tiny, transient life. The way things had happened – the robin taking flight just as the cooshee boat made a bid for freedom . . . It really was almost as if the bird had sacrificed itself for them. Keeping the sluagh occupied just long enough for her and Carla to escape. *Could* it have been Donal?

If it was, he had just saved her life. A third time.

'*What's that?*' Carla's whisper was terrified. '*I can hear something – can you see anything?*'

Heart thumping in response to her friend's burst of fear, Aoife peered back the way the boat had come. She could see nothing but darkness – no distant glimmer of light. There were sounds, but not frightening sounds; natural sounds. Water rippling up against the walls, and distant splashes: probably water rats. The wood of the boat, creaking.

And yet a slight misgiving caught her heart, and it seemed to her that Carla was right. Supposing the sluagh had caught a glimpse of where they'd gone – and returned to tell its master? Perhaps Carla shouldn't be left out here in the dark, alone.

'Come on then – take my hand and I'll help you out. But listen to me – if this guy turns nasty, I'm going to have to *do* something, and I want you to keep out of the way. And then, as soon as we're through here, we're going to get you home.'

CHAPTER SIX

The huge man with the marmalade beard was still sweeping, but now on the far side of the long bar. Three fresh candles were burning on the counter now, with long lilac flames. The shelves behind him were stacked with orange clay cups and a few cans of own-brand lemonade which glinted in the lavender light. At the creak of the river door opening, he turned with a grunt of welcome – but on seeing the two girls in their short black dresses, he dropped his broom with a shocked clatter, and his green eyes, half buried in his hairy flesh, flashed diamond-hard with anger.

Aoife became suddenly, oddly conscious of what she must look like – her short black dress and cardigan muddy and torn; bare feet; her red-gold hair in a tangled mess. Carla was in no better state; her expensive make-up blotched with tears and panic; her beautifully cut hair beginning to lose its shape. Yet it wasn't her the man was staring at as if she were an unwelcome and disgusting sight – it was only Aoife. The next moment, the lower part of his beard began quivering wildly – somewhere inside it his lips were moving – and a slow thunderous roar began to emerge through the thicket of orange: 'Yooouuu . . .'

Carla squealed shrilly. Aoife took a hasty step forwards to place herself between the giant change-ling and the human girl, her palms raised. 'Look, I know we aren't who you were expecting, but we met a friend of yours on the way here, a very brave man called Mícheál Costello . . .'

Now the giant was staring at her with astonish-ment, before taking his whole weight on one massive hand and springing bodily over the counter. This time Carla shrieked aloud and icy power rushed into Aoife's blood – but rather than throwing himself upon them, the man only stood wiping his fingers on the dirty white apron, and then on his spiky orange hair, after which he checked his palms for cleanliness and marched forwards, holding out his huge hand and bellowing: 'Well, the last time I saw your maj-esty you were flying off on some mad ride with a strange boy and there was nothing but mayhem and dullahans after that, and the Beloved left distraught at the altar, and nobody knowing what was going to happen next and the city in darkness all night, and no customers, which is bad for business, and I'll be straight with you, your majesty, I blamed you for making a mess of it all with your faithless ways, because everything was going along peaceful in this city before your man Dorocha decided to bring back the royalty, and I'm a staunch Republican myself, having been brought up in the War of Independence against the English, who are only mad for their queen and her imperial ways. But if our own Mícheál Costello, who is also a fierce Republican man, sees fit to bring the fairy queen to our secret hideout, then who am I not to say ye're very welcome?'

It was Aoife's turn to be absolutely speechless. (Yet why should she be surprised? All Falias had been at that rushed coronation, where the druid had crowned her with a circle of hawthorn and mistletoe. Mícheál alone must have missed it, being on his travels.) Behind her, she could hear Carla squeaking faintly, 'Oh God, you're the *queen* of this place! Oh God, you told me that back in Kilduff. Oh God, that was another thing I didn't believe. Oh God. Sorry. Adjusting.'

The giant was still standing almost to attention, enormous beard thrust forwards, hand held out.

Recovering herself, Aoife stepped up to take the hand and shook it firmly with both of hers. Looking up into his small green eyes, she said, 'I don't feel like a queen and I never knew I was until I was called back to this world, and I'm not even a great believer in royalty myself. My name is Aoife O'Connor, and this is my best friend Carla Heffernan.'

He crushed her fingers heavily, his eyes fixed on hers – while still completely ignoring Carla. The beard trembled again. 'Welcome, your majesty. Wee Peter is my name.' He had a Donegal accent – soft but with an undercurrent of fierce pride. So this was the 'lovely' man of whom Mícheál had spoken – at least, the man who was lovely if you didn't touch his ice cream.

Suddenly conscious of the empty tub in Mícheál's plastic sack, Aoife said quickly, 'And we won't get in your way, because we're only passing through.'

'That's grand, your majesty.' Wee Peter still hadn't stopped gazing at her face. 'I believe the Beloved is out of town, but if you only await him in your mother's tower, he will soon be back to you.'

Despite his initial disgust with her, and his Republican instincts, it seemed to Aoife that he was on her side. Still gripping his mighty hand in both of hers, she said, 'A demon has stolen the boy I ran away with. I want to find Dorocha, but only because I think that's where I can find my—'

'Stop!' He snatched his hand from hers and held it up palm out, as if to keep the sight of her from his eyes. 'Don't be telling me any more! Your business is your own, and I don't want to know it!'

Her heart sank – she had been so sure of him. 'But—'

'No buts! We older changelings have seen too much fighting, between the Great War and 1916 and Independence and the Civil War where brother killed brother. If ye want to fall out with the Beloved, and run off with a strange boy and plunge the whole city into dullahan-infested darkness, 'tis no affair of mine. Let younger changelings decide whose side they're on in your fight. All I want is peace, and satisfied customers.' And he strode past her to the river door, and went running heavily down the steps, calling in a voice that echoed up and down the hidden waterways, 'Big Mícheál! Get yer lazy wee arse out

of that boat! We're down to the own-brand lemonade, I've had a run on the Kimberleys, and I've a
lenanshee-sized *grá* of my own for chocolate-chip ice
cream!'

Aoife threw a quick glance towards the barred
street entrance: every lock would spring open under
her hands in an instant. 'Carla, let's go.'

But there must have been a smugglers' spell on
the door, as there had been on the door to the tomb,
because despite her power the bolts would only inch
aside a little at a time. And before even one of them
had fallen, Wee Peter had come rushing back up into
the bar with a furious cry, booting the river door shut
behind him. 'Where is he? What have ye done with
him? How is it ye have Big Mícheál's boat and Big
Mícheál's bag, but ye don't have the man Big Mícheál
hisself?' He was swinging the heavy plastic sack in
one mighty hand, as if he might hurl it at them like a
stone from a sling.

Carla was shrinking against the wall, white and
rigid with fright. Once more, Aoife stepped in front
of her, steeling herself for a fight. 'I'm sorry for your
troubles, but Mícheál was killed by a pooka.'

'*Pooka?*' He lurched through the tables towards

them, throwing down the sack, jabbing a finger as big and red as a jumbo sausage. Every visible inch of his skin – nose, forehead – was flushed a brilliant beetroot, in violent contrast to the orange beard. '*Pooka?* That's a filthy dirty lie! Big Mícheál was a kind-hearted man, but he would *never* have let hisself be fooled by a pooka. Why, he cut his own grandmother's throat, sliced her open like a squealing pig from ear to ear, rather than risk being eaten by a little old lady . . .'

Aoife stood her ground, fists by her sides, still holding back her power – reluctant to do serious damage unless necessary. She said in calm and – she hoped – authoritative voice, 'I know well Mícheál killed his own grandmother, Peter. This pooka came on us as a four-year-girl—'

'That would have made no difference to him!'

'It didn't! He fought her very bravely! But she got the jump on him, and slashed him across the chest and got his head in her mouth—'

He reeled in horror. '*The pooka ate our Mícheál?*'

'No! We killed the filthy thing, and we buried Wee— *Big* Mícheál good and deep.'

'Ah . . . Ah . . .' At this news, the giant calmed

slightly, and a more gentle grief glimmered through his rage. Tears sprang into his half-buried eyes and sparkled down his beard, and he sank down at one of the many rickety little tables, on a sugán stool that could barely take his weight, and rested his head in his hands. His big shoulders shuddered as he pretended not to weep. 'Ah, Big Mícheál, Big Mícheál, the greatest pooka killer of them all . . .' Clearly Mícheál had commanded a lot more respect among his fellow smugglers than he had realized, despite being convinced they called him 'soft' behind his back. Now Peter was sobbing openly, his beard awash with grief. 'Oh Lordie, Lordie . . . Did ye truly bury him deep? Just the two of ye, two wee girls, to bury him six foot down in the hard earth? That darling man had only a single fear – that of being eaten by a pooka and reborn as a pookeen.'

Aoife wanted nothing so much as to go back to unbolting the door, but it seemed cruel not to take even a few moments to console the weeping giant. With a glance at Carla, who was still white and shaking, she said, 'You're right, it was impossible with just the two of us. But we didn't want the pooka digging him up, so we sank him to the bottom of a lake.'

In a flash, the giant was on his feet again, jabbing and stabbing with his mighty sausage of a finger, his face a terrifying kaleidoscope of clashing colours, his vast hairy eyebrows hurling themselves at each other. 'That's not a true burial! No one throws away a staunch Republican man like an old piece of fish! *That's royalty all over – no respect for the little man.*'

Once more the ice rushed into Aoife's blood – she was going to have to fight him after all . . .

But Carla was darting forwards, shouting fiercely, 'Hey, leave her alone! The lake was my idea and it was an *excellent* idea! Fish and swans are living things, just the same as worms and bees and robins! Mícheál will probably love being a fish, him being so good with the cold! And no pooka will try to get to him in the water – I hit the one that killed him in the face with an oar, and it fell back into the river and melted entirely to pieces, the disgusting animal!'

Wee Peter took an astonished step backwards, lowering his finger and studying Carla in amazement. It was the first time he'd paid her any attention at all. The lower part of his beard twitched. 'Well, I'll be . . . And here was I, making the exact same mistake as any fool of a English royalist – forgetting the little people and talking only to the queen! So you're a mighty pooka-slayer, like our Mícheál, are you? In that case, you must do me the honour of joining me to wish him a speedy rebirth – if indeed he was right, and the Goddess Danu can bring him safely back.' And he sat down again and indicated for Carla to join him at the table – which she did, beaming hugely with satisfaction.

'Carla, we have to go . . .'

But Carla frowned and beckoned her over. 'Mícheál died fighting on our side, and we can't leave without paying him our respects.'

'Spoken like a true Irishwoman!' The giant fished out a leather flask from his apron pocket and slammed it down between them, nearly breaking the table in two. 'And thanks be to Danu, if She truly exists, we have a small bit of hawthorn juice left to wake the man properly, and plenty of supplies.' He reached for the black plastic sack and, to Aoife's alarm, pulled out the container of ice cream with a roar of pleasure. Only, it was empty. Once more, the red tide swept up his neck . . .

Carla was saying innocently, 'It's such a shame about the ice cream, but it was melting very rapidly and we were so grateful to find it, and we didn't think he'd want it wasted.'

Wee Peter's rage subsided, and the tears rose again, refilling his tiny eyes. 'Ah, Mícheál, you will be sorely missed until you are reborn!' He wiped his face with his apron, then brought out a tray of Coke. Cracking open three of the cans, he turned a fourth unopened upside down (saying to Carla, 'And that's for our Mícheál, Danu restore him'), and with a jerk of his mighty beard, roared at Aoife: 'Come on now, your majesty – we've no throne to offer you in this humble abode, but there's a sugán stool awaiting you at our table, if you're not too high and mighty to stoop down to the level of the likes of us!'

There seemed no help for it. And she had to admit to herself that Carla was right – it was only proper for them to pay their respects. If it hadn't been for Mícheál slicing her thumb in the tunnel, Carla would be dead and on her way to being reborn as a vile pooka baby herself. She went to sit beside her friend, on a very badly made stool with very uneven legs.

'Now. Take a mouthful of the American drink, and I'll top her up with the good stuff.' Wee Peter unscrewed and lifted the leather flask of hawthorn juice, but Aoife hastily flattened her hand over her can. She remembered the juice that Donal had poured into her and Shay. It had been a miracle at the time – it had shocked the two of them back to life – but if this juice was anything remotely like Donal's brew, it was unwise to use it for anything other than extreme emergencies. 'We'll stick to the Coke, thanks.'

The flask still hovered in his hand as he winked at Carla. 'The queen has a delicate stomach, it appears, but a hardened pooka-killer like yourself—'

Aoife said firmly, 'No, really, she won't, thanks.'

Disappointed, Carla murmured, 'But it smells nice . . .'

'Trust me, it's not a good idea.' To mollify Wee Peter, who was looking most displeased, she raised her own Coke. 'To Big Mícheál! He died very bravely and I owe him my life.' Which was also true: without Mícheál she would never have known enough about pookas to respond so fast to Zoe's appearance.

'You owe him your life, do you?' Wee Peter didn't seem particularly thrilled by this information. Given a choice between Aoife's life and Mícheál's, he would clearly have preferred things to have been the other way round, but was just too polite to say it. He took a large mouthful of his own Coke before topping his can up with the juice, then screwed the brass top carefully back on the flask and tucked it back into his apron, before lifting the drink over his head – 'To Mícheál! A man who once opened his own grandmother up like an oyster rather than let her get the jump on him!' He took a long pull and shuddered slightly, blinking and shaking his head fiercely like a dog with water in its ears. 'Ah, good stuff . . .' And patted the bulge in his apron. 'A shame 'tis nearly gone. Only one flask remaining after this. But the ladeen who makes it is away hunting the cat-sidhe this past month, and we'll get no more till he returns.'

Nearly choking on her Coke, Aoife said, 'Donal?'

The massive beard twitched, and for the first time he looked pleased with her. 'You know our Donal?'

'A ten-year-old boy with freckles and a big smile?'

'The very one! A grand wee fellow. Did ye meet him out in the wilderness? Is he well?'

The answer stuck in her throat; but in the end there was no need to articulate it – Wee Peter could see it written in her face. Again his eyes welled up. 'Cat-sidhe got him, I'm after thinking?'

Aoife said sadly, 'But we buried him in a really beautiful spot, and the apple trees grew up on his grave so fast, and the apples were really sweet.'

'Were they indeed? Well, isn't that well for them as likes apples.' For some reason the giant looked more angry than comforted. He took out and unscrewed the flask, and helped himself to another drop, larger than the first. 'So now. We may as well wake two children of Danu as wake one.' He lifted the can, saying, 'To Donal, another true child of Danu! Maybe the best of them!' and drank, and whistled a few bars of 'The Foggy Dew'. 'And may the little lad be reborn as something more like himself than an apple.' After which, instead of replacing the flask in his apron, he moodily poured a third drop into his Coke.

Aoife caught Carla's eye and jerked her chin towards the street door, but before they could make a move, Wee Peter grabbed hold of Aoife's forearm, forcing it down on the table. The politeness had entirely gone from him. He said slowly, in his soft, hard Donegal accent, 'I don't pretend to know the ways of royalty, *my queen*, but maybe you might consider the lesser people in future, and not send small children out into the wilderness to catch beasts, on the promise they'll be reborn?'

She jerked her arm away, crying hotly: 'What do you mean by that? I never sent Donal out to catch beasts!'

He tilted his can to the mouth, and looked at her sideways as he threw back his head. 'But was it not your philosophy that made him so brave, my queen? Do you not worship Danu, the Goddess of Rebirth, like your mother before you? The druids teach us, on the queen's behalf: Never fear death, for as a fairy you will be reborn. Lay down your life for your queen and country, because that way lies glory. In the Land of the Young, we will never grow old . . .'

'I don't want *anyone* to die for me!'

He said dangerously, '*Die?* Are you telling me even the queen doesn't believe in transformation?'

'I just mean, I don't want anyone to get hurt, or have to be buried at all!'

He sneered: 'Don't you think, if you come here looking for your boy, and fall foul of Dorocha and his dullahans, there won't be young changelings in their hundreds who choose to throw themselves away on your behalf? And all so you can be like your mother, living in her crystal tower like a cold-hearted lenan-shee, spending all her *grá* on one poor benighted man after the other, while us little people make a living smuggling food?' And he poured himself out another drop of hawthorn juice – and groaned, because the flask was nearly empty.

Aoife was still furiously trying to unlock all the bolts and bars on the street door when Wee Peter came over to her with a bright red, apologetic face. He was holding out the empty flask. 'Take this with you, my queen.'

When she ignored him, he took her by the arm to turn her towards him (Carla snapping, 'Let her alone! Haven't you bullied her enough?'), and pressed the flask into her hand.

She thrust it back at him, furious. 'I don't want it – I don't want anything of yours, I'm not going to involve you in anything.'

'Take it.' He slipped it into the pocket of her black cardigan. 'It's the last drop in there, and it pains me to part with it. But you buried little Donal, and I'd say he'd want you to have it, for emergencies. And here . . .' He handed her an old red shawl, of the type that was worn early in the last century. 'My mother's. Cover your head with this. If you must go walking the streets, you won't get two yards before being recognized – only a fool wouldn't know you. You have the head cut off your own mother – the living image of her.'

She looked at him then. 'You knew my mother?'

He held her gaze with his small half-buried eyes. 'Not knew her, but saw her once. It was near a hundred years ago that the sheóg tricked me down, when I'd gone to look for this very shawl which had got left out on the bog. And when I arrived here, I saw your mother in the street. She was choosing ripe peaches from a stall, and a hundred men around her, and the Beloved watching her from afar. Oh, she was a true beauty, with her turquoise eyes and oval face and red-gold hair . . .' He said with sudden, bitter longing, 'I would have fallen at her feet myself if I hadn't been told she was a queen.'

'Oh . . .'

Wee Peter shrugged. 'And that very night she was murdered in her bed. And I didn't sail with the Tuatha Dé Danann to the Blessed Isles because I didn't care for queens. But in my heart I have always cursed the priest who murdered her.'

Aoife said fiercely, 'He was innocent. Dorocha murdered her.'

His eyes veiled themselves. 'Who told you that? I heard the priest was a jealous lover who couldn't bear that Dorocha was the true Beloved.'

'*Dorocha is the devil.*'

'Every enemy is the devil,' answered Wee Peter calmly, and – ignoring Aoife's quivering anger – he tucked the red woollen shawl around her shoulders. 'And take this too . . .' He pulled a leather pouch out of his linen apron. It was stuffed with the little blue and green enamelled orbs that were used for money in Falias.

'There's no need to give me any money.'

He dropped it into her other pocket. 'Take it, your majesty – you never know when it might come in handy. And it's nothing – ye brought me a bag of smuggled goods, and the Coke alone is worth this amount.'

Stiffly, Aoife gave in to him – 'Thank you' – and went back to opening the bolts; but it was a hard task, fighting the smugglers' spell upon them.

Wee Peter stooped to help her, freeing the last few bolts himself – but as he did so, a sharp knocking rang through the cellar. He straightened up, small eyes darting around. Another heavy knock, as with the side of a fist. The river door shuddered in the wall. 'Did anyone see ye two passing through the gate of flowers?'

Another, louder, knock.

Carla said anxiously, 'We saw an old man and a headless creature on the bridge, but that was before we took the corner . . .'

He swore bitterly under his breath, '*By Danu.*'

'. . . and we had to outrun a big filthy leathery bird, like a shrivelled old geriatric with wings. But I'm certain we took the turning before it could see where we went.'

His beetroot skin paled to pink. 'But the sluagh can see through stone.'

Another knocking. And now an old and quavering voice shouted through the wood: '*Open up, Peter Joseph! Open this door! Hand over the queen – she's as wild as her mother and you know what she was like! Come on now, Wee Peter! I know you don't like to get involved with palace politics!*'

Wee Peter set his hand on the street door – and stood leaning heavily against it, his eyes on Aoife's face. She stared back at him mutely – waiting – sure, somehow, that there was no point in begging.

Carla was pleading, 'Let us out, please, let us out!' She was trying to pull back the last bolt herself, but without any power of her own she couldn't shift it. 'Don't stop us, help us!'

The zookeeper's voice came again: '*I have a dullahan with me, Peter Joseph! And he knows your name and is ready to call it!*'

The giant licked his lips – a dart of red tongue in the immensity of his marmalade beard. Holding Aoife's steady gaze, he said, 'And if the dullahan calls my name, your majesty, do I die? Or am I transformed?'

Knock, knock, knock.

Aoife kept looking straight into his eyes. 'Come with us. There's safety in numbers.'

'What? A number of three?' And he broke eye contact, leaned down and began firmly shoving the opened bolts and bars closed again.

Carla gasped, 'No, let us out!'

Aoife fought to stop him. 'Let my friend go anyway, even if you hand me over!'

'I'm not going anywhere without you!'

But Wee Peter grabbed both their wrists, hissing, 'Ssh! Be quiet! Do you think they would come to the back without guarding the front? Come . . .' And, still gripping Aoife by the arm, he hustled the two girls roughly towards the bar. Behind the counter was a massive flagstone with a bronze ring, which he lifted with a soft grunt. 'Storeroom. Near the back is a crack in the wall. Too narrow for me, but Donal came and went that way, and two skinny slips of girls like ye might just fit through it.'

The knocking came again, and at the same time a thundering began on the front door as well, the massive bronze bars shuddering.

'Aoife, come on – let's do as he says!' Carla fled down the rough wooden ladder.

Aoife paused, a few rungs down, looking up, pulling the cloak tight around her. 'But what about you?'

His big hairy face peered down at her. 'Don't worry about me. I'm going nowhere. Sure, where would the zookeeper get his Barry's Tea without us smugglers?'

'Open the door, Peter Joseph! I know you're awake in there!'

The giant raised his voice to a roar. 'And I know I'm awake meself! How could anyone think they were asleep with this infernal racket going on? Can't an honest landlord get a little rest?'

'*Open up!*'

'That desperate for your tay? Wait there while I get me trousers!'

But as Aoife took another step down, he leaned in to catch her by the end of her shawl and said, low and urgent, 'I'm not a follower of queens or gods. But if you're the queen of rebirth, can you answer me this truthfully? Will little Donal and Mícheál be reborn, as the druid tells us? Or is it just a lie to make the young ones unafraid of dying?'

Her first instinct was to say that she didn't know. Ultan and Caitlin had both told her that fairies were reborn, yet they'd never witnessed it – they only believed it because the druid had told them so. What did she herself know for certain? 'I don't—' But then a different sense of rightness came to her – a feeling that by saying she didn't know, she was being merely stubborn. Blind. Unkind. And anyway, she had a strange feeling that she *did* have the answer – that she had seen it happen. The robin . . . Donal . . . Had the truth of it stared her right in the face? She said firmly, 'They will.'

'Ah . . .' He let out his breath on a long sigh. 'And not just as apples? Will they remember their old lives and who they are, and will we know them?'

Again she resisted the impulse to say she didn't know. Instead, she pictured Mícheál Costello as he died – seeing his wife so clearly. 'We'll know them, and they'll know us.'

'Ah . . .'

On the far side of the counter, a violent battering began, and the sound of splintering wood.

Still kneeling, Peter raised the stone flag in his huge hands, ready to replace it over her head. 'Go on now, quick. I'd rather open up to them than have them breaking down my doors.'

At the bottom of the short ladder, Carla waited for her, pale-faced with fear in the shadows, insisting, 'Come on, come *on*.'

Aoife had nearly reached the floor when Peter called down to her again, his marmalade hairiness filling the trapdoor opening: 'And what Mícheál believed – is it really bad luck to be reborn as the child of a dark creature? A pooka or a cat-sidhe or cooshee? Do we always carry some of its darkness in our own heart, and never find the light again?'

She hesitated, holding the sides of the ladder, looking up, thinking of Donal – and the sweetness of the apples that he had become. 'No, I don't think that's true. I think we take our own nature with us – I think the heart stays whole.' And on impulse, she quickly climbed the ladder again, and pressed a quick, soft kiss to the enormous hairy cheek.

Flushing the deepest crimson yet, Wee Peter said hoarsely, 'Good enough for me. Be off with you.'

And as she fled back down the ladder, he covered the hole with its stone lid, and darkness fell.

CHAPTER SEVEN

After the trapdoor had closed, they were plunged into blackness, and there was a second when Aoife feared she'd done something utterly insane – that she'd walked them into a trap, allowing the smuggler to lock them in a box where they could only sit and wait blindly to be discovered. She could hear Carla panting somewhere in the darkness. Up above in the bar, there was the crash of a door opening, and the whiny high voice of the zookeeper, and the booming tones of the giant . . .

But then her fairy vision sharpened, and she began to make out the shape of the cellar – a cave hacked out of the single quartz crystal of which the whole city was made. Trickles of grey light leaked through a pile of roughly-made wooden boxes stacked at the far end. Carla was standing by the ladder, clearly still blind. When Aoife took her elbow, she started and gave a faint moan.

'It's OK, Carla – it's only me. Come on, I'll guide you.'

Behind the boxes was a space wide enough to slip into, and here was the source of the light: a fracture in the rose-quartz rock, through which several long gnarled roots had thrust themselves, taking advantage of a structural weakness in the crystal. Aoife peered dubiously into the crack – it was deep and very, very narrow. At the far end, a long way off, was a jagged vertical line of pale grey.

Footsteps on the stone ceiling of the cave. Very clearly, the tap of a walking stick, leaving a dotted trail of sound.

'We have to squeeze into this crack, Carla.'

'What crack?'

'Here, give me your hand, feel around.'

Carla did, then said firmly: 'No. Can't fit.'

'I think we have to, Carla. I'm pretty sure I can make it, and you're smaller than me.'

'Smaller upwards maybe, but not *outwards*.'

'That's just in your mind – you're incredibly skinny now. Come on, you go first. I'll push if you get stuck.'

Carla whispered fearfully yet bravely, 'No, I'll go second – if I get stuck, you'll be trapped, and we'll both get caught!'

The dotted line had reached the trapdoor.

Shoving her, Aoife hissed, *'Just get in there!'*

'Oh God . . .' Raising her arms over her head, Carla jammed herself sideways into the fissure, and Aoife squirmed in after her.

Behind and above, a grating of stone on stone. Wee Peter's voice echoed loudly down: 'See for yourself! I told yer! Nobody there!'

The further they pushed in, the thinner grew the crack, like a vice closing on their vulnerable bodies. Aoife began to wish she'd taken off her shawl, to gain a few extra millimetres all round – but there was not enough room now to shrug it off.

Behind, more noises in the cellar. Heavy, soft feet descending a ladder, and Wee Peter shouting desperately, 'There's nobody down there, I'm telling ye!'

Just ahead of Aoife, Carla groaned breathlessly, 'Can't go on.' Bracing herself, Aoife thrust hard with her shoulder. Carla, with a whimper of pain, slid on another centimetre, then gasped, 'Stop! Too tight!'

Aoife shoved again.

'No, stop! Stop! I told you you shouldn't have let me go first! Now we'll just have to pray they don't find us . . .'

Now the darkness was deeper. Carla's body, filling

the crevice, blocked any hint of daylight that Aoife's sharp eyes might have picked up from the entrance at the other end. They stood there side by side, waiting, wedged, unable to move a centimetre. Heavy feet paced the hollow cellar, up and down. A few minutes later, a fierce smashing and breaking started up – the crash of wooden boxes being hurled around. A pause. Silence. And then, from the direction in which they'd come, soft orange light began leaking into the crack – and the hum of flies began to fill the air around them, like the soothing sound of a summer's day. And the abattoir stench of decomposing flesh.

Vomit rose in Aoife's throat. She was jammed too tight to turn her head. She slid her eyes sideways. A large, soft, rotting face had its forehead pressed to the narrow entrance, peering in with eyes that glittered with blue decay, grinning and thrusting out its tongue up which, from deep in the back of its throat, white wriggling maggots crawled.

Trying not to be physically sick with fear and the very stink of the dullahan, Aoife pushed again. 'Move, move!' The crevice was far too narrow for their pursuer, but a dullahan could kill with a name . . .

Carla squealed shrilly, *'I can't! I'm stuck!'*

The rotting head glowed brighter with delight and its vile lips began to shape themselves squashily around a word: 'CAR . . .'

'*Move!*' With a violent spasm of terror, Aoife thrust one more time, and Carla's soft body crashed sideways out of the crevice. Flinging herself out after her, landing painfully among thorns, Aoife plastered her hands over her best friend's ears, blocking the terrible, sonorous cry of the dullahan:

'*Car* . . . *la* . . . *Car* . . . *la* . . . *Car* . . . *la* . . .'

Three times calling Carla to her death.

Carla was groaning underneath her, 'Get off me! Thorns!'

As soon as Aoife released her, Carla rolled over onto her front – 'Ouch! Ouch!' – and went struggling out through the bushes into the open. Following her, Aoife collapsed with a sob of relief on a dewy carpet of grass, face buried in the scented wet, the sun on her back. As her heart-rate slowly recovered, she turned her head to one side.

Carla was already sitting up, inspecting herself for scrapes and scratches; her black dress was ripped and her arms and legs in ribbons, but bizarrely, she was grinning. 'Jesus and Mary, how thin am I, being able to squeeze through there? Thank Christ for last summer's misery diet! One more of Mícheál Costello's chocolate bars and we'd never have made it through. Did we get away without being seen, do you think? Can we have a rest now?'

Aoife laughed into the grass, a touch hysterically – and decided not to terrify her friend with the truth. She just needed to get Carla home before they ran into another dullahan. 'No, I think we better keep on moving.'

'Seriously? Ugh. Grand. Where now?'

Aoife sat up and looked around. The fissure had spat them out into a small orchard of hawthorns, and a thin set of white steps, barely half a metre wide, ran down from the street above. Beyond, the crystal city climbed, layer after layer of sun-touched streets and gardens. Far above, at the summit, was her mother's minaret – a golden pencil in the dawn. 'Home, to Mayo.'

Carla sobbed with relief: 'Oh, thank God.'

'And then I'm going to find Shay.'

'What? No!' Carla's relief turned instantly to horror. 'I can't leave you here in this crazy world by yourself!'

Aoife felt like hugging her – loving her for her

courage. She said firmly, 'No. This is my fight. You're a human. I'm a fairy with powers.'

Carla was breathless with indignation. 'Fairy, shmairy! Not everything is to do with powers, you know!'

'I know you're incredibly brave—'

'I'm not talking bravery either! Any eejit can be brave! I'm talking common sense! Who had the idea about burying Mícheál in the lake? Who told you the boat was hiding when you were about to walk slap into that headless monster? Aoife, I'm not trying to be mean, but you're extremely impulsive and you never— I mean, you don't always think! You need me to think for you!'

'Of course I need you, Carla, but I couldn't bear it if anything happened to you—'

'Nor me you! *I'm not going home without you.*'

Aoife took a deep breath and closed her eyes. Love and frustration battled within her. There was only one way out of this. 'OK. Come on. We can't stay here, anyway.' She got to her feet, holding out her hand, and Carla, astonished at having won the argument, grasped it and allowed Aoife to haul her to her feet.

'Right. Where are we really going?'

'To my mother's tower. Dorocha lives there, and wherever he is, I think this demon and Shay may be there too.'

They climbed from level to level, up high-walled stairways, cutting briefly across streets cobbled in semi-precious stones – lapis lazuli, agate, tiger's eye. At this early hour, all seemed asleep – or absent. Bronze doors were closed. Bronze gates led off the stairways into deserted gardens of fruit trees and marble fountains. On gold-plated roofs, flocks of pink chaffinches and blackbirds poured out their tiny throbbing hearts to the new sun.

Aoife's mind worked as she climbed. Dorocha was out of the city. His own spy, the zookeeper, did not know where he'd gone. Perhaps she should ask the druids about the demon girl – they knew all things, or so they claimed. No . . . Something about the druids made her uncomfortable – they did Dorocha's bidding too willingly. The lenanshees, then? They held themselves as aloof as the banshees. Yet Shay – although his father's human blood ran in his veins – surely counted as one of their own?

But first – the queen's pool. And when Carla, unsuspecting, followed Aoife across the blood-red tiles, she would sink and be gone and, a moment later, find herself climbing out of the hawthorn pool into the first stirrings of the Mayo spring, with tiny green leaves unfurling themselves and the mountain lambs racing in clumps across the bog.

As she neared the top of the next flight, Carla's voice cried very faintly, a long way behind: '*Wait!*'

Aoife turned in surprise – she'd expected Carla to be right behind her, but instead she was slumped against the wall a long way below, head between her knees. By the time Aoife had reached her, Carla was retching from deep down in her gut, and moaning in between convulsions: 'How are you taking the steps this fast? I'm going to *die*.'

'Oh God, I'm so sorry!' After all her insistence on sending Carla home, she'd entirely forgotten the difference in speed and strength between a changeling and a human. She crouched guiltily on the narrow steps. 'I'm such an *eejit*.'

'My legs are cramping. My lungs are agony. I can't even stand.'

'I'll carry you.'

Carla retched again, less violently. 'It's OK, I'll feel better in a while.'

'No, seriously. I'll piggyback you. Climb onto my back.'

'Ah no – you couldn't possibly . . .'

'Trust me, I'm very, very strong. Let me show you.'

'Ah, Jesus.' But Carla scrambled weakly onto her back. 'I must weigh a ton.'

'You do not. You're as light as a feather.' And she raced easily on up the steps, her arms tucked under Carla's knees.

Carla, in between panting, started to laugh so much she got hiccups: 'I can't believe you're doing this! This is crazy! Is this all part of being a fairy queen?'

'Any changeling can do it . . .'

'It's like that scene in *Twilight*!'

'Ssh, not so loud . . .' The nearer they got to the summit of the city, the more anxious Aoife felt about running into another of Dorocha's dullahans. 'Keep looking around you, Carl – keep an eye out for anything moving.' Yet apart from the soft running patter of her own bare feet, the city seemed very still – and now more silent than before, because even the birds on the golden roofs had ceased to sing.

A darkness passed over, cooling the air.

Carla flinched, nearly choking her. '*Oh no, oh God!*'

It was another sluagh, gliding above them like a storm cloud on the wind – not the one that had landed on the dullahan's forearm, but much larger – a twelve-metre wingspan at least. Moments later, the clawed beast rushed forwards, disappearing over the roof tops – no doubt spotting some easier prey in the sunlit open. Carla sighed and relaxed a little, loosening her stranglehold on Aoife's neck. Gasping gratefully for air, Aoife paused on the edge of the next street. Surely not that much further to the summit. She could no longer even see the minaret – it was concealed by the wide blue underside of the lenanshee quarters, its verandas merging with the hazy sky. A very distant lute was playing in these heavens, and a strong scent of bluebells spilled over the edge of the blue balustrade – a waterfall of perfume.

Aoife started out across the street, seeking the next stairway.

And with a triumphant screech, the giant sluagh swooped down on them from behind.

Carla screaming in her ear, Aoife fled round the now quite narrow circumference of the city, past closed doors and gates, and then – just before the clawed hands could rip the girl from her back – threw herself down a waterway that flowed steeply between two houses: a narrow golden gutter down which the red water of the city poured. The shadow was over them again, keeping pace as they raced downwards between the crystal walls of the houses. The screeching old man's head jabbed down at them between the walls, the beaky mouth choked with deformed and twisted teeth.

Aoife yelled, 'We're going to glide! Hold onto my neck!' Letting go of Carla's legs, she flung her arms forward like a diver, and swooped headlong. The sluagh thrust its hooked hands and feet at them, trying to scoop them up; the claws narrowly missed them with every clutch. The golden gutter flowed out from between the houses across a street that was filled by a slowly walking crowd of chattering teen-agers. Aoife swept left and came down halfway into the throng, running forwards in the centre of it. A winged shape swept from above and she ducked, dragging Carla down beside her. Yet the shadow passed over, and when she peered up, it was an eagle – not the magnificent beast of that morning, but a very young and clumsy fledgling, flying slowly and determinedly down towards the valley. Moments later, the sluagh appeared over the rooftops and chased the young bird down several more levels of the city before managing to seize it in its wizened hands and feet, and hurtling on out across the grassy plain.

Aoife rose shakily to her feet, pulling Carla up beside her. 'Are you all right?'

Carla turned her head to look at her, opened and shut her mouth a couple of times, then said in a hoarse, stunned voice, 'Oh. My. God. That was absolutely amazing.'

Aoife was stunned. 'Amazing?' Being chased by a giant sluagh could be described in many ways, but . . .

'He saved us *again*!'

'He . . . What?'

'You see what I mean about you needing me to think sensibly about things? You're so missing the obvious here! The robin sacrificed itself for you and got eaten by an eagle, and then a baby eagle shows up and does the same thing! Coincidence? I'm telling you, it's that little boy you keep on talking about—'

'You think the eaglet was *Donal*?' Shaken, Aoife turned to watch the mighty sluagh powering towards the cliffs with great claps of its leathery wings. Tiny drops of red and gold tumbled from its vicious claws. 'Oh God . . . Do you really think? Oh, Donal, poor Donal . . .' If Mícheál Costello had been right to fear being eaten by a pooka, how much worse would it be, to be eaten by a giant sluagh?

Still panting, Carla said, 'I have to say, if I'm right about this, I really, *really* like that kid.'

Around them, the crowd of changelings hustled on, seeming largely indifferent to the monster that had just passed over their heads. Only a lanky boy of sixteen glanced out towards the cliffs, scowling. 'Hate those leathery things. Where are they all coming from?'

'Don't say "hate". . .' His fellow changeling was an older boy with faint stubble, wearing a soldier's uniform from the First World War. 'We're all one now, we're all creatures of light and dark, united.'

'But the queen is gone.'

Aoife, with a glance at Carla, fell in behind the boys to listen. Perhaps she could learn something.

The soldier lad was saying confidently, 'Stolen away from us, the druids say. The Beloved has gone to fetch her back.'

'But if she genuinely prefers a lad her own age . . .'

'They say she was too young to know her own mind.'

'They *say*.'

'Look, that's why we're here, isn't it? To ask this new teacher the real truth of everything? Stop trying to work everything out for yourself, your brain will melt.'

The throng parted suddenly, flattening themselves against the walls of the street. A long procession of druids in white robes came striding through, beating drums, strumming small gold harps. They were pushing a bronze-wheeled cart on which sat a hawthorn tree in a large clay pot; smoking copper jars dangled on chains from its thorny branches, giving off a poisonous scent. Among the druids was the tall woman who had crowned Aoife. Aoife tightened the red shawl, wrapping it across the lower part of her face. The jars swung and stank; the wheels rattled loudly over the marble cobblestones. Finally the procession passed and the crowd re-formed.

The lanky boy was complaining again. 'What are the druids doing with a hawthorn tree? It's bad luck to dig them up.'

'They're celebrating the Festival of the Dead – the luck is supposed to be bad.'

'Do you think it's true this teacher knows more than the druids?'

'That's what I hear. Only don't go asking questions about wanting to go back hom— back to the human world. Just remember – we changelings don't care about humans any more. We've cut our ties.'

The lanky boy said gloomily, '*You* might have, but I've a girl waiting for me.'

'No, you haven't, Tommy, not any more. We've cut our ties. You're new and it takes a bit of getting used to. But we've cut our ties. This is your home now.'

Other teenagers were coming from all directions now, up different streets and stairways, like festival goers converging. Round the next corner was what appeared to be the crowd's destination – a pair of high golden gates flanked by marble eagles on columns, beyond which lay a long tunnel of white roses, which curved away out of sight. A white-painted board was tied to the gates; it read in neat ochre capitals:

ASK SHE-WHO-KNOWS-EVERYTHING
ENTRY: ONE ORB

A mass of teenagers was already queuing before the sign, some sitting patiently on the cobbles; others restless on their feet. A tall freckled lad wearing a collarless shirt and dungarees was prising a little boy down off the gates, shouting, 'Where do you think you're going?'

'I need to ask, do I have to fight my mam in the war?'

'Where's your money?'

'I don't have any!'

'Then push off!'

'But I need to ask if I have to—'

'Lady Mac isn't free, you know – she's not on show to every passing amadán! She has *expenses*!'

Aoife made a decision. 'Let's go in. Maybe this

teacher will know something that will help us.' She began to elbow her way to the front of the queue, pulling Carla along with her.

The freckled lad guarding the gate glared at the two girls as they came to a halt in front of him. 'Where do you think you're off to? Get to the back of the queue!'

Taking the pouch from her cardigan pocket, Aoife said, 'We're here to see the teacher and ask her a question.'

'One orb each.'

She shook out two of the little blue and green pebbles. The boy took them, with a nod. 'Very good. Now get to the back of the queue.'

'But we're in a hurry!'

He folded his heavy arms and squared his shoulders. 'Wait yer turn – only twenty changelings granted an audience at a time, last lot only just went up, the gate will be open again in half an hour. *Back of the queue.*'

Aoife tipped the full contents of the pouch into her palm. The mound of green and blue enamelled orbs filled her cupped hand. She held them out. 'Is this enough?'

From the way he squeaked, 'Exactly the right amount!' and rushed to unlock the gates – much to the furious discontent of those at the head of the queue – Aoife knew for sure that Peter Murphy, the man who didn't take sides, or hold with queens, must have given her a great deal of money.

CHAPTER EIGHT

As they neared the end of the avenue of white roses, they could hear a loud, harsh voice saying: 'And Aoife – she won't let me call her "queen" she says just because she's a queen doesn't make her any better than me . . .'

Aoife slapped her hand to her forehead, utterly disgusted. 'Ugh! I should have guessed. Famous teacher, my . . . Ugh.'

Carla paused in the act of stepping out into the courtyard. 'You know her?'

'Met her when I first got here, and she's a total header. She has this book which she stole from the druids, but it's in a really ancient language and I don't know if she can read it or whether she's just remembering stuff that the druids have told her before.'

'Do you still want to see her?'

'Not really . . .' Yet sometimes the changeling girl had been right about things – in a strange sort of way. Aoife pulled the red shawl around her face again. 'OK, we'll listen for a moment – but if she's only messing with people's heads, we're not asking her anything.'

The long, rectangular courtyard was tiled in gold – painfully bright to the eyes and far too hot to the feet. Marble statues of extremely handsome men jostled for space between bright blue pools in which golden carp flickered lazily. At the far end was a two-storey building – also gold-plated and constructed lavishly in the style of a temple. The high doors were reached by wide shallow steps, at the foot of which a semicircle of about twenty changelings sat cross-legged. At the top of the steps a muscular girl of sixteen in an ill-fitting dress of kingfisher and peacock feathers, and a necklace of magnificent ruby flowers, was sitting with a large leather-bound volume open on her lap. The girl frowned across the courtyard as Aoife and Carla drew nearer, glanced at the sundial in the corner, but then carried on talking: 'Anyway, the queen says to me, "Choose any dress, help yourself to my jewels, you're my very best friend for ever". . .'

(Carla shot Aoife a look; Aoife rolled her eyes.)

'. . . "you've saved my life a million times so we're

like sisters and I want you dressed as grand as me."
Anyone wants to pay an extra orb, I'll show them the
hundreds of dresses she gifted me. You there, the lad
in the bow tie . . .'

A deep voice from the front said something
inaudible.

Caitlin replied confidently, 'Yes, she's going to
lead us to war against the humans because she's
super-powerful – almost as good as me.'

Carla shot Aoife another look – horrified, this
time hissing, 'A war against the humans?'

Aoife whispered back, 'Don't worry, she gets a lot
of stuff wrong.'

'Are you sure? She sounds very confident . . .'

'Caitlin always sounds confident.'

A murmur was running through the listening
crowd – uncertain, fretful. 'A war against the
humans?'

Caitlin vigorously tossed her bright red plait, the
rubies chinking around her neck. 'Stop saying that
like it's a bad thing! Danu's sake! Have ye all forgotten how your so-called parents treated ye? Don't
ye remember how they kept telling ye that ye weren't
good enough, not like the lovely little human babies

ye were swapped out for? That's what my— Mary McGreevey always said to me, that I wasn't her real daughter but an ugly stupid changeling child that even the fairies didn't want, and how her real *human* daughter' – Caitlin's voice filled with bitterness – 'her precious *real* daughter who got stolen by the fairies would have been this wonderful, beautiful, dainty, helpful, good-mannered—'

A young voice interrupted, 'I actually don't think my mam knew I wasn't hers, because she never said.'

Caitlin snapped angrily, 'You're wrong.'

'But she—'

'*Wrong.* Even if the nurse in the hospital lied to her about the babies being swapped out, your mother always knew in her heart that you weren't her real baby – that's why she never loved you.'

'But she—'

Caitlin sat up, swinging her feet to the steps below, raising her voice to a shout. 'A human priest killed our queen! Now the queen's daughter has been crowned – and soon she will return to avenge her mother and lead us to war! And then we can avenge our own selves on our *human* parents!'

Some cries of excitement, underpinned by another

murmuring ripple of doubt and anxiety. A teenager in a ruffled blouse and velvet trousers shot her hand up. 'So why did she fly away as soon as she was crowned?'

'I told you already – she'll be back soon to marry the Beloved properly—'

'But what about the boy she flew away with?'

'Yes, tell us about him!' exclaimed several girlish voices. 'He was gorgeous! What was his name?'

Caitlin looked uncomfortable. 'Fact, Queen Aoife didn't "fly away" with him, it was just a coincidence they left together—'

'So is he not with her? Where is he then? Has he a girlfriend already? He's so gorgeous!'

Caitlin shouted, 'Stop saying that – none of ye want to go near him even if he'd have ye – he's one of the dark creatures, the son of a lenanshee, and if any of ye kiss one of them, ye'll wrinkle up and die. It's all in here!' She lifted up the big book with its gold- and ruby-embossed cover.

'The son of a *lenanshee*?' Horrified disappointment surged through the female element of the crowd. 'Oh, but he was so—'

'Course he was gorgeous! What part of

403

"lenanshee" don't ye understand? They're all gorgeous, and all deadly, and they don't care about anybody or anything, only getting their own way with anyone that takes their fancy! And that's why Dorocha is making sure that boy you like so much won't go near the queen any more, and then Dorocha and the queen will get married again and lead us to war . . . You there at the back, by the roses . . . What's your question?'

Aoife pushed back her red shawl and looked Caitlin straight in the eye.

Caitlin sprang to her feet, bellowed, 'No more audiences today! Everybody out!' and rushed into the house, the leather-bound volume under her arm.

'Look, I didn't steal them – you said I could take whatever I liked, and then you just disappeared!'

'Tell me what Dorocha has done with Shay!'

Caitlin flung out her arm defensively. 'And there were *millions* of them – you absolutely couldn't miss just a few . . .' The hallway of the mansion was heaped with hundreds of Aoife's mother's dresses – magnificent robes of silk, velvet, lace, feathers, living flowers, encrusted with jewels and pearls. 'Actually, you should borrow one back – that tiny black dress is ridicu—'

'You can keep the dresses! I'm here to find Shay!'

Caitlin's face switched instantly from panic to awed delight. 'Seriously? Oh my God, you're *so* my best friend!' She roared over her shoulder: 'Ultan, get out of bed – it's Aoife and she says I can keep them!' She turned excitedly to Aoife again: 'Did you like the way I'm reworking your story? I'm making you look really good . . . *Hey, you with the stupid hair, get out of my house!*' This last was bellowed at Carla, who was staring in open-mouthed amazement at the piles of dresses. *'This is a private viewing! Stop ogling the stock— I mean, presents!'*

Aoife snapped, 'Leave her alone, she's with me.'

Caitlin looked hurt and furious. 'What do you mean, she's with you? Who is she? Some social-climbing wannabe who's only interested in you now you've turned out to be queen?'

'Where's Shay?' Aoife grabbed the front of the changeling girl's too-tight dress.

'Hey, quit jerking my feathers!' Shoving Aoife away, Caitlin checked herself in a huge sheet of polished copper – crossly fluffing up her moulting bodice and straightening the necklace of ruby flowers. The selkie pearl appeared to be gone, which no doubt explained the absurdly expensive house. 'How would I know where Shay Foley is? I was only making all that up. Fact, I thought he was with you. Has he slipped his chain again already? If I were you, I'd stop shaming myself by tagging around after him every time he cheats on you. It was embarrassing enough the way you dragged him off his last girl-friend at the wedding.'

'*That was his mother.*'

Caitlin laughed mightily, showing the black gap of her missing tooth. 'Oh, right, his' – she crooked her large fingers in the air – '"mother". Is that what he told you? I suppose this new one is' – she air-quoted again – 'his "sister"?'

Aoife had had enough. 'Come on, Carla, there's no help to be had here – let's go.'

But the changeling girl was instantly contrite. 'Wait, stop, you're *my* best friend! What did this demon girl look like? I'll sort out your boy troubles for you . . .' Grabbing up her book from the heap of gold-embroidered wolf-fur capes onto which she'd tossed it, she dragged Aoife by the hand to a green marble table; on it lay a gold platter of what looked like tiny roast chickens, and clay bowls of dark crystallized fruit, and tiny wild strawberries, and silver jugs of a frothy white drink. 'Here, sit – have a roast wren, have a sugar plum, have some hawthorn champagne – it's very, very mild, not like Donal's juice . . . Take off that awful shawl, you look like an aul one.'

'I'm not staying. If you really *can* read that thing, tell me what it says about a demon girl who always steals away the most beautiful boy from the dance.'

'No problem! My only reason for living is to help my best friend the queen with her love life!' Caitlin pushed Aoife onto a marble stool and took another beside her, slamming the leather-bound volume down open on the table between them. 'I've been helping you already, by the way. I've been telling everyone how great you are, even though the Beloved is really, really angry with you right now. You heard me out there, sticking up for you, and explaining you were coming back to marry him—'

'I'm not marrying that devil.'

Caitlin blinked, like Aoife had slapped her lightly in the face. Then said brightly, 'Look, OK, I'm not going to argue with you because I'm your best friend. All I'm saying is, Dorocha's actually quite nice when you get to know him . . .'

'He's the devil, Caitlin.'

'. . . plus he's rich, and Shay Foley can't kiss you without turning you into a prune. Stop, wait! Sit down again, don't get all pissy-arsed. I'm only trying to be helpful . . .' She leafed through the thick yellowing parchment with one hand, while waving her other hand vaguely at the food. 'Have a sugar plum before Fat Boy gets here – he always scoffs the lot in seconds.'

Aoife, struggling to stay calm, didn't sit down again; she stood to one side and said, her voice a little shaky, 'I need to know where to find her before she breaks his heart for ever.'

'Hang on, hang on . . .' Caitlin ran her finger along under the dots and lines of the druidic script; flipping over faint illustrations and faded, half-drawn maps. '"Steals the most beautiful boy from the dance and breaks their hearts . . ." Anything a bit less general? I've known a few like that in my time. Got a name for this one – I mean, an actual name? You're not giving me much to work with here.'

Carla, who was now looking over Caitlin's shoulder, said, 'She was a waitress in a café.'

Caitlin tittered into her hand. 'Ah! Of course. Those demon girls do love wearing waitress uniforms. Pretty?'

'Very long white-blonde hair, and silvery eyes . . .'

'Ooh, Shay Foley, you *bad* thing.'

A deep male voice cried, 'Aoife!' and an auburn-haired teenage boy in an electric-blue shell suit came striding towards them, heading straight for the food.

'Ultan!' Aoife was amazed how pleased she felt to see the plump changeling boy – there was something oddly comforting about the sight of him. He was already cramming two sugar plums into his mouth.

'What brings you back here so soon? And where's Shay?'

'Done a runner already!' Caitlin was still smothering her mirth with her hand. 'With a blonde this time, the type who takes off with the best-looking boy from the dance—'

Ultan choked, spraying sugar from his mouth. 'Seriously? The Deargdue? Well, fair play to Mam for warning me against her!'

After a brief stunned silence, Aoife said faintly, 'Your *mam* knew about this demon?'

He was still coughing, mopping bits of plum from his shell suit. 'She did indeed – talked about little else after I got big enough to go to the discos. I thought it was something she'd made up to frighten me, to be honest.'

Caitlin was flicking through pages feverishly. 'Deargdue . . . I knew that's who your majesty was on about. Dear . . . De . . . D . . . Hmm. Can't see it. Maybe she's under something else. W, for waitress . . .'

'Have we met somewhere before?' asked Carla suddenly. She was staring in puzzlement at the teenage boy.

Ultan smirked, pushing his hands through his thick auburn hair. 'I'm sure I'd remember you if we had met. What's your name?'

(And Aoife suddenly remembered – with a pang of anxiety – how Carla's nan kept Ultan's anniversary mass card on her mantelpiece, and that the change-ling boy had no idea he'd been away from home for thirty years, or that his beloved mother was dead . . .)

'I'm Carla Heffernan. But are you sure I don't know you? I feel like I've known your face for ever.'

Caitlin glared up from her book, incensed. 'What are you, some sort of professional friend-stealer sent to bug me? Leave the boy alone – he's from the country, he's not able for you.'

Ultan said to her tartly, 'Are you still pretending to be able to read that book?'

Instead of reacting to this taunt with her usual furious defensiveness, Caitlin ran her finger down a page before turning it over, saying casually, 'Sorry, why did you say your mam warned you against the Deargdue?'

'Because she always steals the best-looking boy at the dance.' He grinned at Carla while popping another sugar plum into his mouth. 'She was a real Irish mammy – she didn't like the girls being after me. "Ultan," she used to say, "if you see a splendid beour with hair like the barley in your father's fields and eyes like sunshine in the rain, you go and hide behind Father Murphy because you might be all excited thinking she is a fine thing and wanting to buy her a lemonade but she will take you away to her house and lock you up in the dungeon and break open your heart to suck it dry like an orange, and you'll never get to see your loving mammy again."'

Caitlin flipped over another page. 'D . . . D . . . Deargdue . . . Oh, I have it! *Deargdue: Always steals the* – oops, your mammy had it wrong, Ultan! – *always steals the* fattest *boy from the dance.*'

Round cheeks flaming pink, Ultan shouted, 'Stop pretending to read Ogham when you know you can't! And at least my mam was nice to me!'

Caitlin hurled the big book across the table at him, her strong freckled face ugly with fury. 'You read it yourself then, if you're so damn clever, you humanized mammy's boy, you!'

'Oh God . . .' Aoife had sunk back down on the stool, rocking to and fro, her hands pressed over her face. Hot tears dripped onto the marble between her elbows. 'Oh God, oh, Shay . . .' Was Ultan's mother right? Did the Deargdue *literally* break the hearts of boys?

'Stop arguing!' Carla's voice was high-pitched with protective fury. 'Don't you even care she's upset? She loves Shay Foley and now he's been stolen by this Deargdue! You're supposed to be her friends – *do* something! I'm more help to her than the two of ye and I'm not even a changeling!'

Another startled silence fell. A few seconds later,

Caitlin said, in a tense, angry tone, 'What do you mean, you're not a changeling, hey? Are you human, Little Miss Hanger-On?'

Aoife looked up hastily. Caitlin's muscular shoulders were raised like the hackles on a farm dog; she was pointing across Aoife at Carla, who cringed in fright at the sight of the blue flames flickering around the changeling girl's forefinger.

Ultan was protesting, 'Ah now, Caitlin, even if she is—'

'You *are* human, aren't you, you treacherous little—'

Aoife grabbed Caitlin's wrist. 'Leave her alone.'

'But she's human!'

'*Sit down!*'

Caitlin remained glaring at Carla for several more seconds, then slowly, reluctantly, subsided onto her stool. Jerking her wrist out of Aoife's grip, she said plaintively, 'How can you stick up for a stupid human? They're mean and cruel to fairies.'

Taking a stool on the other side of the table and filling his cup with frothy hawthorn champagne – and a second cup for Carla, which he pushed towards her – Ultan said cheerfully, 'Not all humans are like your mam, Caitlin. Sure *my* human mammy used to leave the fairies out cakes and milk, and she called them the good folk.'

Caitlin scowled over at him. 'I hope you told her that was pure patronizing shite.'

'Why would I have said that? I didn't even know I was a fairy myself until I ended up here. Anyway, she wasn't trying to patronize anyone, she had a great respect for the fairies. "Ultan," she used to say—'

'Oh, here we go.'

'"Ultan, if you ever meet a fairy on the road, be sure to move out of their way and be polite. You'll know them by their red hair and their green eyes. They'll grant any human three wishes, so be sure to ask them for yours, and if you've been good to them, they'll grant the three wishes freely, and if you've been bad to them, they'll twist your wish and grant it quair. So never forget to put out the cakes and milk."'

Grabbing a roasted wren and stuffing it into her mouth, Caitlin sneered, 'You know what, your mammy was so wise about everything, I don't know why I bother checking anything in my incredibly ancient, valuable druidic text at all.'

Carla, who had pulled the book towards her from

where it had landed in the bowl of wild strawberries, said under her breath to Aoife, 'Aoife? I wish I could read this.'

Aoife shivered, and the hair pricked on her arms as if someone had walked across her grave; a slight sinking feeling, like a decrease in pressure. It reminded her of the sensation she'd felt when Lois's grandmother was complaining she couldn't see properly with her new bifocals . . .

In between spitting tiny bones out into the palm of her hand, Caitlin was roaring angrily at Carla, 'You get your traitorous hands off my book – it's a treasure of Tír Na nÓg and nothing to do with filthy humans!'

Carla ignored her, bending her head over the book, turning pages rapidly.

'Hey! Give that back!'

But Carla flattened a page, and read out in a loud voice: 'Deargdue: A peasant girl famed for her beauty. She loved and was loved, but the Lord on the hill gave the girl's father a handful of silver coins, and took the girl away from her boy to his house. And there she waited in hope for the boy to rescue her, but he never came. Only her Lord came, who cut through her skin with a small sharp *knife and drank her heart's blood through a hollow stalk of dried barley.'*

The big changeling girl was on her feet, crimson-faced with outrage. 'Stop pretending you can read Ogham script!'

'When autumn passed without a single word from the boy, the girl stopped eating. In winter, she died.'

Ultan muttered, refilling his cup, 'Mother of God.'

'She's making this up, I tell you!'

Trying to listen to Carla, Aoife snapped, 'Be quiet!'

'But she's just a jumped-up social-climbing groupie pretending to be your new best friend!'

'She IS my best friend! Now sit down!'

The big changeling girl's face went white; her mouth twisted. 'No, *I'm* your best friend, it's *me* can read Ogham . . .' She made a fierce grab for the druid's book. 'Give me that, you human scum!'

Aoife also sprang up, furiously wresting the book back out of Caitlin's hands. 'Carla is not scum, she's my best friend, and you know you can't read this yourself, so sit down and be quiet!'

Caitlin stared at her for a long moment, her big mouth working, a suspicious glint of water along her lower lashes – and then stormed furiously away across the room, fiercely kicking aside the piles of gorgeous dresses and screaming, 'I don't care if you are the stupid queen, you're as mean as a human, and you can take back all this cheap worthless shite and give it to your new best friend!' And she charged head-long up a sweeping marble staircase, in floods of angry tears.

Carla said anxiously, 'I didn't mean to upset—'

'Just keep reading.' Aoife's heart was beating painfully. She would comfort Caitlin some other time. Right now she had to know what had happened to that dangerous, damaged beauty.

With one last guilty glance towards the stairs, Carla dipped her head over the book again. '*The body of the poor suicide was left out by the side of the road, and there the boy found her and recognized her and buried her deep in the ditch, and to cover his shame he put no stones on her grave to mark her and there were no stones to keep her down, and so when spring came again, she rose with the grass and came to the boy and pierced a tiny hole into his heart with her knife, and sucked him dry through her barley straw, night after night, until by autumn his agony was over and he was dead.*'

(Ultan gasped, 'Mother of God . . .')

'And then she came for the handsomest son of every nearby townland and they would dance with her, and she would bring them away with her one by one to her house to break into their hearts and suck out their heart's blood through a barley straw . . .'

('My mam was right *again!*')

'. . . and none would see them again in the human world, nor in the Land of the Young, for she cares not for the living, fairy or human, and her only house is Tigh Duinn, the land of the worms, the House of the Dead, or Land of the Dead, from where none can return alive, for once they have crossed her threshold, all are—' Carla stopped reading abruptly; her soft eyes brimmed with tears. 'Oh, Aoife. He's . . . Oh, poor Shay . . . He's . . . Oh, Aoife . . .'

Ultan said with a deep sigh, shaking his auburn head, 'So that's it then. Poor old Shay Foley's dead.'

CHAPTER NINE

Aoife said, 'Wish for Shay to be here.'

Carla went white with shock. 'Wish for . . . . ?'

'Wish for Shay to be here. *Now*. If Ultan's mother is right, you've got three wishes.'

'But Aoife, I can't wish for Shay to—'

Wildly, desperately, hungrily, crazily, Aoife cried, 'Yes you can! Stop wasting time! She's torturing him! Say *I wish Shay Foley was here!*'

'No! Don't!' Ultan was cringing in horror. 'Don't say it – he'll come back with no heart, he'll be undead like in the Dracula films—'

'*Carla, wish it!*'

'But what if Ultan is right? You don't want Shay to come back as a zombie!'

Aoife moaned despairingly at the thought. 'But what if he's not dead? What if she's still torturing him, still sucking at his heart and he's in terrible, terrible agony? Please, darling, please, I'm begging you, if you love me at all—'

Ultan howled, '*Carla, do not!*'

But Carla had broken. Through a flood of terrified tears, she cried in shrill panic, 'I wish Shay Foley was here!'

Aoife's own heart throbbed with a wild, ecstatic joy. She said as calmly as she could manage, 'Your wish is granted.'

Carla dropped her head to the table and wrapped her arms over it, as if Shay in death might swoop down on her like the giant ferocious sluagh, shrouding her in a mantle of black wings. Ultan actually took cover on the floor behind his marble stool.

But Aoife was on her feet – exultant. The hairs were pricking on her arms – and neck, and legs, and scalp – agonizingly sharp and sweet, like her skin was being tattooed with words of love. The drop in pressure that she now knew was associated with granting a wish had left her feeling light and dizzy.

Any moment now . . .

Would he come through the door? Or down the stairs?

She gazed eagerly around the huge room. There were a thousand places in it to hide – it was so cluttered with the dresses, strewn over outsized marble chairs, sofas, tables; polished bronze mirrors leaned against pillars; plump gold cupids were poised on their toes, clutching arrows tufted with gold-painted feathers. The marble stairs swept upwards. She listened for footsteps from above . . .

Nothing.

But surely, any moment now . . .

Beyond, in the courtyard, bird song rose and fell.

Carla raised her head, checking around nervously, her terrified sobs slowly fading as she realized – clearly, to her relief – that the three of them were still alone. Ultan got cautiously to his feet, also peering in every direction, and let out his breath on a long, shuddering sigh. 'Thank Danu that wish didn't—' He checked himself hastily. 'I mean, what a shame the wish didn't work. He was a grand lad, for a lenanshee . . .'

Surely, *surely*, any moment now . . .

Aoife moved slowly towards the open doors. Far above the marble statues and carp-filled pools, the thin finger of the crystal tower burned in the sun, wearing its scented ring of hawthorn. A sluagh circled it, poking its withered head from side to side, surveying the city.

A very long way off, the sound of golden hinges creaking . . . The front gate! As the sluagh disappeared round the far side of the tower, Aoife fled down the steps and across the courtyard to the archway, where she paused at the entrance to the avenue, on her toes, listening, holding her breath . . .

The trellised tunnel of flowers curved away into the distance, humming softly with golden blur-winged bees . . .

Whispering footsteps, far off, out of sight?

No: the distant falling of rose petals . . .

Footsteps; it *was* footsteps!

But so soft, so slow, like the weak, hesitant shuffling of an old, old man . . .

Aoife wavered, poised between fear and longing. Was it . . . ? Could it be . . . ?

Nearer . . .

She was shaking.

Why would her feet not move?

The perfumed trellis curved away; the slow, soft footsteps drawing nearer . . . A movement in the roses, a ruffling of the soft white petals . . . A pale hand, as pale as the petals, crept round the corner, feeling its way along the golden wire that secured the roses to the trellis. And now a shadow fell, trembling like water in the sunlight that fell through the ceiling of flowers.

After the shadow, he came himself.

Dressed all in black, the way she'd seen him last. But not dancing now. Feeble, sick. Walking slowly, so slowly, one hand sliding along the golden wire like a blind man feeling his way, the other hand pressed to his heart . . .

Shay.

In Aoife's mind, she was already running towards him, screaming out his name . . . Yet her feet were still frozen to the ground and she could not speak – she could hardly breathe.

Slowly, slowly he made his way towards her under the drooping, wind-blown roses. Closer, closer. His hand still pressed to his heart. Now his dark green eyes were fixed upon her. Why didn't he smile, or speak? Was he not glad to see her? His skin was as white as the roses that had scattered their petals in his hair, melting into the blackness of it like snow into black water.

'Shay?' At last she had found her voice – it came out husky with grief and longing. 'Shay?' But still she couldn't move.

Behind her, she could hear Carla crying, 'Oh my God, he's . . .' in a high, trembling voice.

'Aoife, don't touch him!' Ultan's warning blurted out shrill with fear. 'That's not him, that's a zombie!'

And still he moved towards her. Slowly, slowly. The silver earring glinted high in his ear. His deeply curved mouth was slightly bruised, as if someone had bitten down hard on a kiss.

'Shay?'

He had nearly reached her. One step away from her. Still he clutched the trellis with one hand, and held the other pressed to his heart. Between his fingers, dark red liquid leaked . . .

'Oh God, Shay, you're hurt – speak to me . . .'

His lips parted slightly. 'Hold me,' he murmured. 'Hold me . . .' He seemed not to have the strength to take the final step. The blood ran down his shirt.

'Oh, Shay, Shay . . .' With a deep groan of joy and fear and sorrow, she took the final step herself, opening her arms.

'Hold me,' he said again, and – closing his dark

green eyes – he fell forward into her embrace. She sank to her knees beneath the roses, clasping him to her . . .

And found herself clutching at nothing.

The howl rose from deep within her gut, animal-like in its desolation. *'Shay! Shay!'*

Carla was instantly beside her, comforting her. 'Poor you, poor you . . . How sad . . .'

'He's gone, Carla! Where did he go?'

'He was a ghost, Aoife! He wasn't really here at all.'

'But at least he wasn't a zombie.' Ultan sounded a lot more relieved than disappointed. 'Ghosts are way preferable.'

Grief and fury rushed in after desolation. 'He wasn't a ghost! He was alive! I felt him! It was like . . .' She pressed her hand to her own heart; it beat on her palm, furiously. *That* was where she had felt him. Alive and real. Yet in her arms, on the surface of her skin, he had been like the mist rising from a river – beautiful and gone. *She should have held him tighter.* 'Wish him back, Carla!'

'Aoife, he was a ghost!'

'Don't say that! It's not true – he's alive! He said to hold him, and I was afraid! I was scared, and by the time I'd taken him in my arms he had slipped away . . . *This time I'll hold him!*'

Ultan was shaking his head. 'Even if you're right, my mam says you can only wish for a thing once, it never works the next time.'

'No. *No!*' Aoife screamed her pain. If she had ruined his only chance of rescue through sheer cowardice . . .'You're just saying that because you're afraid of him! That can't be true!'

'I *am* afraid of zombies – who wouldn't be? But that's not why I'm saying it, and Mam's right about most things . . .'

She seized Carla's arm. 'Carla, do it, I'm begging you. He was here, he was alive, but I didn't run to him, I was afraid and I waited, and then he was pulled back to wherever he is.'

'But he has to have been a ghost, Aoife. The book says he's in the Land of the Dead. Oh dear God, his heart was bleeding and he looked so . . . *ghost*-like!'

'I don't care what he is! *Carla, please.*'

Carla broke down again, weeping with terror. 'I wish that—'

But before she had even uttered his name, to

Aoife's unspeakable joy the distant gate had creaked again, and the shuffling footsteps had begun their slow ascent. She cried, 'He's found his own way back!'

Ultan gasped, instantly scared again, *'Aoife, wait! He might be a zombie this time!'*

But already she was gone – springing eagerly to her feet, sprinting down the long arching tunnel of white roses. This was what she should have done before: run towards him, not stood there trembling like a leaf, as if afraid of what he had become, and then not holding him . . . That was what had gone so wrong.

This time she would hold him and never let him go.

In the distance, a bell was tolling – a church-like sound. *Ding, dong* . . .

'Shay! I'm coming!'

'Welcome home, my queen,' quavered a thin, weak voice. And the little old man in his unspeakable dark green coat came limping through the roses to meet her, his walking stick tucked under his arm.

At the sight of Aoife's face fading from joy to utter horror, Seán Burke couldn't seem to stop laughing. The cooshee scalp he was wearing as a hat slid backwards, but didn't fall off: he wore the long lower jaw of the dog around his neck like a collar, fastened with a twist of wire, so that its yellow lower teeth bristled up in front of his chin. 'Now who did you think I was, my queen? Have you still your *grá* for that lenan-shee lad of yours?'

Recovering her breath, Aoife raised her hands in rage, itching to blast this sniggering little nobody up through the roof of flowers above. '*Where is he?*'

'Such a hussy you are, Aoibheal, like your mother before you—'

She pointed her forefingers . . .

Smartly the zookeeper snapped the upper jaw of the hat back down over his face, the curved yellow teeth of it enclosing the top half of his face like a visor. The bone-white eyes of the dog were now on a level with her own – staring at her with great melancholy, leaking soft jelly tears. Slightly muffled inside the dog's head, like a biker from within a helmet, he said, 'Now, now, my queen – don't you be thinking of abusing a little old man like me. And how can I help you if you blast me to kingdom come?'

She lowered her hands, clenched her fists. 'Tell me what you know about the House of the Dead.'

'Nothing, my queen, although I have to say it sounds pretty self-explanatory.'

'*Where is Dorocha?*'

'Sure what would I know about the Beloved's movements? There might be laws, but he's a law unto himself, that one. I'm a mere lackey.'

Behind her were cries of 'Aoife!' 'What's happening?' – Carla's and Ultan's voices, and their feet racing down the avenue. In the depths of the dog's head, Seán Burke's eyes lit up.

'And here come your little friends to rescue you!' Reaching up with his walking stick, he slammed aside a spray of roses, revealing a patch of sky in which the sluagh could be seen, still circling the tower. Waving the stick through the hole, he cried in his high, shrill, wavering voice, 'Here, bir—'

The blast of Aoife's power caught him full in the chest, where the cooshee claws fastened the fur across his heart, but to her shock he barely staggered. Her second blast didn't even wipe the smile from his half-hidden face, and before she could even summon a third, he had seized her wrist with terrible, unnatural strength, while continuing to quaver upwards, '*Here, birdie! Here, birdie!*'

'Aoife!' Carla came racing round the curve of the avenue, with Ultan right behind her.

Aoife screamed as the zookeeper dragged her away down the avenue. '*Carla, run! Ultan, get Carla back to the house!*'

He grabbed hold of the human girl and brought her to a halt, but for a moment stayed hesitating between doing as Aoife asked and coming on to rescue her instead . . . The sluagh was spiralling downwards, its beaked head jabbing in all directions, seeking the source of the cry.

'*Ultan, go! I can look after myself!*'

Like a helicopter landing, the whoop of leathery wings was shaking the bower of white flowers, sending clouds of petals whirling. Ultan – with a horrified glance upwards – unfroze, grabbed Carla off her feet and ran with her back up the avenue as she beat on his plump shoulders with her fists, shrieking, '*No, put me down!*' Then, just as they disappeared: '*I wish we were both safe home!*'

Instant terror flooded Aoife's heart. No, no . . . Her arms were pricking, as if pins were being forced through her skin from the inside out; within her body, the sinking drop in pressure . . . *No, not me, not me, don't wish me home . . .* Eyes closed, staggering, she fought the sick sensation of the wish being dragged from her reluctant body, like a long ribbon drawn out of her heart. *No, please, God, please, Carla, stop, you go, don't take me, I'll never find my way back here in time to save Shay . . .* And then the mists cleared, and to her relief she was still in the scented avenue of flowers, and still being hustled away by the zookeeper, who was grasping her arm with brutal strength. She craned to look over her shoulder – the avenue was empty and, high above in the hazy golden air, the sluagh was already corkscrewing back up towards the shimmering tower with a bough of roses clutched in its foul claws.

A vicious yank at her arm. 'Wish-granting, my queen?' Seán Burke was peering suspiciously out at her from inside the cooshee head. 'Surely that wasn't a human girl?'

Still nauseous, Aoife panted, 'Of course she wasn't a human – do you think she'd survive here one second if she was? Anyway, I didn't grant a wish. If I had, I wouldn't be here, would I?' (*Please God, I granted the wish 'quair', as Ultan's mam would say. Please, Carla, be safely home.*)

'Hmm . . . That's true. She did wish for you both to be gone home, and you'd hardly pass up a chance to grant that one, I'd say!' But still he looked puzzled – tapping the knob of his walking stick thoughtfully against the cooshee's long thin snout, causing the blind white eyes to leak more jellied tears. 'The druids would be very interested to know if there *was* a teenage human girl in town. The Beloved promised them one for their festival, only he forgot for some reason. Too busy, I expect. The druids were very disappointed – can't say as I understand why. Ye teenage girls are abominable creatures – worse than banshees.'

Aoife's flesh was crawling at the feel of his horrible bony little hand clutching her arm, sliding around beneath the fur of the dead dog. They were nearing the gate, but the fairy power was building up in her veins again. She steeled herself to shake him off and push him out into the street and slam the gate behind him. *This time I'm prepared, I'll smash him . . .*

'Such a shame your little friends turned traitor,' said Seán Burke, grinning at her from behind his visor of cooshee teeth. 'But sure, if you "come quietly", as the guards say, then I won't have this ridiculous palace turned upside down and your big ugly stupid changeling friend – what was her name? Caitlin McGreevey? – and that fat fool Ultan McNeal fed to those hungry dogs you prize so much. And on the off-chance there *is* a human girl in their company, I won't have her delivered to the druids tied up in a big pink satin bow . . . *Or will I?* Oh, that's so much better, my queen! You're actually quite lovely for a teenage girl when you remember to behave yourself – just like your mother!'

When Aoife emerged on the zookeeper's arm – walking tall with fury, her long red-gold hair flying loose and turquoise eyes snapping – there was still a hopeful crowd of changelings sitting against the wall opposite Caitlin's gate. At the sight of her a surprised buzz ran along the row; heads jerked up; a couple rose to their feet. But remembering Wee Peter's contempt for those who encouraged the 'little people' to risk their lives for queen and glory, Aoife jerked up the red shawl to cover her face and ducked her head to make herself seem more of a height with the chortling Seán Burke as he hurried her away.

CHAPTER TEN

The church bell she had first heard in the distance from Caitlin and Ultan's courtyard sounded much louder now. *Ding, dong* . . . A vibrant steady clanging, rising from the heart of the city. *Ding, dong* . . . The sound-waves almost visibly rippling through the blue-gold hazy air.

With inexplicable strength, the old man hustled Aoife on down the long, curving, marble-cobbled streets. The hot sun was high, and their shadows were short and black. The scent of fruit and flowers was strong. Small birds were gathered on window-sills and roofs, but silently. A few teenage changelings lurked in the crystal doorways, but none seemed interested in her or the zookeeper – their faces were turned towards the centre of the pyramid city, listening intently to the bell tolling.

Hugging her elbow and grinning up at her, the old man was saying chattily, 'Rather an imposition on us fairies, don't you think, the way a human can demand three wishes from us? When we go to war against the surface world, we'd better hope not too many of them know about it. Imagine if a fairy said to a human, "I'm going to kill you," and the human said, "I wish you wouldn't." Terrible source of confusion.'

Aoife said fiercely, 'Nobody's going to war.'

The zookeeper guffawed, jerking painfully at her arm. 'Oh yes we are, my queen! There are great plans for war! A grand alliance, between life and death! The worship of roots and shoots, brought into step with the worship of the lead-lined coffin! Change-lings alongside the mighty dullahans! The beasts of the wilderness unleashed! Talking of beasts, what do you think of my magic armour?' He glanced proudly down at his furry dark green costume, with its yellow claw toggles. 'The power of a cooshee coat is wonderful protection, even if it's not the cooshee itself that's wearing it.'

So that was the source of his newfound power – it was stolen from the cooshee he had murdered. It made complete and revelatory sense: the last time Aoife's own power had failed her so dramatically, it was when she'd attacked a living cooshee. Through clenched teeth, she said furiously, 'Assassin.'

He laughed, delighted. 'Ah, now, don't be churlish, my queen – I was acting in self-defence! The youngest was after being very noisy and aggressive.'

The youngest. She fought not to sob, not to show weakness. 'I left them in your care. You said you'd look after them.'

He grinned, peering at her out of the depths of the cooshee head. 'But I *am* looking after them, my queen. The others are very well-fed today, thanks to our enormous friend, the hilariously nicknamed "Wee Peter".'

For a childish, unguarded moment she imagined her poor hungry dogs being fed on crisps and Kimberleys and exclaimed in disgust, 'Cooshees can't live on junk food!'

He howled with mirth. 'Junk food? Is that your opinion of Peter Joseph? Myself, I thought he'd make a healthy mouthful – but maybe you're right; maybe he was more fat than meat. And bone marrow.'

Aoife's stomach lurched. She choked out, 'What do you mean?'

'Ugh, these *incredibly sharp* cooshee teeth keep digging into my poor old face!' Seán Burke adjusted the heavy cooshee skull over his own balding cranium, pushing the elongated jaws further forward to get the sharp yellow incisors away from his cheeks. He set the whole thing back slightly crooked, so that the dog's long green snout ended up twisted slightly towards Aoife, its white, weeping eyes fixed on hers.

'What did you do to Wee Peter?' She was hissing her rage at the zookeeper, but the cooshee's skull trembled from side to side, and for a weird, irrational moment she felt like patting her youngest dog on the head and saying: *I didn't mean you, I know it wasn't you.*

Seán Burke blinked at her from inside its parted jaws: 'Oh . . . What? Oh, sorry, my queen, excuse the mind of an old man. I was distracted by the thought of cooshee teeth and how very, very sharp they are . . .' He laughed again. 'As indeed, was Peter Joseph! Yes indeed – *very* distracted when he saw those teeth – and still attached to their rightful owners! But still he refused to apologize for letting you escape; nor would he redeem himself by joining the hunt for you. I warned him it would be mightily unpleasant to be reborn as a cooshee puppy – that he wouldn't be himself at all, but would take its dark heart for his own, and carry it with him afterwards, into the future. But apparently *someone* had told him that he would remain his own true self, whatever happened to him.'

'Oh, you disgusting, evil, wicked— *You monster!*' But Aoife's heart was swollen sick with guilt. Peter had refused to hunt her down – and he wasn't even a follower of queens. Why had she told him it didn't matter how he died? It wasn't even as if she really knew – she'd only had a feeling that it *had* to be true; that however a fairy was transformed, it would not destroy their basic nature. *All because of the sweetness of some stupid apples growing on a dead child's grave . . .*

Seán Burke was saying chippily, 'Ha! *Me*, a monster? Personally, I blame whoever told Peter Joseph that utter nonsense about a clean rebirth, and gave him the stupid courage to face a cage of half a dozen ravenous cooshees . . . They still have a lot of very big bones to chew on— Danu's sake, what's going on here?'

Their progress had been brought to a sudden standstill by a procession of banshees pouring out of one of the steep alleyways. The tall, beautiful women had their crimson hoods thrown back, and their long hair – a deep, dark red – flowed freely to their knees. Most of them were cradling human babies – the ones they had stolen from the surface world, replacing them in their cradles with fairy children like Aoife herself.

Ahead, the dull, monotonous bell was still ringing – even louder and closer now. *Boom, boom, boom . . .*

The zookeeper was tapping his stick impatiently on the cobbles. 'Ah, that's where they're headed – the temple, for the harvest festival. It happens every seventh year, when the fabric between the worlds is at its thinnest. Come, my queen, we'll take another way to the zoo. You asked to see Dorocha? Well, you're in luck! I have a delightful bedroom set aside for you, with humble servants to wait on you hand and foot until your Beloved returns from his travels.' He dragged her away towards a set of steps cutting downwards to the left, but before they had begun their descent, a group of the black-robed dullahans came up the same steps and glided straight past the two of them – pushing on down the street through the crimson-cloaked throng, which parted as if even the banshees found them untouchable.

The zookeeper turned to watch, intrigued. 'Where are they off to when they should be minding the shop? Lads! Hey, lads!' But the crimson cloaks were closing in again, behind the black.

Jerking Aoife round, Seán Burke began shoving his way after the dullahans, swinging his stick to create space. 'If the lads are off to the Festival of the Dead, we might take a peek ourselves. Sure, we might even enjoy it! What else have we to do to amuse ourselves in paradise? Besides, it will be an education for you, my queen. Observe how the other half worships – not the followers of the Goddess Danu, such as ourselves, but the followers of Death and the Dark Man. This is their cry: *Long Live Death!* You might get to hear it, and don't forget to stand up when you do . . .'

A sudden hope flamed within Aoife, and instead of dragging against his arm, she quickened her pace, helping him force his way through the banshee throng. 'Would the druids know about the House of the Dead?'

'The druids know many things, but they don't tell the likes of me.'

'If I ask them?'

He chuckled. 'I wouldn't go near them today! And while we're on the subject, keep your face covered in the temple – this isn't a festival for the followers of Danu. Pull up that red shawl, then you'll look like a banshee yourself – and I can be your wild beast. Ha, ha – woof, woof! Though I refuse to go on all fours!' Seán Burke tugged his cooshee helmet forward as far as it would go, so that his own face disappeared entirely between the upper and lower jaws of the dark green snout. 'Woof, woof!' He must have turned to look at her from inside the head, because the white eyes of the dog swung towards her, dripping their tears down each side of the snout; the dog's upper lip was drawn back over its thin yellow teeth in a stiff, sad smile.

The banshees paid no attention as Aoife and the old man merged into the throng – their dark eyes were fixed too closely on the stolen babies, which they held wrapped tenderly in the folds of their cloaks. There were round-eyed toddlers as well, clutching the hands of their surrogate mothers; some banshees had charge of both a baby and a toddler – the older child clinging to the banshee's crimson cloak, trotting to keep up with her long strides.

Aoife – thinking of Eva, who had so lately been carried around by a banshee herself – asked, 'Why are they bringing children to the festival?'

From deep within the dog's skull the zookeeper answered, 'Sure, why wouldn't they? Maybe there's clowns and balloons. How would I know? I've never been to one of these myself – it only takes place every seven years, and I've not been here that long. Besides, I don't care for druids. I know we're going to all be on the same side when we go to war, but the mistletoe-and-harp brigade are very clannish, and to be honest with you' – here he lowered his voice to a confidential whisper, pushing the dog's snout coldly against her ear – 'I find these banshees a bitteen creepy, the way they carry them babies around like big dolls. I prefer them headless boyos. They're poor conversationalists, and not the sharpest knife in the drawer, but at least ye know where ye are with 'em – all they worship is death, plain and simple. No taking human lovers like them mad lenanshees, or adopting human babies like them banshees.'

Aoife felt a tug on her shawl – a child was walking calmly beside her, a little boy of around two, gazing about with solemn, long-lashed eyes. He was wearing a child's Liverpool strip and smart white trainers. In her disguise, he must have mistaken Aoife for his own banshee – although her shawl was not as long as the other cloaks, her hair not such a dark black-red, and she was not quite as tall.

The bell was tolling louder and louder now – massive tidal waves of sound.

At the far end of the widening street, hewn from the crystal heart of Falias, stood the vast temple where she had been crowned, and where Dorocha had attempted to marry her. The gorgeous bronze doors, fifty metres high, were open wide. The bronze bell above swung heavily; it was in the shape of a bull, and as wide and as broad. *Boom . . . Boom . . .* Under the bell, the banshees ascended the temple steps, the toddlers clambering and jumping to keep up. The little boy's legs were too short; he began to whimper in panic. Aoife reached down to scoop him onto her hip – it seemed best to bring him along; if she shooed him, he would still have followed her. The zookeeper shot her an amused glance, from under the dark green snout. 'An excellent disguise, my queen – every banshee carries a child!'

As they went through the doors, Seán Burke pulled her to one side against the wall, allowing the banshees behind to pass. The dullahans were already moving to join several others of their kind who stood

443

along the crystal walls of the temple, cradling their decomposing heads in their arms as tenderly as the banshees cuddled their stolen babies. A grey man as insubstantial as a mist at sea drifted past; Seán Burke pointed him out to Aoife, whispering in reverential tones: 'There's yer Fear Liath, a fearsome murderer of sailors.' Other more aggressive creatures were restrained, as if the druids didn't want to risk a blood-bath. A hairy orange grogoch was in a cage, clinging to the bars, its fierce little eyes watching everything. A pooka in real form – relatively small, only about three metres tall – crouched chained by one clawed foot to a pillar of the temple, its black ape arms folded across its hairy chest. A few sluagh, high in the roof, clung to the carved summits of the columns, their wrinkled wings folded around their bodies.

No lenanshees were present – a fact that surprised Aoife. She hated it when Shay called himself a mon-ster, but at the same time – were not lenanshees numbered among the dark creatures? Even Dorocha was wary of them.

The little boy slipped down from Aoife's hip to the floor and stood holding her thumb, watching the pro-ceedings with nervous interest. A banshee paused to gaze at him; she already had a baby in her arms, but she held out her hand to the boy in his Liverpool shirt and clean white trainers and murmured in a deep, musical voice – hungry with the love of her kind for human children, 'Martin, I thought I had lost you.'

With a cry of surprise, he looked from Aoife to her, realized his mistake, and trotted obediently to the real banshee's side, taking hold of a fold of her cloak as she rejoined the procession.

The crimson-cloaked women passed steadily on across the white floor of the temple, reduced to a stream of dark red ants by the vast open space. The enormously high rough-hewn marble altar was empty, but a crowd of white-robed druids – old and young, female and male, with mistletoe and haw-thorn wreathed around their heads and arms – were standing on its lower steps. They swung silver fili-gree lamps from slender chains, which gave off bright purple puffs of incense – even at the back, the scent was strong and dizzying, like the smell of poppies multiplied across a thousand fields.

The druids greeted the banshees as they arrived, taking the babies and toddlers from them, and bringing them away to an area beside the altar where white lamb's-wool blankets were heaped up like snow. As soon as she was relieved of her stolen child, each banshee spun on her heel with a great sweep of her cloak and stalked back across the temple, empty arms held wide, dark red mouth open, keening – a slow, rhythmic cry of despair, set to the steady booming of the temple bell. The long lines of banshees still queuing, still clasping their babies, took up the piercing wail, filling the temple with their grief. The grogoch joined in, screaming its own distress; the pooka rose to its feet, rattling its chains. A gathering of seal-wives still wet from the sea sent up cries like gulls in a storm. The dullahans lifted their rotting heads in mute salute, creating a wave of orange fire around the walls. From floor to roof, from wall to wall, the very air wept, and Aoife's own heart shrank under the weight of all this concentrated grief, and she found herself despairing.

There was no point to life.

No point in hoping that Shay was still alive.

He was in the House of the Dead, unreachable and gone.

Carla was right: he had been a ghost.

His heart had already been bleeding out from

under the hand clasped to his chest. His heart, broken into and sucked dry . . .

At the altar steps, a further commotion. A small, ancient druid, Morfesa, was carrying the little boy in the Liverpool strip up the steps of the high altar; the child had his arms wrapped round Morfesa's neck, gazing anxiously back at the weeping banshee who had relinquished him – her grief had infected him; he too was crying in a high piercing wail.

Aoife said hoarsely to the zookeeper: 'What's happening now?'

He shrugged, peeping out from inside the dog's head. 'Your guess as good as mine, my queen. Reminds me of an old country story about the real reason why the fairies steal human children – to harvest them every seven years at the Festival of the Dead—'

She jerked forward with a cry – *'Harvest them?'* – but he redoubled his grip, dragging her back to his side, crushing her elbow.

'Be quiet! You'll get us thrown out! I want to enjoy the festival!'

'Are they going to kill them? But the banshees love them too much!' She watched in horror as Morfesa reached the altar, where he sat the distressed child on the edge of the stone, and stood fussing with a bowl and a white linen cloth, dipping the cloth in the bowl, then using it to clean a knife.

Seán Burke was saying in her ear, the dog's cold snout pressed against her cheek: 'Don't you know we have to kill the things we love? Sure your mother cast human men behind her like sweet wrappers, until the one that murdered her—'

With a furious cry, Aoife tried again to break free. 'Let me go! I'm going to stop this!'

But again the zookeeper dragged her back, his sharp eyes gleaming out through the grille of yellow teeth. 'What happens here is none of your concern, my queen. It is not your festival and not your religion.' His grip was unbreakable; it was as if her arm was pinned down by the claws of a living cooshee. But above his head, the white eyes of the dog gazed intently into Aoife's face, and she found herself looking deep into the eyes of her favourite dog – and an odd calmness swept over her, and she felt her heart quieten, while around her the waves of grief rolled on – the beautiful, deafening chorus to the dead.

Touching her hand to the green-furred snout,

Aoife said slowly and clearly, 'Let me go. I am the queen. I order you.'

From within the depths of the head, the old man scoffed impatiently, 'You're a mite too young to be giving Seán Burke his orders— *Hey, what* . . . ?' His wrinkled face had sprung fully into view as the cooshee's upper and lower jaws snapped wide open in a ferocious yawn, and he was still saying, startled, 'What the feck—?' when the jaws crunched down again on his cheeks and chin. *'Aaargh!'* Dropping Aoife's arm, the zookeeper staggered in agonized circles, wrenching frantically at the dog's jaws with both hands, silver blood spurting from between the yellow teeth. *'Get off me, ya brute! Call him off! Call him off!'*

But Aoife was already gone, racing towards the massive altar.

The horde of druids circled the base, gazing up towards Morfesa, who was now bending over the child, pressing him gently back against the stone, raising the Liverpool shirt.

Aoife screamed, *'Stop! I order you! I am your queen!'* But her cries were swallowed up in the mighty requiem of sorrow. Louder and louder the banshees shrieked their deafening grief; the bell tolling faster above the doors – *Boom-boom! Boom-boom! Boom-boom!* – shaking the whole vast edifice of quartz. The zookeeper's cries of pain had been cut brutally short, but the pooka was trying furiously to break its chains, and the grogoch was tumbling around its cage . . . Gasping, Aoife thrust and elbowed her way through the ranks of red cloaks, in between the druids – who barely glanced at her – then raced headlong up the altar steps. Morfesa had his back to her; he had stopped cleaning the knife and was holding it above his head, point sideways, testing it with his thumb it for sharpness.

'*Stop!*' She seized his white-clad arm.

The ancient druid turned his gaze to her – eyes dark, malevolent, glazed. He should have known her from her coronation, yet he seemed not to recognize her at all – it was as if he was drugged or blind. He complained in a thin, high, whining voice, 'Who orders me to stop? A banshee, is it? You've given away your child!'

'No I haven't!' Pushing him aside, Aoife swept up the sobbing boy from the altar and clasped him to her chest, ran halfway with him down the steps, shouting to the wailing crimson crowd, 'All of you, take back your children! *Take back your children!*'

The druids at the foot of the steps turned to look up at her in quiet puzzlement, not seeming to know what to do, still vaguely swinging their silver-filigree lamps of incense. A single banshee stepped forward, holding out her arms – and Aoife let the boy slip down to his feet, sending him racing down on his short little legs to his surrogate mother, then stayed where she was on the steps to shout again: 'Take back your children!'

A tough, sinewy hand sank its fingers into her arm and Morfesa spun her round, staring at her with the same dark, malevolent coldness, drawing her back towards him. 'I do not know you.'

Aoife shook her red-gold hair free of the red shawl, and met his blurred gaze with her own turquoise eyes. 'I'm your queen. I order you to stop this harvest.'

Still he stared at her with that strange, wilful blindness, repeating, 'I do not know you.'

'I am the queen of the Tuatha Dé Danann, the queen of the Land of the Young.'

His expression did not change. 'No member of the Tuatha Dé Danann can be recognized in this temple today. This day is not yours.'

But the tall female druid who had crowned Aoife with her own hands was coming up the steps towards them, followed now by the other druids, swinging their lamps. She was urging in an eager, melodious voice, 'Morfesa, this is wonderful! Don't you understand? She has come to us, as predicted! It's the prophecy fulfilled! Every seven years a teenage girl comes to lead the way. We requested that the Beloved bring us a human girl from the surface world, and were angry when he failed, and ordered him to stay away from this festival. We should have been kinder to him in his failure. We should have had faith. A greater hand was at work! It is not possible to force the hand of fate! The prophecy has been fulfilled without our interference!'

Morfesa was shaking his head, frowning. 'No – it is a human girl that is needed, and this one claims she is the queen of the Tuatha.'

'But this is the daughter, not the mother – and is it not well known that her father was one of the Fianna, the human heroes?'

'A hero—'

'But a human one, Morfesa! *Human!*'

The ancient druid's dazed eyes widened in sudden

understanding, and he flung back his white head and called out to the temple roof in a high chanting voice, 'Long live Death! Long live Death!'

The pooka, the grogoch and the zookeeper redoubled their cries of distress, and the bronze bell continued to solemnly ring. *Boom, boom, boom* . . . But the banshee chorus of grief had ebbed in the temple, replaced by a whispering, throaty murmur as the crimson-cloaked women gathered around the little boy in his Liverpool shirt, and began casting longing glances towards their own stolen children. Only the other druids filled the breach, taking up Morfesa's chant: 'Long live Death! Long live Death!'

And while Aoife stood there, utterly confused – what did they mean about her father? Was she really part of some prophecy? – the tall female druid came smiling towards her, and drew the red shawl from her shoulders, letting it fall to the floor, and ran her hand over Aoife's red-gold hair, and carefully placed on it a wreath of hawthorn – not flowering, but studded with red berries. Then pushed her gently back against the altar, and cried loudly but sweetly: 'Lay her on her front to spare her the sight of the knife!'

Suddenly realizing what was about to happen, Aoife made a fierce break for freedom, but there were too many white robes already surrounding her, pressing against her, gripping her by her dress, her arms, her hair, plucking her off her feet, throwing her face down on the high stone table—

'Stop! No!'

A forest of hands pinned her by her legs and arms. A sharp point, just to the left of her spine—

'No!'

A terrible pain pierced her, sinking in through the black cardigan, the dress, into the flesh—

'No! Mam! Dad!'

The knife slid between her ribs, piercing the skin of her heart . . .

'Shay!'

The voice of a ghost, calling on another ghost to save her—

'Shay!'

The knife thrust through her from back to front.

CHAPTER ELEVEN

Down.

Yet she was looking up, lying on her back. On one side, rising monstrously against the night sky, was a vast hulking construction of stone – a sloping façade, fitted together out of crude rough blocks. In the sky above, long streams of stars swirled in spirals like glitter in water . . .

Down.

. . . around a deep hole of intense darkness, revolving slowly above Aoife's head, as if someone had pulled the plug from a bath of stars . . .

Down.

. . . the long, beautiful, bubbling streams of stars spiralling slowly down into the eternal drain.

Fearful of the strange sky, Aoife closed her eyes and, with a deep sigh, stretched out her arms and flattened the back of her hands on cool wet grass – not grass but flowers: poppies, their oily, soporific haze drifting up around her. Overpowering.

So tired . . .

She would sleep, right here, at the foot of this monstrous prehistoric barrow, among the poppies. A wave of torpor swept down over her eyelids like a brush thick with glue.

So tired . . .

And yet she hovered for a while on the edge of her unconsciousness, like a star drifting along the horizon of a black hole.

The back of her hip was resting uncomfortably upon a stone. Eyes still closed, she felt under herself. Not a stone, but a small metal object – a ring. No, a cap . . . Attached to an empty leather flask . . . A vision came bubbling darkly to the surface of her mind: a boy of ten years old with a thick mop of chestnut hair and freckles and bright green eyes. Donal. He had given this juice to her and . . .

Shay.

A trickle of urgency ran through her, but her eyelids remained sealed.

Stay awake.

Shay.

Thick warm waves of sleep, rolling across her brain. She felt again for the flask, and blindly, clumsily, pulled it out from under her and lifted it towards her mouth, fumbling with the bronze cap, spilling what little contents it contained over her chin. In the end, all she could do was lick the cold brass rim, where a single thick drop of juice still clung. It was enough. After a long moment of sickness – heart pounding dangerously – wakefulness flooded her like a cold hit of salt sea, and she gasped and rolled over, rising onto her hands and knees.

On either side, a vast starlit plain stretched away in utter darkness, trembling with shadowy poppies. But before her was the vast stone barrow rising up against the swirling sky, and directly facing her was a pair of upright gateposts, four metres high. A lintel rested across these massive stones, creating a square black entrance to the barrow. There was no door; only this yawning invitation into the dark. Over the stone lintel was a lattice of long bronze daggers . . .

The druid's knife! With a rush of fear, she pressed her hand to her chest, expecting to feel the sharp point of a blade sticking out. Nothing – only a small rent in the black dress, under which her flesh felt smooth and warm. Sinking back on her heels, she felt for the circle of hawthorn berries. The thorns were muddled with her red-gold hair, too painful to disentangle, and after a few seconds she gave up trying.

What was this place?

She got to her feet, still staring up at the lattice of daggers – they were set to form the words: *Tigh Duinn*.

Tigh Duinn.

She knew these words.

Aoife's mind wandered, searching for them . . .

Tigh Duinn.

Yes.

Carla had read it aloud: *And her only house is Tigh Duinn, the land of the worms, the House of the Dead, or Land of the Dead, from where no one can return alive, for once they have crossed her threshold, all are . . .*

Then came the word that Carla refused to speak. And that word was . . .

Dead.

A giddy emotion filled her, as if she'd swallowed hawthorn juice again – dizzying, shocking – two thoughts at the same time, one terrifying, and one electric:

So she was dead . . .

But Shay was here!

Above her crouched the vast House of the Dead – a monster looming against the stars. Heart beating painfully, she took one step closer to the entrance. The high stone gateposts were decorated with carvings – worms wrapped around each other in segmented coils; armoured woodlice and beetles as big as her fists; centipedes. From the dark, a stream of cold air gushed into her face – wintry, bitter and venomous – chilling her to the bone. Tightening the thin black cardigan around herself, Aoife stepped into the icy blast and stood for a moment, head bowed against the wind, waiting for her fairy vision to intensify. Slowly her eyes picked up a ruby glow from further down; a light wash of vermilion and shadow shifted across the walls; her breath seemed to flutter from her lips in ghostly pink wisps like butterflies. Now she could see that the walls of the passageway were carved like the gateposts with the creatures of the earth: woodlice, ants, worms. She took another step. The stone floor sloped steeply downwards. The wind blew strongly up from the depths, freezing her skin.

Another step.

Another.

Twenty more.

Aoife came to the source of the ruby glow: a doorway set in the wall, heavily draped in scarlet wool with candles behind it. The curtain wafted slightly in the breeze. She pushed it aside, just a very little, enough for one eye to see. Within was a small stone bedroom with a clay floor; a high stone bed was placed in the centre with its foot towards the doorway. There were several tall candles set around the bed, most melted halfway down, and a figure was lying there – a long, slender teenage boy, covered to his eyes in a length of the same scarlet wool cloth as the curtain. No pillow; his dark head resting on the bare stone.

Fear held her in place for less than half a second, before longing drove her into the room.

'Shay. Shay, wake up!' She touched his leg through the cloth of scarlet wool. Cold and still. Weak with unshed tears, she moved on up the bed, pulling aside the blanket to gaze into his face. He was lying on his back, with a smile upon his mouth. A beautiful teenage boy, with long black lashes . . . *But not Shay*. Not Shay; some other poor boy . . . His mouth not curved, but straight; his cheekbones high and sharp, the chin pointed, with a scrap of dark beard. He was wearing a dark blue shirt and thin red tie; the tie was loosened and his shirt unbuttoned, revealing his ribcage. From a small hole in the centre of his chest there thrust the end of a small straw – a hollow, dried stalk of barley. Out of the hole a single trickle of dried blood rippled down over his thin ribs and under his arm. His heart must have been pierced long ago by the Deargdue, who had sucked it dry through her barley straw. Shivering, Aoife touched him. Under her hand, his bare skin felt as cold as the clay beneath her feet.

Dead . . . And yet he looked asleep.

She still had the leather flask, and unscrewed the lid, but there was not a single drop left to jolt him into whatever life – if any – might remain. She set down the flask on the bed beside him, and stood thinking. Remembering.

When she and Shay had found Eva lost on the bog, the little girl had been as still and cold as this. Yet Shay had kissed her, and his kiss had stirred a spark, even from the cold ashes of death, and Aoife had reopened the old wounds on both her and Eva's palms and let her fairy blood leak into Eva's veins, and life had come rushing back . . .

In this vast grave, there was no lenanshee to bestow a kiss. On a sad impulse, Aoife leaned down to kiss the dead boy's cold lips herself. Nor was there a knife to slice open her hand or his. Gripping the barley straw between the thumb and finger of one hand, she pressed down the base of her other thumb on the sharp stalk. The point of it pierced the fresh scar left by Mícheál Costello, and a drop of silver blood trickled down the hollow tube, making its way into the boy's heart.

She stood back and watched.

He lay unmoving, his lips still cold and pale. With a sigh, she pulled the blanket over him again, as if by this act she could keep him warm. She turned away, lifted the curtain and stepped back out into the stone passageway.

Twenty metres on, another candlelit room behind a curtain of deep dark blue, and here another boy was lying – this time on his side, his knees drawn up and his hands folded under his cheek. Not Shay. Handsome, freckled, with dishevelled blond hair to his shoulders and thick golden lashes; his full lips slightly parted. He was wearing flared jeans and a faded denim shirt, open to the waist – it must have been forty years since this youth was stolen away by the Deargdue, dancing away from the party across the starlit fields, joyful and in love.

Again Aoife kissed him, and pressed her palm upon the sharp end of the straw that rose from between his ribs.

Somewhere in the bowels of this house of death was the demon who had done this evil.

The passageway twisted and turned on its way downwards, and other corridors with other rooms led off to right and left, and Aoife followed each to the end before retracing her steps. So many bedrooms, all with cold clay floors and cold stone beds. So many cold boys – so many cold, dead boys. Auburn hair, with copper lashes laid on pure white skin. The dark skin of the western coast, with hair so black it shimmered blue. Sometimes a blond head, a strong Viking look. And the clothes they were wearing spanned not just decades but centuries; millennia. The thick plaid cloaks of clansmen; the silken cravats and lace cuffs of young gentlemen from a romantic age; the darned trousers and bare feet of peasant boys; suits for

Sunday best, with a flower – now dead – in the lapel. Hair carefully cut and brushed. Boys heading for feasts and parties in search of sweethearts.

And they had found her time and time again – the beauty with hair like fields of barley, and eyes like sunshine on a rainy day. A serial killer who for two thousand years had conducted this orgy of revenge – murdering (over and over again, in her mind) that single cowardly boy who had abandoned her so long ago, when her father sold her for a handful of silver coins.

Each time Aoife saw a dark head, she was terrified to gaze upon the face – but over and over again, the victim was not Shay. So she would linger to kiss a mouth or cheek, and let a little silver blood drip into an unknown heart, and then move on down the twisting passageways that stabbed this way and that into the heart of the house. Lifting the curtain of room after room. So many dead boys that even though she only gifted one drop of blood to each, she grew light-headed. Sometimes in the side corridors there were steps, and spiders hung invisible veils across her way, smothering her, and rats ran over her naked feet. But she didn't care – it seemed a very long time since she had been frightened by something as innocent as a rat.

The air grew colder and more bitter; she pulled the cardigan tighter around her. Pointless. The chill was deep within her bones.

The central, widest passageway sloped ever steeper, plunging like a crooked spear into the bowels of the earth. It was now so cold, that her feet were briefly frozen to the stone with every step, and her hand to the wall; her eyelashes were heavy with crystals and her lips were sealed together – held by a film of ice like glue. But she couldn't turn back, not ever – not until she had found Shay in one of these many, many rooms . . .

Not until she had found the demon killer.

She had turned several corners since the last bedroom, and its soft weak candlelight had faded behind her. Despite her fairy vision she began to have to feel her way, one hand on the wall of stone.

And then the corridor ended.

For a while she stood there, so deep within the earth, under the weight of clay and stone and death, both palms resting on the stone wall ahead of her . . .

The wind had stilled, and only the cold remained.

He was not here, in all this place.

Go back.

But her palms were frozen to the stone.

Go back.

She could hear faint distant noises.

Far, far behind her, a soft padding, as of many feet. Unknown creatures restless in the dark. And ahead of her, as if within this stone wall, a rustling, as of the summer rain shower rushing across a barley field . . . Or a vast cage of birds . . . Wings . . .

Go forwards.

Ripping her palms from the ice, she swept them in slow, steady arcs across the invisible wall, willing it to unlock. A dull trickling sound came from deep within the stone, like gravel pattering down, and then the mighty slab of rock cracked open, just a fraction – a very high stone door.

She pushed, with frozen hands.

Slowly it opened, just enough to let her through.

Light swelled from within. Flickering lilac shadows of a golden fire.

And the sound of wings fluttering. Hundreds of wings.

CHAPTER TWELVE

Twenty or thirty small perfumed fires were heaped in bronze baskets around the cavernous room – from these rose shimmering clouds of gold, crimson and lilac sparks, wafting up towards the roof where thick rafters of blackened bog-oak burst from the high clay walls. Along these rafters clustered the ranks of wrinkled, leathery sluagh – at least a hundred of them – clinging with both claws and wizened hands, so densely crowded together that they could barely move. Only the tips of their wings rustled, like bunches of dried leaves, as they peered down from the shadows with glinting, hungry eyes.

Aoife remained momentarily frozen in the narrow opening, in her bare feet and short black dress and thin black cardigan, gazing with wide turquoise eyes up at the living, fluttering roof of wings. Every sinew in her screaming: *Turn back. Run.*

She did not run.

Instead, she lowered her gaze.

There was a stone dais in the centre of the room – not high, but very wide and deep; it was spread luxuriously with purple silk, pillows embroidered with long centipedes in gold thread, brass lamps in the shape of curled woodlice, and scattered with poppies, torn up by the roots and trailing crumbs of earth. On this strange bed two lovers sat facing each other – their attention so utterly focused on each other's faces that neither of them had even noticed Aoife standing there. The girl's hair reflected all the sparks of the basket-fires, so that it appeared not barley-white but the same red-gold colour as Aoife's own; her white dress, also stained with firelight, clung to her. Facing her, his knees drawn up, was a beautiful dark-haired young man wearing a long black coat which flared out around him on the stone. The girl was leaning forward, both hands resting on the young man's slender waist, gazing up into his eyes. The young man's long pale fingers cupped her cheek and stirred in the sheaf of her firelit hair, so that it trembled like a field of barley at sunset, catching the evening breeze.

Beside the bed was a tall carved chair, of the same blackened bog-wood as the rafters. There was a third figure sitting in the chair – but the high back, carved to represent a nest of worms, was almost fully turned towards the door, so that all Aoife could see was a strong hand, resting on the arm – a hand, a wrist, and the black cuff of a sleeve.

The soft warmth of the fires melted the ice on Aoife's lips and eyelashes; it ran as water down her cheeks and chin. She took a step forward, through the narrow opening.

Finally noticing the intrusion, the Deargdue glanced towards the door – then widened her silver eyes and bared her pretty teeth with a faint hiss. Her companion, following his lover's gaze, looked at first bewildered by the sight of Aoife – then briefly guilty, as if he'd been caught doing something he shouldn't. But in the end he just laughed and rose to his feet, holding out his hand, saying in that light mocking tone of his, 'My queen! Come join us!' And above him, the sluagh leaned forward on their perches, with hungry interest.

Turn back. Run.

Aoife took another step. The unseen figure in the high-backed chair still did not move. His strong square fingers curled down over the arm of the chair.

There was a pale line around his wrist where the sun had not kissed his skin.

Dorocha also remained where he was, standing on the stone bed – smiling, eyebrows raised. 'You've caught me, Aoibheal! And I confess my sin. But you must admit, you gave me good reason to betray you. You yourself are as fickle as your mother. Come!' He was still holding out his hand. 'Tell us how you found your way here— Oh!' His beautiful face lit up, delighted. 'The hawthorn berry wreath upon your hair! How lovely! Morfesa made you his teenage sacrifice – am I right? So that's how he decided to get his own back on me, the cunning old fool. And all because you saved that foolish, fanciful, nasty-minded . . . What was her name? Lois?'

The pale line where the sun had not touched him, because he'd been wearing the golden locket . . .

Around your wrist, a narrow line
of paler skin
because you once were mine . . .

'Shay?' Heart weak with hope and fear, Aoife drew closer, running her hand over his, circling her fingers around the pale line, touching for the soft throb of his pulse. She moved around the chair to face him. He remained utterly still, hands resting on the arms of the chair, gazing at the Deargdue. He was even paler than when she had seen him last, under the white roses – his hurt mouth still bruised by a bite, or an angry kiss. His black shirt torn open. Sunk between his ribs was the creamy stub of barley straw; the dried blood drawing a straight line over his flat stomach, into the waistband of his black jeans. Head slightly on one side, dark green eyes on his beautiful demon. A dust of spider's web across one cheekbone.

Now sitting cross-legged on the pillows, the Deargdue picked up an ivory comb from beside her and ran its sharp teeth through her fire-tainted hair. She said in a discontented voice, 'Beloved, make her go away. The lenanshee boy is your gift to me, and I don't want her touching him.'

Dorocha soothed her: 'Hush, my dear one, let's just watch her try to wake him. It's as good as any show.'

'Shay?'

His dark green eyes were filled with tears – but how old were the tears?

No pulse beneath his skin.

Leaning closer, she pressed his hands – so strong, and now so cold. 'Shay?' Her voice was thick in her throat. 'Shay, can you hear me? Shay, it's Aoife . . .'

His mouth was curved, as it always was, at rest. On a groan, she bent to kiss it. Behind her the Deargdue snapped, 'Restrain your pet!'

Hands seized Aoife's arms from behind; Dorocha lifted her high above him, spun her round, and a split-second later smashed her headfirst onto the cold clay floor, where she lay half blinded by pain and shock, stunned and winded. Above in the roof, the sluagh shrieked in excitement and cracked their leathery wings like whips, clapping their wrinkled hands, hanging onto the rafters only by their claws.

Before her brain could stop spinning, and her lungs rasp back to life, Dorocha had dragged her roughly to her feet, pulling her round to face him. 'Apologies, my queen.' His hand pushed back her red-gold hair with a pretended sigh of concern; his other hand supported her, his palm flat against the small of her back. 'But no kissing. *No kissing*. The boy is my gift to my Deargdue – not to you.'

Still literally breathless, Aoife stared up into his

eyes – that midnight waste of stars. Again he touched her hair – and for just a moment his empty gaze held a fraction of true tenderness. 'Ah, so like your mother . . . So beautiful . . .'

Instantly she felt the sickening pull of him, her silver blood like streams of stars whirling down into the drain.

Down.

The un-empty emptiness beyond.

Down.

Shay.

Her lungs ripped apart; her dry lips parted; air flooded in. She stammered, 'One kiss . . . One kiss.' It was all her dazed mind seemed able to fix on at this moment – it was her light in the dark. One kiss, and if Shay was alive . . .

Dorocha was smiling knowingly. 'You think if you kiss him, you can fly, and escape me? I can assure you it is too late for that. His heart is broken, Aoibheal. He is beyond all rescue.'

Grief sank through her like a stone. 'Not true.' And yet, of course it was. She was too late: he was gone cold. There was no chance of escape for either of them now – whether he loved her or not. And yet she repeated stubbornly, 'One kiss.' It was all she could hope for. A beautiful pinpoint of light, shining in the darkness; the tiny spark that pulled her on.

Dorocha said, with utter contempt, 'Your mother's blood must be very strong in you, Aoibheal, if the desire for a kiss could bring you this far, this deep. I always knew the queen was a lenanshee, but I thought the *grá* would be less strong in the daughter.'

Again Aoife's lungs seemed to empty, as if he had smashed the breath from her once more; again she stared.

His mouth twitched with humour; stars dancing in his eyes. 'You never guessed, did you? All that heroic denying of his *grá* for you, and yet there was never any need for him to leave your side, never any need for him to be afraid of loving you. If you'd stayed with him, and he with you, he might have been strong enough to resist his sweet demon lover. But now it is too late for kisses.'

She should have known.

He shook his head, amused by her despair. 'I know, I know – how could you not have guessed? A fairy queen who keeps a servant to bring her human lovers of her choice, and then casts them aside when they are done? Aoibheal, if you'd only looked in the mirror, you would have seen her eyes, the turquoise eyes of the lenanshee. Your mother's eyes . . .' And with a rough change of mood, as if enraged by that memory, Dorocha shoved her backwards, so that she sat down suddenly on the edge of the stone dais.

Behind her the Deargdue sighed and yawned, cat-like, and combed her hair in the light of sparking fires.

Dorocha stood before Aoife with his feet apart, in his soft red boots; he took the rainbow ring from his pocket – the ring with which he had tried to marry her. Aggressively, he tossed it up in the air before her – a band of living flames. 'Your wedding ring, Aoibheal! I found it on the temple floor, where you threw it away.' He winked at her, twisting it between finger and thumb – 'It will melt the flesh of your finger to the bone, my queen!' – before tossing it aside onto the dais, where it twirled away in a trail of multi-coloured smoke, leaving a scorched spiral across the stone. 'However, I've decided I don't want to put myself though *that* again.' He paused, checking Aoife's face for her reaction, and sneered. 'Confused, my queen? Did you think I wanted Shay Foley dead so I could marry you? Ah no, my dear – nothing so romantic. It is all about revenge. The moment I have married my new darling, she will suck out the last of your lenanshee lad's heart while you watch— Oh, don't even *bother*, Aoibheal.'

She had made a fierce effort to get up, the ice-power flooding into her veins. Again Dorocha flung her easily aside; this time she landed clumsily spread-eagled at the foot of Shay's chair, her cheek resting against his unmoving knee, her hand on his shoe – an old black Adidas trainer, with broken laces tied in a short frayed knot. Her power draining away, in dark despair.

'Stay down.' Dorocha gave her a sharp kick in the thigh. 'And listen to what I have in store for you and yours. Just because I am happy to relinquish you does not mean I don't require my revenge. After your boy, we will come for your family and your friends. The banshee will reclaim the sheóg Eva, and the druids will *adore* your little friend Carla. As for those human parents who raised you so badly—'

Aoife made another effort to rise, tears of horror pouring from her eyes. He kicked her again. 'I said, stay down!'

In the tear-blurred corner of Aoife's vision, the Deargdue had paused in her combing, raising her head and saying – in a voice as sweet and musical as when she was the waitress in the lonely cliff-side café: 'But Beloved, I want this boy to last for ever.'

Turning towards her, Dorocha smiled very brightly. 'My love, I will get you a hundred more – a thousand more where he came from!'

'But none so pretty . . .'

'We will sweep through the human world and take every boy from every house, and you can keep them all as long as you like!'

She pouted. 'But this one was your wedding gift to me. How can you take back a wedding gift?'

'I have another! The queen of the Tuatha Dé Danann will be your hand-maiden. She will live here for all eternity, and help you bleed your boys.' He wheedled, honey-tongued: 'Won't you adore that, my hungry love? You – a human peasant girl before your father sold you, and your boy abandoned you, and your lord transformed you – you, my love, having as your servant the queen of the Tuatha Dé Danann?'

The Deargdue's silver eyes had brightened, but

still she hesitated, eyeing Aoife, slumped broken against Shay's knee.

Clearly guessing the reason for her hesitation, Dorocha urged, 'The queen's powers are nothing to yours, my love, and never will be. The queen will never be sixteen – she will never leave this place. When we journey to the surface together, we will leave her here in chains, with only your cold, dead boys for company. Come now. Marry me, kill the boy, and she is yours.'

But the beautiful demon only began to comb her hair again. 'I don't know. Perhaps I don't want to marry you. Perhaps I think my boy is prettier than you.'

'Ah . . . You have wounded me.' Dorocha said it carelessly, yet with a hint of injured pride.

'Besides, my boys won't like it if I am wed. They adore me.'

This time he was more surprised than hurt. 'But your boys are dead . . .'

She frowned, worrying at an invisible knot in her hair. 'The dead love me.'

'But my love, they're dead.'

She was starting to smile now. 'So? You have no heart.'

'Which is why I am the only man for you! Marry me—'

In a burst of petulance, she pointed the ivory comb at Aoife. 'How can you ask me to marry you, when only yesterday you were prepared to marry *that*!'

'Aha . . . Is *that* is the reason for your cruelty?' Smiling again, he stepped up onto the stone bed, stooping to seize a handful of the poppies with which it was strewn, bending over his Deargdue with a bunch of wilting flowers. 'Will I make you a pretty speech?'

She turned her face away from him, smiling again.

Dorocha stood over her, shaking the poppies, showering her with petals from the flowers. 'I admit, I had a vision once – a union of the living and the dead. But only for the sake of war, I swear! I did think to marry the queen of the Tuatha Dé Danann, because the changelings would follow her, and the beasts obey her. But then, I thought to myself – why should I saddle myself with a sulky child?'

Glancing up at him from under her gold eyelashes, the Deargdue said scornfully, 'You didn't think anything of the sort – she ran away from you with that pretty boy.'

'Ah! You are cruel!' Leaning down, Dorocha struck her lightly on the cheek with the remaining stalks. 'That humiliation was my punishment for trying – as always – to force the hand of fate. Ask the druids – there's probably a prophecy in it somewhere. Failure gave me time to reflect on my position.'

She mocked him: 'You've abandoned war?'

He laughed and shook his head. 'No, my love! But it is you I need by my side, to strengthen me – you, with your power to crush the hearts of the young, even while they fall in love with you.' He fell extravagantly to his knees beside her. 'Come with me, my poor, abused, beautiful, barefoot peasant. We are the king and queen of death.'

The Deargdue seemed interested now, finally laying aside the comb. 'But the changelings – will they follow you without her?'

He caught her hand and kissed it. 'They will follow anyone. They are mere children, teenagers – they'll swallow any nonsense in their lust for glory. The druids have taught them that a human priest murdered the queen. I will train them to thirst for human blood – just as I have the zookeeper training the beasts of the wilderness, feeding them on living flesh.'

'But the children and the beasts won't be enough—'

'We have our own cavalry, my love! The dulla-hans, the sluagh. All the dark creatures will follow us to the surface of Connacht when they realize what is to be gained in spoils. I will promise the druids a thousand girls for sacrifice. The banshees will have as many human babies as they can carry. The beau-tiful lenanshees will have as many human loves as they desire.'

Her head still lying against Shay's unmoving knee, Aoife felt her heart swell with unbearable grief. She had thought she could make a difference – but she had been a pawn, a disposable nothing. Carla's sweet, dear voice trickled through her mind: *I'm not trying to be mean, but you're really impulsive and you don't always think properly about what about you're at.* Her darling best friend, who understood so much.

All Aoife had thought about was Shay. Following her own impulsive heart, and in the end failing eve-ryone, including him.

Oh, Shay. What am I going to do?

She pressed her cheek against his knee, trying to draw some strength from him through her skin. She had to escape. She had to warn her parents and Carla of the war that was coming – she had to get back to them; she had to protect them. She tried to judge the distance to the tall narrow door, leading away into the dark. If she could even summon the energy to crawl, while Dorocha was absorbed . . . Yet how could she leave Shay behind? Above, the sluagh shuffled and peered, keeping their own watch, rattling their wings, opening and closing their beaked mouths, their small, mean eyes observing her: pinpoints of reflected firelight in the shadowy roof. Behind her, the confident murmur of Dorocha's voice pleaded his case for love and war.

Beyond was the tall stone doorway, slightly ajar into the darkness.

And beyond the doorway, sounds.

Soft, soft . . .

She lifted her head . . . It was the distant padding she had heard before, when she was standing outside that same door in the utter dark.

Soft, soft . . .

The shush of naked feet?

A paleness shimmered in the darkness.

The leathery wings of the sluagh were fluttering; their deformed beaks and pinpoint eyes also turning towards the doorway, puzzled . . . A single, smaller sluagh tumbled from the rafters and circled awkwardly, its leathery wings tipping the walls, its eyes vivid green in the firelight.

Behind, the Deargdue gave a small, ecstatic sigh. 'I *do*.'

And Dorocha murmured, 'Let me hold you—'

And the heavy stone door swung inwards, pushed open by many hands, and pouring into the fire-lit chapel came the hundreds of cold, dead boys.

They came on across the wide clay floor towards the bed – soft in their bare feet, more and more pressing in from behind, out of the dark, out of the endless curtained rooms. The Deargdue was crying with agitated pride: 'I was right! They still love me!' And Dorocha, incensed, was shouting, 'Who woke these vermin?'

'They love me, even though I killed them! They still love me!'

'They're nothing to you! Get rid of them! *Send them back to their graves!*'

But still they came on – those at the front now crawling up onto the stone bed; pushing aside, with their slow tide, the silks and cushions, the lamps and flowers.

Hidden in the centre of the flood, Aoife knelt, holding Shay's own cold hands. 'Shay? Can you see me?' But his dark green eyes gazed over her shoulder, as if he longed to join the press of silent boys now pulling at the demon's hands, her feet, her dress. The Deargdue was shrieking – a thin, high mixture of ecstasy and fear – as they tugged her this way and that. Dorocha, snarling with rage, was kicking and slapping them aside: *'Get back! She's mine!'* They rose, and came again.

'Shay?' The sharp stub of straw protruded from his chest; she drew it gently out. He sat forward and cried out, clasping his hand to his heart. She pulled down his head and kissed him.

Even this far beneath the earth, Aoife could taste the flowery scent of the Mayo air on his lips, and the salt of its sea. And as her mouth pressed against his, she felt a pull, a draining away of herself – but not in the way Dorocha sucked the strength from her. This was a giving, not a taking away. *I am a lenanshee, giving life.* She kissed him again, and again came that subtle pull. On the third kiss, his curved lips moved beneath hers. Gasping, she staggered to her feet, dragging him up beside her, supporting him towards the door. He stumbled beside her, not looking back. Among the tall sea of dead boys, none paid the two of them any heed. Slipping out into the steep, sloping passageway, leaving behind the frenzied cries of the demon and Dorocha's incoherent rage: '*Get down, I command you! Obey me! You are the dead!*'

Shay slowed to barely a walk, his head lowered, his shoulder pressed to the wall – he seemed barely conscious. 'Shay, come on!' If they could make the surface, somehow she would get them home. She kissed him again. He recovered a little, and staggered on, leaning against her. They were passing open archways now, the curtains ripped down, blankets tossed aside, candles kicked over. Room after room. The cold wind blew at their backs, hurrying them on.

Rustling the curtains.

Fluttering . . .

Not curtains – wings. Hundreds of wings, coming up fast behind them.

With a groan of horror, Aoife tried to force Shay on. 'Run! Run!' He stumbled with her through the dark; she with her arm around him, supporting his weight.

Wings, louder . . . Louder . . .

He staggered again, and this time she stopped and pushed him against the wall. 'Kiss me! We have to fly!' Pulling his mouth down on hers, her arms around him . . . If there was any *grá* left in him for her at all, any faint ghost of his old desire . . . She sought it with a kiss, seeking that flood of lightness, the joyous power of flight . . .

Hooked hands and feet seized Aoife round the waist, wrenching her off her feet. She fought and kicked and screamed in her despair. Her captor swept on, hard, thin, wizened arms wrapped tight around both her and Shay. The dark shadows of the passageway flashed past; other wings were beating against the walls behind her; other beaks slashed at her feet, hands clawed at her bare legs. Starlight ahead . . .

Out.

The sluagh continued to climb towards the dark

whirlpool at the centre of the stars. Pouring out of the barrow behind them came a long black stream in clamorous pursuit, wings slicing the air. But the sluagh who was carrying them spat and howled, as if to say '*Mine!*' until slowly, one by one, the others gave up the chase and peeled away, drifting in circles like flakes of soot, back down to the poppy fields, now so far beneath.

Aoife no longer dared struggle, because if the sluagh released them, the fall to the ground would be too great. Below, the immense stone barrow was shrinking to a dot. The dark poppy fields stretched out for all eternity under the swirling stars. Shay's cheek was against hers; he was crushed into her arms by the grip of the sluagh. Breathing. Alive. And lost.

She had saved him – and saved herself – for this:

To end it together, in the most horrible, painful way possible – dumped into the stinking nest of a sluagh, there to be eaten alive, torn limb from limb.

She wondered, in her desolation: would they be reborn as sluagh – and would they know each other? As the queen of rebirth, she was supposed to understand these things. She knew nothing. Far below, the dark world turned as the sluagh continued its steep ascent. Its arms were gripping her so strongly she could hardly breathe; but with what breath she had she began to cry – painfully, childishly – stupid, point-less, despairing sobs. And still with its foul arms clasped around them, the solitary sluagh continued to fly upwards, with great sweeps of its leathery wings – *whoop, whoop, whoop* . . . Up into the swirling vortex of the stars.

CHAPTER THIRTEEN

And still the sound of wings: *whoop, whoop, whoop* ...

With a shuddering cry, Aoife awoke, thrashing about in the . . . Not a foul, blood-spattered, bone-filled nest, but a soft white bed of linen and lamb's wool. A large, strong hand was shaking her gently by the shoulder. She struggled into a sitting position, then hastily pulled the blankets to her chin. Someone had taken her clothes, and she was naked – clean, perfumed and washed, with her hair softly curled and combed around her shoulders. '*Caitlin?*'

As if in a very odd sort of dream, an extremely elegant version of the changeling girl was standing beside Aoife's bed, wearing a lace dress that fitted perfectly; there were bluebells threaded through her bright red hair, which was loose around her shoulders, and she was holding a plate of honeycomb, sloe berries and tiny dark biscuits. 'Eimhear sent me to wake you.' Caitlin's usually harsh, piercing voice was surprisingly muted and gentle.

'Who's Eimhear? Where's Shay?'

'Shay's mother – and Shay's not woken up yet, but he's grand. There's a whole load of the girls watching over him, the bold things.'

'Oh, thank God.' Aoife made a joyful move to get out of bed, then remembered she was naked. 'Where are my clothes?'

'Eimhear's on her way with something for you to wear.'

'Caitlin, where *are* we?' Overhead swayed bright copper birdcages, tinkling together, shaken by caged nightingales singing. An arched doorway led to the sunny outside world, made misty by azure translucent drapes; a distant flute was playing. The crystal floor was scattered thickly with bluebell flowers. The heavy scent of the flowers; the singing of the birds; the pale azure light shed by lamps of bluebell oil; even the fact that Caitlin was acting in such a restrained fashion – everything seemed more hazy and dreamlike than real . . .

'We're in the lenanshee quarters. Do you like my dress? The girls insisted on me wearing it, although I don't think it's as nice as the feather one you gave me. I have to warn you, they're extremely fussy here

about every single little thing – what you wear, hold
loud you talk, the way you move . . . It's a lot of fuss
to make about not actually doing anything at all . . .'

Whoop, whoop, whoop.

Aoife glanced around fearfully, her heart
contracting – the noise of wings seemed so loud, and
coming rapidly closer. And yet Caitlin appeared
utterly unconcerned. It must be the stress of everything that had happened imprinting that dreadful
sound on her mind . . .

Whoop, whoop, whoop.

Setting down the plate of honeycomb and biscuits, Caitlin was saying, 'Here's your breakfast – the
berries are a bit sour, so dip them in the honey—'

'Caitlin, get down!'

A vast black form had hurled itself against the
gauze drapes from outside, slashing and tearing with
its claws, screeching at the top of its hideous, grating,
old-man's voice to get in. Shrinking back against her
pillows, Aoife raised her hands, icy power pouring
into her fingers . . .

Rushing towards the archway, Caitlin cried, 'No,
stop, don't hurt him!'

'It's a sluagh!'

'He's our friend!' The ugly creature had got itself into a terrible tangle of gauze, battering frantically with its leather wings. 'He brought you and Shay back here from the House of the Dead – apparently ye blasted up through the sacrificial altar like a mad moon-rocket thing . . .'

'*Be careful of it!*'

'It's not an "it", it's a "him". Come here to me, you silly thing.' Caitlin began gently extricating the creature from the drapes – and, despite Aoife's horror, it didn't attack her but, once freed, clung to her like a child with its wizened legs and arms, wings folded around her like a giant leather cloak, its head on her shoulder, beaky mouth opening and closing, crooning now instead of squawking. An old man's head, although its eyes were vivid green. Caitlin carried the creature across the room towards an inner door, staggering slightly under the weight of it. 'Come on now, Donal, I'll get you something to eat.'

Dazed, Aoife said, 'Donal?' She pulled the soft lambswool covers back up to her bare shoulders.

'It's the eyes remind me of him!' Caitlin paused to beam at her, heaving the sluagh higher in her arms. 'Fact, I'm pretty sure this *is* him. After he dropped you off, he came to fetch me, obviously because you needed me to look after you. Gave me a terrible fright when he crashed in through the window and grabbed me – before I realized who he really was. You're cute, aren't you?' She dropped a kiss on the wrinkled dark forehead. 'I know it seems a bit fast for him to get this far on the rebirth front, but I checked in the book, and because Shay is a lenanshee and kissed Donal before he died, the book says everything would go unusually fast, and if a sluagh ate something which had eaten something else which – et cetera—'

Aoife cried out in amazement as everything fell into place. 'You're right, Caitlin – you're completely right!'

'I know I am, I read it in the book – which I really can read, by the way.'

She remembered – she owed Caitlin an apology. 'I'm sorry for upsetting you the last time. I never meant to say you couldn't read it – I'm sorry—'

'No, you're grand, because actually' – Caitlin turned slightly pink – 'I wasn't very good at reading it, believe it or not. But it's all right now, because I got hold of one of the human children that the banshees stole from the festival – there's been a huge row between the banshees and the druids, by the way; I'm not sure exactly what happened – anyway, I got this kid to wish I could read the book—'

'Oh, genius!'

'Thanks . . . And I must say, the English edition is completely different. Between you and me, it wasn't a human priest who murdered your mother at all, but Dorocha himself. So my new advice to you is, you'd be better off not marrying him after all. I'll go and tell Eimhear you're awake.'

'Caitlin, wait—'

'What? Donal is really hungry – I need to go get him some food.'

'What about Carla?'

The changeling girl looked surprised. 'Sure, didn't you make her wish herself back to the human world because she was no use to you in this one, not like me? I was just coming outside to see what the racket was when she shouted her wish, and *poof!*'

Aoife laughed with relief. So the wish had been granted. 'And Ultan?'

Caitlin's face darkened. 'Went with her.'

'Oh God . . .' Aoife stopped laughing. So that was

494

how she'd granted the wish 'quair': she had sent 'both' of them home. Just not herself and Carla. She'd sent Carla and Ultan. 'I'm so sorry, that was my fault. I hope he didn't mind . . .'

Hugging the sluagh version of Donal against her as if for comfort, Caitlin said bitterly, 'Don't be sorry – he always did have a thing about humans, and I dare say he'll be much happier with that fancy friend of yours, with her stupid fancy hair.'

'I'm sure he'll be back soon. I'm sure he'll miss you.'

Caitlin looked grudgingly pleased. 'Maybe he can get some other dumb human to wish him back.'

'Maybe he can!'

'Although according to the English edition—'

Behind Caitlin, an inner door opened – a honeyed slab of amber, full of shadowy flowers. A lenanshee with long black curling hair and turquoise eyes appeared, wearing a dress of rich ivory lace that came to just below her knees, and carrying in her arms another similar garment. She said in a soft, musical voice, 'Aoibheal?'

It was strange – it was the first time someone had called Aoife by that name without it seeming entirely wrong. She sat up straight under the blanket. 'That's me.'

'I am Eimhear.' Shay's mother drifted into the room – then drew aside with a dismayed shudder as Caitlin rushed out past her with the sluagh: the changeling girl with her big shoulders hunched up to her ears and her hand shielding the creature's ugly face, as if that way the two of them could avoid the disapproval of fastidious beauty. Still shivering delicately, Shay's mother sat down beside Aoife on the bed, and gazed smiling into her face, laying the dress she'd been carrying across Aoife's feet. 'Do you remember me at all, Aoibheal?'

'I saw you in my mother's tower, and in the temple.'

'I mean, from when you were a little girl. Your mother was my dearest friend, Aoibheal – and you look so like her! You have her eyes, and her hair – the exact same colour, like the winter sun.'

Tears roughened Aoife's throat. It was unexpectedly lovely to hear someone other than Dorocha – or even poor Wee Peter – speaking so intimately of the queen. She said, 'I really look like her? What was she like?'

'Very powerful. Very beautiful. Her own mother was a lenanshee, and her father was of the people of Danu. Passion and magic combined – a perfect queen for the Land of the Young. And now here you are, and it is as if she walks again! We will be such friends, you and I.'

Aoife glanced towards the open archway, where the gauze drapes now hung ragged, revealing the outer world. Beyond was a crystal promenade, across which poured a sea of azure light from many arch-ways. And from above fell the long sunset shadow of her mother's tower, cutting a thick black line across the promenade and the city below. The day was passing. She had to get home. The queen's pool was only a short distance above her head – she could climb to it from here, up the carved walls of the city, as she had seen the lenanshees climb before. She had to get back to the surface world; if war was coming, she had to protect her family. 'I have to go – I have to warn—'

She stopped. Dorocha had been very confident the lenanshees would join his war. *They are also dark creatures, the lenanshees.* So she said instead, 'Is Shay awake yet?' And then, remembering, 'I know you told him to stay away from me . . .'

Eimhear was fussing with Aoife's red-gold hair, straightening a lock of it over her shoulder. 'Only when I feared his *grá* would destroy you. But I now know that the lenanshee is as strong in you as in your mother. Why else would you follow him all the way to the House of the Dead? That is the *grá*. Do you wish to see him? He's beyond that door . . .' And the lenanshee held out her elegant white hand, and then withdrew it with a smile and said, 'But first, put on the dress.'

Shivering with impatience, Aoife drew the ivory silk over her head, and over her body, then stood and pulled it down to her knees.

The lenanshee stopped her halfway to the door – 'Wait!' – and, standing behind her, made a few last adjustments to Aoife's hair with an ivory comb strangely like the one the Deargdue had used. Aoife stood very still, tense, heart beating strongly. The figure of Eimhear was reflected softly in the smooth amber of the door. Seeing her in that white dress, and holding the comb, it was hard not to be reminded . . . *They are also dark creatures, the lenanshees*. Eimhear let Aoife's hair fall from her hand, and Aoife ran towards the door again – but this time stopped of her own accord, turning back. Something in her mind . . .

'Eimhear, how long did you know my mother?'

'Many thousands of years.'

'Then did you know my father too?'

'Ah, your father . . .' Eimhear smiled, slipping her arm through Aoife's and walking with her to the door. 'Your father was a handsome boy of seventeen when he chanced on your mother, washing her red-gold hair in the soft water of a pool surrounded by hawthorns. She looked up at him and smiled as she wrung the water from her hair – and that was the end of everything for him. He forgot his mother, his father, his brothers and sisters, his duties as a young warrior of the Fianna. And when your mother slipped feet first into the pool, he threw aside his cloak and sword and followed her. Ah, that was a true love story, Aoibheal – beautiful and tragic and short! He could not withstand the *grá* – but in the way humans live on, one after the other, he lives through you. Lenanshee passion, Tuatha magic, your father's stubborn recklessness – all are combined in you, Aoibheal. The human in you travels to the Land of the Dead, but the lenanshee heals the deepest wounds, and your fairy blood can bring you home again – or take you further on to distant places: the Blessed Isles, beneath the wild sea, where no human or lenanshee has ever stood.'

Beyond the amber door was a larger communal chamber scattered thickly with bluebell flowers, and here and there were low-backed sofas of pale birch, heaped with white cushions embroidered with blue flowers and butterflies. Lenanshees reclined in twos and threes on the sofas, but more sat cross-legged on the bluebell-strewn floor, combing their long black curls. In the centre of the chamber, one of them was playing a flute made of green reeds – a melody Aoife didn't truly recognize yet which seemed strangely comforting and familiar, as if it was a song sung to her as a child.

Near the flute-player lay Shay, stretched out on a couch, half hidden by one of many light gauzy curtains that floated in the air like drifting rain. A crowd of young lenanshees sat around him, watching him sleep. Eimhear drew Aoife across the room to the couch, and whispered the other girls away, and pulled the soft gauze aside and stood gazing down on her son. He lay breathing gently on his back, still pale;

one sun-browned arm cupped around his head, his long black lashes resting on his strong cheekbones. At rest, his mouth was deeply curved. The pale line around his wrist . . .

because you once were mine . . .

With sorrow and joy in her heart, she leaned over him.

'Shay?'

His eyes fluttered open for a moment – then closed.

She dropped to her knees beside the couch and touched her finger to the line around his wrist. He shuddered slightly, as if her touch was wrong. She grieved, knowing who she was not. The Deargdue was so utterly beautiful that even the dead had come crawling to her feet.

His eyelashes trembled on his cheeks.

Where was he, in his mind? Lying here on the couch, he was still dressed in the black clothes he had worn to the Halloween dance. *Dancing . . . Dancing . . . His lips buried in her white-blonde hair . . .* His curved mouth was still bruised by the demon's kiss.

Aoife touched her finger to his lip, and watched the bruises fade.

Again his dark green eyes opened, and rose slowly to her face – the golden depths of them glimmering like sunlight striking a woodland pool. They travelled across her face, her hair. She stroked the curve of his mouth once more.

This time his lips parted slightly, and closed on her fingertip – the lightest of fragile kisses.

A trickle of love; a warmth against her skin. 'Shay?'

He met her turquoise eyes, and held them for the longest time – then, very lightly, winked.

'*Wahu*, Aoife.'

I WISH TO ACKNOWLEDGE:

For their invaluable advice and constant support:
My son Jack and daughter Molly.

For being such insightful readers and also hilarious company:
My daughter Imogen and son Seán.

For being my love:
My husband Derek.

For launching the first book with such a moving speech:
Una.

For all the walks and wine:
Sinead.

For being ready for anything:
Aideen.

For being as steady as rock:
Cathy and all her family, especially Joe – an exceptional friend.

For all the tea and setting the world to rights:
Julie – and Liam, whose heart will never leave Ross.

For fabulous editing:
Kelly Hurst.

For equally fabulous copy-editing:
Sophie Nelson.

Also my thanks to Tom Rawlinson – and welcome aboard, Claire Hennessy.

For being wonderful agents:
Marianne Gunn O'Connor, Vicki Satlow.

For great advice as always:
Kate Kerrigan.

Also:

Everyone who came to the first book launch, especially Sara Bourke, who despite having a car run over her foot still managed to make it. And Lorraine for taking over the serious work while I concentrated on the frivolous stuff. And Mary Butler and Bernie Costello, without whom etc. You know what I mean.

And:

For being himself:
Tim Lacey.

For being herself:
Rachel Falconer.